Memories of County Clare

Elaine M McMahon

This is a work of fiction. Names, characters, and incidents either are the product of the author's imagination or are used fictitiously. Any resemblance to actual persons, living or dead, or events, is entirely coincidental.

Copyright © 2020 by Elaine M McMahon

All rights reserved. No part of this book may be reproduced or used in any manner without written permission of the copyright owner except for the use of quotations in a book review.

First paperback edition June 2020

ISBN 978-0-578-68383-6 (paperback)

Published in the United States by Elaine M McMahon

To Michelle and Jeffrey
For believing in me

Chapter One

At daybreak, Niall and Patrick hitched the horses to their caravans in the dim gray light. Their cousin, Danny McMahon, came galloping down the road in a cloud of dark dust, his cap riding precariously on the back of his head.

Patrick looked up. "About time you got here!"

"Hey!" cried Danny. "The sun ain't up over the hill yet, so it's still plenty early."

Niall's eleven-year-old son, James, grinned. "Da says you'll be late for your own funeral!"

Danny dismounted and led his horse to Patrick's wagon. "Yeah, well, I'd rather have it chasin' after me than offer m'self up to it!" He was smaller in stature than the O'Brien men, but well proportioned. Though only in his mid-twenties, his air of reckless confidence belied his size. He feared no one and more often than not, ended up on the wrong side of mischief. Bright blue eyes set off his freckled face, and the curly hair that hung unfettered over his ears lent him an air of perpetual boyishness.

He tossed his bedroll into the back of the wagon and helped Patrick hitch up his horse.

The two wagons were piled high with supplies: baled hay, feed, cooking pots, and the few tools they would need.

Patrick laughed and punched Danny's shoulder playfully. "You'll probably be the death of us first!"

The four of them were heading to Doolin a day ahead of the rest of the family to set up camp for the weekend gathering. Many more would join them there to erect the temporary horse pens that would straddle the River Aille.

A still sleepy Saraid, in a loose cotton chemise, approached them with a hamper of food and a jug of ale to slake their appetites on the way. She passed the jug to Niall and stowed the hamper under the seat of his caravan. After hoisting the jug into the back of the caravan, Niall, his dark hair falling loosely to his shoulders, wrapped an arm around her waist and bent his tall frame to kiss her goodbye. He smiled into her grass-green eyes and touched a finger to the dimple in her cheek. "You be careful on the road."

Saraid and the rest of the family would leave later in the day and travel half way, spending the night in Ennis with Doc O'Hickey and his wife, Martha. That way, all their traveling would be done in the daylight hours with less fear of meeting up with highwaymen along the road.

"Sure ye've no need to be worryin' about us." She pushed a strand of her long auburn hair behind her ear with one hand and playfully squeezed his thigh with the other. "John and yer mother will be with us, an' I'll have my knife if there's any trouble. I'm just hopin' we can find ye when we get there."

Niall nodded. He and Saraid hadn't been back to Doolin since Bridget had been born, four years before. The trip was more difficult now with so many of them.

"Yeah, there'll be hundreds there," he said as he tied his hair back with a leather cord. "Don't try to take the wagon over the Burren, just stick to the road. One of us will be watching for you and lead you to the camp. In any case, we'll try to set ourselves up near the horse pens by the river."

"All right, then," Saraid said as she waved them off. "See ye tomorrow!"

James softly played his penny whistle as the men headed north along the River Shannon to Killaloe. The mist that covered the river drifted over parts of the road, slowing their pace. The only sounds were of the wagon wheels grinding over the pebbled road, the awakening birds chirping in the trees overhead, and squirrels scurrying in the blackthorn that grew along the river bank. He'd hoped to see some rainbow trout 'dancing on the water', but the river was barely visible. "Da," he asked, "how far does the Shannon go?"

"It starts at the northern edge of Clare," he answered. "It flows south to Limerick and then west to where it meets the Atlantic waters in the Shannon Estuary, then on to the sea."

James watched as a few boats headed downstream, some with their cargo shrouded by fog. "Why are no boats going upstream?" he asked.

"Some do, but not much further than Killaloe. The river is passable here, but further north, past the Lough Derg, it's only two feet deep in places. Barges would get run aground. There's talk of building canals from Dublin to Athlone, to the north, for trade. The only problem is that they have to figure out how to deepen the Shannon to make it passable. Then they could make an inland trade route all the way from Dublin, then by boat to Limerick, and then west to the ocean trade routes to other countries."

James nodded and, losing interest in the subject, went back to playing his penny whistle. The mist had begun to lift as they arrived in Killaloe. Patches of sunlight began to glint off the new stone bridge with its seventeen arches that spanned the river to Ballina on the other side. The two towns were almost identical and, in both, were the sounds and smells of a new day beginning. Lit candles could be seen through the windows of the harness shop, the butcher, and the tanner. The yeasty aroma of fresh bread wafted over them from the open door of the bake shop. From the river, men prepared their fishing boats to head downstream in search of salmon.

They made a stop at the bakeshop where Niall had a quick conversation, in hushed tones with the baker, who nodded his head. "I'll be there," he said softly.

The men munched on their sweet bread as they continued on their way. They skirted the western side of the Lough Derg before heading west on the well-traveled road to Ennis, the halfway point of their journey. Once they came to the edge of town, they stopped to eat the picnic Saraid had packed for them, and to rest and water the horses. The large town was filled with shops and taverns and was, as always, busy with travelers clogging its narrow cobbled streets.

"Will we get there before dark?" asked James.

Niall looked to the sky and judged that the sun would be with them for several more hours. "Probably, but by the time we get near to Doolin, there'll be plenty of folks on the road with lanterns. We'll be able to see well enough."

"What exactly is the Burren?" James asked.

Niall eyed his son and chuckled over the long stream of questions he'd asked along the way. He realized that the lad had been quite young when he had last been to Doolin and too excited to pay any mind to the lay of the land. Now, he was old enough to be able to take it all in and retain the memory. Remembering how patient his own father had been during his young years, he explained what he could.

"The Burren is what they named the entire northwestern section of Clare. It's a barren landscape, composed of limestone that encompasses more than one hundred square miles. It was formed by huge mountains of ice called glaciers that moved across the land gnawing away at all the soil. It left nothing but flat limestone, filled with cracks called grikes. The flat chunks of limestone that remained are called clints. Years of melting and rain deepened the grikes and created all the caves that run under the Burren. The underground water eventually found its way to the sea."

James tried to digest all this information. "Do people live there now?" he asked.

"Of course they do," said Patrick. He took a bite of a chicken leg as he watched caravans and open wagons pass by them on the road. Many people were walking with bedrolls tied to their backs. "Looks like we'll have a good turn out."

"Do they have farms in Doolin?" asked James.

"Nah, mostly just some goats," said Danny. "They eat the grass growin' outta the grikes."

Patrick added, "There's some strange flowers growing there, too."

"You can't do any real farming in Doolin," said Niall. "There's not much good soil. Most of the men are fishermen."

"Yea, ye got to own a boat," said Danny. "Or own a tavern!"

Patrick chuckled at Danny. "And you'd be the one to know about that!"

James nudged Danny. "Did you bring your dancing shoes?"

Danny laughed. "Does a leprechaun wear a hat? O'course I did! An' I plan on out-dancin' every one of ye!"

They all grinned and shook their heads at him.

James puffed out his chest. "I've been practicing really hard and I bet I can beat you this year!"

"Enough talk of dancing," said Niall, wiping his hands on his britches. "Let's get going."

Chapter Two

John O'Brien set his leather satchel on his neatly made bed. He caressed the supple leather, noting that it lacked the scratches and wear of most travel bags. Not surprising when you were too tied to the workings of the farm to do any traveling. This weekend would be a welcome relief. For the first time in several years, the entire family was traveling to Doolin for the annual *'Céilidh'*, a gathering, of the O'Brien clan. The clan included, among many others, those tribes with the names Kennedy, McMahon, Hogan, O'Casey, and McGrath.

For the last few years, only Patrick, the youngest of three O'Brien brothers, and their neighboring cousin, Danny, had made the time to take the trip. This year, all of them, including his eldest brother, Niall, with his wife, Saraid, their four children, and their recently widowed mother, Kate, would be going, too. By wagon, his trip from the farm to Ennis would take several hours. Spending the night with the good doctor and his wife would be delightful.

John found himself smiling as he thought about the upcoming activities ahead. Doolin might not be a great place to live but the vast flatness of the Burren lent itself to the many festivals and dance competitions that were held there throughout the year. Aside from the blaring music and dancing, the gathering families could find men in need of work to hire for the harvests. It also gave young people a chance to mingle and search for mates, which they had difficulty doing when farms were separated by so many miles and long hours of farm work.

As he packed clean clothing into his satchel, John caught movement out of the corner of his eye. He moved to the window and stood in the beams of sunlight that streamed through the glass. He watched his mother climb the hill to the family burial plot and felt a pang in his chest. She was still struggling with her grief, probably always would.

In the months since his father had passed, she had withdrawn into herself, speaking little, refusing to let anyone see her cry, becoming short-tempered with Saraid and the children, especially with Saraid.

John went to his desk and picked up his leather-bound journal, thumbing through the pages as he walked back to the bed. The family scribe had brought all the volumes of their family history to them a few months ago after his father died. The scribe's failing eyesight and lack of male heirs prevented him from continuing as the family record keeper. The volumes contained charts of their ancestors that went back hundreds of years to the legendary High King of Ireland, Brian Boru, who had freed the Irish from 800 years of Viking oppression.

John had found the charts informative but sterile, containing nothing of the heart and soul of the people who had come and gone before, the high notes and low notes that created the melodies of their lives. He had used his natural bent as a writer to begin a fresh volume with anecdotal memories of his ancestors as well as stories about his present-day family. It was his hope that, someday, generations from now, someone would pick up this book and be able to understand what their lives had been about here.

John started to put the journal into his satchel then paused, went back to the window, and stared up the hill. He could just make out the figure of his mother, sitting on the bench among the headstones, her head bowed. Perhaps if he joined her, he could use the journal as an excuse to coax her into talking about her early years at the farm.

He knew it must have been difficult for her, an Anglo girl from a wealthy family in Dublin. After a chance encounter, she'd been courted for two years by James, his gregarious father. The ensuing chaos in Dublin had finally convinced her to marry him and make the move to the family farm in County Clare. Though the farm was actually a small estate, it was still a farm with crude elements, and hard work was needed to make it run properly.

After John finished packing, he picked up his quill and a small pot of ink, and tucked the journal under his arm. He descended the stairs, went out the door and climbed the hill.

Chapter Three

A pair of wrens sang out as they flew overhead, bringing Kate back from her reverie. She sat on the old bench, blinking, staring off into the distant fields without focus. It had tired her to climb the long slope and she had dozed for awhile. When she awoke, the mid-summer sun had arrived at its zenith and the day had grown hot and dry. Her long fingers were still wrapped around her white ruffled cap that held the now-wilted bunch of wildflowers, picked as she walked to the family burial plot. Kate sighed and looked over the many headstones, each with the surname O'Brien, the dates of their births and deaths chiseled into the flat grey surfaces. She tossed flowers onto the rounded earth of her husband's grave.

James O'Brien had passed away just three months ago, and Kate felt the pain of his loss more deeply than she ever thought she might. And anger, too, that after almost forty years together, he had left her to face the austerity of Clare without him.

The gentle breeze disheveled her hair as she looked out over the acres of stone walls that divided the land. The sharp scent of pastures filled with sheep and cattle mingled with the sweetness of wheat and hay that stood waving gently, waiting for harvest.

Tears trickled down the creases of her face as she pushed an errant strand of gray from her eyes. Kate put the cap back on her head, the ruffling shielding her eyes from the sun's glare.

She felt a sudden deep desire to go home . . . to Dublin. If she were honest, she knew that there was nothing left for her there. Her parents had passed away long ago, and her brothers had moved back to England decades before, after their factories were destroyed in the riots.

"Mother?"

Kate started, quickly wiping her face as John reached the cemetery and stood before her. His tall, lanky frame was a mirror image of her own. She gazed into his face, the high cheekbones, the thin straight nose. His golden brown hair and eyes were hers as well, though his tied back hair lacked her curls. "Hello, John."

He set his journal on the edge of the bench, his quill and a small jar of ink beside it. Sitting, John wrapped an arm around Kate's shoulder, giving her a gentle squeeze as he stretched out his long legs and crossed his feet.

"Are you all right?" he asked.

Kate took in a settling breath and nodded without meeting his eyes. She motioned to James's grave. "I just wanted to tell him that we'd be going to Doolin." She shook her head. "I'd really rather stay home."

"You know the clan will be honoring him there. You need to be with us."

"I know," she sighed. "It just seems so far to travel, and there will be so much noise."

John chuckled, "That's your English roots calling it 'noise'. We Irish think of it as a raucous good time. It will also be a fun time, especially for the children. We could all stand to have a few days away from the work here. I know I could." He was thankful that they had two good men to oversee the farm in their absence.

They had been preparing for this trip for weeks now. Metal arcs had been attached to the wagon beds and canvas tarps tied over the tops to create the caravans that would hold all their necessary goods and provide, if need be, a sheltered place for them to sleep.

John opened his jar of ink, filled his quill, and opened his journal across his lap. He turned to a clean page and began to write.

"What are you writing about today?" asked Kate.

John shrugged. "I've just finished writing about how you and da met in Dublin." He chuckled. "That must have been really something."

Kate turned her face away from him and dabbed her eyes. "So what is it you want from me?"

"Can you tell me what it was like for you when you first came here? It must have been difficult."

Kate looked away, her heart aching. How could she describe how isolated she had felt? Her mind flooded with the echoes of her husband's laughter, his patience, the simple joy he found in day-to-day living. She had found his boundless energy exhausting at times, but she had admired his optimism and strength. And, always, he had coaxed a laugh from her.

"He was such a good man," she finally whispered.

John chuckled. "I know this is hard for you, Mother; but surely, you can do better than that. I want to know about you."

Kate sniffled and took a deep breath. *I need to do this.* "When he first brought me here, I couldn't understand why he loved this place. It all just seemed so desolate to me. All these endless green hills were so foreign to me after living all my life in a busy city." She stared at the white clouds that dotted the clear blue of the sky, trying to remember their early life together. "I was so overwhelmed by everything."

John kept silent, hoping she would continue. In time, she did. He picked up his quill again to record her words.

"Mostly, your father surprised me. He had always talked about what a glorious life he had and convinced me that we would be happy here. He'd added on to his cottage so we had our own place. It was clean but so much smaller than my home in Dublin. He made sure there were carpets and panes of glass in the windows and shelves for my books.

"For the first year, I spent a lot of time sitting alone, reading, or doing embroidery, waiting for his long work day to be done. I was a bit surprised that he had so many books of his own. I had been taught that the Irish were mostly an ignorant bunch that couldn't even sign their own names. Your father's people weren't great scholars, but they were educated and well-spoken."

John chuckled at that. Because of his mother, he and his brothers had been given an exemplary education. He, alone, had always preferred to bury his nose in a book than to work the crops. He had made one trip to Dublin to see Trinity College and had come away with a deep longing to be part of that community of scholars. The ache had never left him.

Kate had insisted that the boys spend time each day learning how to read and do mathematics from the books she had brought with her from home. She fully expected that one day, when they were old enough, they would go to Trinity College to study. Their father would have none of it when they were needed to work on the farm. No amount of ranting by Kate or threats of leaving had changed his mind. Instead, he compromised and allowed Kate to hire a tutor who came to the farm two afternoons a week disguised as a peddler.

Since the Anglo-run Parliament's enactment of the Penal Laws in the late 1600s, education for the Catholic Irish was forbidden. Undaunted and clever, the Irish formed 'hedge schools,' where clusters of children hid behind hedges, in barns, or in the woods to receive their learning. Often, it was banished priests who became the teachers. Aside from the basics, the O'Brien boys also read both English and Irish literature, history, and studied maps of the world. From Paddy, the Catholic priest who had lived with them for years as a hired hand, they learned Latin and Greek.

Kate continued the voyage through her memories.

"The O'Briens tried to make me feel welcome but they were as leery of me as I was of them. They all worked hard on the farm and had no time to waste on keeping me company. While the men worked in the fields, the women cooked meals, made jams, grew herbs, salted meat and churned butter for market. At harvest time they worked in the fields, too, and flailed the wheat and put it in sacks. The wheat became their main tax crop when they gave up growing flax. I didn't know how to do any of those things . . . and I felt it beneath me to soil my pretty clothes and learn.

"Your father never berated me for it, though. He'd work hard all day and even though I could see how tired he was, he always brought me a posy of wildflowers. I expected him to devote all his evenings to me—just me. But here, everyone would gather in the evenings and sing and play their penny whistles and dance. I couldn't do their fancy steps and I didn't know the songs."

Kate rubbed her hands over her face to wipe the tears that were flowing freely now.

John thought about telling her that she needn't say more, but she began to speak again so he continued to write.

"After several months of my pouting and complaining of loneliness, your father finally lost patience with me and took me to task for it. He didn't get angry often, but when he did, I listened. He said that if I was going to stay here as his wife, I had to learn to live here. Eventually, I gave in, packed away my smart dresses and began to wear the same simple clothes as the rest of the women. And I learned how to work. My first calluses were a painful shock to me. The women took great pleasure in teasing me, but they weren't mean. Overall, they were very kind to me, and patiently taught me the things I needed to do. It was very humbling. Eventually, I even learned to dance."

Kate's tears had stopped and she shook her head. It had taken the dance master years to convince her to try. Remembering when he was just a child, watching his mother struggling to master the steps, John couldn't help but smile.

"I remember a day early on when he took me for a walk through the fields. He used his shillelagh to ruffle the tall grasses, warning the quail nesting there of our approach. When they flew from the grass, I screamed and he just laughed. He gently parted the fronds to show me the nest with its creamy white eggs hidden there. Then we walked on and he pointed out the different insects–crickets, praying mantis, mosquitoes–and told me how they benefitted the land. He knew the names of all the butterflies and birds that I had only ever learned about by reading books. It was quite different to see them as living, breathing things. I had never seen a real cow or sheep or pigs. He was impervious to the smell of them and how it carried over to himself."

The slightest hint of a smile touched her lips. "It occurred to me after a while that I no longer even noticed the smells because they had seeped into my pores, too."

"Then the babies started coming. He was so proud that Niall had his dark hair and blue eyes. He would carry Niall around the farm on his shoulders and point out all the boundaries of his land, telling Niall how it would all be his one day. He carried his pride and his bearing, as well as his sense of fairness."

Kate stiffened, as she always did, when thinking about Niall's wife, Saraid. She had detested the woman from the moment she had first seen Niall dancing with her on that hot July night in Doolin so many years ago. This barely literate girl from Kerry that her son had gotten with child when she was only seventeen was so beneath him! It was another reason she hated traveling to Doolin; it made that memory fresh. Kate shook her head and continued.

"When you came along," she went on, "I was afraid you would be left out, but your father's capacity for love was boundless. He was very proud of you, though you never took to the land like he did. He respected your good sense and ability to figure things out. He was happy that you had such a great love of books and had a good mind for math, like me.

"Once the farm became his, he gave in to my pestering and allowed me to use my talent for figures to keep the ledgers, but he never liked it. He didn't consider it women's work."

John coughed to clear the lump in his throat and set down his quill. "I always felt that I let him down somehow."

Kate whipped her head towards him. She grabbed his hand and gave it a shake. "Don't ever feel that way! We were both proud of you! Not everyone is born to work the land. He was very happy when you took over the accounts for the farm. He knew that you would have made a great teacher, too."

Kate chuckled, her mood changing again.

"Then Patrick came along and your father became as silly as a boy again. Patrick was the happiest child we had ever seen, and your father enjoyed every minute with him and every laugh. Patrick carries your father's joy of living in every bone of his body, his gentleness, too. Where he came by his great size, we'll never know."

Kate folded her hands in her lap and sighed. "The three of you boys are the best of him."

John knew she had said all she was going to. "Thank you, Mother. Are you ready to come back to the house? It's almost time to leave."

Sighing, she rose and took his arm. "Talking about him has eased me some."

Chapter Four

"So, Patrick," said Danny as they traveled through the countryside. "do you have anyone in mind yet?"

Patrick didn't understand what he was asking. "What are you talking about?"

Danny burst into laughter. "Sure ye know exactly what I'm askin'! I hear this is to be yer big passage to manhood."

Patrick's broad face blanched and then turned a vivid red all the way up to the dark curls that shot out from his head in wild abandon. He glowered down at Danny, his blue eyes glinting with anger. "I don't see that it's any of your bloody business!"

"Oh come on now, man! Sure ain't it the whole reason for ye comin' to Doolin this year? To wet yer wick?"

Patrick let out a breath. He was embarrassed to be discussing this very private matter, but he knew that Danny wouldn't let it be.

At twenty-eight, Patrick still hadn't been with a woman and had taken more than his share of teasing over it. It wasn't that he didn't want to. There was little opportunity to meet women in their small village, and none who held any fascination for him.

Patrick was also uncomfortable with his size. Unlike his lean brothers, he feared his large body would scare off any small woman. He was well over six feet tall, with a massive chest and shoulders. His arms were the size of a smaller man's thighs, while his own thighs were broad and muscular as tree trunks.

Patrick shook his head. "I probably won't."

"Why the devil not?" asked Danny.

"Because I don't know anyone!" Patrick didn't want to talk about it anymore and flicked the reins to make the horses go faster.

Danny hung onto his hat as the horses leapt forward. Still laughing, he continued to tease his cousin. "I could fix you up with a fair colleen—or *two* if you like."

Patrick gave him a disgusted look. "I probably couldn't even handle *one*!"

"Oh, don't be goin' all shy now!" Danny teased. "Sure I know just the place! And just the girl! When we get settled in, we'll go see Annie at the Shamrock! She'll know just how to be takin' care of ye."

Patrick got red in the face again. He knew who Annie was. He remembered the little barmaid from when he and Danny had gone to Doolin by themselves the year before. *She was a minx, that one. Sassy as they come.* "I wouldn't know what to do with her. Besides," he sighed, "I'd probably crush her!"

"Yeah, ye're kind of big, but maybe she likes a big man! Besides, she knows more about it than the two of us together. Sure ye might have to toss 'er a coin or two, but it wouldn't get complicated."

"What are you saying?"

"You know just what I'm sayin'. She ain't the kind of girl yer gonna marry but she'll show ye a good time an' teach ye the ropes."

"I don't know," replied Patrick, shaking his head. "We'll see."

Chapter Five

When the men's wagons reached Lisdoonvarna, they veered off the main road to follow the River Aille, which ran west, right on through Doolin.

"Ewe," said James. "What's that awful smell?"

"Sulphur," replied Niall. "There are mineral springs here. People come to bathe in the waters for the healing. There's to be a celebration here, too, for a good harvest."

"Seems to me it would make you sicker," said James, making a face.

The Doolin campsite was well lit by scattered firelight and lanterns under a moonless sky. Though they were still too far from the coast to hear or see the surf, a tinge of salt-laden air floated over them. They heard music and hammering as they came upon the men who were already gathered in groups. Some were securing lengths of wood with nails and wire to make the enclosures for the horses on both sides of the river. Others hauled bales of straw on their backs and spread them out for the horses. The scattered weeping willows that hung over its banks, graceful fronds swaying in the breeze, would provide the horses with a bit of shade as they enjoyed an endless supply of fresh drinking water. The fragrant yellow gorse in bloom along the river bank shone bright gold in the lantern light. On the far end of the campground, another group of men were hammering together the tables and benches where the women would ply the wares that they'd created over the winter months to sell or barter for things they needed.

Wagons were spread out across the Burren in a large circle, leaving a wide expanse in the center for the dance competitions. The winners would be given the honor of competing to dance in groups before the Irish Parliament at Easter time.

Small peat fires glowed across the limestone landscape where the individual clans settled together. Many displayed their coat of arms in front of their wagons. Some had already prepared their cooking areas and the smell of fresh meat cooking drifted through the warm night air.

James was wide-eyed as he took it all in. "This is amazing! I've never seen so many people!"

"Just you wait until tomorrow," said Niall, stretching his aching back and looking out at the hundred or so men in their vicinity. "When all the women folk and children arrive, it will be chaos for sure."

As they began leading the horses to the river, a voice called out. "Niall!" exclaimed Charles MacNamara, as he held out his hand. "It's good to see you!"

Niall grinned and clasped the older man's hand. "Good to see you too, Charles!"

The MacNamara family owned most of the land around Doolin and were astute enough to offer the space, for a modest fee, to different groups for musical festivals throughout the year. It was good business, bringing much needed coin to the taverns and the townspeople who would not survive without it. The people who lived in the area often rented out their beds to strangers in the warmer months while they, themselves, slept outdoors with their goats. The precious income would pay for the food to get them through the long, quiet winter.

MacNamara pulled Niall aside and lowered his voice. "Just wanted to give you a warning."

"What's that?" asked Niall.

MacNamara looked around, to make sure he wouldn't be heard.

"Seems to be some trouble afloat. Word got out about the meeting, so the sheriff's going to be keeping a close watch on the doings. They're threatening to arrest any dissenters."

Niall nodded. There was no need to ask what the older man was referring to. Political meetings among the Irish were always fraught with danger. He was disappointed that word had gotten out so soon; but with so many involved, it was hard to keep secrets.

"Thanks for letting me know. We'll keep a watch out."

Niall, tired of the useless misery besetting many of the Catholic Irish, had decided to use his influence to try to do something about it. He had worked for months to set up a clandestine meeting between the heads of the clans. He had hopes of uniting them to find a peaceful way to stave off the onslaught of new taxation and punitive laws that stripped a man of his right to provide for his family. He hoped to initiate this before the Irish fell, once again, into small useless rebellions that only caused more death. He had enlisted Willie Hayes, the young dance master, to help spread the word as he taught dance throughout the countryside.

Willie was only too happy to promote Niall's cause. He traveled far and wide to the selected few that Niall had chosen to find a peaceful resolution for his people. Under the guise of dance, and his liberal use of boyish charm, Willie moved about freely and was welcomed by rich and poor alike. He had even traveled to Dublin and met with Henry Grattan to deliver into his hand a letter, written by Niall, pleading for his help.

Grattan, a young rising star of the Anglo-Irish Parliament, was known for his considerable expertise at oratory. He was as disenfranchised by English rule as were the Catholics. Those who had been loyal to England were being as unfairly taxed as the Irish and were forming dissenting groups of their own. After thinking on Niall's proposal for a few days, he decided that it might benefit his own cause to at least meet with the man.

Chapter Six

Saraid squinted into the late-day sun as they traveled the last miles to Doolin, pulling at the ruffle of her cap to shade her eyes. There were so few trees here that relief was impossible to find. Her cotton top was clinging to her body, streaked with sweat and the grime of the dusty road. Her head was pounding from listening to Fiona's incessant whining. She'd had enough. Saraid rubbed her jaw, which she realized was aching because she had been clenching her teeth for miles. "Fiona!" she snapped. "Can ye just keep yer bloody mouth still for five minutes?"

"What do you mean?" cried Fiona. The ten-year-old girl was stunned to have her mother speak so harshly to her. Her green eyes filled up and her lower lip began to quiver.

Saraid sighed and shook her head. Being cooped up in the wagon for the better part of two days with three children was hard on all of them. Thankfully, Liam and Bridget had fallen asleep for the last hour, and she had only Fiona to listen to.

"Please don't be cryin', Fiona," Saraid pleaded. "I didn't mean to be yellin' at ye."

"Then why did you?" Fiona wailed. She crossed her arms over her narrow chest and made a dramatic pout, her lower lip sticking out, pink and wet.

Saraid sighed and thought that Fiona's lips looked like a fat slug. "Because I'm weary, and ye've not stopped talkin' since we left Ennis!"

"Well, what else am I supposed to do? There's nothing to do but sit here. How long before we get to Doolin?"

Saraid bowed her head. *Dear sweet Jesus,* she whispered to herself. *Please keep me from doin' bodily harm to this child!*

Exasperated, Saraid snapped the reins to get the horse moving faster to catch up to John and Kate. Once she did, she called out to them. "John! Pull over!"

Once John had guided his caravan to the side of the road, Saraid got alongside him. "Can Fiona ride with ye for awhile?"

Kate looked at Saraid with stern disapproval. "What's the matter?" she asked.

Saraid muttered, "I'm just needin' a few miles of peace and quiet."

John looked at Fiona, who was still pouting, and then at Saraid whose eyes were pleading. "There really isn't much room," he said softly. "The back of the wagon is full."

Kate shifted on the seat. "She doesn't take up much space. She can sit beside me."

Saraid sighed with relief. "Thank ye, Kate."

"Humph," muttered Kate. "No need to thank me. I'm not doing it for you. Fiona will be better off in our wagon since you have so little patience."

Fiona turned her face so her mother wouldn't see the smile that played on her lips.

Saraid ground her teeth together to keep from sputtering.

John lifted Fiona into their wagon. "We'll be there soon, little one."

"How long is soon?" asked Fiona.

"It's only a couple more miles to Lisdoonvarna." He nodded to Saraid as he spoke to Fiona. "I think either your da or Danny will meet us there near the springs."

Kate knew that her own patience with Saraid was sorely lacking, but she just couldn't help it. The worst of it, for her, was that since

James had passed away, the big house now belonged to Niall. He had wasted no time moving his family in. She still flinched when she thought of the day-to-day commotion and noise Saraid brought into the house. Two women in the same house was difficult at best, but with Saraid, it was impossible. Kate thought about moving herself into Niall's smaller house, but she was determined to stay where she was. She'd be damned if she would leave her own home!

An hour later, they saw Danny on horseback, waiting at the edge of the road, talking and laughing with a throng of men. "Hey!" he called out. "Ye finally got here!" He rode over to them and dismounted.

"Where are Niall and James?" asked Saraid, looking around at all the unfamiliar faces.

"They're in deep conversation about some horses so he sent me to fetch ye." He reached up and squeezed Kate's hand. "How's my best girl?" he asked, his eyes twinkling.

Kate's mouth twitched as she did her best to hold back a smile but it escaped her anyway. She shook her head. "I'm hardly your *girl*!"

"Ah," Danny laughed. "Ye'll always be my girl."

He turned to John. "Follow me and I'll lead ye to camp."

The last mile was slow going and noisy. The air was heavy with salty moisture from the sea and the smell of cook fires and ale. A cacophony of pipes and whistles competed with fiddles and voices singing a discordant number of melodies at the same time. Several couples were already dancing reels in the meadow. The celebration had begun.

They reached the camp and parked the wagons. Saraid's sister, Maureen, and her husband, Michael Roark, were joining them with their twins. Their wagon was there, but it was empty

"Have ye seen my sister?" Saraid asked Danny.

"Yeah," he replied as he helped John unhitch the horses. "Maureen's taken the twins and gone explorin', an' Roark went off with Niall and Patrick. They should all be back soon enough."

Saraid smiled, filling with happy anticipation, her foul mood lifting. It had been over a year since she had seen her sister and she was looking forward to it. They would be coming back to the farm with them for two weeks to help with the harvest.

Danny and John took the horses and led them to the pens. Beyond the fences, naked children were splashing and laughing as they played in the shallow river.

Kate was happy to see that the men had fashioned a simple table and a couple of wooden benches near their wagons. She set a folded blanket on one, sat herself down and looked out over the meadow. *So many people!*

Saraid lifted Bridget and Liam out of the wagon and set a blanket on the ground for them to sit on. She opened a cloth sack and gave them each an apple. "Ye sit yerselves right here now and don't be wanderin' off."

Saraid was pleased with the fire pit the men had created by stacking small flat pieces of limestone and other rocks around a larger slab of limestone. The men had erected a spit, as well as braces to hold the cooking pots, by pounding iron rods into the fissures between the stones. Chunks of peat were stacked beneath the pots to be lit as needed for cooking. One of the pots was already filled with fresh cold water. She scooped her hands into it and splashed water over her face and neck and wiped away the grime of the trip with her skirt.

Patrick had brought one of his freshly slaughtered pigs and had it slow-roasting on a spit over a second fire, the fat dripping and sputtering into the low flames. The pig would roast throughout the night and into the next day before it was ready to be eaten.

Fiona asked, "Can I go to the river?"

Saraid shook her head as she unloaded sacks from the wagon. "Not until your da gets back."

"You never let me do anything!" Fiona whined.

"Sure yer quite right, missy. Especially when ye're havin' such a smart mouth." She grabbed an ear of corn from one of the sacks and tossed it to Fiona. "Here, catch! Ye can help get the corn ready." She emptied the sack onto the blanket and handed Liam and Bridget ears of their own to keep them busy.

Fiona flinched and let the corn hit the ground. "I don't want to peel corn!" She began crying again.

Saraid squeezed her eyes shut and clenched her hands together. "Fiona," she said softly, willing her daughter to look at her. It was so difficult not to scream at her in front of Kate. She bent over until her eyes were even with Fiona's, cupping the child's chin in her hand. "Tomorrow will be yer special day. Are ye forgettin' already yer new dress that I worked on for months? I did that just for my special girl. And yer new shoes? Only ye got special new shoes."

"Can I put my dress on now?" she asked, though she already knew the answer.

Saraid sighed. No matter what she said, it would not be what Fiona wished to hear. "If ye be puttin' it on now, it will only be ruined for the dancin' tomorrow."

Kate made an attempt to mollify Fiona. "Come here, child."

Fiona sniffled and went to her grandmother who wrapped her in a gentle hug. "Your mother is right, in this." *Much as I hate to admit it,* she thought. "Tomorrow will be soon enough to wear that special dress." She pushed the damp strands that had escaped Fiona's long braid from her face. "Tonight, we'll go to bed early and tomorrow, we'll all be happy to watch you dance."

"There ye be!" cried Maureen in greeting, as she and the three-year-old twins rushed toward them.

"Maureen!" Saraid squealed. She rose from the blanket and ran to her sister with open arms. They clung together until the twins started pulling on their mother's skirt, demanding her attention.

Kate took the opportunity to go to her caravan. "I'm going to lie down for a while." Her head was aching and her legs felt weak.

Saraid barely glanced at Kate as she walked to her caravan, sensing nothing amiss. She leaned down and ruffled the boys' hair. "How are ye, my darlin' boys? Look how big ye got!"

It was easy to see that the women were sisters. They were both petite, if roundly built, with sturdy legs and the same wide smile and dancing green eyes. They both wore their dark auburn hair in a single thick braid that hung nearly to their waists.

Maureen pulled away and offered Saraid an over-flowing basket. "I've brought ye some wild onions an' fresh parsley, an' I found some thyme growin' out there on the Burren."

"Happy day," said Saraid. "Let's mix the herbs with some honey and pour it over the pig."

"Boys!" cried Maureen as she pulled the twins back from the cooking fire. "Watch ye don't be gettin' burned"

She turned to Fiona and gave her braid a light tug. "Watch them for a bit, won't ye Fiona, so I can talk with yer mother?"

"I can't now," said Fiona peevishly. "I have to peel the corn."

"Fiona!" cried Saraid as she mixed up the glaze. "Mind yer manners! Just sit 'em on the blanket with ye and give 'em each an ear. They can help ye."

Fiona's lips tightened into a trembling, angry grimace, tears welling up in her eyes, yet again. "How come it never matters what *I* want to do?" She flung down her corn and stomped to the back of the wagon.

Saraid began to follow after her but Maureen held her back. "Just let 'er go." She furrowed her brow as she watched the unhappy girl sit on the ground and bury her face in her hands and sob. "She's not a very happy girl, is she?"

Saraid shook her head as she slowly poured the savory mix over the pork. It sizzled and the fire spit as the glaze dripped down to the flames. "No," she sighed. "An' she got so excited about comin' here an' the dancin' that she wore herself out jabberin' about it." Saraid shrugged as she watched her daughter "She's stuck in that place of being too old to be little and too little to speak her mind without hearin' about it."

Maureen tilted her head to one side, pondering Fiona. "It might not be that at all, ye know. Sure there's always been a fierceness about that one—*determined* to have her own way, if nothin' else," she added with a chuckle. "She'll be a force to deal with in a few years."

Saraid smiled, but as she stared at her daughter, she realized that Maureen had given voice to her own fears. "Ye know," she said pensively, "I believe ye may know her better'n she knows herself right now. Can't ye just see her goin' off bare-fisted against our mighty enemies with that smart mouth?"

Maureen laughed heartily at the vision but said in all seriousness, "I hope for her sake . . . and yers . . . she outgrows her anger at the world."

Saraid laughed despite her weariness. "Sure I pity the boys who try to charm her in a few years because she'll be havin' none of their blarney." She shrugged her shoulders. "Yet, who knows, she might surprise us."

Chapter Seven

Sean and Tommy Callahan, young brothers from County Kerry, were showing off their race horses in a small grove of pines a short distance from the pens. The dozen or so men gathered around them were all asking questions at the same time.

"What breed is this?" asked Niall, running his palm over the horse's compact back.

Tommy, thin and sinewy, his light hair falling over his eyes, sat astride his mare who was chomping on a hedge of gorse. A light scent of coconut filled the air as the horse chewed on the yellow flowers and leaves. Slightly inebriated, he spoke with the great enthusiasm only a sixteen-year-old can muster. "They's called an Irish Sport horse. We been breedin' thoroughbreds with the draught horse for a few years now. Then we breed the new mares with other o' the new ones. This year we added a Connemara stud, too."

"How big do they get?" asked James as he marveled at the size of the beast.

Sean, two years older and not as lean, stroked the nose of his black stallion, keeping a loose hold of his bridle. "They actually come out three ways. The smallest one will carry a lighter man like Tommy here. Then what we got the most of is a middle weight for carryin' the average rider. Sometimes, you might get a larger one that can carry a man big as Patrick here, but that's a rare one."

Tommy took up where Sean left off. "The draught's a strong and steady horse an' the thoroughbred is good an' fast an' has endurance, too. We got a few good colts this spring. We're hopin' to breed em' with some Andalusian stock next year."

Sean added, "Yeah, that'll give em' more strength and stamina. The equestrian riders like em' too' cause they're great jumpers an' perform well." His love of the horse was evident as he stroked his smooth coat. "We're talkin' a really good lookin' horse here, too."

James, clearly puzzled, asked, "What's an equestrian?"

Sean chuckled. "They's rich folks that make horses do fancy jumps and steps for show."

Tommy held the reins close as the mare started to prance. He patted her flank, pride radiating from his face. "This one races like the wind. Ain't no stoppin' 'er once she gets goin'."

"I've heard of horses like these but I've never seen one," said Roark. His own plough horse could pull a plow or a wagon but race like the wind? Never.

"You can see for yourselves tomorrow! We's gonna be racin' down through Fisherstreet in the mornin' to show off what they can do."

Patrick reached up and stroked the stallion's arched, muscular neck. The horse stayed calm under his hand and snuffled at his tunic, giving him a little nudge. "I'd like to see that!"

"Can we see the race, Da?" James's young face radiated excitement

Niall smiled and ruffled his son's hair. "I don't see why not."

Jack Cleary, portly owner of the Shamrock Tavern chuckled. "Like the wind, you say? Maybe we should be makin' a wager as to which one will win."

Seamus Flynn spat on the ground, gave Jack a mean look. "An' I suppose you'll be holdin' on to all the coins?"

"What's wrong with that?" Jack asked. "You can all come over to the tavern after the race and we'll settle up. In fact, why don't you all come by now for a pint on me?"

Seamus licked his lips, already tasting a fresh mug of ale. His pocket was empty and a free drink sounded good to him.

Tommy smiled. "Sounds all right to me!"

Niall and Patrick exchanged a look. The last thing they needed was another drink.

Another man among them got serious minded and looked to Sean. "Ye'd best be hidin' a few of these horses so the Anglos don't go takin' 'em all at tax time or raise yer rents again."

Tommy, red-faced, jumped from his mare. "Don't even talk like that!" The rage he always carried just beneath the surface manifested itself into a tirade. He began to pace, his arms waving as he spoke. "They already took everythin' my family ever had! My great-granda and our people had to run halfway across this feckin' country with just the clothes on their backs and a couple of ponies! That feckin' bastard Cromwell gave his soldiers the land that should 'a been *ours*," he yelled, pointing to his brother.

Lord Oliver Cromwell, sent by the English Parliament to quell the last of the Irish rebellion in 1649, was fanatical in his hatred of the Irish Catholics and took great pride in bringing them to their knees, leaving naught but butchery and smoke in his wake.

Sean stepped in front of his brother and grabbed him by the shirt. "Easy, Tommy! There's nothin' to be done for it now."

Tommy shook his fist at the sky. "By God, I'll kill every last one of 'em before they take this horse from me!"

"You need to quiet down," said Niall.

Seamus shared Tommy's rage. He got in front of Niall's face and sneered. "Not everyone's well off, ye know. Can't blame the lad fer bein' angry. I am, too! Molly and me got *nothin'* left." He had been drinking heavily with the Callahans for most of the day and his eyes were bleary, his breath foul.

Niall scowled. He had no use for Seamus, drunk or sober. It didn't help that Seamus was married to Saraid's childhood friend, Molly. He saw him as a poor provider with no ambition other than to serve his own needs. He tried unsuccessfully to ignore him.

Seamus kept on carping. "Our da had three acres left, just like his brothers. We farmed it all together just so we could try to fill our bellies. When he died, Henry and me got just over an acre each— that's it! Then we couldn't pay our taxes and them greedy bastards took the last of it."

Tommy felt energized by Seamus's rant. "We should join up with the Whiteboys an' see how them landlords like it when we tear down their fences and wreck their stone walls!"

Jack stood back, a small smile playing on his mouth as he took in the spectacle. *Isn't this interesting?* he thought to himself. *Maybe if I keep the antagonism going, we'll have some real excitement!* "You gonna kill off their cattle, too?"

Tommy was taken aback. "I ain't plannin' on killin' nothin!"

Jack laughed and scoffed at Tommy. "You wouldn't last a single day as a Whiteboy! You've nothin' for brains and your big mouth would be heard all the way to Dublin!"

Tommy raised his fist to strike the man but Patrick grabbed his wrist and held fast.

Jack backed away and put his hands up in a placating gesture. "I was just sayin'—I meant no harm."

Niall tried to bring calm to the group but they talked right over him. They didn't want to calm down; they felt that all their resentments were valid.

More than a dozen years before, small bands of young men in the counties of Limerick, Tipperary, Cork and Waterford roved the countryside, all wearing white shirts. They dug up confiscated farmland, destroyed orchards and wrecked fences and stone walls that penned in cattle. They posted demands that these lands not be re-rented for three years and that people stop paying the tithes to the Anglican church.

The government response was to make a concentrated effort to round up the dissenters, many of whom were imprisoned or hung.

Now, the increasing poverty was bringing a resurgence. Larger, more organized groups of angry young men were striking back with more deadly force against the unending oppression.

Tommy's eyes filled. "You don' understand what that Cromwell did to my family! The only reason my great-granda survived was 'cause he an' my uncles were in Ballinasloe, lookin' to get new ponies! They was comin' home to Wexford an' they kept meetin' up with all these sorry-lookin' people, runnin' fer their lives with just the clothes on their backs! All of 'em carryin on weepin' and tellin' 'em tales."

Sean spoke quietly. "When they crossed the river Barrow, they started seein' the smoke an' everythin' in ruins. Thatched roofs burned away, fences busted and livestock all killed or dyin'. They was right scared when they rounded the last bend in the road to find everythin' they owned gone. The barns and stables were burned to nothin'."

He began to pace, rubbing his stomach, barely able to contain his grief. "An' that weren't the worst of it," he whispered. "The air was stinkin' from the horses that got trapped an' burnt up in the stables. The thatched roof of the house was nothing but inky black strands an' the ground was all charred." Tears rolled down his face and he wrapped his arms around the stallion's neck. The other men stood silent and uncomfortable around him.

Sean's eyes glittered and he paused for a deep breath. "The worst part was findin' their kinfolk layin' dead and rottin' in the dirt; their wives and children stripped naked and raped, their hair singed off. They was helpless against Cromwell's men and their swords an' guns and torches. The men was too broken to even cry. All they could do was bury 'em."

Sean leaned against his stallion and said nothing more while the men around them looked away, each with memories of the tales of their own families' struggles in those long ago years. The horses nickered quietly, as if in sympathy, while the birds sat silent in the boughs overhead.

Even Jack was silent, unwilling to provoke them further.

James was the first to speak. "Did they stay there?"

Tommy took a deep, sobering breath and shook his head. He related how the Callahan men, three brothers and two young sons, left the life they had known and made the long trek west to County Kerry where they had family that would help them.

The journey was difficult and they had to forage and hunt for food. On a good day, they snared a rabbit to roast over an open fire or caught fish with their bare hands in the pristine streams. Other days they survived on berries and edible roots as they silently made their way to the western counties of Ireland that had been spared Cromwell's tyranny.

The horses and ponies managed quite well on gorse and wild grasses and the fresh water from plentiful streams along the way. At night around the campfire, as they finally shared their tears and anger with other travelers heading west, they found some short measure of solace in the playing of their penny whistles and the low singing of their mournful Irish songs.

It took four generations for the Callahans to recover and rebuild their families and their horse farm. They were a tight-knit clan, determined to eke out a life despite the ravages of their past. Their rage and deep feelings of loss were as ingrained as their tenacious sense of survival.

Jack could see that the men were getting restless, some beginning to walk away. He reminded them of the offer of a free pint as he too walked away.

Niall put his hand on Tommy's shoulder. "Look, I know your family suffered, as did many others, and I'm sorry for it. Instead of burning yourself up over what happened over a hundred years ago, try remembering that they had the courage to survive. You have a life today because of them and their sweat. You have no idea who might be roaming around and hear what you're going on about. Keep on with the threats and you'll end up hung for it."

Tommy, shrugging away from Niall's hand, scoffed at him, still too angry to get it through his thick skull that Niall was right. "Who's gonna hear us out here? Are ye afraid of 'em, Niall?"

Niall stared hard at Tommy but kept silent, refusing to take the bait.

Patrick gave Tommy's arm a yank. "Don't be challenging him, you dim-wit!"

Tommy tried to free his arm but Patrick's big hand held fast until he stopped struggling. He finally managed to stand still and just sulk.

The few remaining onlookers, edgy and tight-lipped, broke away from them. Muttering their farewells, they set off for their wagons or to the Shamrock for their free pint.

Once they were alone, Niall placed his hand on Tommy's shoulder and spoke calmly and clearly. "Look at me, Tommy." He waited patiently until the young man finally faced him. "You're only sixteen. You have no idea yet how your temper can wreck your life. This is about more than just what you want this minute." He paused, trying to find the right words without revealing too much. He decided not to tell him about the meeting that would take place late that night. "Things will happen for the better at the proper time."

Tommy tried to shake free but Niall's hand dug deeper. "I wasn't done. You will wait until after the *Ceilidh* to do whatever it is you're so hell-bent on doing. You will not put our families in danger with your quick mouth or your stupidity. No more talk of the Whiteboys."

Tommy eyed him defiantly, then sighed. "I hear ye."

When Niall was satisfied that the arguing was over, he patted Tommy's shoulder. He nodded to James and began walking back to the wagons, Patrick and Roark following.

Chapter Eight

Danny hollered out, "There ye be!"
Niall looked up to see Danny coming toward them through a noisy throng of clansmen milling about their cooking fires. The air was heavy with smoke and the smell of fresh fish and meat cooking. Niall's stomach growled and he realized how hungry he was. "They've arrived, then?" he asked, relieved. He shrugged off the tension in his shoulders and vowed to put away his foul mood.

"Sure they have," Danny replied. "I've been sent to fetch ye for dinner."

"Good!" cried Patrick. "How's the pig doing?"

"Smells right good. Saraid cut off some of what's done on the outside and left the rest to cook 'til tomorrow."

When they came into camp, Niall tried to nuzzle Saraid with a warm greeting but she was too weary and frazzled from the journey for his touch. "Not now!" She ached for his embrace to soothe away the rigors of the journey but instead, she squirmed away from him and busied herself with helping Maureen put dinner on the crude table.

Thick slices of crackled pork sizzled on a platter. Corn, with butter melting over the golden ears, was heaped in a large earthenware bowl and a tin plate was piled high with sliced apples. Chunks of potatoes were scraped from a pot where they had been roasting in pork fat over the fire and seasoned with plenty of salt and parsley.

Bemused, Niall stood beside Roark and John while his younger children accosted him with squeals and affection. Bridget stood bouncing on her little legs and reached her arms up. He swooped her into his arms and tickled her, making her giggle with happiness. Liam hung on to his legs and he ruffled the towhead's hair. Suddenly, just like that, Niall's mood was lifted back to joy. He searched for his mother who was nowhere to be seen. "John? Where's mother?"

John looked around the gathered family and then realized that she had not returned from her nap. "She lay down for a bit. I'll get her."

When John and Kate arrived at the table, Niall noticed that she seemed not herself but bit his tongue. They all settled in to eating and between mouthfuls of the succulent pork and the rest, plans were made for the next day.

"We're going to a horse race tomorrow!" exclaimed James.

"What's this about a race?" asked Saraid.

James spoke animatedly to the others about the Callahans and their horses and the big race the following morning at Fisherstreet, the small community on the outskirts of Doolin.

"I don't want to go to a horse race," mewled Fiona.

"I do!" cried Liam.

"I thought we were setting up the tables in the morning," said Kate.

Niall turned to Saraid. "Did you remember your lace?"

Saraid nodded. The fine examples of her work were stacked to bulging in a linen sack in the caravan. She was hoping for some good sales this year. She'd also brought a box of linen pouches filled with dried herbs, most for healing remedies. "I'd like to see the race, too."

She turned to Kate. "If I help ye set up the tables, would ye sit durin' the race? An' since Fiona don't want to go to the race, she could help ye 'til I get there. I'll be takin' Bridget with us so you won't have to be watchin' her too."

Fiona began to complain but Sariad silenced her with a hard look. "You can collect the coins." It was a bribe but Saraid knew her daughter well.

Fiona finally had something to smile about and her eyes twinkled. The girl loved to handle coins and knew how to figure the worth of them.

Kate's lips twitched at how cunning Saraid was. "I'm sure Fiona and I can manage things for a while."

"Good." replied Saraid. "That's settled then."

Roark licked his fingers of pork grease. "We're still goin' to the sea, too, aren't we?"

Patrick nodded. "As soon as the race is over. We'll have to get there while the tide's still out if we're wanting any clams."

"Are we going to get a boat?" asked Liam."

Niall shook his head. "If we get there early enough, we can roll up our pants and walk out on the sandbar."

"We'll have to be quick about it," said Danny. "Sure ye don't want to be out there when the tide starts comin' in!"

***

Sean and Tommy stood alone in the small grove of trees with the horses. Sean got a whiff of salt coming across the meadow with the cooling breeze off the Atlantic. It made the hot afternoon bearable. He looked to the cloudless blue sky as he wiped the sweat from his brow and judged it to be about dinner time. "Sure he makes sense, Tommy." When his brother didn't respond, he grinned and gave him a friendly punch on the arm. "Look, let's just get through the day. How 'bout we go to the Shamrock and get us that free pint and cool off a bit."

Tommy shrugged as they mounted their horses, a smile twitching at the corners of his mouth. "Sounds good to me."

Sean was relieved to see Tommy's anger finally subside. The last thing they needed was trouble. "Come on, man! Maybe we can git some wagers on the race! An' the dancin' too! Ye know I'm gonna beat yer ass off on the doors!"

"Hah!" Tommy snorted. "Ye cocky bastard . . . y'ain't got a prayer!"

Chapter Nine

By sunrise on Saturday, the morning fog that usually floated over the coastline of Doolin had burned off. The village of Fisherstreet was bathed in brilliant sunshine under a clear cornflower sky. The rowdy crowd lining both sides of the road was filled with anticipation, casting their bets for the horse they hoped would win.

Midway on the route, Niall and his boys and Saraid, with Bridget in tow, stood a few feet behind the crowd with Roark and Maureen and their twins. Danny and Patrick, who stood closer to the road, beckoned to Niall to join them for a better view. Niall shook his head and hoisted Liam to his shoulders.

Suddenly, everyone grew silent as a man's arm shot into the air. The sun glinted off the black steel of the gun barrel held aloft at the starting line. The young racers struggled to hold the great horses back as they pranced and neighed, anxious to start.

"Just fire the bloody gun!" cried Tommy Callahan.

A single gunshot blast echoed through the village, and the crowd erupted into a roar of shouts as the horses came tearing down the road.

One ear-piercing cry went through the crowd like a knife as Bridget, hands over her ears, escaped Saraid's grasp and ran blindly through the people blocking her path.

"Stop!" Saraid hollered after her young daughter. "Bridget! Don't run! Oh dear sweet Jesus, someone stop her!"

Saraid screamed Bridget's name again and again as she chased after her. All she could see was the mop of reddish-blond curls as the child careened between the bodies in front of her.

Niall dropped Liam to the ground and pushed aside everyone in his path to chase after Bridget, too.

"Bridget!" he screamed, his heart pounding as he ran through the crowd toward the road.

The throng of cheering people were deaf to their shouts as they watched the horses speeding towards them.

Bridget tumbled barefoot through an opening in the crowd onto the narrow dirt road and froze. Terror filled her green eyes as the two giant horses, their legs taller than she, came racing straight towards her, their hooves kicking up a cloud of dust in their wake. She huddled there on her knees, her mouth agape but unable to utter a sound. The crowd was too stunned to act in time, or without being injured themselves, when they comprehended what was happening.

The Callahan brothers saw Bridget spill into their path but had no way to stop the full out gallop of the massive horses. Without a word between them, they swerved to the left, just as Niall's hand grabbed a fistful of Bridget's tunic and yanked the terrified child out of harm's way. The crowd cheered, and more than one woman began to wail and weep as Bridget was pulled to safety.

Niall, his eyes squeezed shut, breathed deep to calm his thudding heart, clutched the now sobbing child to his chest. "Your da has you, little one." His voice cracked. "Don't cry."

Bridget looked up at her father, tears still shimmering in her eyes. "I was so scared, Da!"

Saraid reached them, the race forgotten. She clung to them both, still breathless with fright as tears coursed down her cheeks.

"Oh Niall, she could have been killed," she cried. "God bless those boys that they saw her in time."

Niall snapped at Saraid, unable to hold back the anger he felt. "Why weren't you holding on to her?"

Shock flushed her face. "How can ye be blamin' me for this?" she cried. "Of *course* I was holdin' on to her! I had her hand in mine but she took off like a sprite when the gun went off!"

Niall closed his eyes and nodded as he put an arm around her shoulder. "I'm sorry . . . I was scared too." He had wanted to blame someone for the near tragedy and she was nearer than anyone else. He pried Bridget's arms from around his neck and handed her off to her mother who held her close, gently wiping her tears with trembling fingers.

"No harm done to ye, my darlin' girl," Saraid said, patting Bridget's curly head. "Sure ye're alright now."

Niall looked around for James and Liam. "Why don't you take her back to the caravan and lay her down for a bit. I'm going to go find the boys. The race must be close to done by now."

Saraid gazed up into the vibrant blue of his eyes, relieved to see no more of the accusation or blame in them. His rebuke had been like a slap. In the bright light she noticed for the first time that lines had begun to creep around his dark lashes; and with his hair tied back, fine silver strands glimmered at his temples. Thirty-four was not old for a man as fit as he was, but working the fields and caring for the livestock was not an easy life.

"What?" Niall asked quizzically as he bent to kiss her cheek and tug on the long braid that hung like heavy rope beneath the ruffled edge of her white cap.

Saraid's smile was wide, the dimple in her left cheek deep as she gave him a mischievous grin. "Not a thing, my love," she said. She shook her head to push away her lusty thoughts.

He leaned in again, grinning, and whispered near her ear, "Hold that look for me." He gave her ample bottom a quick squeeze. "I'll see you in a bit."

Saraid chuckled, feigning wide-eyed shock at his familiar, playful touch. She was filled with an aching tenderness as she watched him walk away from her. There was an easy grace to his tall, lean frame that made her belly quiver. She smiled softly, knowing how well-muscled he was beneath the loose white shirt and snug britches, his feet tucked into soft summer boots. He charmed her still. Together for fifteen years now, she marveled at how the flirtatious start of their relationship, begun right here in Doolin, had grown and deepened over the years, despite Kate's pettiness. She struggled every day not to show Kate how much it hurt her to be such a constant disappointment to her.

Saraid walked slowly back to the caravan, her long crimson skirt swaying as she rocked Bridget in her arms. By the time they reached the campsite, she was humming and doing small dance steps. Saraid lay Bridget down on her side in the caravan, tucking the child's favorite blanket around her. It was a light-weight yellow wool with a soft ribbon binding.

Saraid began singing an old lullaby:

> *Rest tired eyes awhile . . .*
> *Sweet is thy baby's smile . . .*
> *Angels are guarding and they watch o'er thee.*
> *Sleep, sleep, grá mo chree . . .*
> *Here on your momma's knee . . .*
> *Angels are guarding . . .*
> *And they watch o'er thee.*

Bridget's eyes fluttered shut and her thumb found her small mouth. Her fingers toyed with the binding that she held against her cheek. Saraid continued the lullaby, gently stroking Bridget's back. The old song calming herself as well as her little girl.

> *The birdeens sing a fluting song . . .*
> *They sing to thee the whole day long . . .*
> *Wee fairies dance o'er hill and dale . . .*
> *For very love of thee.*

Outside the caravan, she spied her boys coming toward her. Seven-year-old Liam, all rosy cheeks and twinkling blue eyes under a head full of blond curls, was fairly bursting with excitement as he ran headlong toward her.

"Mam!" he squealed breathlessly. "You should've seen those horses when they came roaring over the finish line! They were so fine!"

Saraid held a finger to her lips. "Hush, my little one," she chuckled, looking at his ever-cheerful face. "Ye'll be wakin' yer sister."

"Tommy Callahan beat Sean by just inches," said James as he came up to them. Her elder son, a tall lanky boy, all dark-haired and blue-eyed like his father, grabbed an apple from the basket in the caravan and took a large bite. "They were amazing to watch," he said as he chewed, wiping the dripping juice from his chin with the back of his hand.

Bridget began to whimper and Saraid gently rubbed her back. "How 'bout ye boys help me sing her back to sleep for a bit?"

James tossed the apple core and wiped his hands on his pants before reaching into the caravan for his tin whistle, and Liam's willow branch whistle, as well.

As the boys began to play, Saraid continued the melody..

Dream, dream, grá mo chree . . .
Here on your momma's knee . . .
Angels are guardin' they watch o'er thee . . .
As you sleep may angels watch over . . .
And may they guard over thee.
The primrose in the sheltered nook . . .
The crystal stream the babblin' brook . . .
All these things God's hands have made . . .
For very love of thee.
Twilight and shadows fall . . .
Peace to his children all . . .
Angels are guardin' and they watch o'er thee . . .
As you sleep . . .

May angels watch over and may they guard o'er thee.

"Thank you, my loves," she whispered. "Sure that was right lovely."

Liam craned his neck to see his young sister who was once again soundly sleeping. "Mam, is she alright now?"

Saraid ran her fingers down the boy's cheek. "I'm sure of it, Liam. She just needs to rest a bit and she'll be right as rain. Do ye want to be restin' a bit yerself? We've a big afternoon ahead of us."

"No Mam," he replied with whispered excitement. "I want to go to the ocean and see the boats!"

"Not now Liam. I'll need ye and James to stay here with Bridget while I go fetch yer gran and Fiona."

James balked. "Da said we could go! We're to be getting the buckets for the clams and fish!"

Niall arrived with Roark and Maureen as the boys pleaded their case. "What's going on here?" Niall asked.

Saraid said, "I need the boys to watch over Bridget while I go fetch Kate and Fiona."

Liam looked to his father, pouting. "We want to go with you for the clams!"

Maureen waved her hand in the air. "I'll stay with Bridget. Let the boys go."

"Are ye sure that's not a bother?" asked Saraid.

"Not at all. Ye go on, then." Maureen nodded to the twins who were clinging to her skirts with sleepy eyes and fingers in their mouths. "Sure my babes be needin' a lay down, too."

Patrick and Danny came to the wagon with buckets in hand.

"Are we goin' to be off sometime today?" asked Danny.

"You hush up," said Saraid. "Be off with the lot of ye, then."

The men and boys happily set off for the shore.

Chapter Ten

Saraid smiled to have a few minutes to herself as she walked across the Burren to where the women were selling their wares. Saraid enjoyed the feeling of the damp grass between her toes as she walked barefoot across the campsite. She lifted her face to the sun that had risen higher in the sky, admiring the few lacy clouds that were drifting by. This was her favorite time of day when near the sea and she embraced it, ignoring the rising humidity. The air had the fresh tinge of salt and she could hear the gulls crying out in the distance as she imagined them searching for their dinner in the quiet surf of low tide. Music carried from all corners of the camp and she greeted all who called out to her with a wave and a smile. Knowing that she would be back on the quiet farm soon enough, she looked forward to all that would transpire over the next two days.

She was totally unaware of the effect she had on the people she passed. She had a natural earthiness about her that was at once both lusty and innocent. Many women envied her, wishing they could be more like her. Most men envied Niall, thinking of what a delight she must be between the sheets.

Saraid arrived at the end of the camp where many of the women and girls had spent the morning sitting at tables with their handmade wares to sell or barter. She nibbled on bits of bread dotted with fresh butter and jam or drizzled with honey, all the while swatting at the flies that were drawn to the sweetness. At other tables, she ran her fingers over bolts of wool and linen that had been woven over the winter. The annual summer gathering was one of the highlights of their year and a good time to accumulate some of the stores needed to replenish their larders.

Saraid sniffed at herbs wrapped in pieces of thin cotton and tied off with string, knowing that hers were better. She came from a long line of healers, women who still clung to some of the pagan ways and knew the medicinal properties of herbs.

Her own specialty, though, was the lovely crocheted lace that she made during the long winter evenings with linen thread and a thin steel crochet hook, working by the light of the fireside and a small lantern on the table. She had been taught by her mother and her grandmother, and was now teaching the art to Fiona. Her grandmother had been one of many impoverished women taken in by the good sisters at the convent in Youghal, in County Cork, after being driven from their homes by the Anglos. The small intricate pattern pieces required concentration and dexterity, but when sewn together, were awe-inspiring in their beauty. She had put her skills to work this past winter to fashion an exquisite lace ascot for Willie Hayes as a barter for their dance lessons when he had made his trek to their village.

Saraid chuckled to think how miffed Martin Clancy, the reigning Dance Master of Clare, would be when he saw it. She thought Martin, with his bright attire and fancy scrolled staff, was a prissy fool of a man. She did have to agree, however, that even at fifty, he was still the fiercest dancer in Ireland, able to outlast men half his age.

Saraid spied her childhood friend Molly Flynn and her children, sitting not far from Fiona and Kate, and eagerly made her way over to her.

"Ah Molly!" she exclaimed, clapping her hands with joy. "Ye've saved me some of my favorite black raspberry jam!"

Molly, a babe sucking at her breast, laughed brightly as she lined up the half dozen jars she had set aside. "Sure I set aside most of it until I saw ye comin'. God knows there'd be hell to pay if I din't!"

"The other folks will have to make do with the crabapple jelly and bramble jams because I'll be takin' all of them!" She pulled more coins than needed from the small cloth bag tied to her waist and set them before her friend.

Molly quickly gathered up the coins and added them to the others in her bag. She was more grateful than she could say for her friend's generosity.

The women around them joined in with teasing and laughter, happy to be away from their monotonous daily routines. It lifted their spirits to be among so many of their women friends, just to get caught up on gossip and news.

Saraid hugged her old friend. She couldn't help but notice that Molly's pale blue eyes were ringed with shadows. Her cheeks, though still sprinkled with a smattering of freckles, were much thinner than when she'd last seen her. Molly shifted the baby to her other breast, her belly straining against her tunic.

"What? Again?" asked Saraid. "When are ye due?"

Molly blushed. "Ye know that man o'mine," she said. "Sure we'll be havin' a houseful. This one," she said, laying a hand on her bulge, "should be arrivin' late fall."

Saraid eyed the three children sitting at Molly's feet, the eldest wearing a shabby make-shift tunic. It was clearly one of Molly's cast-offs and hung off the girl's shoulders. The other children were naked. All of them were thin, smudged with dirt and unkempt.

Saraid shook her head. "I don't know how ye can do it every year," she said.

Molly shrugged. "There's not much I can be doin' about it, now is there?" She fingered the crude wool blanket in front of her. "I'm earnin' some money workin' for the wool weavers."

Sariad frowned at her friend. "Molly, ye don't want to be gettin' caught working for O'Connell," she said quietly.

She knew the Irish were forbidden to export their wool. Even so, there were merchants who bought wool from the sheep herders at the big Ballinasloe Fair in the fall, and then paid the Irish women to comb and spin it into yarn in their homes. Very few women had looms large enough to weave the wool so it was then taken to weavers in the larger towns.

Molly's smile faded and she asked Saraid where she'd heard about this.

Saraid shrugged at her friend and waved her hand in the air. "It isn't much of a secret among us that he's quietly shippin' it out to Portugal and the West Indies."

Molly laughed, unconcerned. "Just look at this blanket, Saraid. Sure it ain't very good . . . too coarse," she went on, "but I'm learnin', an' at least we'll have warm blankets fer the winter."

"An' what're ye doin' about the children when ye work?"

"Sure I take the babe with me an' Seamus watches t'others." Molly looked lovingly at the baby boy in her arms and the young girls sitting around her on the ground with their penny whistles and dirty feet. "I have to do what I can for 'em," she said sadly. "Seamie's gettin' right discouraged. We din't have enough land left to keep the sheep fed, so we sold the last of 'em a month ago. Thank God we had potatoes! Then we come up short to pay the taxes, so they took what land we had left."

Saraid was stunned. "I didn't realize ye were strugglin' so! What are ye goin' to do?"

Molly shrugged and lifted the baby to her shoulder, patting his back, not meeting Saraid's eyes. "Seamus is hopin' to find work here to get us through. Sure we ain't like ye folks with life so easy."

Saraid shook her finger at her friend. "Don't be forgettin' that we're now leasin' our land, too. Not bein' taxed on the grazin' land is the only savin's we get." She paused, shook her head. "Sure bein' an O'Brien may still count for *somethin'* 'round here, but heaven knows what." Saraid sighed. "I thank God every day that up to now, Niall's land has been fairly safe."

Molly couldn't hide the trace of bitterness in her voice. "Ah yes. This is *O'Brien country*, after all."

Sariad struggled to hold her temper. "Molly," she said tightly. "It isn't like yer problems are Niall's fault."

Molly let out a sigh. "No . . . an' at least Niall din't become a Protestant just to keep his land like some of them others."

Saraid looked away, discomfited. She'd looked forward to seeing Molly again, but now, she felt eager to be away from her and her self pity. She spied Kate, who was beckoning to her with a look of agitation on her face, a sullen Fiona sitting beside her.

Molly bowed her head with shame, tears smarting in her eyes. "I'm sorry, Saraid. I know Niall ain't at fault."

"Let's leave this be," Saraid said abruptly. "It looks like my mother-in-law is havin' a time of it with Fiona over there." She gestured to where her daughter and Kate were sitting. "Sure there's just no pleasin' that woman." Saraid felt weariness replacing the joy she had felt only moments before. She gathered up the pots of jam, then kissed Molly's cheek and said good-bye to the little ones. "Fiona looks a bit bored an' out of sorts. I'd better be gettin' over there."

Turning back to Molly, she asked, "Will we be seein' ye for the dancin,' tonight?"

Molly nodded, a smile back on her thin face as she rubbed her belly. "Won't I be a sight?"

Chapter Eleven

There were very few bags remaining of the herbs that Saraid and Fiona had spent days preparing: meadowsweet, calendula, nettles, dandelion leaf, willow bark, and feverfew among others. All were used to heal and ward off sickness, infection and soothe headaches, aching muscles and stiff joints. These folk remedies, passed down from one generation to the next, were necessary for the farmers and peasants who were spread out over too many miles to see a doctor unless there was a life and death emergency.

"I see the herbs sold well, Mam," Saraid said to Kate as she set down the pots of jam.

Kate nodded. "They did. I sold a bit of the lace, too, but not much else." Kate gestured to the lace. "I bartered some of your doilies and lace collars for more spools of linen thread and a new wool blanket. Those collars seem to be a big hit with the young ladies," she said begrudgingly. "One woman really liked this tablecloth," she added, running her fingers over the lace, "but in the end she said it was much too dear."

Kate hated giving Saraid her due over her talent with lace. Her own long fingers were knotted with arthritis and could not handle the slimness of the hook. Neither could she thread or maneuver small needles for sewing or mending because her vision was also beginning to fail. It grated on her to have to rely on Saraid or Fiona for these simple chores.

"That it is, Mam," replied Saraid. "We'll not be sellin' much of it here, but it'll do better at the fair in October. Folks'll have a bit more coin after sellin' off their cattle and sheep. Sure they'll be gettin' more people there from Dublin an' Limerick, too, who'll have more coin to spend. This is just to put a thought in people's minds."

Fiona's head rested on her forearm on the table, "How long do I have to sit here?"

Kate, frowning, raised her eyebrows to Saraid and shook her head. "It's a terrible thing for a young girl to have to sit for so long with her grandmother."

Fiona sat up and cast baleful eyes at her mother. "My cousins don't have to sit here. They're all getting ready for the dancing."

Saraid chuckled at her willowy daughter whose deep auburn hair, when loose, hung well past her shoulders. Today it was neatly plaited, which made her large green eyes stand out on her round face. "An' how did ye do with the coins, Fiona?"

Fiona shrugged as she rattled the box. "I counted them right."

Saraid picked up the brightest penny and pressed it into Fiona's palm. "Thank ye fer yer help."

Fiona grinned, unable to hide her surprise. "For me?"

"Yes, my daughter, fer ye."

"Can we go now so I can put on my new dress?"

"Are the fairies in yer feet gettin' eager, Fiona?" her mother asked.

"Oh yes, Mam!" Now, she was fairly bouncing on her seat. "I can't wait to dance!"

Saraid placed her hand under Fiona's chin and raised it to have her full attention. "Patience, my daughter. The dancin' is only a wee part of the day. We have a lot to do yet."

Fiona wrinkled her brow and whined. "But, *Mam!*"

Saraid shot her daughter a look that required no explanation.

Kate's smile was a tight line on her tired face as she looked at the two of them. "What have you done with Bridget?" she asked, looking around for her favorite grandchild.

"Oh!" cried Saraid. "We had some excitement with Bridget! She bolted into the race crowd when the gun went off and landed in a heap in front of the horses!"

"Oh my God!" cried Kate, her hand pressed to her heart. "Is she all right?"

Saraid stiffened, fighting off the guilt she still felt. "Niall was just able to grab her as they went hurtlin' past!"

"How could you let such a thing happen to that poor child?" Kate demanded, glaring.

"It wasn't to be helped, Mam. She bolted off like the very devil was chasin' 'er when that gun went off. I ran right after her."

Fiona jumped from her seat. "Did she get hurt?"

Saraid shook her head. "She's fine, but it gave us an awful scare." She gave a quick kiss to first one forehead and then the other, trying to reassure them. "I laid her down in the caravan and she's asleep, but I need to be gettin' back."

"You left her *alone?*" asked her mother-in-law accusingly.

"No, no, Mam! I would *never* do that!" she answered quickly, averting her eyes so that Kate wouldn't see the hurt in them. "Maureen and the twins are with her." *She always thinks the worst of me!*

Saraid quickly gathered up the remaining bags of herbs into a shallow wooden box that had been stored under the table. "Let's go back to the caravan, an' Fiona, ye can help me get the cook pot goin'. Then we'll get ye ready for the dancin'."

Fiona clapped her hands and squealed with joy, then jumbled the spools of thread into a cloth bag.

Kate stood and carefully laid the folded lace tablecloth into a linen sack. As she began layering the remaining lace trimmed hankies and collars on top of the doilies, she ran her hand over her aching forehead and swayed slightly. "I didn't realize how tired I was."

Saraid grabbed her arm to support her. "Are ye all right then, Kate?"

"I'm fine now . . . just had a bit of dizziness." She shrugged off Saraid's hand and continued stacking the pieces of lace and putting them into another sack. She regretted snapping at Saraid and attempted, begrudgingly, to make peace. "You have done a lovely job with these lace pieces. Neither my fingers nor my eyes could ever manage these patterns."

"Thank you, Mam," Saraid murmured quietly. She was surprised to hear Kate pass on a kind word. It was the first nice thing Kate had said to her in months. Saraid was pleased that Kate could acknowledge her skill, but it didn't soothe the insults accumulated over the years.

They said good-bye to the other women and headed back to the campsite. Saraid carried her sacks of laces on top of the box of herbs and jam; Fiona, the sack of thread; and Kate, her new woolen blanket.

When they arrived at the caravan, Kate passed a hankie over her brow and then tucked it back into the sleeve of her dress. The blanket she carried weighed next to nothing, but, suddenly, it felt heavy.

Maureen was sitting on a blanket beside the caravan where Bridget still slept. Her own children were napping beside her.

Saraid motioned to the caravan and whispered, "Is Bridget all right?"

"Aye," answered Maureen. "An' I was about to doze off m'self."

Kate sighed. "Thank the Lord that she's all right. I don't know when I've been so tired. I think I'm going to go rest for a bit." She turned and walked away to her own caravan, clutching the new blanket against her chest.

Saraid watched her go and was mindful of telling Niall about Kate's dizziness when he came back from the sea. For now, she put the thought to the back of her mind. She was pleased that Fiona was so happy about the new dress that she had so carefully stitched herself. Using red, yellow and green linen threads, Saraid had spent many weeks embroidering the Celtic symbols to the bib front and full skirt of the white cotton dress. Her daughter would do her proud in the competition.

For months, all the neighboring children had gathered in their kitchen after supper to practice the steps that Willie had taught them. The table and chairs were pushed to the walls, and the children would break out their whistles and the men their fiddles. The music and tapping would echo out over the hills and fields along with their laughter as they sang and tapped into the evening. Children enjoyed cups of apple juice while the adults enjoyed mead and homemade ale, made with fermented corn, honey, spices and herbs. The brews were not very potent but they did ease the strains of the day.

Fiona knelt on the blanket and was just about to untie the bundle that held her dress when the men arrived with their buckets of fish and clams, salt water and sea weed sloshing over the sides.

"Watch out!" cried Fiona. "You'll get my dress all wet with that stinky water!"

Saraid quickly picked up the bundle and handed it to Fiona. "Please put this away before it gets ruined."

"But *Mam*! You said I could get ready for the dancing!"

"*Not now*, Fiona! I told ye we had some things to do first. It's not time yet."

"*But Mam!*"

"Mam!" cried Liam as he ran to her. "You should've seen all the boats!" It was his first time to see the Atlantic Ocean and he was properly amazed. His fair cheeks and nose were sunburned but he seemed not to mind.

Danny laughed. "Wait 'til ye see it at high tide! Now that'll be excitin'!"

"Aye," she agreed. "And did ye find some good clams for our dinner?"

The twins, awakened by all the noise, ran to the bucket of clams and began tossing them at each other. Maureen chased after them while Roark chuckled and hailed their throwing arms.

"Sure we did! We walked on a sand bar and dug in the sand and there they were! And Da let me row the boat! And the ocean is so *big*!"

"More like you *tried* to row the boat," teased James.

"Got us some oysters, too," Danny called out.

Fiona, jealous of the good time the boys had became teary once again. She stomped away and threw the bundled dress into the back of the wagon. "I hate you!" she cried. She climbed into the wagon and cuddled next to Bridget and closed her eyes. Within minutes, she had stopped sniffling and was soundly asleep.

Saraid rubbed her brow and felt a headache growing larger by the moment. *I need a cup of mead, but I'll settle for feverfew and chamomile*, she thought, looking around for her box of herbs. If she could find a spare moment, she would make some tea to calm herself.

"And look! I got some shrimp!" Liam said, holding out the small bucket he'd carried with him.

Danny and Patrick began scooping clams out of the buckets and tossing the good ones into a large cauldron.

Saraid called out to them. "Be sure to save the salt water. I'll be needin' it for the stew."

John and Roark laid two large white fish on the table and prepared to gut them.

Niall watched Saraid struggling for composure while the confusion of so many conversations roiled around her. "Saraid," he said, setting down his knife. "Let's get some pails of fresh water from the river while they tend to the fish."

She huffed out a breath and took his hand. "Sure," she sighed. "Let's do that."

Niall called to the boys. "Liam and James . . . you help Danny and Patrick go through the clams. Throw out any that are opened."

Liam asked, "Can we eat the open ones?"

"No, no, no," said Saraid. "They'll be makin' ye sick."

"But I'm hungry!"

James laughed. "Nothing new about that!"

Chapter Twelve

Niall found a quiet section of river away from the horse pens, set down the pails, and swept Saraid into his arms. He strode knee-deep into the river, bent his knees for leverage, and tossed his unsuspecting wife into the air.

Saraid screeched as she sailed aloft, her arms flailing, before landing with a loud splash, and disappearing under the water. She came to the surface sputtering and coughing up the water she had swallowed and gasped for air.

She railed at him, stumbling as she tried to find her footing in the rocky riverbed. "What the bloody hell did ye do that for?"

Niall laughed, pulled her into his arms and hung on tight as she tried to break free of him. He dove under the water and found her mouth with his as they squirmed against the bottom. When they surfaced, they were both laughing and dripping.

Saraid faced him as she wiped the water from her eyes. "I don't know whether to be throttlin' ye or huggin' ye!"

His eyes sparkled with humor. "I thought we could do with some cooling off." He ran his fingers over her dark nipples. They were tightly peaked from the cold water and clearly visible through the white muslin of her smock.

She drew his hips close and felt his erection pushing against her belly. "Humph," she said. She twisted away from him and tried to wring the water from the thin fabric that clung to her breasts.

As they climbed out of the water, Niall said, "Tell me what's got your ire up."

Saraid sighed. "Tis Fiona that's all out of sorts."

They sat on the river bank, nearly invisible under the draping fronds of a willow tree, and Saraid worked to squeeze the water out of her skirt. They were just far enough away from the noise of the campground to be able to talk without raising their voices. A flash of orange caught her eye at the river's edge. She turned to see an elegant Monarch butterfly, its brilliant wings aflutter, dancing from one wild rose to the next. The bright pink blossoms with their golden centers were in sharp contrast to the dark of the river.

"What's got her so upset?"

Saraid turned her attention back to Niall and shrugged. "More like what *isn't* upsettin' her. She's got nothin' on her mind but dancin' in her new dress. She don't understand that we've things to do before the dancin'. An' then I told her she couldn't go with you an' the boys to the sea 'cause I needed her to watch the younger ones so I could talk to Maureen."

Niall chucked. "Is that all?"

She elbowed him. "Don't be gettin' me all riled up again!"

He drew her close and they were quiet for a moment. "Is she coming into her woman's time?" He rubbed her arm as she nestled against his shoulder.

"Oh God! Don't even be thinkin' of *that* yet! She's only ten!"

"It was only a thought."

She studied his face for a moment, detecting something in his eyes that she couldn't explain. "What is it Niall?" she asked. "Ye've had somethin' preyin' on yer mind ever since ye came back from yer talk with those men." She hung on to his arm as he tried to shrug her off. "Niall O'Brien, don't ye even be *thinkin'* of havin' secrets from me!"

Niall stiffened beside her, his face grim. He stared into her eyes, wondering how much she'd understand. He sighed and then looked away from her and shrugged. "People are a bit on edge about the meeting. There's talk that we're being watched."

"Maybe ye should be forgettin' it for now."

"No, I can't." he said. "I had Willie deliver a message to Dublin to ask someone important to come and talk to us. The man agreed, even though it's dangerous for him."

Saraid furrowed her brow. "An' who is this *important* man?"

"Henry Grattan. He's an Irish Patriot and just been elected to the Irish Parliament."

Saraid was shocked. "Ye've asked an *Anglo* to come here? Jesus!" she exclaimed. "Why the devil did ye take such a chance?"

Niall hesitated, then decided that it was pointless not to tell her the truth. "The Anglo-Irish aren't happy with all the new taxes and trade restrictions, either. The war in the American colonies is draining the British coffers so they're taxing the devil out of everyone. He's working toward changing the laws and getting more independence for the Irish government without bloodshed. We'd all benefit."

"If ye ask me, I think ye're goin' to have trouble convincin' the Catholics to go along with that."

Niall nodded. "Perhaps, but too many Irish are being forced from their land and wandering with empty bellies. They've got nowhere to go. There's serious trouble coming and not a lot to be done about it," he said quietly. "The Whiteboys are starting up again and Tommy Callahan was shooting off his mouth about joining up with them."

"Bloody Christ!" she swore. "What, in the name of all that be holy, was he even thinkin?"

"That's the devil of it," Niall said, spitting the bitter taste of it from his mouth. "He'd already had a few pints in him and he wasn't thinking at all."

Saraid held him close and whispered in his ear. "Sure he'll spoil all yer plans if he don't get arrested first."

Niall, resting his head against hers, was pensive. He thought about telling her that Seamus Flynn was of the same mind but decided to let that be.

"The rebels aren't too close to us yet, but they're talking about some major retaliation again in Limerick and Tipperary."

Saraid grew tense as the import of what he was saying sunk into her mind. Limerick was just across the River Shannon from their own farm, too close not to be worried about it. "I thought I heard somethin' about trouble with the Whiteboys once before."

Niall nodded. "Yes, years ago. It was just some small things of no account in some isolated areas. Nothing to get anyone too excited. But now, they're becoming more organized and making demands. If you add someone like Tommy to the mix, someone is going to get seriously hurt . . . maybe even killed."

"Can you keep Tommy calm today?"

Niall sighed, picked up a handful of pebbles and tossed them into the river. "He seemed somewhat steadier when I left him. His brother, Sean, has a pretty good head. Hopefully he'll have some control over him. I'm going to be talking to him again later to be sure."

"Promise me that ye'll be careful."

"No need to think I won't." He got up and held out his hand. "We should be getting back."

Saraid nodded and took the hand he offered. "The sooner we get the chores done, the sooner Fiona can get her bloody dress on."

They each filled a pail with fresh water and, hand in hand, they walked back to their camp.

Patrick sliced a sliver of crackling skin from the pig that had been roasting since the day before. Dripping fat, mixed with the honey and rosemary glaze, still sputtered in the embered coals of the peat fire. He breathed in the smoky sweet aroma and closed his eyes in ecstasy as he licked the hot grease from his fingers. Slowly roasted pork was his favorite meal. He would gladly forego the fish to heap his plate with the succulence of the pig.

He opened his eyes to see Niall and Saraid approaching with their pails of water. He pointed to a cast iron cauldron suspended over the fire. "I just put the salt water on for you."

Niall added the fresh water and, using metal tongs, lifted a hot stone from around the fire and added it to the pot. "Is one stone enough?" he asked Saraid.

"Aye. We can add another later. Sure we don't want the fish cookin' too fast." She laid a clean piece of linen on the table as she looked around their empty campsite. "Where are the others?"

"Maureen, Roark and Danny took the children for a walk to see if they could find some berries," he answered. "Mother's resting and John is working on his journal."

"Did Fiona go with them?" asked Saraid.

Patrick shook his head and grinned. "The imp is sleeping. Seemed best to leave her be."

Saraid nodded in agreement. She laid one of the gutted white fish on top of the linen and stuffed the cavity with wild onions, seaweed and a handful of fresh thyme and salt. She rolled the fish in the fabric, tied it securely with twine and gently set it into the pot. While Niall filleted the second fish and cut it into chunks, Saraid added in the clams and oysters from the bucket of seafood. Then she cried out with pleasure at the dark crustacean stretching out its claws at the bottom of the bucket. "Ye didn't tell me we had a *lobster*!"

The men shared a grin. "It was meant to be a surprise," said Niall. "I know you enjoy it, but there's just the one so you'll have to share it."

"Ha!" she said. Mindful of the claws, she carefully lifted the lobster from the bucket and admired its size. "Sure we'll need to keep it out of the pot 'til the water is good an' hot."

Chapter Thirteen

Blaring horns and pipes sounded across the meadow as several well-muscled young men came into the clearing. With one fellow at each end, they carried seven scarred wooden doors, free of their hinges and latches, that the tavern and shop owners had removed from their establishments. They laid six of the doors side by side in two even rows to accommodate the dancing feet of the clan. One door was centered in front of the rows for the dance master.

The Scotch-Irish bagpipers in their kilts and tams, and the Irish with their smaller uillean pipes, had been playing for over an hour, revving up the hundreds of eager, happy folks who were making their way to the open circle. Flutes, fiddles and small bodhrán drums added a sense of urgency and wild excitement to the fun.

Niall lifted his eyes to the clearing and tried to get into the mood for the afternoon's festivities. The tension he'd felt after his heated altercation with Tommy Callahan was slow to leave him, even after a dunking in the river. He was still feeling uneasy and hoped the rest of the day wouldn't be marred by the younger Callahan's righteous anger. He was also hopeful that Grattan would be able to inspire peaceful resolution to the problems that so many were facing.

"Looks like they be settin' up the doors," said Danny as he and the others arrived back to the campsite. Their small pails were mounded with red raspberries. "Time to be gettin' on our dancin' shoes!"

The younger children's faces and hands were smeared with red juice from the berries they had eaten along the way. Maureen and

Saraid both worked to clean them up before they changed them into their dancing clothes.

Fiona bounded up to her mother when she heard the blaring horns. "Is it time, now?" she asked, hoping not to be disappointed yet again.

"Yes, dear daughter," answered Saraid. "It is finally time!"

Fiona squealed with joy and made a dash for her *ceilei* costume. It was Fiona's first formal dance dress and she was flushed with pride. She ran her fingers over the embroidered symbols of her heritage and became dizzy with excitement. Once in her dress, she picked up the matching cape and special Tara brooch and ran to her mother for help to put them on.

Saraid finished tying Liam's small hornpipe shoes on his feet and pinched his cheek. "Go see yer da now, my little man," she said with a smile. She beckoned Bridget to follow her and started to walk toward the caravan. Bridget clapped her hands though she was too young to understand what all the excitement was about. Saraid stopped in her tracks as Fiona appeared before her.

"Ah, my beautiful daughter." Saraid felt her chest tighten with pride at the sight of Fiona in the remarkable dress. She gazed into her flushed face and chuckled. "Ye'd be a bit excited now, aren't ye?"

"Oh yes, Mam!" she exclaimed, bouncing up and down in place as she handed her mother the cape and brooch. "And you're going to be dancing, too, with Gran and Auntie Maureen?"

Saraid nodded and, smiling, put a conspirator's finger to her lips. "Aye," she whispered. "Later tonight, but don't be tellin' yer da. It's a surprise!"

Fiona beamed as Saraid carefully fitted the matching cape around her slim body. She wove the sharp pin of the brooch through the fabric of the cape and dress on the right shoulder, adjusting the folds to drape down over Fiona's back. Using dark green to line the cape had set it off beautifully. The amethyst stones of the brooch were embedded in silver scrollwork and glimmered in the sunlight. Saraid ran an affectionate hand over her daughter's neatly plaited braids, a mist coming softly to her eyes. "I'm rememberin' when my mam gave me that brooch," she said quietly. "I was just yer age. It's been in my family for generations so we need to be takin' special care of it."

Fiona nodded. "I know it's special. Thank you," she said, twining her arms around her mother's neck and placing a kiss on her cheek. "Did your stomach feel sick like mine at your first dance?" Fiona asked, her confidence suddenly faltering.

Saraid chuckled and held her daughter close. "Of course! But do ye know what my mam told me?"

Fiona shook her head, too excited to speak.

She gave Fiona's tummy a quick rub. "She said it were all the happy fairies inside me just itchin' to get out and dance with me!"

Fiona laughed, her eyes sparkling, and knew that was just what it was. She took a deep breath and ran off to join her brothers.

Saraid picked up Bridget, setting her against her hip, and gave her a small ring of silver bells. She turned to Niall. "Are the boys all set?"

Niall had just finished tapping short nails into the toes and heels of his own hornpipe shoes, as he'd done earlier for James and Liam. The nails would make all the tapping against the doors more pronounced. He smiled and kissed Bridget's cheek. "As ready as they'll be on this day or any other. They're looking pretty sharp in their new britches," he said. "They've already gone over to their group. Martin and Willie will be tossing the coin to see who goes first any minute now, so let's get moving."

Saraid chuckled. "Sure the young ones are so determined, even if they stumble a bit."

Niall agreed, wrapping his arm around her. "It's the most fun of the day, really."

Saraid reveled in his embrace but pulled back after a moment. "I think James is going to surprise everyone this year. He's been practicin' with such determination."

"Of course," he said with pride. "Didn't I teach him everything I know?"

They began walking over to the crowded area around the doors where music was blaring. People were singing and clapping their hands in the bright afternoon sun as if they hadn't a care in the world. They passed by the couples who were still dancing reels, the four couples squared off, dancing to and fro, changing sides and partners to the lively music.

This heady musical respite from their daily cares and hardships was embraced with a joy known only to Irish hearts. Forgotten for the moment was the struggle to put food on the table and the heavy rents and taxes to be paid with crops and livestock that they could ill spare.

Niall took Saraid's hand and raised his voice against the pandemonium surrounding them. "Let's just have some fun!"

Chapter Fourteen

The two dance masters flipped a coin to see who would perform first. Willie won the toss and led his youngest dancers to the platform. The musicians stilled and awaited his signal to begin the song he had chosen for them to play.

Willie Hayes, a twenty-six-year-old dancer from Tipperary, had worked hard to earn the title of Dance Master. He stood hatless but resplendent in his gold waistcoat, frothy lace cravat and black britches. Silk stockings covered his legs, and black hornpipe shoes covered his feet. He took his position on the first of the doors for the simple jig he would perform with the beginners. He faced the dozen young boys and girls with a smile and a wink from his light blue eyes. Willie, his sun-streaked curls ruffling in the breeze, held his oak staff in front of him, gently fingering the carving on its length as he spoke to the children. Though this was to be his first organized dance showing in preparation for the October fair, he was confident.

The easy, joyful people of Ireland had been so welcoming to him and his blind fiddler, Freddie, as they made their scheduled wanderings throughout their countryside. Host families would share their food and provide lodging, most times in a snug loft, for a week at a time. Sometimes, they slept in their caravan, or occasionally, in their bedrolls under the stars. Villagers would gather at the host farm to share in the lessons for a sixpence each. These evenings were filled with music, dance, and laughter.

No one seemed to know when the custom began for the dance masters to have a blind fiddler. When performing, the blind man would sit on a three-legged stool with an upturned hat at his feet to gather coins tossed by an appreciative audience.

Willie gazed at the children before him, all so earnest and guileless that he could not help smiling at them with affection. He caught Saraid's eye on the edge of the crowd and gave her a two-finger salute as he fluffed the lacy cravat at his neck. She beamed at him and did a little curtsy to acknowledge his pleasure.

"Are ye ready now, boys and girls?"

The children, ages five through eight, all nodded, shifting from one foot to the other with eager anticipation. They were dressed in an assortment of tunics, britches and kilts, many with bare feet that would never do at a formal competition. Since these youngsters were beginners, Willie didn't begrudge them. He understood that many, in their poverty, had never had a pair of shoes.

"Well then," Willie said. "First, I'll be showin' ye the steps to be remindin' ye of how they're done. Sure it will be just like we did with yer lessons. All of ye learned the same steps. When I stop and rap my staff on the door, then ye will dance along with me. Ready now?"

The children stopped fidgeting and stood perfectly still, straight as you please, their small arms at their sides. He turned his back to them and gently tapped Freddie's bow with his staff. Freddie began to play a merry jig and the rest of the musicians followed his cue. The crowd began to sing and clap their hands in perfect tempo as Willie did the simple Irish jig.

Toddlers in their parents' arms shook their *craebh-ciuils*, the little branch with tiny silver bells tinkling sweetly. Others blew discordant melodies on their penny whistles.

Once Willie had completed his run through, he turned to face the children. He tapped his staff to the door plank, and the young ones joined in for a lively first attempt at performing. The gaiety of the crowd grew as the young fellow next to Liam lost his footing and tripped right off the end of the planks, causing the other children to giggle. Unperturbed, he quickly leapt back onto the door with a red-faced smile. Though he tried to catch up, he was completely out of step with the others. Laughter echoed throughout the meadow, and the crowd cheered them on until they finished to rousing applause.

Martin Clancy stood imperiously at the sideline, the broad brim of his red hat casting gray shadows across his hard face. He pursed his lips and shook his head. His tall thin frame was accentuated by the tight black britches and ostentatious purple waistcoat, buttoned high against a bright gold and green striped cravat. His staff was made of a fine black walnut, liberally engraved and embossed with gold leaf. The crook was embellished with his name on one side, and his title, Grand Dance Master of Clare, on the other.

When he removed his hat to fan his face, wisps of grey hair escaped the thin tail at his nape, creating a featherlike nimbus around his head

As Willie relinquished the doors, Martin put his hat back on his head and gave Willie a curt nod. "Now you will see how it should be done."

Willie refused to be disheartened by the pretentiousness of a man who was so stern and unbending. He gave Clancy a mocking bow, sweeping his arm toward the doors. "I'll look forward to it," was all he said. As he stood in the crowd to watch the performance, Willie muttered under his breath, "Bloody ass!" Those near him chuckled in agreement.

Clancy's young pupils stood rigidly in place as Martin stared from one to the other, commanding their attention. One little girl of about seven stood rock still, her lips trembling and her eyes filling. Clancy pointed at her and then to the grass. The child ran to her mother and began to sob. There were boos and shouts from the onlookers.

"Hey Clancy," shouted one. "This is a party not a funeral!"

Several others murmured their disapproval as the child's parents quickly enfolded her and wiped away her tears.

Unfazed, Clancy turned his back to the remaining children. Using his staff, he jabbed Hank, his fiddler, in the ribs to signal him to begin. Hank cried out and there were shouts from the crowd, but the blind man began to play and the other musicians joined in. Clancy moved precisely through the steps and the children followed with not a smile among them, dampening the joviality of the crowd. When they were finished, the children scampered with relief from the doors to raucous cheers from the parents and others in the crowd.

As Clancy left the stage, Willie told him, "If that is how it's done, I hope I never learn!"

Chapter Fifteen

After the first set, Hank followed clumsily after Martin toward the Shamrock Tavern. He cursed his name, flailing one arm, and banged his cane against the dirt path with the other. "I'm warnin' ye Clancy! Don't even be thinkin' of pokin' me again!"

Martin stopped and turned. Staring coldly at Hank, he grabbed him by the neck of his shirt and dragged him off behind a large outcropping of rock, out of sight of the crowd. He pushed the mewling man roughly to his knees and struck him sharply with his staff.

"You sniveling pile of goat dung! You *dare* to raise your voice to me?" Martin stood over him and scowled. "Do you remember how we met, Hank?" he asked cruelly. Then he tossed some coins on the ground in front of him. "Go have a pint and get your wits about you before the next round of dancing." Then he turned away and left Hank huddled in the dirt.

Hank cowed at the sight of the coins. The memory of what they stood for would be forever etched into his mind.

Hank was nine years old. His family had been trying to eke out an existence in the fetid slums of Dublin. His da had been caught stealing food and was carted away, never to be seen again. His mother had too many little ones to be able to look for work, and most of the time they felt the pain of hunger.

He had been such an innocent boy, trying to help his mother, and thought himself so clever. Pretending blindness, he'd taken his da's sole possession, a fiddle, and sat on a corner near the better part of Dublin, playing his heart out, begging for coin. Occasionally, a passerby would be so disarmed by his innate talent that they would toss a coin or two into the ragged cap at his feet.

Hank bowed his head, remembering how he'd been caught out . . . .

***

Someone tossed more coin than usual into Hank's cap. Without thinking, he glanced down to count the coins. He heard a chuckle and quickly looked up and spotted the man who was grinning at him from the shadows of the alley in front of him. Realizing his mistake, he got to his feet and grabbed his cap. He tried to run but the man was too quick.

Martin grabbed him by the arm and wouldn't let go as he'd squirmed and kicked to try to get free, all the while trying to protect his precious fiddle.

"Let me go!" he cried, helpless, tears coursing down his hollow cheeks. "I got to be gettin' home to me mam."

"Not so fast!" cried Martin, who openly stared at Hank's body with fascination. "Oh, I think you'll do quite nicely, lad," Martin cooed. "What's your name?"

"Hank," he whispered. He was suddenly breathing hard, filled with an unknown fear. The look in the man's eyes paralyzed him. He clutched his cap and fiddle tight to his chest. He was no match for a fully grown man and there was no one nearby to help him.

"I'll accompany you home," Martin said softly. "Lead the way or I'll see to it that you go to the sheriff. I imagine that he'd be only too happy to consider your begging akin to stealing since you aren't actually blind."

"Please, sir," Hank begged. "My mam needs the coin to feed us!"

Martin gave him a whack on his back with his staff to show him he meant business. Tears sprang from Hank's eyes as he lead Martin through the maze of narrow, garbage-lined streets of the tenements.

"This is it," Hank mumbled as he stopped in front of a weather-beaten door.

Martin struck his staff against the aged wood until it was opened a crack by a harried young woman who looked far older than her years.

She gasped as Martin pushed his way in and flung Hank to the floor.

Hank's mother tried to brace herself against the stranger and to shield the younger children. "What do ye want?" she cried. Martin glanced around the single windowless room, taking in the lack of furniture, the pile of ratty blankets against the wall, and the reeking chamber pot in the corner. The stub of a single candle cast eerie shadows on the bare walls, accentuating the despair of the hovel.

"Where is your husband?" Martin asked.

"I think he's dead, sir," she whispered.

Martin pointed to Hank. "I caught this one begging for the blind."

Hank stood motionless, filled with shame for having been caught. "I'm sorry, Mam," he said quietly.

Fear plain on her face, she laid a shaking hand on Hank's shoulder. "Are ye goin' to be turnin' him in?"

"Oh, I think not," he replied, his eyes mocking her. "I think I'm going to take him off your hands. I'll even pay for the pleasure," he said as he upended a pouch of coins that tumbled onto the dirt floor around her feet.

Hank's mother gasped, afraid to count the coins. It was more than she had seen in her lifetime. She clung to Hank as the boy wailed. "Sure ye ain't talkin' of makin' a slave of my boy!"

Martin laughed derisively. "Not a slave, no," he answered calmly. "I plan to take advantage of his talent. As it happens, I'm in need of a fiddler . . . a blind fiddler." He gave Hank a knowing look. "Since you already know how to play the part, it should be easy for you."

"I don't want to go!" cried Hank as he clung to his mother. "I ain't really blind!"

Martin smiled at the two of them. "That is correct." He then turned his attention to Hank.

"I'll will hold your little secret and keep the sheriff from your mother's door. They would blame her for what you've done." He paused to let his words sink in. "Do you want that?"

Hank felt trapped. He looked up into his mother's sad eyes and didn't want more bad luck to happen to her. "No," he said in a small voice.

"Very good," said Martin. "From now on, you'll be my blind fiddler. I fully intend to become the Grand Dance Master of Clare, and you will help me to achieve that. In return, you will not go hungry, you'll have a clean place to sleep, and you will earn some coin for traveling with me." He nodded to Hank's mother. "He may even earn enough to send some coin home to you."

He returned his gaze to Hank. "I will supply you with clothing befitting your position which you will pay for, over time, out of your earnings."

Hank could tell that his mother was torn as her eyes shimmered with misery. To have to choose between him or the coins should have been easy, but he knew that he was lost when she nodded her head in submission.

She stared at Martin with squinting eyes, fearing what it was that he really wanted with her young son. "You'll be givin' me yer promise not to be hurtin' my boy."

Martin chuckled softly and Hank wondered why he was so amused.

Martin stepped closer to his mother and squeezed her arm tightly enough that she whimpered. "I'll see to it that no harm comes to him as long as he follows the rules." he said as he let her go.

"Will he ever come back to us?" she asked.

Martin just shrugged. "We'll be heading for Clare today, so it's not likely he'll be back any time soon."

Hank's mother wrapped Hank in a tight embrace and whispered in his ear. "Ye go with him, Hank. Ye'll be out of this sorry place and ye'll be havin' a chance!" She wiped away his tears, even as her own flowed. "Ye be brave now!" she said as she uncoiled his arms from around her neck. "Ye go be a grand fiddler an' send yer mam some coin so we can all be beholdin' to ye!"

Now, thirty years later, Martin had achieved his goal and Hank had paid the price. Hank hung his head in shame and wiped the tears from his eyes. His mother had chosen the coins over him. She had chosen to have one less mouth to feed.

No one knew what had happened to the previous Grand Dance Master of Clare. The likeable man had just suddenly disappeared and Martin had been right there, a skillful, determined, ambitious dancer, to take his place.

Martin had groomed Hank slowly, and with great care. He had become a truly gifted fiddler and the perfect foil to the man's dancing abilities. He taught Hank the value of obedience and kept his promise of food, shelter and clothing. He also tossed a few coins his way but never enough to survive on his own for more than a day or two at a time.

There was never anything left for Hank to send to the mother who had become, in his memory, prey to her own desperation. Hank became Martin's victim, again and again, in ways too painful and shameful to speak of. The abuse had lasted for so many years that Hank lacked any sense of pride in himself. Once he became a man, Hank no longer held any fascination for Martin, and the older man found younger boys for his depraved pleasures.

Now, near to forty years old, Hank had no life left in him; his hair had grown sparse and his fingers were becoming painfully knobby.

Before long, he mused, he would probably not even be able to play his old fiddle.

Morose, he gathered up the hated coins that Martin had thrown at him. He spat on the ground and limped into the Shamrock. He carefully laid his fiddle and cane on the bar, lined up some coins beside them, and asked Jimmy, the old bartender, for a pint.

"Ain't ye playin' fer Clancy today?" Jimmy asked.

"Yeah, but I be takin' a rest," he answered. "Willie's up next so I got me a few minutes."

Jimmy slid a mug of ale to him and tossed one of Hank's coins into the box beneath the bar. "Can't say as I be blamin' ye none, Hank. I hear that man's a beast."

Hank's eyes burned, his mouth sagged, and his shoulders slumped. He quickly downed the contents of the mug and pushed it toward Jimmy with another coin.

Keeping his eyes blank, he caught sight of Martin in the mirror over the bar and slowly shook his head from side to side. He seethed as he watched Martin order a drink from the barmaid, then stroll over to the table against the wall that was heavily laden with food. He clenched his teeth as Martin filled a small plate with cold shrimp and savory tomato sauce.

His anger continued to simmer as he downed two more pints in quick succession. He watched as Martin slowly plucked the glistening pink morsels from their shells and dunked them into the pool of sauce before slowly sucking them into his mouth.

Hank's stomach growled with hunger but there was no time to eat a meal before the next performance. Somehow, he would find the courage to avenge his years of abuse. He banged his mug against the bar. "Jimmy!" he called out. "I need another."

Jimmy stood before him and sighed. "Take it easy man. Ain't ye had enough yet? I'm thinkin' ye need to slow down if'n yer goin' to play that fiddle."

Hank stared straight ahead with rheumy eyes. "There ain't never goin' to be enough." He rose unsteadily from the bar, tucked his fiddle under his arm, and taking up his cane, limped away, swaying a little as he went out the open door.

He found his way back to the circle where Willie was chatting with some of the clan folks before the next performance. He plunked down on his stool, setting his fiddle beneath it, and dropped his cane on the ground beside him. All the ale he had consumed in a short period of time had his head spinning. He folded his arms over his knees and lay his head upon them. Within minutes he was snoring, oblivious to the crowd, the music, or the clatter of feet against the doors.

Chapter Sixteen

Willie once again took his place in front of his students. The children, ages nine through twelve, lined up shoulder to shoulder on the dance platform. Fiona was in the first row with the other young girls in their colorful ceili dresses. James took his place in the second row with the other boys, some in the plaids of their clans, some in britches, all wearing their black hornpipe shoes with nails tapped in.

Willie looked out over his students, confident that they would not disappoint the crowd. The youngsters stood there, every pair of eyes focused on him alone. Their arms were straight to their sides, hands loose, backs straight, and their feet in position to begin. Willie led the first movement and the children, hard shoes clicking and clacking against the wood surface in absolute precision, followed in kind. Their lips twitched and their eyes twinkled as they kept step for step with Willie, who tried to show encouragement and approval without bobbing his head. Then, suddenly, the musical pace increased, and feet moved faster and faster, harder and harder. Sweat began to form on their young faces, the doors began vibrating, and the thunderous sound drove a flock of small birds from the trees. The applause and shouting nearly drowned out the sound of their hard-tapping shoes.

Fiona, joy radiating on her flushed face, and James, so serious in his concentration, were both dazzling in their delivery of the steps. Liam, beside his father, clapped and whooped, dancing to his own rhythm.

Saraid, with Bridget on her hip, bobbed to the quickening beat of the dancers' feet, pride filling her as she watched James and Fiona perform. She was so drawn up in the excitement that she didn't realize that she was mindlessly biting on her knuckle until it was raw.

Kate watched Saraid and, unable to control her disgust, pulled Saraid's hand from her mouth, startling her. "What on earth are you doing?" Kate demanded. "Chewing on yourself?"

Saraid flushed with embarrassment, wiped the small trace of blood on her skirt. She glanced quickly at Niall and then back to Kate. "Sorry. I was so caught up I didn't know I was doin' it."

With a final stomp, the dance ended and Willie was beside himself with pride. He stood there and laughed with tears in his eyes as he gathered the breathless young people around him and praised each one, sharing in their joy. "You were magnificent! Each and every one of you!"

Niall gave his mother a stern look before joining in the cheering of the crowd.

Kate turned away from him, not caring that she had made her disapproval known. She could not fathom what Niall could possibly find attractive about this woman whose mannerisms were no better than that of a common wench. It pained her that Saraid took so little interest in improving her actions, her speech, or her mode of dress. Thank heavens that because of the years she, herself, had spent teaching them, her grandchildren were more like Niall.

"Ah Fiona!" Saraid cried as her daughter ran into her open arms. The laughter and cheering of the crowd droned on as she hugged her daughter tightly. "Sure I'm so proud of ye!" Then she reached for James who had just been released from his father's embrace.

"And *you*, my young man! Sure ye'll be king of the boards in no time!"

James beamed, sweat still trickling down his face. "Yeah, but now I'm just thirsty!"

Saraid turned to Niall. "I'll be off with the children now to get them some tea and to check on the fish. An' I'm needin' to get some bread started."

Niall held his mother's arm as she turned to accompany them. "Stay a moment."

Kate opened her mouth to object but his cold look stopped her.

* * *

As Martin Clancy and his next group approached the boards, Willie looked him in the eye, waiting for the remark that was sure to come. Martin just stared at him for a moment, then merely nodded and turned his back on him to face his own students.

A groggy Hank placed his old fiddle under his chin, waiting for the signal to begin.

Willie was a bit stunned but, nonetheless, took the lack of comment as a sign of approval. He walked off, a huge grin on his face. "Ye just wait, Clancy," he murmured under his breath. "Soon it'll be only ye and me dancin' on the boards!"

The dancing duel between the two men would be the highlight of the competition.

Chapter Seventeen

Niall, his hand still firmly grasping his mother's arm, began moving away from the crowd, walking with long strides to the far end of the meadow near the river's edge.

Kate struggled to keep up with him. Looking left and right to see if anyone was watching them, she hissed. "Let me go! You're dragging me along like a common dog!"

"Not yet." He spoke quietly but with determination, his anger barely controlled. He finally stopped some distance away near a large outcropping of rocks and the shade of a lone tree. When he was sure that they wouldn't be overheard, he let go of her arm and faced her with steely eyes. "You will tell me now what it is that makes you so hard against my wife!"

Kate began to shake. In deference to her husband, she had been biting her tongue for years but she refused to cower in front of her son any longer. "You were foolish to take up with that woman in the first place!"

Niall clenched his jaw. "That *woman* is my *wife*!" He began pacing in front of her.

Kate shook her fist in his face. "You let her trick you into marrying her so she could have a better life than she had with that band of heathens she comes from! You deserved so much better!" she spat out angrily. "She has no grace and can barely read or write her own name!"

Niall stopped pacing and stood in front of her, his jaw dropped in disbelief. "Tricked me? How can you even *think* that?" He began pacing furiously again, flailing his arms. He thought to tell her that Fiona was secretly teaching her mother to read but pushed the thought away. At this point, it didn't matter. "I married Saraid because she was my love, not because I had to! I wanted that babe as much as she did, and I was certainly not going to make a bastard of him."

Kate stood rigid with her chin stubbornly lifted, no longer willing to control her rage. With high color in her angular face, she began yelling at her son.

"I've spent all these years trying to understand what you see in her, to accept that she is little more than nothing!"

Niall strode toward her but she held up a hand to stop his approach. She struggled to lower her voice. "I've stayed silent all these years hoping that some sort of civility would rub off on her, but breeding cannot be put on like a cloak. Your father may have been taken in by her, but I am certainly *not*!"

"Mother," he said, his jaw tight. "We both cried when our son didn't survive his birth. Saraid's a good woman. She's kind and loving, a good mother to the four happy children that we are blessed to have. Saraid works tirelessly with me every day to run the farm without complaint . . . *ever*! There's no woman alive who could make me happier than I am!"

Kate, with a wave of her hand, continued to send barbs into his heart. "Fiona is not happy! I have spent my days trying to teach her how to be a proper young lady, something she cannot possibly learn from her mother. She is moody and unappreciative of all that I am trying to teach her!"

"Mother," Niall asked quietly, "did it ever occur to you that she is unhappiest when she is with you?"

"How *dare* you say this to me?" Kate's rage caused spittle to spray from her lips. "If it weren't for me, they would all be ignorant wretches like their mother! And so would *you*! How is Fiona ever going to find a proper husband, running around in the fields with dirty feet like some wild colt? Most of the time she dresses like a boy and even strong soap and lye aren't enough to clean her up!"

Niall couldn't help it. He chuckled, dumbfounded. "A *husband*? She's still a *child*! She *should* be running about the fields, free to explore and have a bit of fun!" He shook his head, unable to fathom where his mother's thoughts were coming from. "A fancy dress wouldn't do her much good in the fields, or the barns either!"

Kate buried her face in her hands. For years, she had dreamt of taking Fiona to Dublin. She wanted to introduce her to the world of museums, the great library and beautiful parks filled with flowers. She would be able to meet proper people who lived in well-appointed homes. She craved sitting again in the afternoon, to tea being served from a fine English china pot with proper biscuits. Fiona deserved all these niceties, too, and more. His blindness was just too much.

With little care for the consequences, she spat out her wrath with an old Gaelic insult. *"An té a luíonn le gagharaibh éireoodh le dearnaithib!* If you lie down with dogs, you'll rise up with fleas!" Kate watched Niall's face go white. He recoiled as if he'd been slapped. She knew she had gone too far, but was too proud, too angry, to back down.

"*Mother*," he said, anger burning in his eyes, his voice a bitter rasp. "Now you insult my *children*? When we get home, you will remove yourself from what is now *my* house! You can move in with Patrick or John, or into my old place. Or better still, move back to Dublin where you came from, so I'll not have to look at your ugliness ever again."

Kate's chest was heaving as she fisted her hands into her hair, loosening the coil at the nape of her neck. The long strands of hair that blew around her face made her look like some mad, raving hag. "You think to put your mother out of her own home?" A bitter laugh escaped from deep within her. Then she went deadly calm, staring at him with icy eyes. "Little that it is, it is still mine."

Niall began to tremble, addled by how crazed she had become. He reached out a hand to try to calm her, but she wrenched away from him. He bowed his head for a moment, breathing deeply to settle himself. Unwilling to do more to appease her, Niall began to walk away, then paused, and turned back toward her. "Be very careful mother. *Is í ding féin a scoileann an dair.* It is a wedge of itself that splits the oak. By rights, now that my father is dead, the house is mine to do with as I wish. And I wish your hateful self gone."

Niall turned away from her, squared his shoulders, and without another look in her direction, walked back to the meadow.

"I will not go quietly," she vowed, anger still roiling within her. "You will pay my son," she whispered. "You will *curse* the day you put me out."

* * *

A short distance away, hidden by a large outcropping of rocks, Jack Cleary stood silent and still. A small smile played upon his lips as his eyes narrowed on Kate. *Well, well, well,* he thought. Maybe there was a way to use this upheaval to get the proof he needed against Niall O'Brien and his secret band of rebels.

Unaware of the man in the shadows, Kate stood where she was, feeling a chill cover her in the shade of the whispering leaves overhead. She watched her very angry beloved son walk away from her into the sunlight on the dirt path. Only when Niall was out of her sight did she allow herself to let out a keening wail, the fiercely controlled tears finally spilling from her red-rimmed eyes.

A sudden numbness began in Kate's face and her limbs grew weak. She blinked away her tears only to find her vision still blurred, the trees and the ground beneath her faded and distorted. Dizzy, she leaned against the rough bark of the tree behind her, slid to the ground and closed her eyes. As panic clutched at her, she began to pant. Kate rubbed her shaking hands against her face, trying to bring back some feeling. Her head began to throb and her confusion mounted. She couldn't understand what was happening. In fact, she had trouble thinking at all. After a few moments of struggling to keep her wits about her, a deep shuddering sigh escaped her lips and her ragged breath began to even out.

"James . . . oh James," she whimpered. "I'm so bloody tired. How could you leave me and let it all come to this?"

Without James, she felt as empty and haunted as the Burren. She closed her eyes, wanting to give in to sleep, praying that her discomfort would subside. Then her husband's smiling face floated before her, his lilting brogue whispered in her ear. He reached out his hand and she gladly raised hers.

"Mrs. O'Brien? Are you alright?"

Kate gasped, staring wild-eyed at the heavy-set man standing there with her hand in his. She yanked her hand away, her heart pounding with fear. "Wh . . . who are you?" she demanded.

"Jack Cleary, ma'am," he responded quietly, with a brief bow. "Don't you remember me?"

She was groggy from her half-sleep reverie. The sun at his back was shining in her eyes and she couldn't make out his features. She drew up a hand to block the brilliant light and though he came more clearly into view, his features were still blurry.

He reached a large hand down to help her up. "Can I be of some assistance?"

She recoiled with a shudder. *My God,* she thought. *Who is he? I don't even know where I am!* "I cern'ly don nee sistance!" she snapped, struggling to regain her feet.

He took her elbow anyway and she tried to shake him off. "I own the Shamrock Tavern. I believe you've been there a few times over the years."

Kate took a deep breath and blinked her eyes, trying to will away the cobwebs from her mind. She stared off into the distance, not wanting to look at him. *Why can't I speak,* she wondered? She swallowed and willed her words to be clear. "You star'led me, is all. I was hav . . . ing a rest from all th . . . th . . . the noise." Her fingers were clumsy as she tried to fix her hair and put her cap back on her head.

Jack tried not to smile. *Of course you were.* He had been watching her for better than a half hour from his hiding spot and knew that something had definitely happened to her. Her speech was slurred and there seemed to be some stiffness on the left side of her face. His original thought, to use her anger as a foil for gathering information about Niall, was overridden by the fact that she was actually in some unstable condition. Abandoning that idea for the moment, he decided on a new course of action. Perhaps a drink, some food, and a bit of kindness would soothe her and he would be able to gain her trust.

"I was just heading back to the tavern to see about the dinner I'm putting out for the crowd. It would give me great pleasure to escort you back to your people," he said kindly, offering her his arm for support.

Kate began to move away from him but quickly realized that her legs weren't very steady. Her steps began weaving as she fought for balance. She quietly took his arm, but there was no gratitude in her eyes as she struggled to speak. "I s'pose tha . . . wou be k-k-kind of you."

She tried to shake off the panic that was rising within her, the sense of confusion, her double vision, and the shakiness in her limbs. *I have to get out of here!* It was obvious to her that she couldn't manage it on her own. It would be utterly shameful if she fell down. She couldn't even remember where she was or how she had gotten there. All she knew was that she had to get back to her family. Her family . . . *something had happened . . . what was it?*

He feigned ignorance of her condition. As they walked slowly down the path, he chattered on about the great gathering, the music, and the dancing, though he knew that her mind was elsewhere.

Kate wished he would just shut up. Her mind was spinning. What on earth was happening? She stared into the cloudless blue sky. She heard the sparrows and the finches squabbling in the gorse along the river bank, took in the crowded campsites, the cacophony of instruments, voices and laughter of the crowd up ahead. She caught sight of Niall and his brothers, began to quiver, suddenly remembering bits of the bitter confrontation. Her cheeks reddened and Jack felt her hand tighten on his arm as she spied her kinfolk.

Having overheard the ugly words between Kate and her son, he knew she might be persuaded to avoid them for a bit. "Would you like to come to the tavern and have a pint? Or perhaps a glass of wine?" He might still succeed at his original plan if he could isolate her for a few hours and treat her kindly. *Yes indeed,* he thought, *this might turn out perfectly after all.*

Since Kate didn't feel strong enough yet to face Niall, she turned to Jack and tried to get her lips to smile. She slowly lifted her eyes to meet his and stifled a shudder. *What a disgusting little weasel of a man,* she thought. *I must be truly mad.* "I thin' I could ma . . . nage a glassss of w-w-wine," she said tightly.

Chapter Eighteen

"Where were ye?" asked Saraid as Niall ambled up to her. Bridget was clutching her mother's skirt with one hand and sucking her thumb with the other. "It's just about time for yer turn on the doors."

Niall gave her a forced smile as he closed his eyes and drew her close. "I had something to take care of. Are Patrick and John here yet?"

"Aye," she replied, raising her voice over the blare of the horns and fiddles. "An' where is yer mother?"

Niall looked away from her. He picked up Bridget and gave her a squeeze, trying to act as if there was nothing wrong. "She'll be along," he said, evading the question.

He hoped that his mother wouldn't make a liar of him. She'd hurt him deeply with her diatribe and he honestly didn't care if he ever saw her again. He pondered on how he was going to explain it all to Saraid, but didn't want to think about it right now. The other children arrived and he set Bridget down. He rubbed Liam's shoulder as he chatted with Fiona and James and asked them to cheer him on. "Let's see if your old man still has what it takes!"

Niall thought, *Maybe some good foot stomping will get rid of this anger.* He hoped so. He gave a sideways glance at Saraid as they joined hands and walked through the crowd. She was his life. There had never been a day or a night in their years together that he hadn't felt an ache in his chest at the sight of her, the touch of her. The sense of joy he found in her smile was equal to the pleasure he found in the lingering scent of rosemary and lemon verbena that she rinsed through her thick hair in the stream after bathing. He was still enticed to passion by the sparkle in her eyes when she teased the fatigue from him after a long day. To lay with her and feel her own passions ignite was all a man could ask for. And the children . . . four beautiful children; each one healthy, strong-spirited; each so different, yet each reflecting her goodness. He felt such pride in his family . . . and pain that his mother couldn't appreciate how much Saraid gave to all of them.

Niall took his place on the dance platform with his brothers and shook out his arms to loosen the tension in them. Another dozen men, including Danny and the Callahan boys, were itching to start. "Hey Roark!" he called out. "Get up here!"

Roark, standing with Maureen and the twins, shook his head. "My knee's actin' up. I'll just watch ye make a fool of yerself!"

Willie stood before them, giving Niall a questioning look.

Niall clenched his jaw, nodded that all was well and waved a hand in frustration. "Just get on with it!" he cried. John and Patrick stood to either side of Niall and jostled him good naturedly with their elbows.

John made a striking figure in his traditional white shirt and dark green tie tucked into long black pants. A cape, made of the same green, draped over one shoulder. "All right then brother," he teased. "Let's see what you can do with those big feet of yours."

Patrick joined in. "Yeah, I heard you dance like an old woman!"

When dancing, Patrick's large frame was surprisingly graceful. He was dressed more casually in snug britches and a loose, sleeveless tunic of soft brushed leather that accentuated the bulging muscles of his arms.

Niall's temper was simmering just beneath the surface, but he went along with the teasing and just shook his head. "Yeah, I'll be outlasting you two and then you can eat your blarney for dinner! I was dancing before you ever saw the light of day!"

Willie, with a word to Freddie, began to dance a short solo in front of the men as Freddie played. On cue, the men moved shoulder to shoulder to make room for Willie, who hopped onto their doors and fancy-stepped around them. He hopped back onto his own door and nodded to the other musicians to begin.

Harps, fiddles, hand drums, pipes, horns, accordions and tin whistles all began with an easy tempo and the men joined in the dancing. The excitement grew as snare drummers appeared from behind the Shamrock Tavern and suddenly began their loud rhythmic accompaniment. The crowd roared with glee and surprise at the new addition to the music. The pace of the dancing picked up as did the volume of the music.

For the next ten minutes, the men gave it their all.

Niall moved his feet with precise and insistent clicks and clacks against the battered wood, combining light toe touches with hard foot stomps in perfect timing with the other men. They were all crossing their ankles forward and back, kicking their bent knees to the side, forward and back, followed by high straight-legged kicks to the front and more of the fancy hard clicking and clacking of their shoes, all in perfect syncopation.

Soon, the fast intricate steps had Niall's heart pounding. Sweat ran down his back until his shirt lay wet against his skin. Dripping tendrils of hair glistened against his reddening cheeks. His anger gave way to the intense concentration needed to keep pace with the others and soon his spirit began to lift.

The men began to tire and pant. John unhooked his cape and tossed it to a laughing Saraid. Tommy Callahan was streaming sweat, a look of sheer determination gritty on his face. Danny was grinning from ear to ear, caught up in the competitiveness of the dance. Patrick, alone, seemed to be taking it all in stride with each step as easily done as the one before.

The crowd was cheering and yelling and clapping at the group of dancers. The drums beat incessantly, the horns blared and the fiddles whined as they all got caught up in the noise and the frenetic tempo as the afternoon sun beat its own heat upon them. The scavenging gulls cried their displeasure, scurrying to find free space to fly, away from the noise.

As the grueling minutes continued to pass, energy began to lag, and one by one, they dropped from the doors. John collapsed laughing in the grass at Saraid's feet while others pressed hands to their quivering knees and struggled for breath. Danny, beet red, his shirt soaked with sweat, finally succumbed, too. Soon, it was just Niall, Patrick, and Tommy left standing to dance with Willie. The tapping became yet fiercer, the drums louder and the faces redder, the frenzied crowd continuing to cheer them on, becoming exhausted and sweaty themselves with each passing moment. Even Patrick finally conceded defeat, tumbling into a groaning heap on the grass, leaving Niall and Tommy to finish the battle.

After another five minutes, a spent Willie waved off the drummers to signal the end of the number. Niall and Tommy collapsed on the doors, exhausted, gasping for breath, unable to speak.

Tommy finally rolled over and gasped. " I could . . . a . . . coulda . . . beaten ye."

"Not . . . today," Niall rasped, his thighs burning and cramped. Laughter spilled from his parched throat. "Not today, boy-o!"

After a few minutes, Niall was able to sit up and wipe the sweat from his face, oblivious to the crowd that was still laughing around him. He was finally feeling relief from the tension that had plagued him earlier.

The excitement over, the crowd dissipated. Some headed to the taverns, some to their dinners and a much needed break from the noise and festivities. The grand finale between Willie and Martin would take place after a few hours of rest.

Niall got to his feet, wincing at the pain in his knees. He flung his arm around Saraid's shoulder with a groan. He swept Bridget into his arms and she wrapped her arms around his neck, looking up at him with delight. "Da!" She shook her *craebh ciuilli* at him, the tiny bells tinkling. "You dancin' and dancin'!"

Liam, James and Fiona, all smiles, joined in the praise, so proud of their father for lasting so long. James and Fiona, after dancing themselves earlier in the day, were especially proud of the endurance he'd shown to put on such a performance.

"Golly, Da," cried James as he patted his father's back, "how did you ever last so long?"

"I could hardly believe that was you, Da!" cried Fiona.

Saraid looked deeply into his eyes, tilting her head to the side. "Where did all that come from? Ye were dancin' like St. Patrick himself was callin' yer name!"

Niall let out a muffled laugh against her hair that was warm from the sun. "That's a very good possibility!" He drew away from her and sighed, hearing his brothers calling out to him. They were on their way to the Shamrock with Danny and Roark.

"I need me a pint," he said, kissing her forehead.

"Go along then. Ye've earned it." She brushed a stray lock of hair from his forehead. "I'll take the children back to the camp. Maureen and I will finish puttin' dinner together."

As Niall walked over to the tavern, he saw Jack Cleary coming down the path alongside the river, his hand at Kate's elbow. He motioned to the other men to go into the tavern. "Go set me up with a pint. I'll be right along."

John mopped the sweat from his brow with his sleeve and nodded, only too happy to get out of the midday sun. Patrick used his big hands to wipe away the drips from his hair and face, then wiped them on his tunic, leaving dark imprints on the soft leather before disappearing through the door.

Niall leaned casually against the door frame beneath the large green shamrock on the signage. Squinting against the sunlight, he watched Cleary and his mother approach.

The man was smiling and chatting away in a low voice to Kate, who had slowed her usual long stride to match his slower rolling gait. Her back was ramrod straight, her eyes expressionless, her mouth slightly contorted but not smiling.

Niall wasn't sure what to make of the scene but felt unease creep through his gut and prickles at the nape of his neck. There was something about his mother's bearing that didn't look quite right. She seemed to have recovered somewhat since they'd argued and he noted that her hair was neatly back in place beneath her cap.

Jack wore an exaggerated smile as they approached the open doorway. "Ah, Niall . . . I've just invited your mother to have a bit of wine with me. Would you like to join us?"

Niall eyed the man with suspicion. Though Jack gave the appearance of congeniality to the clans, most people believed that he was sympathetic to the English cause and that he was spying on the Irish rebels in their midst. Niall wondered what the bloody fool had up his sleeve to be spending time with his mother. He studied Kate's face carefully, trying to assess what was going through her mind, sensing that something was, in fact, amiss.

She stared back at him, unspeaking, and then raised her chin with a hint of defiance. The challenge in her eyes dared him to make an issue of Jack's invitation.

"Is that what you want to do, Mother?" he asked softly, forcing her to speak.

Kate struggled to answer, her voice an indecipherable whisper.

Niall cocked his head closer to her. "What was that you said?"

Kate, panic rising within her, bowed her head and coughed loudly into her fist to clear her throat, and hopefully, the cobwebs of confusion clogging her mind. *Something is wrong with me*, she thought.

She couldn't give in to it, refused to shatter. She'd not give Niall the satisfaction of knowing how he had addled her mind. Determination filled her and she used it to pull herself together. She raised her face and stared haughtily into Niall's questioning eyes. "I said it would be lovely to share a glass of wine with Mr. Cleary." The exertion it took to say so many words exhausted her and she feared she would faint. She hung on just a bit tighter to Jack's arm. "Can we get out of this bloody heat, or are we going to just stand here?"

Niall choked back a laugh, shocked to hear her unlikely choice of words.

Jack laughed heartily. He was encouraged that Kate seemed to have recovered her faculties and he used it to his advantage. "Perhaps you would like to have some supper with me," he said jovially. "We've prepared quite a banquet for our guests, if I do say so." He turned his eyes back to Niall and added, "You and your family are welcome to join us, as well, Niall."

Niall heard the words as a challenge and refused to accept. "No thanks," he replied tightly, pushing himself away from the door frame. "We're just stopping in to wet our whistles. We'll see to our own dinner at the camp." He cocked his head towards his mother. "We've got us a whole pig to feast on, as well as a pot full of fish."

Kate turned her face away from Niall, intent on ignoring him.

"Mother?"

Kate spared him a glance.

"Enjoy your wine," he said. I'll come for you when we're ready to leave."

Chapter Nineteen

Patrick and John stood just inside the tavern entrance, trying to adjust their eyes after being in the bright sunlight outside. Window panes covered with salty haze did little to reflect the dim light from the candled lanterns that hung about the room. After a moment, they spied Danny waving to them from one of the tables against the far wall, and they eased their way across the gritty planks to join him.

The noisy tavern was filled with hungry musicians, couples, families and single young people; some laughing, some singing, others sharing ribald limericks. Most were imbibing tankards of ale or glasses of whiskey. Others were greedily partaking of the feast that Jack had supplied. They weren't about to ignore free food. Here and there, a lone chap sat drinking by himself, watching the crowd.

Danny had found an empty table and grabbed a mug off of Annie's tray as she passed by him. He greeted the others with a quiet warning. "Keep an eye on some of them that's sittin' alone. I'm thinkin' they might be Anglo spies."

"We'll keep an eye on them," said John as he scanned the crowd.

Patrick sat heavily and rubbed his knees. "I don't know about you, but this body is tired."

"Me too," sighed John.

Danny laughed as he looked around the room for the barmaid. "We'll get Annie over here and she'll set ye to rights."

Patrick looked up at the rough hewn timbers that were draped with old fishnets across the ceiling and shook his head. "Don't be starting with your malarkey. I'm not in the mood."

The netting held dried starfish, conch shells and large opalescent abalone that had been gathered over the years along the Doolin shore. Buoys, paint-stripped from years in the sea, hung from twisted coils of rope on the walls, along with a few old lobster pots, silvered and brittle with age.

Danny, grinning, put his hand to his chest and pleaded innocence. "I was only talkin' about gettin' ye a mug of ale to quench yer thirst, man!"

John was chuckling, too. "Make sure that you are, my friend."

The bar itself was Jack Cleary's pride and joy. It ran all along one side of the room, the dark wood gleaming. Jack waxed it himself on a regular basis to protect it from the salt air. The front of the bar was adorned with three large shamrocks that had been carved into the wood and painted a vivid green, edged with gold, to match the one that hung over the entry way. The stools were filled with patrons and people standing behind them waiting for drinks.

The smells of grilled meat and fish hung heavy in the close quarters, mixing with the haze of pungent pipe tobacco that wafted through the air and drifted out the open doorway. Greasy fingers made short work of roasted ribs and chunks of chicken grabbed up from platters. Steaming pots of chowder, lamb stew and thick slices of oat bread graced one of the heavily laden tables at the back of the tavern. The other table held platters of cold shrimp, crab and clams, and a bowl of savory sauce for dipping. Sharing space on the tables were bowls of boiled potatoes, turnips, carrots and cabbage.

When she wasn't serving spirits to the boisterous crowd, Annie replenished the food from the kitchen in the back room.

Annie Muldoon was a coltishly built young woman of seventeen, slim hipped with pert high breasts and long, slim legs. Her shocking red curls hung heavy down her back. Today, her hair was loosely bound with a bright blue scarf that matched the one she had knotted around the narrow waistline of her long skirt. Her simple cotton smock was filmy with age. It stuck to her curves as perspiration flowed freely down her skin from both the heat in the room, and the exertion of serving so many in a timely fashion. Her blue eyes twinkled with merriment as she filled the room with hearty, deep laughter. A full generous mouth was accentuated by deep dimples in her cheeks when she smiled.

Niall wove his way through the tavern, waving to old friends and distant relations. He joined his brothers who were already seated at a table with Roark and Danny.

Some of Danny's kin had come from Killdysart and were sitting at the next table, sharing tales from home. "Hey cousin, I see no one's locked you up yet!"

Danny laughed heartily. "They'd be havin' to catch me first!"

"They's still sayin' ye did 'er wrong."

Danny had left home a few years before when an irate father came after him, accusing him of defiling his homely young daughter. "There's no way I was marryin' that hard-faced girl! I ain't never touched 'er!"

Mugs of ale were lifted. "*Sláinte!*" they cheered.

Everyone joined in the laughter but Niall. Ever aware of his surroundings, he noticed that Martin Clancy, sitting a few tables away from them, had stopped eating, and had turned towards them.

Martin scowled, his eyes like dark pebbles. When he saw Niall staring back at him, he quickly turned and pretended to ignore them, but listened hard to catch any glimmer of conversation.

Niall watched as Tommy Callahan, behind them, set down an empty pint and began working on another. His brother Sean gnawed ravenously on a chicken leg. He made a mental note to speak to Tommy again later.

One of Danny's elder kin asked about the meeting that was to take place later that evening.

Niall quickly shook his head and made eye contact with the other men at the table. "We need to keep the conversation on the light and social for now," he whispered. "I think we've got us a listener."

Danny casually turned his chair and, leaning his elbow on the table, crossed his leg. He let his gaze randomly scan the room as he drank his pint.

Patrick, seated beside Niall, also gave a casual look about the tavern but saw nothing amiss. "Who would you be talking about, brother?"

Niall replied, "I could be wrong, but I think Clancy's got an ear cocked in our direction."

Just then, Annie came by, her skirts swishing between the tables. She quickly removed the empty pints and took orders for more, deftly out-maneuvering Danny, who tried to get his arm around her tiny waist to pull her into his lap.

"Sure I'll be havin' none of yer shenanigans!" she said.

The men howled with laughter while Patrick's face began to burn red behind his smile. "But Annie," he teased. "You'll be breaking his heart now, don't you know?"

"What heart?" She scoffed with a blushing giggle, as she continued to weave through the tables, grabbing empties as she made her way to the bar. She called out their order to Jimmy, the barkeep, and quickly picked up a full tray of drinks for another table.

Moments later, Annie leaned against the end of the bar and wiped her sweaty face with the hem of her skirt. She loved the excitement this big clan get-together brought to the quiet fishing town. The coin they tossed her way was plentiful, too. Part of her hoped to meet some special young man who would take a fancy to her and take her away from this desolate town.

She had given both Patrick and John O'Brien particularly coy smiles and a wink, hoping that one of them might show some interest in her. She didn't bother thinking seriously about Danny. She knew that he just wanted to play, and she desperately wanted more. She did have her eye on Patrick though, hoping that he would remember her from last year. He had been so painfully shy around her then, turning bright red around his ears and face every time she came near him. She'd barely been able to get a word out of him. He certainly seemed more playful this year. He was a really large man, she thought, like a big bear! Her heart began fluttering as she closed her eyes and tried to picture them together. Sighing, she shook off the romantic thoughts and faced reality. She had nothing to offer to someone as grand as Patrick. He probably wouldn't give someone like her the time of day.

Annie would do most anything to get out of Doolin. The constant smell of fish, the barrenness of the Buren, and the hopelessness of her lot were oppressive. She had only her mam left now that her father and her only brother had drowned. A sudden storm had come upon them at sea, capsizing their fishing boat too far from shore to be saved. The broken up boat and their bodies had washed up beneath the cliffs a week later. Her kin were almost unrecognizable after being ravaged by the rocks and sea predators. Though two years had passed, Annie's mam was still grieving, and Annie couldn't hope to fill the void of their loss. There was no way she could leave her to manage on her own.

She did her best to keep her mam going, but it was exhausting just to get a meal into her. Many a day after working in the tavern, she found her mother still sitting where she had left her in the morning; still in her rocking chair by the window, inebriated on mead; still in her flimsy soiled robe, her wispy hair matted and uncombed. She spoke little, if at all, to her daughter. Her tired eyes were red and swollen from tears that didn't stop leaking from them. Annie had no clue as to who was bringing the intoxicating mead to her mam, but swore she would do serious damage to whomever it was when she found out.

***

"Hey Annie!" cried the barkeep. "Wake up over there and get these pints! They ain't going to be servin' themselves now, are they?"

Annie blinked back to attention and silently cursed her mother for disturbing her concentration. She pasted a smile on her face and ambled over to the bar with swinging hips to fill her tray once again. "And where would these be goin', Jimmy?"

Jimmy gave a soft curse. "Ye'd be the one puttin' in the order, so damned if I know! I got enough to do keepin' up with 'em that be sittin' here at the bar. I got no time to keep track of yer tables!"

Annie flushed with temper but silently loaded the mugs of ale onto the tray. As she surveyed the room, she spotted Tommy Callahan waving his empty tankard into the air. Her face brightened and she happily sashayed back to their table, serving the mugs around to each of the men. When Annie served Patrick, she bent a little lower, showing a curve of soft breast beneath her gauzy smock. She slowly raised her eyes and met his dead-on.

His eyes were shining and his breath caught in his throat. The sight of her pink-tipped breasts caused a sudden painful throbbing in his groin, leaving him tongue-tied. He'd never dealt with a woman as fetching and brazen as Annie.

As an unexpected shyness enveloped her, Annie quickly swept away from their table and made her way back to the bar.

***

The other men at the table hooted with laughter. Danny nudged Patrick and playfully teased him. "Sure I think she's sweet on ye, man! Y'ain't goin' to pass that up are ye?"

Patrick gave him a dirty look that shut the smaller man up. "She's a nice girl and you just leave her be."

John chuckled. "A nice girl? *Truly?*"

Niall nudged John. "Let him be." He turned to Patrick. "Why don't you see what time she gets done and ask her to join us tonight for the tales around the fires?"

Patrick shrugged. "I don't know . . . ." Then, looking from one to the other, he added in all seriousness, "If I do, you'd better be decent to her or I'll break your bones."

John nodded and let out a quiet sigh. He wished a woman would have that effect on himself. He lifted his tankard and sipped at his ale. He would never have anything of the farm to call his own. Nothing to offer a wife. No sense to even think about marriage. He drained the last of his ale and pushed the mug to the center of the table with the other empties.

Chapter Twenty

Jimmy hollered over to Annie as she set the glasses on the bar. He pointed to a table in the back where Jack was sitting with a woman she didn't know.

"Jack wants ye to set 'im up with two settin's, all nice like, fer dinner with his lady friend. He even wants a cloth on the table."

She was shocked. "An' where am I to be gettin' a fancy cloth in this place?"

Jimmy reached under the bar and took a small brass key out of the till. "He said there's a cloth in the bottom drawer under the old desk in his office. Make it snappy now, and don't be snoopin' in the desk."

She looked over at Jack who was paying rapt attention to the woman at the table. She stared at their glasses of wine. *He must have served up the decanter of wine himself,* she thought, as she made her way to the back room. Annie had never been inside Jack's private office before.

The room was not very large but it was comfortable. There were kegs of ale and crates of liquor stacked against the rough paneled wall in the back. One of the walls had shelves that held supplies on the bottom and various personal memorabilia on those above; a small collection of books with leather bindings, some china figurines, and a large glass bowl filled with various seashells and bits of smooth sea glass.

Annie crossed to the desk, hastily wiping her fingers on her apron before running them over the supple surface of the leather chair.

Bending her head, she sniffed with pleasure, knowing she had never smelled or touched something as rich as this before. She carefully moved it away from the desk. The leaf of the desk was down, loose papers piled on its surface. Her fingers were itching to explore all the marvelous nooks and crannies at the back of the desk to see what was hidden there. As she pushed the papers back to close the leaf, a single loose sheet fell to the floor. Though she hadn't had any schooling, her mam had taught her to read some, and she could tell that it was a list of names. As she sounded out the letters, she could make out that one of the names was Danny McMahon, and another, Niall O'Brien. Callahan's name was there, too. She placed it back on the pile, and closed the leaf, not having time to give it another thought.

When she unlocked the drawer, she found several pieces of fine linen. *Where the bloody hell did these come from?* she wondered. She chose a soft damask cloth of rich cream and two matching napkins. After re-locking the drawer, she pocketed the key, and returned to the front room.

As Annie approached Jack's table, she could tell that the woman had some breeding and acted accordingly, with her best manners. "Good afternoon missus," she said with a small curtsy. "My name would be Annie, and I'm happy to be of service to ye."

Jack held both glasses of wine in one hand and the decanter in the other to allow Annie to put the cloth on the rough table. Kate merely nodded while Annie placed the napkins in front them.

It had been Jack's plan to mingle among the patrons; to listen and observe, hoping to pick up some stray bits of illicit conversation. Though his plan had now changed, he thought the outcome might be even more beneficial.

Jack was making an effort to act the suave gentleman, which Annie found quite amusing.

His broad girth barely fit behind the table, his waistcoat bulging around the copper buttons that strained to hold his belly in place.

Beads of perspiration dotted his balding head, running into the ring of wiry red curls over his ears.

Jack turned to Kate. "How about if I have Annie fill a couple of plates with a variety of things for us? Then we won't have to deal with all the folks around the tables."

Kate nodded, silently relieved that she wouldn't have to struggle to keep her balance while walking with a plate of food in her hands. Though she felt some better, there was still some quivering in her legs. She wasn't really hungry, but perhaps some food would settle her stomach.

Jack turned to Annie. "All right then." He waved his hand towards the buffet tables. "Fill up a couple of plates and bring some smaller plates as well for Mrs. O'Brien and myself."

Annie blinked in surprise as she addressed Kate. "Would ye be mother to those fine O'Brien men over there?" She pointed across the room to where the brothers were laughing boisterously, lifting their pints in a toast.

Kate raised her eyes to look where she pointed. Only Niall was silent, staring at her with obvious puzzlement. Scowling, she asked, "Would that be any of your concern?"

Annie blushed, deeply affronted. "Excuse me missus . . . I was just payin' a compliment to you on havin' a family of such fine dancin' men. I saw a bit of them havin' a go on the boards earlier." She braved a glimpse at Kate, and seeing that the woman was embarrassed, felt better. "Ye should be right proud of how amazin' they are. That's all I was sayin'."

With that, Annie turned on her heel and marched petulantly to the buffet. She grabbed two plates and manipulated them perfectly, her fingers evenly splayed under the two, her thumb pressed on top of where the two rims overlapped. She piled one plate with chicken legs, slices of beef, and some pork ribs. On the other, she added some cold shrimp, cooked clams, chunks of lobster, and a ramekin of butter. She filled another plate with bread and vegetables, and carefully carried it all back to the table. She set the plates down on the table in front of Jack and rushed back to the table for their individual plates and utensils.

Annie surveyed the table, happy with her presentation. "Will ye be needin' anythin' else?"

Jack waved her off. "That should be enough to keep us busy for a while. Go take care of our other guests. Oh, and Annie . . ."

"Yes, sir?"

"Send another round of pints to the O'Brien table and be sure to tell them that I sent them free of charge." He nodded to Kate, as if waiting for her approval.

Kate sighed. *What a poppycock he is!* She had a vague memory of Jack being a skinflint of the first order. *I wonder what he wants of me? I hope he isn't expecting me to be grateful!* She shuddered, regretting her decision to accompany him into the tavern, but it was a little late now. She wasn't about to cause a scene. Instead, she decided that she would try to eat something, and then make her escape back to her caravan so she could sleep.

Chapter Twenty-One

Martin poked through the empty shrimp shells on his plate to make sure there wasn't one more morsel hidden among them. Satisfied, he pushed the plate aside and lit his pipe. Gazing around the room, he observed everything that was going on in the tavern. His eyes came to rest, once again, on Jack and Mrs. O'Brien.

What the hell does Jack have up his sleeve, carrying on with the O'Brien woman? Doesn't he know how it would look? He tried to catch Jack's eye, but the man was pointedly ignoring him. The deliberate slight made him fume.

Martin had much to tell Jack and it needed to be done while many of the clan were here together for the weekend. He had gathered some interesting tidbits on his travels that incriminated Danny McMahon with the recent damage unleashed on the estate of one of the land barons in Limerick. It was up to Jack to pass the information on to the sheriff and his men who were camped to the north of Doolin. They were just waiting for the word to round up the rebels. His mood grew fouler yet as he gazed towards the bar. He spotted Hank, hunched over his ale, looking maudlin, as usual. Martin sighed and decided that tonight he would tell Hank that he was done with him. Time to move on. The long trip back to Dublin would give him the opportunity to find a replacement. A young fiddler would be far more eager to please and would offer new opportunity to fill his needs.

That decided, he turned his gaze back to the O'Brien men who were carrying on as if they hadn't a care in the world. He'd paid an exorbitant amount of coin to find out that it was Niall O'Brien who had organized the secret meeting that was to take place later that night. He needed to be stopped. The thought of Niall being caught out thrilled him. He couldn't wait. Loud voices drew his eyes to another table.

It was Tommy Callahan who was creating a ruckus. He needed to be made an example of, too. He had heard that the hot headed Tommy was itching to be in cahoots with the Whiteboys. *Bloody fool!* Maybe if they hung the boy in public alongside O'Brien and McMahon, the others would fall into line and forget their thoughts of rebellion. Their bravado was just that. There was no way they could accomplish anything but temporary inconvenience to the baronies.

He needed to be careful not to tip his hand. If they found out about what he himself had been doing, his own life wouldn't be worth a copper. All the information he had been collecting over the past months was astounding. Many of those poor Irish that he met in his travels through the outlying reaches of the counties had no idea that he had moved his allegiance to the side of the Anglo landowners. As he plied his trade with his dancing shoes, Martin ate their food and drank their ale, slept on their filthy straw-filled mattresses. All the while he maintained a civil tongue and smiled politely as he taught them to dance and listened to their endless chatter. For some reason, despite the poverty of some, they still managed to laugh at their own foibles and dance with abandon. They were despicable, dirty, uneducated fools, too ignorant to know how miserable they were. Martin snorted. The same could not be said of the O'Brien men. *They were too smart for their own good!* It angered him that the O'Brien clan had so much because of their bloodline, while he had to struggle, year after year, to maintain his lifestyle.

The small O'Brien estate now fell under the purview of the Baron of Thomond, himself an O'Brien, and brother to Niall's grandfather.

The baron had held onto his thousands of acres by denouncing his Catholicism and paying homage to the Anglican Church. Then he had absorbed and held the deed to the prime acres along the Shannon owned by Niall's family. The baron softened the blow by leaving hundreds more acres as a wooded buffer around the farm. Only then had he given up some lesser acreage to the Anglos. To Martin, this was a ploy to keep the prime acres from the Anglos until such a time when the Catholic O'Briens were once again allowed to own land.

When faced with how difficult living could be in County Clare, most of the Anglos became absentee landlords. They were only too happy to leave the Irish to the working of the land while they collected crops and tax revenue.

Martin had fallen out of favor with the Baron years ago when he'd approached the man for information about the religious and political leanings of James O'Brien and his sons. Since the Baron now spent most of his time abroad trying to acquire more property and wealth, Martin felt he had a better chance of finding the sons complicit with the rebels.

He tried once again to gain Jack's attention and was angry that the man was still acting like he was invisible. He decided that he'd been ignored long enough. Rising abruptly, he stalked over to Jack's table. With a stern nod to Kate, he turned his attention to Jack. "I need a moment of your time."

"Can't you see I have a guest?" asked Jack, not pleased to be interrupted.

Martin spoke through clenched teeth. "I need to speak to you privately."

"Now's not the time."

Kate shrank back in her seat, trying to distance herself from the venom in Martin's gaze. Her heart pounding, she started to rise from her seat. She had no desire to be part of this quarrel. "Perhaps I should leave you to your discussion."

Jack laid a gentle but firm hand upon hers on the table. "You'll do no such thing, Kate." His eyes were like steel when they met Martin's. "Whatever it is, it can wait until later this evening."

Martin banged his staff against the floor. "I suggest that you make time now!" he hissed.

"And I suggest," Jack retorted angrily, rising from his chair, "that you leave the tavern now before I have you thrown out!"

Martin bit his tongue though his thoughts were murderous. He was not oblivious to the hush that had begun to creep over the nearby tables. Soon it would spread across the room as people sensed the possibility of a fracas. Without another word he spun away from the table and headed for the door. *How dare Jack speak to him like this! He would make the fecking fool pay for his disrespect! Who does he think he is?*

Tommy Callahan was in his cups. He had yet to eat anything and the four pints he had consumed heightened his emotions. He was still grousing to his brother and the others about the possibility that Martin Clancy could be working for the Anglos. He was alternately morose and teary eyed over the plight of his ancestors, then suddenly angry and explosive. Sean kept trying to calm him down and keep him quiet. Patrick had tried cajoling him out of his ill temper, but was getting nowhere. John tried to mind his own business but wasn't having much luck with that once Tommy started waving his arms around and yelling.

Danny decided he'd listened to Tommy sputtering long enough, and grabbed the younger man by the front of his shirt. "Ye be shuttin' your feckin' mouth right now, ye sorry bastard, or find somewhere else to sit!"

Niall eyed Sean and motioned towards the door. "We don't need the attention he's drawing to the rest of us."

Then Niall stiffened as he watched Martin get up from his chair and approach Jack's table. Jack's anger was palpable across the room and Kate looked tense. The tables around them grew silent as their argument grew louder.

The others were too engrossed in the trouble with Tommy to realize what was going on across the room. Niall was ready to rescue his mother when Martin abruptly turned and began stalking across the room towards to door. Niall let out a breath when his mother seemed to recover from her discomfort.

Martin shot a look of contempt at Tommy and the others as he passed by them.

Tommy, uttering obscenities, tried to lunge at Martin. His brother quickly grabbed him by the arm and tried to force him back into his seat.

Danny grabbed Tommy's other arm and shook him. "Are ye daft, man?"

Patrick quickly grabbed onto the back of Tommy's neck and pushed his face down to the table. He refused to let go, despite Tommy's cursing and lashing about, until Martin was safely gone. He pulled Tommy back up and calmly looked him in the eye. "It's done. If you know what's good for you, you'll get something to eat and cool down."

Tommy struggled to free himself of Patrick's grasp but remained seated, muttering about Martin under his breath. "That traitor needs to die."

"Most likely he does," said John, "but you'll not be the one to do it."

"Yeah, well . . . *somebody* needs to take care of 'im!"

Danny swore as he tipped his mug and drained it. "Don't be worryin' yer head about it."

Niall sat in silence, his eyes riveted on his mother. The noise and laughter once again swirled around the tavern, the revelers oblivious to the dramas playing out around them in the room.

Patrick released his hold on Tommy, and sat back in his chair. Tommy continued to sputter, then just shook his head and remained quiet as he picked up his pint. Seeing that it was empty, he shoved the mug across the table where it tipped over and rolled to the edge. Danny grabbed it before it could hit the floor.

"Hey little brother," Sean pleaded. He reached for Tommy's arm, pulling him up from his chair. "C'mon . . . let's get outta here and go for a walk before ye be startin' somethin' stupid."

Tommy angrily shook him off and dropped back into his seat. "I'll be a'right. I'll get somethin' to eat."

"Yeah, ye will but we're goin' out for a bit of air first," said Sean, as he dragged Tommy from his chair and headed for the door.

Danny rose as well, tossing some coins on the table for Annie. "Sure we've killed enough time in this stink hole." He gave Patrick a big grin and a friendly punch in the arm. "Ye should see if Annie wants to come to the fires tonight for the story tellin'."

Patrick shook his head. "I don't know man." He looked around the room for Annie but she seemed to have disappeared. Then he saw a flash of bright red hair as she stopped at Jack's table. "What in bloody hell is our mother doing sitting with Jack?"

All eyes turned to the table across the room.

"What's happening?" asked John, craning his neck. He was stunned to see his mother sitting there, unease clearly on her face. "Why is our mother sitting with *him*?"

"I can explain," answered Niall hastily as he began to walk across the room.

John grabbed Niall's arm as he followed him. "You knew she was here?"

Niall shook him off. "I'll tell you about it after we get her out of here," he replied.

"Mother?" asked John. "Are you all right?"

Kate nodded, grateful to see her three sons. Her thoughts swam in her head. *I need to get out of this wretched place! I need some fresh air! I need to sleep!*

"Of course she's all right," said Jack, fighting to control his temper. *Damn Martin!* He had ruined all his plans! "I wouldn't let anything happen to her. We're just about to have a bit of dinner, as you can see," he said, waving his hand over the plates of food.

John began to seethe. "Come along, Mother," he said as gently as he could manage. He offered her his arm and helped her to stand. "We've a big dinner set at the camp."

Jack held his anger in check and politely rose to his feet and addressed Kate. "Perhaps we can do this some other time."

Kate and her sons turned their backs on him and left the tavern without uttering another word.

Jack watched them leave the tavern and sank heavily into his chair. He wanted nothing more than to throw all the plates of food after them. People at nearby tables were staring at him, some with smirks on their faces as they talked in hushed tones. This enraged Jack even more.

"What are you looking at?" he yelled, as he got up and stomped past them. He headed out the door determined to find Martin. "I'm going to kill that bastard," he muttered.

Jack searched the campground until he came upon Hank, inebriated and dozing on his stool. He gave Hank a shake, demanding to know where Martin was. Hank could do no more than babble and had no idea where Martin was. He dropped his head back to his chest and began to snore loudly. Jack picked up Hank's cane, ready to throttle him with it, but there were too many people watching. Instead, cane in hand, he stormed away, asking others if they had seen Martin. Someone thought he had seen him walking towards the bay. He hurried off in that direction and was breathing hard from the exertion when he got there. He ducked behind a monolith as he saw someone else approaching the bay. He had no choice but to wait until they left. All the while, he continued to fume.

Chapter Twenty-Two

Martin stormed from the tavern, rage eating at him as he elbowed his way through the crowd. His breathing became labored, his chest tightened like a vise. He stopped and leaned against a hitching post, sucking in air until his breaths evened out. *This will not do,* he thought as he wiped the sweat from his brow. He decided to walk down to the bay to settle himself. Slowing his pace, he ambled through the village of Fisherstreet, past the woolen shop, the smithy, two more boisterous taverns, and then crossed the bridge over the little culvert that awaited the incoming tide.

The sun beat on the rotting flesh of clams in their broken shells and the drying seaweed trapped in the rocky crevasses. The squawking gulls and a horde of flies swarmed over the fetid mess and would remain there until the salt water flowed over it. A few errant gulls hovered over him as he neared the bay and he waved his staff into the air to scare them off.

Though the wide brim of his hat shaded his eyes, the sun's reflection off the water was strong and made him squint. The seascape was fairly empty of people as most were eating or resting up for the remainder of the day's activities. *At least there is no music blaring here,* he thought. The solitude was welcoming. He would be able to think more calmly about all that was on his mind.

He gave some thought to Willie. It pained him to admit that the young man was a talented dancer. He feared that Willie might well best him when they competed later in the day. *I can't let that happen! I must find the strength to defend my title!* He wondered if Willie was passing messages among the Catholics, exactly as he himself had been doing for the Anglos. Perhaps he could use this information to get rid of him, too. He would have to bring this up with Jack before he headed back to Dublin.

Martin finally reached the bay and carefully climbed down the slippery, tide-worn rocks, using his staff to maintain his balance. Here at least, the dried seaweed and broken bits of shells lay submerged, the air free of the putrid smell of the culvert. He sat on a large, flat stone just above the water's edge, and carefully secured his staff in the wet sand between the rocks behind him. He slowly removed his brogues and stockings, setting them on a higher slab of rock. Sighing deeply, he eased his swollen, aching feet into the cold salt water and massaged the bulging veins in his calves. The tide was known to come in with sudden force, but for now, the waves were gently lapping, the foamy residue sluicing over his feet and between his toes. Martin removed his hat and, closing his eyes to the sun's glare, raised his weathered face to let the ocean breeze cool his skin and scalp. He was weary. It was taking him longer and longer to recover from the arduous dance routines. It struck him like a blow that his dancing days might be coming to an end. He had come a long way since those early years in Dublin.

Ahh Dublin. Martin chuckled to himself. He too, was from the poor streets of the city but he hadn't let that deter him from what he wanted from life. He'd been blessed with dancing feet like no other and was determined to be a success. He'd wanted riches, adulation and the respect he would garner as a master of the dance.

It took money to establish oneself with the right clothes and connections. In the dark of night, he'd become a talented thief, sneaking in and out of moneyed homes where he pocketed jewels and small fancy items that he could easily sell on the streets. His first purchases with the ill-gotten coin were a decent waistcoat and a proper pair of dancing shoes. He also had to train himself to act the part; to remove the rough diction of the streets from his vocabulary; to affect the mannerisms of those of a higher station; to fit in without being caught out for the wretched queer he really was.

Once he felt confident that his metamorphosis was complete, he had positioned himself on the better street corners and danced for delighted passersby, paying whomever he could find to play the fiddle for him. Before long, he had become a fast-footed sensation and was invited into aristocratic homes for the amusement of the rich. He determinedly charmed both men and women, unabashedly prostituting himself to his inebriated hosts and hostesses. The leverage and the blackmail were profitable. It was also dangerous. Eventually his victims had had enough and, banding together, turned on him. He knew he had to get out of Dublin . . . and fast.

It was when he was hiding out in the slums that he had come upon young Hank and his luck had changed again. Their journey across Ireland to the county of Clare offered many opportunities to establish himself. The boy had been more than adequate as a fiddler and over time had filled many of his personal needs as well.

Hank's innocence had been a welcome challenge, keeping him entertained and satisfied for years. Since the boy was too far from home and too scared to ever find his way back, he'd not had any choice but to submit. Once he had outgrown his youth, Hank had become no more than a whipping post. That, too, had filled a perverse need. As time passed, Martin made certain that the young boys he desired were waifs of the streets with no one to wonder about them, no one to cry foul.

Martin had done whatever was necessary to achieve his dreams of greatness and no longer feared exposure for his perversions. The aristocrats he had used and blackmailed in his youth were long dead and their secrets had died with them. For decades, he had been the master of his own fate. Having achieved his goal, his behavior with his new benefactors became above reproach. He was no longer reviled and was, instead, feted by the masses, as he felt was his due. When he returned to Dublin, he would be wined and dined for months before putting on a command performance before Parliament with his best students. He was ready to enjoy a few months of rest and being spoiled. He was, after all, the best dancer in Ireland!

Martin shook his head. Hank was becoming too difficult, starting to fight back. *Yes, it's time to let the sniveling sod go.*

The food and ale he had consumed made him feel lethargic. The distant sound of a softly played pipe wafted on the air like a lullaby and the hypnotic sound of gently rolling waves soothed away his anger. *There is nothing as calming as sitting by the sea.* He dropped his chin to his chest and, with a sigh, closed his eyes.

Martin never heard the quiet footfalls that crept up behind him as he sat dozing. He never felt the heavy end of the shillelagh ram into the back of his skull, never cried out with sudden, unbearable pain. He never tasted the spray of blood that spewed from his nose and mouth, spattering like scarlet raindrops into the swirling white foam at the water's edge. He toppled forward, landing face down in the deepening sea, a trail of red flowing behind him. Within minutes, the fast-rising tide began drawing him away from shore over the now hidden rocks of the bay, the crushing current dragging him down into its unforgiving depths. Martin's shoes and stockings soon followed. All that remained was his red hat, bobbing aimlessly away on the water's surface and his staff, nearly submerged between the rocks.

Jack was breathing heavily, hardly believing what had happened. His emotions wavered between fear and exultation. His eyes smarted with tears that refused to fall. It was moments before he was able move. Distant laughter startled him and he spun towards the path. He quickly looked around to make certain no one had witnessed the crime. Jack realized that he was still holding Hank's cane and tossed it aside.

He grew dizzy and sat down behind a rock where he wouldn't be seen. He covered his head with his hands. *What am I going to do? Think, man! Think!* Then it came to him. He could sneak into Martin's room at the hotel and steal his money. *God knows he won't be needing it!*

Then he would have enough to disappear. *Yes!*

Trembling, he scanned the water to make certain that nothing of Martin remained. The staff was no longer visible between the rocks. Before he hurried from the bay, he muttered to the gulls squawking overhead, *"Go n-ithe an cat thú is go n-ithe an diabhal an cat"* May the cat eat you and the devil the cat!"

Chapter Twenty-Three

Saraid waved at Niall as the O'Brien brothers and their mother approached the camp. "It's 'bout time ye be gettin' here! Dinner's ready!" She was puzzled by their grim faces and flustered that not one of them acknowledged her.

Niall held up a finger as he passed by and said, "Wait."

She grew more puzzled when, after the brothers helped Kate into her caravan, they continued on towards the river. She became alarmed as John and Patrick began confronting Niall with raised voices. They were obviously angry about something.

* * *

"So Niall," said John, his teeth clenched. "Tell us how mother came to be with Jack Cleary."

"Yeah, Niall," said Patrick. "What was she doing with that snake?"

Niall sighed and guessed he had better get on with it. "After the kids danced, she said yet another hateful thing to Saraid and I'd finally had enough of it." He snapped a twig from an overhead branch, tossed it into the river and watched it bob on the current until it disappeared.

"That's it?" demanded John. "There has to be more!"

Niall nodded. "I pulled her away from the crowd and we went at it good and hard. Her words were cruel enough that I've told her to leave my house."

John screamed at this brother. "How could you say that to her! She's our mother!" John, always the closest to their mother, was appalled that Niall would even suggest such a thing, never mind mean it.

Niall eyed both his brothers before replying with a voice that was as brittle as ice. "She insulted not just Saraid, but me, and our children, too. *That* I cannot forgive!"

Patrick asked, "And just where is she supposed to go?"

Niall shrugged with a nonchalance he did not feel, and tried to speak without the venom that was still choking him. "I told her that she could move back to Dublin to be with her own kind if she had a mind to."

John waved his arms in the sticky air. "But, it's her *home!*"

"Actually," Niall replied, biting on the words, "Now that Da is gone, it's *my* home. If you're so worried about her, perhaps she should move in with *you*."

John laughed incredulously at the thought. "Where is she supposed to sleep? Now that your brood has moved into the main house, I have only the cottage!"

While their father was alive, John had enjoyed the spacious rooms and comforts of the main house. Once Niall became the heir in residence, he'd had to move into the cottage to make room for Niall's family. He was still trying to adjust to the smaller, more rustic space.

Patrick, torn between both brothers, tried to play peacemaker by changing the subject. "Look, we can't be throwing mother to the wolves now can we? But aside from that, I still want to know about Jack Cleary. What was mother doing with him?"

"Yes, Niall," exclaimed John, pacing back and forth. "You were going to tell us what she was doing with that bloody ass." He stopped and jabbed a finger into Niall's chest. "Does it have anything to do with that argument you had with her?"

Niall sighed, mentally exhausted from the strain of the argument.

As he swatted John's hand away, he looked across to their camp where Saraid stood watching them. She began to approach and he motioned for her to stay away. He watched her spin on her heels and march back to the camp. He shook his head with resignation, knowing that, later, he would have to deal with Saraid, too. "I think something must have happened to mother after I left." He shrugged his shoulders, feeling some guilt in spite of his anger. "When I went over to the tavern, I saw her walking with Cleary, and he seemed to be holding her steady. Her face looked a bit strange and she seemed to be struggling to speak."

John's eyes glistened with rage. "You bloody bastard!" He made a fist and punched Niall full in the face.

Niall spun around and was about to return the blow when Patrick grabbed them both by the scruffs of their necks and held them apart. "Stop it!" he screamed, his arms straining with the effort. "Are you both insane?"

Niall twisted away from him, wiping the blood that ran from his nose with his sleeve. He stood still while John flailed his arms and tried, unsuccessfully, to hit him again.

"You should be ashamed of yourself!" screamed John.

Niall took a slow steadying breath before trying to explain. "Look, John. I can't undo what happened, but I spoke to her when they arrived at the Shamrock to see if she was all right. She was adamant that she was fine, insisted that she wanted to sit with him, and I didn't want to create a scene. I kept watch of her while we were in the tavern, and she seemed to have shrugged off whatever was ailing her, so I let her be."

Though John was still steaming, the argument had left him weary. He tried to temper his words as he defended his mother. "She hasn't been right since da passed on . . . I'll give you that. I like Saraid . . . I do . . . but she and mother are like two snakes in a pit with each other. It's hard for her having all of you in the house."

Patrick decided that enough was enough. He could smell the food and he was hungry enough to eat the entire pig himself. "Look, can we leave this for later? Food's ready and I'm going to starve to death if I don't eat soon."

Niall and John just stared at their mountain-sized brother, and then they chuckled in spite of themselves. Agreeing to talk again after the final competition, the three of them walked back to the camp in silence.

Saraid and the others were anxious to eat and began to cheer as the men approached. She and Maureen had spread the wagon tarp on the ground to use as a dinner cloth. Saraid, trembling from the brothers' conflict, did not look at Niall. "Sure it's 'bout time ye finally decided to join us. I was beginnin' to think we'd be eatin' all this food ourselves."

Patrick laughed. "Not on your sweet life, woman." He pointed towards James and Liam, issuing them an order. "Get me that big platter and help me with the pig."

"Niall?" asked Saraid. "Is yer mother not joinin' us to eat?"

"She had her dinner at the tavern," he replied quietly, not meeting her eyes. "She's going to rest for awhile." At Saraid's questioning gaze, he added, "I don't want to talk about it right now. It's a touchy subject."

"Ye're not serious?" she asked, finally looking at him.

"I surely am," he replied, shaking his head.

"Look at me!"

He raised his eyes to hers for a moment before looking away. "Let it be for now. She'll be along soon enough."

Saraid huffed out a breath. "An' where's Danny? Didn't he come back with ye?"

Niall looked around then shrugged. He'd been too caught up in his own problems to keep tabs on Danny. "I honestly don't know. He left the tavern before we did."

As he left her to help Roark with the dinner pot, she vowed to get to the bottom of it all.

Patrick began carving chunks of the black-crusted pig while juices dripped and sizzled. The strong aroma of honey and rosemary tickled his nostrils and made his stomach growl with anticipation. He licked his greasy fingers and sighed with pleasure. "Now boys," he said as he offered each of them a small strip of the succulent pork. "This is heaven itself."

James popped the hot meat into his mouth and licked his lips as the fatty juice ran down his chin. He grinned broadly at his uncle and said, "Oh man . . . this is so good!"

Liam held the strip in his fingers and slowly sucked the juice from the meat. He, too, smiled and nodded in agreement.

Niall and Roark carefully removed the large pot of simmering fish from the fire and carried it over to the tarp. Maureen admonished the twins to stand back as she set down a spare pot. The men poured some of the hot liquid into it, to save for soup, before dumping the rest of the pot onto the tarp. Some of the broth ran over the edges and the rest seeped through the tarp leaving the fish and shellfish in a pile. The bright red of the lobster was colorful contrast to the black shells of the mussels and the pink of the shrimp and crabs. John poured out a smaller pot of red-skinned potatoes while Roark emptied another filled with gleaming ears of golden corn.

Niall slid the whole fish onto a small platter and cut through the string and cloth that bound it together. With two small sticks, he carefully spread it apart and drew out the spine in one long strip, then set down the platter with the rest of the meal.

Young Bridget did her part by distributing the bowls around the edge of the cloth. While Saraid added melted butter to the bowls, Fiona added a board of bread, fresh from the stones around the fire, which Maureen sliced. The younger children's tunics were removed to eat bare-chested. Saraid and Maureen chuckled together, wishing they could do the same.

Saraid stood with her hands on her hips, satisfied with the looks of their feast. "All right everybody, let's eat!"

Mugs were filled with ale from a keg and mead from a jug for the adults, and sweetened tea was poured for the children.

No one bothered with utensils. Everyone just dropped to the ground, greedy hands reaching for everything at once. They scooped the succulent morsels of clams from their shells and dropped them into their butter before casting the empty shells back onto the tarp. Crab legs were cracked with stones to retrieve the tender meat within. The ears of corn and chunks of potatoes were dipped into butter and sprinkled with coarse salt before finding their way to hungry mouths.

Patrick passed the platter of pork and grinned as slices went directly from platter to mouth.

Maureen moaned with pleasure. "Patrick! This is delicious!"

Niall twisted the back from the head of the lobster, hot broth running out onto the cloth. He cracked the claws with a small rock and tossed the pieces back into the pile. He bent back the tail fin, tossing that as well, before shoving his fingers into the cavity and forcing the pink-white tail meat out the other end of the shell. After cutting it into pieces, he added them to the pile where they disappeared as soon as they hit the cloth.

Saraid grabbed a claw and carefully removed the shell, pulling the meat from it in a single piece. She dunked it into her butter and, noticing that Niall was watching her, tipped her head back and slowly sucked it into her mouth. His face flushed with discomfort. She grinned, licking her lips seductively, in hopes of teasing him out of his foul mood. She was rewarded by his chuckle before he dug into his own food.

James had cut and whittled some thin willow branches of their bark. They used these to push and dig the lobster meat from the knuckles that they couldn't reach with their fingers. John passed the platter of flakey fish around the circle with the warning to watch for tiny bones.

There was little conversation, only sounds of pleasure as they slurped clams and crabs, and chewed on the tender fish and pork. Sticky fingers scooped up the green roe from the lobster that had oozed onto the tarp. When the large pieces of lobster were stripped clean, they scraped their teeth against the narrow legs, sucking every last bit of meat from the small shells. All the while, butter and pork fat dripped from their chins and juices slid down their forearms. A bucket of river water and a pile of clean rags sat on the ground at the end of their picnic area to clean the grease from their hands and faces once they were done.

The sun was still hours away from the horizon, and the heat of the day added to the euphoria of the meal. The constant onslaught of music had finally stilled; the exception being the occasional sweet trill of a penny whistle or pipe, as people filled their bellies and then napped or chatted quietly in the mottled shade under the scattered trees. After an hour, there were deep sighs around the circle and the occasional noisy belch, with Patrick and Liam competing to see who could voice the highest praise for the excellent meal.

Chapter Twenty-Four

"Danny will regret missin' all this food," said Maureen as she soaked a rag to wash the twin's faces. They squirmed and giggled as she scrubbed the grease and char from their cheeks and then tweaked their noses.

Roark shrugged. "Danny's a big boy. If he's hungry, it be his own fault."

"I have a surprise," cried Fiona. She ran to the back of the caravan and returned with a bowl filled to the brim with fragrant red raspberries. "I picked these myself!"

"Me too, me too!" cried Bridget, because she had helped with the picking and had the scratches on her thin arms and legs to prove it.

There were several groans from those with sated bellies, but no one could resist the sweet, freshly-picked fruit. As they were lounging on the grass with their berries, Willie Hayes approached them.

"Hey Willie," Saraid called out to the young dance master. "We've still got a bit of fish and berries here if ye'd like to join us."

Willie nodded and grabbed a handful of berries, popping them one by one into his mouth. His eyes smiled his pleasure while he savored them. He looked to the men and asked, "I don't suppose any of ye have seen Martin?"

"Not just now, Willie," replied Niall, looking around the camp. "He was in the Shamrock a while ago but he left before we did."

Patrick asked, "You ready for the big competition?"

Willie laughed and did a little jig. "Martin's lookin' a bit worn out. I'm thinkin' that I might just beat 'im this year! That is, of course, if I can find 'im."

Niall was puzzled. "What are you saying, Willie?"

"Well, he seems to have vanished into thin air. No one's seen 'im for over an hour."

Patrick laughed. "Maybe he's left town and you'll win without working up a sweat!"

Willie shook his head. "I'd rather win fair and square! I've practiced long and hard since I embarrassed myself last year."

"Ye did no such thing, Willie," cried Saraid. "Sure he's just been doin' it a lot longer and knows how to pace himself."

"Actually," said Willie, "maybe he's just dozed off somewhere, gatherin' his strength. I should do the same." He waved goodbye and they called out their wishes for a big win that evening. Then he meandered off between the wagons, chatting with other folks still at their picnics.

Saraid and Maureen scavenged what seafood could be saved from the tarp, swatting away the flies that had been gathering around the leftovers. They put all of it into the pot of broth while Fiona cut up and added the few left over potatoes. Roark took his knife and scraped the remaining kernels of corn from their cobs into the pot as well. The rest of the shells, cobs and bones were left in a pile on the tarp.

Patrick drew up the corners of the bundle, yanked it off the ground with one hand, and grabbed a clean bucket with the other. "I'll go get rid of this and bring back some fresh water."

"Can I come with you?" asked Liam.

"Not this time, little one. I'm going to be stopping at the tavern to see about Annie."

Maureen kidded him, punching his arm. "Finally goin' to take the plunge, are ye?"

Everyone laughed and voiced an opinion on how to woo the young barmaid. He waved off their laughter, red-faced. "She'll probably have to work, or already have someone else to meet up with."

"Don't know until you try, Patrick," said Niall, slapping him on the back. "I think you just might be able to convince her to join you."

Roark laughed easily, enjoying Patrick's discomfort. "Sure, man!" he cried. "How can she resist such a big, strong example of Irish manliness?"

The teasing continued for a few more minutes before Patrick had had enough, and turned away from them and headed down the path.

"Wait up, Patrick," said John. "I'll go with you." He grabbed two corners of the tarp and the two of them drifted off towards the bay with the garbage swinging between them.

* * *

Niall sat leaning against a wagon wheel, chewing on the end of a long piece of grass. Saraid plunked down beside him, laying her face against his thigh, and stared up at his troubled blue eyes.

"So, *Mo Sheare*. Are ye going to tell me what's goin' on or are ye goin' to keep it all to yerself?"

Niall gazed down at her and wrapped his arm across her midriff. He rested his hand beneath her breast as he bent to kiss her forehead. "It's not a good story," he said quietly.

"Tell me anyway."

"I didn't like the way my mother spoke to you."

"When?" she asked, searching his face.

Niall couldn't believe that she had forgotten his mother's harsh words. He turned away from her eyes and looked at his carefree children, chasing after each other in the meadow. He returned his gaze to Saraid and felt a fierce pang of love. "When she pulled your hand from your mouth."

"Oh, that was nothin'," she said, flipping her hand in the air.

Her acceptance of the slight hurt him. He struggled with telling her the truth, but he did.

She was silent, never looking away from him as the story spilled out in fits and starts. When he was done, they both sighed.

After some minutes of silence, Saraid finally spoke. "It's a sad thing yer tellin' me," she whispered, "but some of what she speaks is the truth."

"Don't say that!" he cried, fresh anger spilling from him.

Saraid grabbed his arm as she sat up. "Hush! Nothin' is goin' to make that woman like me. That don't mean we have to be like her! I know it pains ye, but the only thing that makes any matter to me is that it don't come between us!"

Niall tried without success to have her feel the indignity as deeply as he did.

"I could try to be as she wants me, but in the end, it might bloody well kill me. An' even if I could, it won't change nothin' 'bout how she feels 'bout me!"

Niall couldn't understand how she could be so forgiving of his mother's venom.

Saraid began to giggle.

"Why are you laughing?"

Her green eyes twinkled with merriment. "There's more than one way to skin a cat," she replied. "I'm not near as nice as ye think I am! She'll not be gettin' to me, Niall."

"What are you thinking to do, *A Ghra?*"

"I'm plannin' on smotherin' her with kindness! We're all goin' to keep livin' in that house. She'll not see any pain on my face, an' she'll hear no nasty tongue in my mouth! It will make her crazy!"

Niall laughed in spite of himself and hugged her close. "Are you sure?"

Saraid shrugged her shoulders. "If she chooses to stay, then this is how it's gonna be."

***

Willie finally reached his own wagon and saw Freddie asleep in the shade beneath it, his fiddle close by his side. No one along the way had a word to say about Martin being seen anywhere. Yawning, he removed his waistcoat and folded it neatly, feeling instantly cooler. He loosened the fine lace ascot that Saraid had made for him and laid it carefully on top, once again marveling at her fine stitchery. He yawned again as he removed his shoes and lay down on top of the blankets in the wagon, propping another under his feet. *Lord, I'm tired!* He closed his eyes. Niall had about done him in on the doors and it felt good to get off his feet.

He thought about the day's activities; and, to this point, he thought that all had gone well. So much drama in the camp this year! The young rebels were getting more organized and more vocal. Soon there would be more to be angry about. The circuit he traveled week after week was proving that.

Back and forth across the countryside, carrying messages and instructions, he found more and more people on the roads looking for shelter and food. Many, like the O'Brien family, had more than enough to last a long time, though taxes were eating up some of their reserves, too. *It must be strange to have an uncle as your landlord . . . especially one who was feigning allegiance to the Anglos.* He knew that people were beginning to suspect this was so, though they had no proof yet. The Earl of Thomond was a cagey fellow, paying the taxes forward as he was supposed to. Some of those peasants who didn't know what the Earl was doing, were still itching to burn down his estate and wreck his land. Willie sighed. He needed to watch his own back. He couldn't be of help if he was found out. The combination of the heat and the dancing finally won out, and he drifted off to sleep.

Chapter Twenty-Five

Patrick and John were too anxious to rid themselves of the garbage to do more than wave to the revelers who called out to them as they meandered along the road. There would be plenty of time for conversations later when everyone gathered in the evening for the annual telling of the tales. Patrick knew that John had tagged along to talk about Niall and their mother. Hoping to divert his attention, he asked, "Does the road seem wider to you?"

John, deep in thought, paused and looked at the road as if seeing it for the first time. He shrugged. "It's no wonder with the hundreds of feet that have trampled over it the last few days. After a brief silence, John blurted out, "Niall can't just throw mother out of the house!"

Patrick had already decided to take the high road in the controversy, reserving judgment and blame until all sides of the argument could be heard. "Look, I don't think he would actually do that. He's really angry though, and can you truthfully blame him for that?"

"Blame has nothing to do with what's right or wrong! He's wrong in this! Mother should be allowed to live out her days in her own home!"

"You know, John, mother could live for another twenty years or more. What are Niall and Saraid supposed to do? Should they have to build another house? And where would they be putting it? We need all the land we have left for grazing and planting."

"Maybe they could enlarge the cottage where they started."

Patrick laughed and slapped his brother on the shoulder. "It could take a lifetime to get that done! Besides, you're living in it now and Paddy's living in the only other cottage." He looked up and spied someone up ahead climbing up from the rocky shoreline and making tracks toward the village. Wondering if it was Danny, he called out his name. The wind blew his voice back and the man, too far away to hear him, quickly disappeared down the road.

"I don't think that was him," said John.

The sound of the waves crashing over the rocks increased in volume, and minutes later they were at the bay. It was fast approaching full tide. Pounding surf sent sprays of salt water skyward as they crashed against the rocks, then settled, swirling, into the crags between them.

They hung on tight to the tarp as they eased their way down among the rocks to get as close as they dared to the water's edge.

"Let me take it down," yelled Patrick. He took the odorous tarp and stepped gingerly over the remaining slick rocks, struggling to keep his balance in the knee-deep water. He waited until a large wave was receding to pitch the contents into the air while still gripping one corner of the tarp. Shells, bone, gristle and cobs flew aloft and splashed down, quickly swallowed by the spume. Patrick clung to the tarp as the next wave crashed over it. He nearly lost his footing as the spray soaked him.

John wrapped an arm around one of the jutting rocks and yelled. "Patrick! Give me your hand!"

Patrick grasped John's hand for ballast as the undertow threatened to drag him into the roiling water. When it finally ebbed, he yanked hard on the tarp and drew it back over the rocks.

"Jesus!" he cried. "A man could drown out here!"

They climbed back to drier land and worked together to wring as much water as they could from the tarp before folding it.

John took the bundle and tucked it under his arm. "So, where are you heading now?"

Patrick shrugged as he tried to brush the wet from his arms and his tunic. The breeze quickly dried his arms and legs, the salty residue that remained making him itch. "I guess I'm heading for the tavern," he said, scratching at his skin.

"To see about Annie?" John asked with a grin.

A flush bloomed over Patrick's face. "Like I don't have enough to worry about!"

John gave his shoulder a friendly shake. "Just do it!"

They said good-bye and John headed back to camp.

* * *

As Patrick turned to head in the opposite direction, something on the bank caught his eye and he bent to pick it up. It was a cane. *Hmmm,* he thought. *Why would someone leave this here? Wouldn't they be needing it?* He turned it over in his hand and found the name Hank crudely carved on the knob. There were too many Hanks around these parts to know offhand who would be the right one. He decided to take it with him to the Shamrock and leave it with the old bartender, Jimmy.

He whistled a lilting tune as he walked, harmonizing with the tin whistles and pipes that blew softly from the campground. His stomach became jittery as he neared the tavern and he held up outside the door. Part of him wanted to forget the whole thing and go back to the camp. And part of him didn't. He finally took a deep breath and entered the Shamrock. He could see Annie sitting at the bar with a pint of ale, chatting with Jimmy and some other people. He watched her for a moment, filled with anxiety. He also felt desire rippling through him as she bantered and laughed with the men who sat on the stools beside her. He gripped the cane and decided to use it as an excuse for being there. He crossed the room, slid his bulk between two of the men seated there, and ordered a pint from Jimmy.

He tried desperately to act nonchalant as he turned towards her, saluting her with his mug. "Hey there, Annie."

Annie's breath caught in her throat and her cheeks turned crimson. "Hello there, Patrick. What brings you here at this hour?"

He held up the cane. "I found this at the bay. There was no one around so I thought I'd leave it here with Jimmy."

Jimmy held out his hand. "Give it here." He looked it over and nodded his head. "This looks like it belong to that Hank feller what plays fiddle for Martin. I'll see he gets it."

Patrick nodded and turned his attention back to Annie.

She lifted her eyes up to his with clear invitation and smiled. "You be wantin' anythin' else, Patrick?"

Patrick felt his ears burn. He was torn between wanting her and hoping that she would be working all night. He had no idea how to act around this vixen. He only knew that he wanted to be with her. Her eyes were as blue as heaven itself and they twinkled like stars. Her blush was as enchanting as the rest of her. "I was wondering if you would be working much longer."

"And why would ye be wantin' to know that?"

"Well . . . " He paused and took a breath. "I was wondering if you'd go to the fires with me tonight and, you know," he stammered, "listen to the tales?"

Annie choked back her ale, laughing, and then seeing his discomfort, realized he was serious. Her heart began pounding. *Oh dear, Lordy! Ain't this what I been hopin' fer?*

As she shrugged with a confidence she had difficulty carrying off, her dimpled smile filled her rosy face. "Well, I s'pose I could be doin' that, since I'm all done fer the day."

Patrick tried to act casual, too, but he wasn't any good at pretending, either.

The air between them was filled with tension, their pulses racing. "It's way too early for the fires, and Martin and Willie have to dance yet." He needed to bathe and find a clean tunic; one that didn't stink of food and sweat. "I can come back for you."

Jimmy piped into the conversation. "The way I hear it, it's lookin' like there ain't gonna be no more competition."

Patrick looked at him. "And why not?"

"Martin seems to be among the missin'."

"Willie said much the same when he came to our camp. How can he be missing? He was dancing just a bit ago."

Jimmy waved a hand. "Hank was sittin' here mumblin' an' cryin' in his beer, sayin' he couldn't find 'im anywhere. O'course he's a blind one, so he can't right be seein' nothin' anyway."

"Well, I'm sure he'll turn up. He won't miss a chance to stomp against Willie."

Annie nodded absently, her mind spinning. She needed to get home to see to her mam, make sure she was fed and settled for the evening. "I have to be goin' home to check on me mam; make sure she's got some food fer the evenin'."

Her mind was beginning to fill up with thoughts of her and Patrick . . . *together! I need to be checkin on m'self, too*, she thought, *and be gettin' the stink of the bar off me. This is my big chance!* "I'll be back here in a couple hours," she said. "Would that be to yer likin'?"

Patrick nodded, relieved. All thoughts of Martin left his mind. He'd done it! Now, if he could just get through the evening, he might get a chance to be alone with her. *Oh my God! She said yes, so I'm already lucky!* He hoped everyone would leave them be and not be making fun. *God, they had better not!* He drained his pint and tossed a coin to Jimmy. "That would be very much to my liking. I'll be back for you." He gave Annie a grin and strode out of the tavern. As he walked back to the camp, he passed by Hank, sitting on his stool with his fiddle, calling out to people as he heard them passing by.

"Martin!" Hank called out. "Are ye there, Martin?"

"Hey Hank," said Patrick. "Have you lost Martin?"

"Who's that there?"

"It's Patrick O'Brien here, Hank."

"I ain't seen 'im in quite a while. Not like 'im to be runnin' off when he got more dancin' to do."

Patrick felt pity for the man. He looked so lost. It had to be tough to be blind. It was then that he noticed that Hank's cane was nowhere in sight. "Where's your cane, Hank? Did you lose that, too?"

Hank almost fell off his stool, so startled was he by the question. *Dear Lord,* he thought, *my cane! Now what am I gonna do?* Sputtering, he shouted, "My cane? Ain't it right here?" He leaned down, groping the ground around him as if he couldn't see for himself that the bloody cane was gone. "Somebody took my cane! How am I goin' to find my way 'round without it? Now who'd be takin' the cane of a blind man?"

"Take it easy, Hank. I saw a cane lying on the ground down by the bay. I just left it with Jimmy at the Shamrock. Maybe it was yours."

"Now, what was it doin' down there?" He kept staring straight ahead, desperately trying to maintain his ruse of blindness.

"I have no idea, Hank. Maybe it's yours and maybe it isn't. Do you want me to go get it and bring it back to you?"

"That would be right kind of ye, Patrick."

Hank breathed a sigh of relief when Patrick headed off. He lowered his head to his hands and wept quietly. He had to sit there and wait for Patrick's return to figure out how he was going to get through the rest of the day. More likely, how to get through the rest of his life. But first, he needed his cane. His brow furrowed as he wondered who had taken it, and why? He couldn't imagine that Martin had taken it, the ruse of his blindness worked for both of them.

Hank sighed and wiped his eyes. He wanted nothing more than to leave this place. He knew in his heart that his time with Martin was over. Suddenly, he sat up straight, realized that this might be his last chance to get away. He needed to think clearly. *Where am I goin' to go? How am I goin' to get along? What if Martin doesn't show up at all?* Then he would have no money at all to make his escape, and Martin owed him plenty. Maybe when it got dark and everyone was at the fires for the tale-telling, he could sneak into his room at the hotel and find some money to make his escape. No one would miss him until the morning. Maybe Martin was afraid that Willie would beat him at the competition and he had taken off. If so, there would be no money to be found.

With new-found determination, he fought to clear the cloud of ale from his mind. Once he was away from Doolin, he would ditch the cane and no longer make the pretense of being blind. That would be disguise enough to get away. Maybe he would head east and find his family. His stomach was knotted in fear. For too many years, he had been beholden to Martin for his existence, little as it was. He would be *free!* He had no idea what that actually meant, but he was ready to find out.

Patrick retrieved the cane from Jimmy and returned to Hank. "Here you go, Hank," he said, placing the cane in the man's hand. "Does this feel like yours?"

Hank made the motions of sliding his hands over the cane to get the feel of it. Relief washed over him as he fingered his name in the wood. "This is it! I'm right beholden to ye, Patrick."

"It was a pretty mean thing for someone to do to you, Hank."

"It don't matter none, now." Hank placed his old fiddle in its worn case, rose and tucked the stool under his arm. "I think I'll take me a wander, now . . . see if I can be findin' Martin."

"Well, be mindful not to be losing your cane again."

Chapter Twenty-Six

Patrick watched Hank walk up the path towards the hotel, scraping his cane side to side in the dirt, carefully working his way around obstacles. Patrick looked into the clear blue sky, then closed his eyes and whispered, *thank you,* to the God he knew watched over him. He always tried to be mindful and forgiving of the frailties of others; always tried to be thankful for how lucky and blessed he was in this life.

Now, he thought, *if I could just figure out how to romance Annie without thinking about marriage, I'd be more than lucky.* Being the youngest son, he was well aware that the land would never come to him. After Niall, when the time came, the land would go to Niall's son, James. Until things changed in Ireland, he had no hope of buying land for himself or the family he hoped to have one day. It wasn't so bad though. He and his brothers worked the large amount of acreage together, and he felt pride in what they shared between them. Niall never acted like it was all his and they shared the profits between them. Not that there was a lot left. Most of what remained went back into the purchase of more livestock, seed for crops, and the repair or replacement of equipment and tools.

Still, there was enough for his needs. He had a large comfortable bed that he had built himself from smooth planks of oak. It took up much of the space in his two rooms. Over a few years' time, he had meticulously carved the headboard and posts with intricate Celtic symbols and a trailing garland of small leaves. He had hand sewn a thick piece of sail canvas into a mattress that he packed tightly with fragrant straw to comfortably support his height and weight. His belly was always filled with food that Saraid and his mother prepared for all of them. *Yes*, he thought, *I am comfortable; and, for the most part, happy.*

His small stone house faced southeast, giving him a view of the forest where game was plentiful. When winter came and the trees were bare, he could just catch a glimpse of the river Shannon in the distance. The salmon and trout he caught there were large and plentiful. *What else could I want?* He sighed with an ache in his gut, knowing exactly what was missing. He wanted someone like Saraid to make him laugh; someone to warm him on cold nights; and children. He wanted love. He knew he was not alone in his wishful thinking. There were many men like himself in Ireland who remained unmarried well into their forties, dependent on their families, their own dreams unfulfilled.

Patrick walked off the main road to a narrow footpath that ran through the trees. He came to a small clearing where the stream that flowed parallel to the meadow widened and deepened into a quiet pool before tumbling down a rocky barrier to meander once more. It was a serene spot disturbed only by the sound of a lone flicker pecking for insects in the canopy of boughs overhead. The sun that filtered through the branches reflected on the surface of the gently flowing water as dragonflies skimmed and danced upon its surface.

Patrick stripped off his tunic and shoes and waded into the crystal clear water, a school of minnows scattering around his feet. When the water reached his thighs, he sat on the smooth silty bottom and lay back to dunk his head. While submerged, he scrubbed at his bearded face and his thick hair, working his fingers through the tangles. He sat up and shook off the excess. He cupped a mouthful of water, swished it through his teeth and spit out the pulpy residue of his dinner. His big hands scooped up silt from the stream bed and rubbed the grit over his taut body. Muscles rippled across his shoulders, down his arms, and beneath the thick matte of hair on his chest, on down to where it narrowed below his flat stomach.

As he submerged once more, he thought about Annie and an erection stirred and throbbed. Relieving himself was tempting. In fact, he thought it would be better to do so than to carry his unappeased desire with him when he went back for her. As his hands worked, he pictured Annie, her small, perfect breasts peeking out from her bodice. After only a few strokes, he began panting. A grinding ache quickly built in his groin, streaked like lightning down his thighs, and his buttocks grew taut. Patrick inhaled sharply, squeezing his eyes shut as he rubbed faster, throwing back his head, every muscle in his body tensing, screaming for release. At last, he convulsed forward, Annie's name exploding from his lips in a guttural whisper of longing as he ejaculated into the water. Lightheaded, he drew in great gulps of air until he was breathing normally again and had stopped quivering. He stood and made his way to the grassy bank, scraping away the excess water from his skin. Patrick stood like a golden god in the sunlight, reaching out his arms to the warm breeze that quickly dried his tanned skin. Sighing, he pulled on his soiled tunic and shoes and made his way back to the camp. Once there, he dug his way through his caravan to find a clean garment.

Fiona came upon him as he was pulling the fresh tunic over his head. "Oh!"

Patrick unabashedly pulled the tunic down over himself and turned to face her. "Hello, little one."

Fiona had seen nakedness between her parents and considered it normal, but her young eyes had never seen Patrick without clothing. It seemed different somehow and she quickly looked at the ground as her face burned. She was distracted and relieved when James and Liam trotted up behind her.

Patrick eyed the sling shot in James's hand. "What have you got there, James?"

"My da made it for me!" James hoisted a rabbit by its hind legs in his other hand. "Look what I got!"

Patrick tensed when he saw that the rabbit was stunned but still breathing. "Set it down, James."

"But I want to show it to my da!"

Patrick slowly took the rabbit from his hand and carefully knelt on the ground with it. He softly stroked the rabbit's back as he held it in place on the grass. "Easy as you go, little rabbit," he said softly, examining the small cut on its head. "You'll live to run another day." The children knelt beside Patrick as he continued to soothe the creature whose heart was beating wildly. After a few moments, the rabbit calmed enough to shake its head and move its legs. Patrick set it free and it scampered away into the brush. "There now," he said to James. "No harm done."

"Why couldn't I keep him?"

"Is your belly aching with hunger, James?"

James scuffed his foot in the grass. "No, I'm not hungry."

"Then why would you want to be killing a living thing?"

"We could've had it for dinner," he said sullenly.

Patrick sat in the grass with the children and tried to explain the order of things. "God put lots of animals here to fill our bellies, but we have to have respect. We don't kill animals just for the sport of it, or to go to waste on full bellies. If we do that, then when we are hungry, and we need the food, there might not be any left."

Filled with guilt, James hung his head. "I know. My da taught me that. I just wanted to surprise him, is all."

Patrick lifted the boy's face. "This is important, James. Didn't he also teach you about making a clean kill?"

James shrugged. "I forgot."

Patrick knew this discussion was really Niall's job but he needed to impress James with the importance of it, right now. "Listen up, James, and listen well. You don't ever leave an injured animal to hurt or suffer. If you have a mind to kill it, then you kill it fast. You gut it right off so the meat doesn't spoil, and you skin it to make use of the hide. You don't go wasting any of it, you hear me?"

Fiona and Liam had been sitting quietly as Patrick talked to James, but now Fiona, disturbed by the conversation, rose and took Liam's hand to pull him up. "C'mon Liam, we should be getting back to the wagons." They began walking back to where the others were gathered. "Let's get the marbles out and have a game."

James put the slingshot into his pocket as he and Patrick walked together behind the others. "Are you going to be telling my da about the rabbit?"

"I don't think we need to tell him about it as long as the lesson is learned and abided."

Relief surged through the boy and he sighed. "Thanks. I won't do it again."

Patrick ruffled the boy's hair. "Then, that's all that matters. Tell me, what else has been going on at the camp?"

"Da was playing at some hurling with Roark and some other men up the road."

"Didn't you want to try it?"

James shook his head. "It's a bit rough for me. I'm not big enough yet." He started to laugh. "Mr. O' Casey got Da in the shin with the sliothar, so Da broke his hurley!"

Patrick grinned. "I wish I could have seen that!"

The smell of chowder wafted in the air as they joined the rest of the group. Patrick noticed that the tarp had been draped over the wagon, the sides loosely flapping in the breeze to dry.

"Heard you got a good one in the shin," said Patrick.

"I'll live, but it hurt like bloody hell. So, did you talk to Annie?"

"I did."

"Well damn, man! Give me the details! How did it go?"

Patrick threw his hands in the air. "It's no big deal! It's just a campfire!"

Niall laughed. "Easy, brother! I'm just asking."

"She said yes."

Niall clapped him on the back. "Good job! It's about time you got up the backbone to find a woman." He cocked his head and eyed Patrick from head to foot and nodded approvingly. "I see you even cleaned up a bit."

Patrick swatted Niall's arm. "Of course I did! I was stinking of fish and sweat." He fiddled with the tarp, adjusting the canvas, and then stood quietly for a moment. He turned to face Niall. "The problem is," he said quietly, "I haven't got any idea about what I'm to be doing with her."

Niall fought the temptation to laugh as Patrick looked to be genuinely flummoxed. "Just act like yourself. She knows you're no scoundrel. If she said yes, then she wants to be with you, too."

"I'm afraid of embarrassing myself."

"No need to be thinking like that." Niall chuckled and patted Patrick's shoulder. "She probably knows more than both of us! She'll show you."

Patrick shot his brother a disgusted look. "I should just forget about it and stay here."

Niall shook his head and let go of Patrick's shoulder. "Look, don't pay me any mind. For God's sake, you're almost thirty years old! Just go and have a good time. Don't force it. If something happens, it was meant. If not, you haven't lost anything."

Patrick sighed. "All right. Maybe I'll head back to the Shamrock now, and have a pint to calm myself."

As Patrick headed back to the village, Saraid approached Niall, a sleepy Bridget straddling her hip.

Niall rubbed the child's curly hair affectionately. "How's my pretty little fairy girl?"

Bridget gave her father a tiny smile as she continued to suck on her thumb, tucking her head into her mother's neck.

Saraid rubbed her small back. "I'm goin' to lay her down for a bit; and myself as well."

Niall nodded. "How's my mother doing?"

Saraid shrugged. "I gave her some chamomile tea and it seemed to settle her a bit. She's asleep in John's caravan."

"In that case, maybe I'll rest my eyes for a while, too. It's going to be a long night."

Chapter Twenty-Seven

Hank finally made it up the hill, silently cursing Martin with each step for choosing to stay in the fancy hotel. His hip and leg ached from the climb. He sat heavily on the bench outside the lobby to rest before attempting to climb the stairs to Martin's room. Well-dressed patrons of the hotel sneered as they passed by him and he figured he had better move. He entered the hotel and stood in the shadows, waiting for a clear path to the stairs. He wanted to call as little attention to himself as possible.

Keeping his eyes blank, Hank watched the activity around him. The hotel was alive with people coming and going and servers rolling trays of food into the busy dining room. His stomach rumbled with hunger, but he knew he would never be welcomed among them. With his shabby clothes, he would stand out like a sore thumb. The bar looked inviting, but he didn't dare to go there, either.

After a few moments, no one seemed to be paying him any mind and he made a quick, if painful, trek up the stairs. He thanked God that Martin's room was on the second floor and not the third. When he arrived at the door, he looked around nervously to make sure he wasn't seen as he used his pocket knife to pick the lock. Though he shared the room with Martin, he had no key. He also had no bed. He slept on the floor in his bedroll while Martin enjoyed the firm mattress on the four-poster bed.

The room was tidy, the bed made, and clothes neatly hung from pegs in the small closet hidden behind a drape. He wished he could sleep in the big bed under cool sheets for a few hours before making his escape. Lord knew he needed to rest up before he could think of heading out away from Doolin, but he had no idea how much time he had. If Martin didn't show up soon, he knew that someone would come looking for him to see what he knew about his disappearance.

Hank pushed aside the drape, looked at the row of Martin's clothes, and smiled. If he got cleaned up, he might be able to fit into some of the dance master's outfits. Nothing too fancy, but something better than his own shabby clothes. It had been a long time since Martin had provided him with anything new.

First, he had to find the money. He wasn't leaving without what was owed him, and maybe a bit more. He looked in the drawers of the dresser and the bedside table, but found nothing. Then he went through the pockets of the clothes hanging on the pegs and still came up empty handed. Nothing under the mattress either.

"Damn it Martin! Where did ye hide it? I know ye got money here someplace." He looked under the bed and discovered Martin's satchel. "Aha!" he exclaimed. He pulled it out and set it on the bed and carefully undid the broad straps. He removed a lone pair of hornpipe shoes and examined all the compartments. Still nothing. Then his rummaging hand found a slight tear in the frayed edge of the fabric on the bottom where the seam had been hand stitched. He carefully cut the stitches with his knife, gently pulled away the fabric, and found the false bottom. Beneath it was a wad of bank notes neatly stacked beside a drawstring bag full of coins.

"Well lookie here," he chuckled softly. "Ye weren't as smart as ye thought ye were!"

Hank decided against taking the banknotes but took great pleasure in the jangle of the coins as he dumped them out of the bag. He spread his handkerchief on the bed and made a nest of copper and silver coins. He hungrily eyed the few gold coins, but knew he would have a hard time explaining where he got them. "Don't be gettin' all greedy now, Hank," he said to himself as he carefully tied off the cloth and hid it deep inside his bedroll.

With regret, he placed the rest of the money back into its hiding place. Depending on how things went, he didn't want to be accused of stealing the lot of it. The amount he took would be more than enough to keep him fed for a while. Since he had no needle and thread, there was nothing to be done about the stitches but to stuff the edges of the cloth tightly into the bottom. Hank wished he could take the satchel with him but was afraid it would cause unwanted attention. He put Martin's shoes back into the bag, re-fastened the straps, and put it under the bed where he had found it.

Next, he went through Martin's shirts and britches, picking out what he would change into, given the chance. He decided that he would also take Martin's grooming tools, as he had long admired the silver-backed hair brushes with their fine horsehair bristles. There was nothing else he would have any use for.

Hank removed his dirty clothes, rolled them into a ball and stuffed them into his bedroll. He would have to take them with him, but once he was far enough away, he would get rid of them. Pouring fresh water from the ewer into the heavy basin, he used Martin's soap to clean away a week's worth of sweat and grime. He even scrubbed his hair. Rubbing himself briskly with a thick towel, he began to giggle. He felt that he had washed away years of grief and pain and his heart pounded with joy.

Now he would sleep for a bit. When it got dark, if Martin was still among the missing, he would make his escape.

He gave in to his desire for comfort and climbed naked into the soft cool sheets of Martin's bed. He exhaled with pleasure as he let his head sink into the plump goose-down pillow. He was almost asleep when fear started gnawing at his gut. *What if I get caught? What if someone recognizes me when I leave the hotel in Martin's clothes?* "Stop it!" he hissed to himself. "It'll be dark and no one will see me. I'll be long gone before anyone comes lookin' fer me." Still unable to sleep, he cursed and rose from the bed, carefully arranging the covers to look freshly made. He went to his bedroll, pulled out his dirty clothes, and climbed into the years-old bedding, vowing to get rid of that, too. He wanted to be rid of everything that reminded him of his current life.

Eventually Hank slept, though fitfully. Gentle dreams of home and his mother interwove with nightmares of a sneering Martin hovering over him with his staff ready to strike him. His breathing became labored and he began to shake.

Suddenly Hank realized that someone was knocking on the door. Panic seized him as he jumped up and looked quickly around the room. He started talking to himself. *What in bloody hell should I do? Should I answer?* He stumbled in the dark, realizing that hours must have passed since he lay down. Then he stood still and took himself to task. *I can be here! I sleep here every night!* He quickly grabbed his dirty clothing and hurriedly put them on as the knocking started again.

"Who's there?" he called out, as he drew on his pants.

"Is that you, Hank?"

"Yeah, it's me. Who are ye an' what do ye want?"

"It's me, Jack Cleary. Is Martin in there?"

"No, he ain't here." His stomach clenched as he cracked open the door.

Jack, regarding him with suspicion, pushed his way into the room and looked around. He took in the neatly made bed, the general tidiness of the room, and noticed nothing amiss. "What are you doing here, Hank?"

Hank stared straight ahead. "I was sleepin'! I ain't got no clue where Martin is."

"You're looking a bit uneasy, Hank. Why are you in the room by yourself?"

"I ain't uneasy! I was just sleepin' and ye come poundin' on the door! Scared me half to death!" Hank's legs were trembling. He was almost as afraid of Jack as he was of Martin. He took a breath and tried to pull himself together. "Until Martin come back, I got nothin' to do, so why shou'n't I wait here fer 'im? That way he won't haf'ta come lookin' fer me."

Jack slowly paced the room, stopping at the foot of the bed, where he fingered the coverlet. He hadn't expected Hank to be in the room. He had thought he could slip in quickly and find Martin's stash since no one had a clue where Martin had gone to. *How should I play this? I need to get rid of Hank.* Then he could search for the money. Unless Hank had already found it and was planning to take off. Would Hank be hanging around if he was guilty of some malfeasance? He didn't know. He would take one more walk around the meadow, check with a few of his spies to see if there was any word about Martin. He hoped that his body had not turned up yet. Then, he would come back and press Hank harder to find out what he might know. He would also be able to say that he had found Hank in the room by himself. If asked, he could blame any theft on Hank. How could he explain his own arrival at Martin's room? He would simply say he had been looking for Martin.

"I don't think Martin would be pleased to find you in here on your own."

"And just where else would ye be suggestin' I be?"

Jack suddenly had an idea. "Tell you what, Hank." He dug into his pocket and pulled out a couple of coins and tossed them at Hank who, caught by surprise, grabbed the coins in mid-air.

Hank froze and felt the blood drain from his head. He had just made a terrible mistake

Jack laughed at the look on Hank's face. "I caught you out, Hank! I've been waiting a long time for this."

"It was Martin's idea, not mine!"

"Actually, Martin told me about you a long time ago. I went along because it served my purpose to have this little secret. Now, if you know what's good for you, you'll get out of here before I call a constable."

"Fer what would ye be doin' a thing like that? I ain't done nothin' to ye!"

"Who knows, Hank?" Jack smiled inwardly as an idea spun in his head. "No one seems to be able to find Martin. Perhaps you've done something to him."

"I already told ye!" Hank cried out. Fear clutched at him. All his dreams were fast heading for the dirt, like the rest of his miserable life. "I ain't got no clue where Martin got his self off to!"

Jack spoke calmly as he continued to stare at Hank. "I think you best be taking off right now, and don't come back. Get as far away as you can before they come looking for you."

Hank was terrified that Jack would start searching his things and find the coins and the hairbrushes. Then he was a dead man. He began to whine. "Why're ye doin' this to me? I ain't never done nothin' to you!"

Jack despised weakness in a man. He felt nothing but disgust for Hank as the man limped about the room.

"If you aren't out of here in the next two minutes, I'll take great pleasure in setting the law after you and you can spend the rest of your life in jail."

"But . . . but I ain't done *nothin*!" he cried out desperately. His scalp felt like a hundred fire ants were chewing every hair from his head. His heart banged like a drum and bile rose from his stomach, threatening to land in a slimy pool at his feet. He ran for the chamber pot and dry heaved until, weak-kneed, he collapsed into a ball on the floor. Tears stung his eyes and his voice was a hoarse whisper. "I told ye before. I ain't got no clue where Martin got off to. For all I know, maybe ye already know the answer to that."

Too late, he regretted his words as Jack gave him a sound kick in the hip. He grit his teeth from the pain and tears fell, but he refused to cry out.

With a look of disgust, Jack pulled Hank up by his hair. His voice became quietly malevolent. "You get out of here right now or I'll make sure you never see another sunrise."

There was nothing left for Hank to do but to hastily wrap his precious fiddle in his one remaining change of clothes and roll it up in his bedroll. He slung the strap over his shoulder, grabbed his stool by one leg and, leaning on his cane, slowly limped to the door. He paused in the entryway and gazed thoughtfully at Jack. He opened his mouth as if to say one last thing but, at the look on Jack's face, decided to say nothing more.

Chapter Twenty-Eight

When Patrick met with Annie at the Shamrock, they decided to go for a walk across the Burren before heading to the campfires surrounding the meadow. They took a lantern in hand as darkness would be falling soon. For now, a hazy sun still hovered just above the horizon, and a mist obscured the Aran islands across the bay. Sweat that glistened on their foreheads and arms began to evaporate as they neared the shoreline and the sea breeze wafted over their skin.

The flat limestone clints were threaded with fissures from which sprouted rich patches of wildflowers. Butterflies flitted from the tall stems of blue campanula to oxeye daisies and brown-eyed Susans.

As Annie picked a few daisies, she shouted a warning to Patrick as he bent to pick some white sea campion.

"Don't be touchin' them flowers!"

"Why not?"

Annie pushed strands of wind-swept hair from her face. "Folks call 'em devil's hatties. They say they be temptin' death if ye bring 'em inside yer house."

They continued to walk side by side, neither knowing just what to say. Patrick tried to stay calm and not allow his libido to overtake his common sense. He didn't want to scare her. Neither did he want to feel inadequate. But oh, how he wanted to touch her! His brothers didn't think he should worry about how she felt. They were sure that she would have no expectations beyond a few moments of pleasure.

Annie struggled with feelings of hope that she could make him care for her, yet worried that he would think her unworthy. Finally she asked, "Have ye ever been to the caves?"

"Not in many years. You?"

Annie nodded. "I ken show ye my secret cave if ye like. Nobody knows 'bout it but me."

"And what cave would that be?"

She gave him a full grin. "Ye'll see!" She grasped his hand and pulled him along the descending rocks that led down towards the water's edge.

Patrick, feeling lighthearted in her exuberant presence, was happy to let her lead the way. He was trembling and not unaware that the solitude of a cave would present an opportunity for the kind of intimacy that he'd yet to experience.

Flocks of gulls and puffins soared overhead, then dove into the sea, appearing seconds later with fish flopping in their beaks. Annie carefully guided their way down the rocks and through wild brush until she stopped and looked up to his face. "Are ye ready for a surprise, Patrick?"

He looked into her sparkling eyes, swallowed, then nodded.

Hand in hand, she led him past a scrubby patch of blackthorn and fragrant honeysuckle until they reached a narrow crevasse, quite hidden from view unless one knew it was there.

Patrick barely squeezed his bulk through the opening, his tunic scraping both sides of the rock walls.

As they entered the cool darkness, Annie said, "It's a long way in, so light the lantern."

He stopped and groped for her breast but Annie slapped his hand away. "Not yet, Patrick! I want ye to see my treasure first!"

Patrick sighed, struck a match against the limestone, and lit the lantern. They continued through the passage, the walls widening and growing damp as they went deeper into the cave.

He yelped, ducking as a whoosh of black wings skimmed his head, seeking the deeper darkness.

Annie laughed. "It's just bats, Patrick. They won't be hurtin' ye."

Patrick shook his head. "What's so special about this place? Bats or no, it looks pretty much like every other cave."

"Ye just wait. I'll not be disappointin' ye."

Annie led him for a few long minutes, deeper and deeper into the darkness until they reached a curve. Patrick suddenly stopped, seeing the glow of light ahead. "Someone's here!"

"Not likely. Turn off the lantern, now. It's my surprise!"

She pulled him forward another few feet until the passageway suddenly swelled into a high-vaulted cavern where the source of light was revealed overhead. "What do ye think? Ain't it *grand?*"

Patrick stared up to the light in stunned silence. Suspended from the ceiling of the cavern was a broad stalactite, at least a dozen feet in length. It glowed pale amber in the rays of the late afternoon sun that somehow permeated the rocks at the top of the cave. The chamber was filled with the echo of gurgling water from the river that ran beneath the rocks under their feet.

"What in the name of Jesus *is* that?"

Annie was smug at the look of awe on Patrick's face. "I don' rightly know an' I ain't never heard nobody talk about it, neither."

He shook his head, still filled with wonder. "How did you ever find this place?"

"In truth?" She shook off the bad memory with a shiver. "I was runnin' away from Jack Cleary. He was wantin' more'n I was willin' to give 'im. He followed me out o'er the Burren and when I slid down the bank, there was the entrance. I snuck in an' just kept runnin' through the dark 'cause he was after me. I'm guessin' that even if he found it, he coun't be fittin' through so he finally gave up. When I come 'round this last corner, I coun't believe it. I felt like God hisself was watchin' o'er me!"

Patrick reached out and put his arm around her. "Have you not asked anyone about it?"

"*No!* I don' want to share about it with nobody!"

He looked down at Annie's face in the dim light. There was a luminescence reflected there, a purity that juxtaposed with the kind of life she lived. "You shared it with *me*."

"Yea, well, if ye don' already know, ye be about as special to me as that damn thing shinin' up there."

Patrick bent down and touched his pursed lips gently to hers, whispering against the softness of her mouth. "Thank you, Annie, it's the best gift I ever *got*."

Annie's heart swelled, the ache in her chest nearly unbearable as she leapt into his arms. She wrapped her legs around the expanse of his thighs and grabbed fists full of his hair as she brought her lips to his. His mouth was tightly puckered and grinding into hers until she abruptly pulled away.

"Patrick! Go easy or ye're gonna be mashin' me mouth clean off me face!"

He froze, feeling lost until she brought her face close to his again. Smiling, with her legs still wrapped tightly around him, she took his lips in her fingers and wagged them playfully. "Don' be puckerin', let 'em be soft and floppy-like." Annie brought her own soft mouth back to his and pulled away again when he started to get too forceful. "Ye gotta learn to play, Patrick.

"Keep yer lips soft an' then just sorta suck gently on me mouth. Like this . . . ." She moved in slowly and let her mouth flutter softly over his, drawing on his lips with her own.

Patrick, rather than being upset with her chiding, was enchanted that she could be so guileless. There was nothing mocking in her words and her eyes showed nothing but warmth. It took a few tries, but he was determined to please her. He knew he got it right when he heard her sigh as she relaxed against him. His spirit soared. Then she began to lick the inside of his mouth with her tongue and gently nibble his lips with her teeth.

His breathing quickened, everything inside him ached with an aroused yearning that weakened his knees. He wanted to kiss her forever, but his need gave way to impatience. He wanted her, now! He fumbled with her skirt, pulling it up over her thighs, marveling at her soft skin, the tensile strength of her young body as she struggled to pull his tunic over his belly. Ignorant of preamble or consequences, he tried to plunge into her, then groaned as his body betrayed him, his seed spilling sticky and hot down her thighs without ever entering her.

"No!" he cried out, letting her slide down until her feet touched the ground. He turned away from her to lean against the wall of the cave, hanging his head with shame. How could this happen? He'd wanted so badly to be with her and now he was angry and disgusted with himself. It was bad enough that his cock didn't match the size of the rest of his body, but not being able to perform at all really shook him. "I'm sorry," he whispered with a shuddering breath.

Annie stood rock still, anticipation draining from her limbs. Though shocked, she somehow knew that the chance she wanted with him depended on how she handled his embarrassment. She tentatively reached out and stroked his arm. "It's all right, Patrick."

He tried to shrug her off but she persisted, her voice a bare whisper. "I'd just like to be askin' ye if this be yer first time?"

"Of course not."

She saw through his shame, knew that he was lying, and decided that this was not going to be the end of them. "Sure ye just got too excited is all. I don' want to be soundin' like I know it all 'cause I surely don', an' it woun't be sayin' too much good fer me if I did, would it, now?"

Patrick turned towards her and allowed her to embrace him, grateful for her lack of judgment. "You've nothing to be ashamed of,

Annie. You're a sweet girl, and it is I who disappointed *you*."

Annie eyed him with dismay. *A sweet girl?* If he only knew! He *must* know that she had been with other men, more than she cared to admit to. She'd even been grateful to take the coins they tossed her way afterwards. With her father and brother gone, there was no money to pay for food or to pay the rent on their shanty. She was trapped here. With the state of her mother's mind, she couldn't leave her to search for a better life. It fell on her to provide for them anyway she could. She'd accepted that this was her lot in life . . . for now . . . and swallowed back any feelings of shame that haunted her afterwards. She continued to hope that, one day, someone would come along to save her from this wretched life.

And there before her was Patrick, looking at her as if she was some fragile flower to be handled with care. In her heart, she ached to be that flower, to feel clean and worthy. There was no bloody way she would have him feel inadequate. "I can assure ye that I'll not be allowin' ye to do any such thing!" She swatted him playfully and held out her hand. "Give me yer tunic."

He hesitated, never had he felt so exposed. He looked into her eyes and seeing no pity or amusement there, pulled the tunic over his head and handed it to her. She reached out with trembling fingers and caressed his naked shoulder.

"Ye're a fine lookin' man, Patrick, an' I plan on takin' full advantage of ye." She gave him an impish grin before she lay his tunic on the ground. "Now lay on yer back so I can take a good look at ye."

Patrick did as she asked, his stomach quivering with uncertainty.

She eyed the magnificence of his body in the pale light; the broad shoulders, the matte of soft curls that ran from his sculpted chest, down his flat belly, and nested around his quivering manhood. She marveled at the length and strength of his arms and legs. He took her breath away and she purred her appreciation.

"You're not a bit shy, are you?"

"Not usually . . . but today . . . maybe a bit."

There was a slight tremor in her voice, and he knew from her trembling that she wasn't nearly as brave as she would have him believe. This was a relief to him and he took a breath, trying to relax, willing to let her lead the way. He set the extinguished lantern to the side. There was enough ambient light from above to see without it.

Patrick grew uncomfortable with the frankness of her gaze. "Are you going to keep staring at me or are you going to let me look at you, too?"

Annie silently undid the cord that held back her wild red hair, let it cascade freely about her flushed face and arms. Wonder filled him as she slowly untied her long skirt, letting it glide down her legs. She stepped out of it, rolled it up and placed it under his head, never taking her eyes from his. Then, as he watched, she undid the strings of her bodice, a smile playing on edges of her mouth. She lifted it over her head and tossed it aside. She stood naked before him, back straight, her shoulders drawn back, waiting for his acceptance. *Please God, don' let him be disappointed.*

Patrick marveled at the way the soft light played on her slim torso, creating luminous patterns on the crests of her small breasts and shadows between the length of her legs. He reached up and tugged on one of the burnished curls that hung like a veil over her skin. "You're so beautiful, Annie." He drew her down to him, grateful and filled with longing.

She lay beside him and gloried in the feel of his arms as they came around her and drew her close. His hands traveled over her back and hips, his mouth softly searching hers as she had shown him.

Drawing his head to her breast, she whispered, "Now kiss me here . . . like ye kissed my lips."

Patrick marveled at the wonders and reactions of her body; how she pulled his head away when he got too exuberant, how she clutched at his hair and held his face close when he was too gentle.

She arched against his mouth when he lapped and drew her taut nipple into his mouth with care. For both of them, each sensation was new and shimmering. A feeling of rightness and ease came over them as the moments passed by, and they grew comfortably warm in the damp chill of the cave. When he moved to mount her, she stopped him, whispering, "Not yet." He groaned with want but did as she wished.

"I have another secret place," she whispered, guiding his fingers between her thighs to explore the soft wetness there.

"Oh, sweet Jesus!" Patrick was at once overcome with desire, and he grabbed at her with rough fingers.

Wincing at the abrasiveness of his touch, Annie pulled his hand away. "Easy, Patrick . . . just softly now." She held his fingers and gentled his touch, guiding them to the swollen nub that was now throbbing. She began to moan, arching against his hand, aching to have him within her.

Stroking the stubby length of him, she waited for growth to match the hardness there, but it didn't come. She hid her disappointment, hoping that desire would be enough to make their coupling possible. She rolled on top of him and floated her body over his, barely skimming his skin. She rained kisses on his neck and shoulders, slid her tongue over his taut nipples and down his belly.

Patrick wanted to scream from the maddening sensations sweeping through him. When she eased her mouth down even further, he moaned and begged her to stop before he released again. She raised herself up and slowly slid onto him, knowing that once again, there wouldn't be much time.

"Don't move, Patrick," she said with quiet urgency. "Let me do it. You'll be lastin' longer if I just rock for a bit."

He still struggled between his instinct to overtake her and his willingness to allow her to take the lead. He took a shuddering breath and lay still.

Annie began to rock slowly against him, hungry to be filled by him. She tried hard to hold him inside while he groaned and sweat beaded his face. Close to the end of his endurance, he began to push against her. Within seconds, he cried out and it was over. Patrick lay panting and sated while she, laying atop him, suddenly felt desperately alone, her body still aching with want.

Annie whimpered and Patrick became alarmed. He held up her face and made her look at him. "What is it, Annie?"

She shook her head, knowing if she spoke the truth, he might think her wanton or worse, feel less about himself.

"Annie, *please*! Tell me what's wrong. Are you sorry to be with me?"

She opened her eyes and looked into his, tears trickling down her cheeks. "I could never be sorry to be with ye, Patrick. I want to be with ye more'n my life."

Patrick was so confused. Something shattered inside him to see the sadness in her eyes. "Then tell me why you're crying."

She sat up, still astride him. She lay her hands aside his face and searched his eyes. "Are ye sure ye want to be hearin' a thing that might make ye think less of me?"

"Annie, you have to tell me. I'm lying here, happier than I've ever been in my life, and I want you to be happy, too!"

She hesitated a moment longer before giving in to her throbbing need for release. "I'll show you how to make me happy," she whispered.

Lifting herself slightly, she took his hand and brought it once again to the slick tender ache between her thighs. She guided his fingers in a slow stroking touch as her hips swayed against them. In just seconds, her body grew taut and she began to cry out with pleasure. As the ache began to crest within her, she shifted over his long fingers and impaled herself upon them, rocking her hips hard against him again and again. The release rose from her toes, exploding through her like the thunder of a spring storm rumbling through the mountains. Wild hair flying, she flung her head back, gasping her joy as it raged through her. She finally collapsed upon him, the aftershocks of her violent orgasm quivering through her.

Tears sprang to his eyes as he clung to her. "Well, *damn!*" he cried. Then laughter bubbled out of him, echoing throughout the cavern.

Annie froze, the blood draining from her head. She fought a wave of dizziness as she struggled to her feet, standing before him on shaky legs, her hands balled into fists. She glared at him, her pale skin turning blotchy with rage. She kicked out at him, screaming, "Why are ye laughin' at me?"

The sight of her standing there in all her naked, disheveled glory made him laugh all the harder.

Annie roared, too, her fury combined with confusion and shame. Suddenly, the joyful leap of faith she'd taken only moments before had her plunging into a freefall of betrayal and despair.

"How *dare* ye be laughin' at me!" She fell upon him and began to pummel him about the head with her fists. "I'll *kill* you for this! I *hate* ye! I *hate* ye!"

Patrick struggled to choke down his laughter, trying to catch her hands before she did him serious damage. "OWWW!" He yelled to drown out her shrieks. "Stop it! Oh my sweet, sweet girl! I'm not laughing at you! I'm *delighted* with you!"

She stilled her assault, gulping air, one fist yet raised to strike out again. In the dull glow from overhead, she could see his cheeks were reddened from her blows. Her hair hid most of her face as she eyed him warily, not sure what he was saying. Her voice croaked in her throat as angry tears streamed down her face. "Ye'll be needin' to explain that to me, then."

He sat up and brushed the damp tangled hair from her face, hesitated, then plunged ahead. "Oh Annie, you were right. I've never been with a woman before." He gestured to his now flaccid cock. "I know I'm a bit lacking, and I was afraid a woman would laugh at me. I had no idea a woman could do what you just did, or how fully amazing it would make me feel to be part of it." Then he grinned broadly and reached out his hand to her cheek. "Can we do that again?"

Stunned, Annie stared down into his eyes, wanting desperately to believe him. As much as she struggled against it, everything inside her began to shift like an ebbing tide. For the first time in her young life, she dared to hope that, maybe, she finally had a safe place to lay her head; that she could let out the breath that she had been clutching in her lungs for all of her life. Now, the ache in her chest had nothing to do with pain. Instead, she felt the soft glow of tenderness that yearned to reach out from every muscle, bone, and pore of her body to the big man who was no longer laughing, who looked up at her with moist eyes. She tried to fight the feeling, not willing to let the tide of love sweep her out to a strange sea without knowing if she would ever be able to come back from it.

He reached out a hand to her and whispered, "Stay with me, Annie."

She closed her eyes for a moment, still struggling to believe. Then, finally, smiled. Her faith returned and with it, her sense of humor. She cupped her hands beneath her small breasts and gave them a jiggle. "I'm a bit lackin' m'self."

This time, his laughter only warmed her. She lay down beside him, nestled in his arms and sighed with relief. As hours passed, the light above them faded away and Patrick relit the lantern.

They drifted in and out of sleep, continued to reach out for each other, exploring the mysteries of their bodies and emotions.

When Annie finally pleaded for rest, Patrick closed his eyes and tried to sleep. The trickle of subterranean water and their soft breaths were the only sound in the stillness surrounding them.

He knew they should be heading to the campfires to hear the

tales. The family would be wondering where they were. Yet, he hated to break the spell by moving.

For the first time, Patrick understood the depth of Niall's passion for Saraid, the mystery of their quiet smiles, the joy they shared over simple things. He thought of his father and marveled that he might have felt the same for his wife. Perhaps the loss of such feeling was why his mother had grown so harsh.

Suddenly, a deep sadness crept over him and he didn't know why. His eyes filled and he squeezed them shut, swallowing hard against the burning lump in his throat. He gathered the sleeping Annie closer to him and began kissing her gently. His tongue traced her lips and trailed down her neck until he found her nipple. Sucking softly as a sated babe, he drifted into sleep.

Chapter Twenty-Nine

After leaving the hotel, Hank wandered to a nearby tavern for a pint of ale before setting off on his journey. *No way could he show up at the Shamrock!* He needed to tell one person of his innocence before high-tailing it away. It would be tough going in the dark. Maybe he could hide in the woods until daybreak. He sighed with relief to see Willie and Freddy at the bar. Freddy had been his only real friend for many years. Both had left their families long ago to fiddle for their keep. The difference was in their masters. Willie had always treated Freddy kindly and with respect. He had been kind to Hank as well.

Using his blind persona, Hank let his cane guide his way through the dimly lit tavern, calling out for Martin as he limped along.

"Hey there, Hank," Willie called out to him. "Come join us. Freddy and me are just enjoyin' a pint." He took Hank's arm, directing him so he could sit between himself and Freddy, then motioned to the bartender to get Hank a pint, too.

Hank sat down heavily and let out a weary sigh. The benefit of a few hours sleep had been lost after the altercation with Jack.

Freddy nudged him with his elbow. "What's goin' on with ye, Hank? Still no Martin?"

The bartender pushed the cold pint against Hank's hand to let him know it was there.

Hank nodded his thanks and guzzled the lot of it straight down. His fist pressed against his chest as he emitted a loud belch. He sighed, pushing the tankard forward, and dug a coin out of his pocket for another. "No . . . no Martin."

"Well now, don't that beat all?" Freddy replied. "We was fixin' on beatin' the two o' ye straight away!"

Willie studied the tremor in Hank's hands and the twitching around his eyes. "Not like ye to be a gulper, Hank. Has somethin' happened?"

Hank bowed his head and shook it side to side. "I think I'm about to be blamed for somethin' I din't do." He put his face in his hands and began to weep quietly.

Willie placed his hand on Hank's shoulder, gave it a gentle squeeze. "Tell me what happened, Hank. Maybe I can help ye."

Hank shuddered and wrapped his hands around his pint. "I was alone in Martin's room and Jack Cleary caught me out! He started askin' me a bunch of questions, all suspicious, like maybe I did somethin' to Martin. He said he was goin' to send the constable after me if I din't start runnin' and git outa town."

"What does he think ye did to Martin?"

Hank railed. "I got no clue! For all I know, Martin could be fine or dead somewhere." He took a deep breath and tried to calm himself, nervously rubbing his hands against his legs before continuing. "Jack's got somethin' else on me though . . . "

Willie stared at him in silence, waiting for him to continue, while Freddy fidgeted with his mug. Hank continued to sit, his shoulders shuddering to control his tears.

Willie finally asked, "What is it, Hank?"

"Oh sweet Jesus, help me," he cried softly. "He knows I ain't really blind!"

Freddy jumped up from his seat and groped Hank's shirt until he found his neck. He squeezed Hank hard and shook him, making Hank's teeth rattle. "All these years!" Freddy was screaming now. "I thought ye was my *friend*!"

Willie struggled to separate the two, pleading for the men to quiet down even as Hank grabbed at Freddy's hands, frantic to free his windpipe and catch a breath. As they struggled, Hank's arms began to flail and he caught Willie in the nose. Blood streaming down his face, Willie had no choice but to strike Freddy in the back of his head with his fist, causing the blind man to crumple in a heap on the floor.

The tension in the room was rising as other drinkers began rising from their seats to see what all the trouble was about. The bartender started yelling for the men to stop or he'd throw the lot of them out. He was no stranger to skirmishes in the tavern but wanted order before the crowd started taking sides, causing a free-for-all. He loved a good brawl as much as the next man, but he was too tired after the busy weekend to have to be sweeping up any more glass or broken tables.

Willie apologized for the disturbance as he wiped his bloody nose and carefully lifted Freddy from the floor. "I'll get 'em out of here," he said, tossing some coins on the bar. He turned his attention to Hank who was still rubbing his neck as he tried to catch his breath. "Are ye all right, Hank?"

Hank nodded silently, even more ashamed, if that was possible. "I'm real sorry," he rasped, hanging his head. "I just ain't no good to nobody."

"No time for that now, Hank. Get yer wits about ye! We have to get out of here right now." Willie hoisted Freddy's arm around his neck and half dragged him towards the door.

Hank humbly followed them out into the misty twilight. There was a haze beginning to waft over the night sky that would turn to fog before the night was over. Music was barely heard as they neared the clearing. There were still some young people dancing, but the older clansmen were busy finishing up the ring of campfires for the tale-telling.

Willie veered off the path to the caravans, where he gently laid Freddy onto his bedroll beneath the wagon.

Freddy moaned and tried to sit up but Willie gently held him down. "Stay still, Freddy."

"Wha . . . what happened?" he asked as he rubbed his sore head.

Hank knelt beside his old friend and took his hand. "Freddy," he said quietly. "I ain't never wanted to lie to ye." Tears choked his bruised throat. Freddy, covering his eyes with his sleeve, said nothing.

Hank continued, "All these years . . . ye been my only friend."

Freddy shrugged away Hank's hand. "If we was friends, then why'd ye lie to me all these years?"

Hank let Freddy's hand drop and laid down on the dirt beside him to ease the ache in his hip. He sighed wearily. "It's a long story, and I was too ashamed."

Willie sensed how difficult this was for Hank. "Do ye want me to leave so the two of ye can work this out?"

Hank shook his head. "Ye might as well stay."

It was a few moments before Hank swallowed down the ache in his chest and began to describe how he had met Martin on the dirty street corner in Dublin when he had been a child of nine. "My da was in jail for stealing food. My mam couldn't work 'cause there were three more younger'n me, one a new babe. My da done taught me how to play the fiddle and it come natural-like to me. So . . . since we had nothin' to eat, I took to pretendin' to be blind and went to the street corners where them that's better off liked to walk. I'd sit there all day on me stool with me hat on the ground, and play 'an smile fer all them rich folks. Sometimes they'd be generous, tossing a copper into my hat 'cause I was so small and played so good. At the end of the day, I'd run home and give the coins to me mam. She'd go off in the dark and come back with food."

He paused as thoughts of his mam filled him. She'd been so pretty once. Then the hard times came. The worry, fear, and empty bellies growling at night in the small, dank room had aged her and she looked no different from all the other beggars on the street.

"When I had a good day, things were better while we waited for my da to finish his time on the road gang. We din't have nothin' really, but at least we was together. Then we heard that he got hisself killed tryin' to break out of the work camp." Hank wished he could forget the rest of it but he wanted Freddy to understand.

"One day I was playin' and someone tossed a bunch of coins in me hat. I was so surprised that I looked quick to see an' I got caught out. There was this man lookin' at me and smilin' all nasty like. He threatened me and dragged me home to my mam. He told her he was goin' to Clare to be a big dance master and he was needin' me to be his blind fiddler. He told her if she din't let me go with 'im, he'd turn me in."

Hank hung his head and tears slowly dribbled from his eyes as he wrung his hands. "My mam knew we'd be in big trouble cause I weren't really blind. Then he held out a bunch of coins sayin' it were my first wages. My mam din't know what to do 'cause she was scared fer me . . . but she was needin' that coin real bad fer t'others."

There was a long silence and then Freddy nudged him. "So yer mam made ye go?"

Hank nodded. "Yep. She made him promise to take good care o' me and told me to be brave. She thought my life would be better far away from Dublin but, it just weren't so."

Willie sat beside him with his legs drawn up and rested his head on his arms. He was dreading the rest of Hank's story. He had suspected Martin of abuse for a long time but had never felt it his place to intervene without being asked.

Hank shook his head. "At first he was almost nice to me. He bought me some new clothes, got me a haircut, and my belly was full. We played music in lots of places and people was right kind to me, tossin' plenty of coins." He paused, letting his fingers trail through the sandy dirt under the wagon. "I got none o' that though. Martin tossed me a coin sometimes, but mostly, he kept it all for hisself."

When Hank raised his face, Willie saw the light fade from the man's eyes as he stared off to his distant memories. What remained were the deep hollows of despair.

Hank sighed in resignation. "Not long after we got to Clare, Martin started doin' things agin almighty God to me, an' if I tried to fight 'im off, he beat me and did it to me anyway. Every day . . . he made me bleed. I should'a been stronger and fought back. I should'a run away but I had no coin an' no place to go. I was too far from home an' so lost." Tears continued to course down his cheeks and drip off his chin onto his shirt. He was without a thought to wiping them away.

Freddy lifted a hand to reach out to his friend but drew it back when Hank flinched against his touch.

Hank took a deep breath before continuing. "So today, me and Martin had a blow out behind the Shamrock. I swore it was the last time he was gonna raise a stick to me! He told me I ought be *grateful* for all he done fer me over the years! Can ye believe that?" Hank picked up a small stick and flung it. "I followed him into the tavern and had me a few pints. I watched him in the mirror while he ate an' I couldn't believe the hate in my heart. After he took off, I decided I was goin' to his room and git the coin I got comin' to me and then leave here."

Willie asked how he had gotten into the room.

"I picked the lock . . . it weren't hard."

Freddy and Willie both asked what had happened then.

Hank decided not to tell how he'd helped himself to the money and used Martin's things. "Well, I laid down to sleep for a bit and that's when Jack come to the room and starts askin' what I was doin' there, and he goes acusin' me of doin' what-all to Martin." He went on and described how Jack had tossed the coins and caught him out for not being blind. "So now I gotta run but I got no clue about any place to go. I thought about goin' home to Dublin; but my family's prob'bly long gone by now, and I know I ain't got the strength to walk all that way."

Freddy asked, "Did ye check the stable to see if Martin's horse n' carriage is still there?"

Willie thought for a moment before asking any more questions. No one had seen Martin since early afternoon when he had eaten at the Shamrock. Some thought they had seen him walking down the road toward the shoreline, but no one had seen him return. At twilight, a search party had scoured the campgrounds with lanterns, to no avail. The rocky shoreline was too dark, the tide too high to be able to search effectively, so they gave it up until morning.

Good thing, too, thought Willie. With Niall's big meeting only hours away, they didn't need anyone watching their movements. With any luck, none of them would have to bear Martin's presence again. He doubted that Hank could have mustered the courage or the physical strength to harm the man. That said, what was to become of Hank if suspicion were cast his way?

Hank shook his head. "I ain't had time to check on nuthin'. An' what would I be doin' with a fancy carriage but makin' people think I was stealin' it?"

Willie shook his head. "Ye're right Hank. The carriage is too easy to recognize. Ye might get away with the horse though."

Hank sighed. "Even if I got the horse, where would I go? I'm needin' to hide til mornin'. Elsewise, I'll get lost in the dark." He looked around the campsite nervously. "I can't be here when Jack comes lookin' fer me."

Freddy reached out to find Willie's arm. "Can he stay with us?"

Willie shrugged. "Let me think on it." He wasn't sure how deeply he wanted to get involved in this mess. He needed to protect himself and Freddy, no matter how much he pitied Hank. "Let me wander a bit . . . see if I can figure somethin' out and get some help for ye. Maybe ye should set yourself in the wagon and get some rest. Ye'll be needin' yer strength." With that, he rose and headed over to the meadow, threading his way among the families to look for Niall.

Hank looked at Freddy and asked, "Are ye still my friend?"

Freddy sighed, his own thoughts a jumble in his mind. Yes, Hank had lied but maybe he would have done the same in his shoes. God knew his life had been a sight better than Hanks. "Yea, I guess we's still friends. Jus' don' be lyin' to me no more."

Chapter Thirty

All that remained of the music was the sound of crickets chirping over the landscape and the soft lilt of tin whistles, small harps, and flutes to accompany the story tellers. The humid day had given way to an overcast sky, a misty moon and a few stars winking through the cloud cover. Thin wisps of fog had begun working their way inland, promising a damp night.

The rampant odor of sweaty bodies was defused by the sweet smell of crushed meadow grass that lingered in the balmy evening air where only a faint breeze off the coast stirred. After two long, noisy days and nights, the throngs of revelers were finally spent. They were happy to sit lazily around the dozens of small campfires that provided light around the meadow, resting their full bellies, tired legs and blistered feet. They enjoyed their jugs of mead and ale or flasks of Irish whiskey as they gossiped among themselves, waiting for the story hour to begin.

The ability to tell a story is a gift. Whether it be with the lilting cadence of a limerick or the telling of bygone tales of battle, nowhere but in Ireland, and especially County Clare, does the story become a melody. Gently rolling brogues magically transform mere words into mesmerizing lyric; at once lulling and hypnotic to the audience, be it of one rapt soul or a hundred. It is no wonder, then, that an organized story hour around a campfire becomes an event filled with anticipation.

The mysterious disappearance of Martin Clancy became a tale of its own. There was the low rumble of whispers shared behind hands that hid the lips. From one mouth to the next, the tale grew and was expanded upon with a multitude of proffered explanations for his disappearance. Emotions ran the gamut between a euphoric *'good riddance'* to *'he probably took off 'cause he knew Willie would beat 'im on the doors'*. There were more than a few whispers that *'maybe somebody killed 'im'*. No one among them was grieving the loss.

From the edge of the meadow, Roisin, a small, plump woman, walked slowly through the trampled grasses to the center of the circle, her uneven gait aided by the use of a briar-wrapped shillelagh. The heavy knob of the handle had been filled with lead when crafted many generations ago, and over the years, had been used as a powerful weapon when needed.

She was known to young and old alike simply as 'Auntie Ro'. No one knew from whence she came, only that she had always appeared among them to enchant the little ones. In her soft melodious voice, she told the children stories of quick-flitting fairies with gossamer wings who spread fairy dust over their meandering dreams, and of impish leprechauns creating mischief and mayhem with their rainbows and promised pots of gold.

Her white hair was parted in the middle, plaited and coiled on either side of her head like two bulbous ears. Her cheeks, ruddy and round as apples, perched beneath blue eyes that twinkled with merriment and mystery, belying her age. No one knew exactly how old she was, but guessed her to be at least eighty, perhaps more. Her long shapeless shift of black cotton, frayed at the hem, was covered by her signature rainbow-hued shawl, knit from hundreds of bits of multicolored yarn. She held the edges of her shawl away from her body and, smiling, slowly turned to face the surrounding crowd. Auntie Ro chanted softly, nodding to the heads of the clans, her signal to gather the children around her. As she completed her turn, throngs of children ran laughing and clapping to sit at her feet. Mothers and older children carried wailing babies and anxious toddlers who, quite soon, ceased their cries and fussing, content to sit and be amused and captivated by the lilting brogue of Auntie Ro. Always soft-spoken, Roisin commanded earnest silence by the sheer intensity of her animated features as she narrated her tale:

> *In a shady nook one moonlit night,*
> *A leprechaun I spied*
> *In scarlet coat and cap of green,*
> *A cruiskeen by his side . . .*

Willie watched the spectacle and chuckled, shaking his head as he elbowed Niall. "Isn't she somethin'?"

Niall, too, chuckled. "She sure is. Question is, what?"

"Was she around when you were younger?"

"I can't say as I remember a time when she wasn't here, but I've no clue who she belongs to."

> *Twas tick, tack, tick, his hammer went*
> *Upon a weenie shoe,*
> *And I laughed to think of a purse of gold,*
> *But the fairy was laughing, too . . .*

They continued to watch how Auntie Ro entertained the children and the adults who had settled themselves in an ever-growing ring around her. Saraid and Maureen were there with Liam, Bridget and the twins, as well as Molly and her brood. Fiona and James had gone off with cousins of their own age to the far side of the circle.

Niall noticed that Molly's husband, Seamus, was deep in discussion under the trees with John and Roark. John didn't look too happy, and Niall wondered absently what that was about.

Willie looked around. "Where's Patrick?"

Niall wiggled his eyebrows and leered playfully. "He went off to fetch Annie but he's been gone for hours. They should have been back here by now." As he looked around the meadow, he said, "I wonder what's keeping them."

> *With tip-toe step and beating heart,*

> *Quite softly I drew nigh.*
> *There was mischief in his merry face*
> *A twinkle in his eye . . .*

"Actually, Niall," Willie said softly as he looked around for eavesdroppers, "I'm glad for a moment alone with ye. There's some trouble brewing."

"What kind of trouble?"

Willie motioned Niall to follow him into the shadows beyond the firelight. Then he explained what had happened to Hank and the threats made by Jack Cleary.

> *He hammered and sang with tiny voice,*
> *And sipped the mountain dew;*
> *Oh! I laughed to think he was caught*
> *But the fairy was laughing, too . . .*

"I want to help him but I can't draw any more attention to myself. Cleary already suspects me of spyin' and Martin very openly shows his disregard for me.

Niall shook his head. "What do you think really happened to Martin?"

"I fear he's come to a bad end. Danny came by and went to check on Martin's horse and carriage. They're still here so he hasn't left on his own. Danny's pretty ticked about the lot of it. He went lookin' to have a word with Jack. Sure he's thinkin' of gettin' Hank out of here later tonight. We don't want to see Hank punished for somethin' he didn't do."

"Are you so sure of his innocence?"

"I'd bet on it. He may actually have his vision and his hate of Martin, but I can't see him havin' the strength or the opportunity to have carried out a bad deed. I've asked around and many people vouched for him. He was seen by others all day long sitting on his stool. He even slept for a few hours right by the doors, waitin' for Martin to come back."

> *As quick as thought I grasped the elf*
> *"Your fairy purse," I cried,*
> *"My purse?" said he, "'tis in her hand,*
> *That lady by your side . . .*

"Well, it's too late to mount a search now. We'll have to wait until first light. Where is Hank now?"

"He's asleep in my caravan. Freddy is keepin' him company. He'll get word to me if there's any trouble before I get back."

"Well . . . let's give it 'til morning and talk more about it then."

> *I turned to look, the elf was off,*
> *And what was I to do*
> *Oh! I laughed to think what a fool I'd been*
> *And the fairy was laughing, too . . .*

Willie turned to walk away, then stopped. "Niall . . . ," he whispered. "Do ye think Martin's disappearance has anythin' to do with the meetin' tonight?"

Niall looked startled. "I never gave that a thought!" His forehead creased with worry. "I sure hope not! This meeting is too important."

***

John shook his head, barely containing his disgust. He was getting really tired of people like Seamus coming around looking for an ill-disguised handout. "We've got no place for you."

"I ain't lookin' fer charity! I know ye're needin' help with the hayin'. We could sleep in the barn and I could work fer our keep." He had been drinking most of the day and his speech was slurred, his hands visibly shaking.

Roark snickered as he took in Shamus's bleary eyes. "Shape ye're in, you couldn't get through a single day of hard work."

"Ye got no cause to be sayin' that to me, Roark!" Seamus slapped his cap against his britches, struggling to keep his temper in check. "It ain't none of yer business no how!"

John pushed back his cap to wipe his brow, then put his hands on his hips. "What happened to your farm, Seamus?"

"We lost our land, what little was left." He began to whine. "It ain't my fault we cou'nt pay the feckin' taxes! After feedin' Molly an' the kids there weren't nothin' left to pass along."

John wanted to end this conversation. "So why aren't you hired on with anyone?"

"I work when I can! That's why we come here . . . so I could find work! Nobody wants to give me a chance!"

"Look at yourself!" cried John. "You come here stinking of ale and looking like you haven't bathed in a month! I don't know how Molly puts up with you!"

Roark was disgusted. "I noticed ye've banged her up again. Seems to me, if ye stayed out of the pubs and left her be once in a while, ye'd not be havin' to worry about feedin' 'em all." That said, Roark stomped back to the circle to find his own family

Seamus yelled after him. "Don't ye be talkin' 'bout my family like that! There's nothin' to be preventin' it if yer a good Catholic." He wasn't about to tell them how much he resented the feckin' brats . . . and Molly, too. He wished he was rid of the lot of them. He felt his eyes tear up and wiped his hand across his eyes. All he really wanted was to get into his wagon and leave them all behind. Start a new life somewhere else.

John decided that he'd heard enough. "Look, Seamus, I don't want to hear anymore. It isn't up to me anyway. The land belongs to Niall and the decisions about the farm are his to make."

Not one to give up easily, nor to be bound by pride, Seamus continued to grovel, clutching on to John's arm. "Could ye be puttin' in a word with him then? I'd be nothin' but grateful."

John shook him off angrily. "I'm not getting involved in your problems so stop begging and just leave me be." He stalked off muttering to himself as he headed back to the campfire to find Niall.

"Yer goin' to be mighty sorry fer talkin' to me like that, you selfish bastard."

Seamus knew he'd hear much the same from Niall. Maybe Molly could talk to Saraid. She owed him that much. He hated to admit it but they were fast growing desperate. If they didn't get some help soon, they wouldn't last the winter. It wasn't all so bad before his da passed over. The division of the land among four brothers made each parcel too small for sustenance. His brothers were too selfish to share and share alike as the O'Brien's had managed to do. His poor hut with its sod and mud roof had been cramped but now even that was gone. He couldn't think about how much worse it was going to be once the new baby came and the others got bigger. A well-thatched barn with hay for sleeping on would be a whole site better than living out of the wagon like they were doing now. Molly might stop carping at him, too. He was so sick of listening to her whine about how she worked so hard with her wool; and he knew that with a new baby, she wouldn't have time to do much of anything to help out. *Sure, Molly, make me feel even worse!* Seamus couldn't think about it anymore. He needed a pint to make the pain of his failure tolerable. He fingered the last of the coins in his pocket as he headed to the Shamrock.

Chapter Thirty-One

Jack muttered under his breath as he left the meadow, passing by the Shamrock on his way up the hill to Martin's room. He had hoped to make a perfunctory swath through the crowd and quickly return to the hotel. Hank seemed to be nowhere in evidence; hopefully, the idiot had taken his advice and left town. It seemed that everyone wanted to stop his progress and talk about Martin's disappearance. The bastard deserved all that had happened to him. Approaching him in front of the O'Brien woman had been the last straw. Whether she'd been in her right mind or not, he couldn't afford to have anyone suspicious that his tavern was the main drop off point for the many informants in Clare, as well as those along the coastline from Galway to the north, and Kerry and Cork to the south. The information that he culled was then funneled to Ennis and then on to Dublin. He was well paid for his trouble and wasn't about to have the piteous likes of Martin Clancy louse it up now. Over the last five years, he had saved almost enough to get out of this hell-hole. Then he could go back to living among the well-heeled folk in Dublin, where he belonged. If he could get his hands on Martin's money, he could leave as soon as the weekend was over. Once the crowd left, Doolin would once again be a quiet fishing village until the next festival in the fall. Feigning business in Ennis, he would leave Jimmy and Annie to run the place. What the hell; they needed the work. By the time they figured out that he wasn't coming back, he would be long gone. They could keep whatever money they collected . . . it wouldn't be much anyway.

Jack entered the hotel and quickly climbed the stairs to the second floor. He pretended to be searching for his room as a couple passed by him in the hallway. After they had turned the corner toward the stairs, he went to Martin's door and quietly let himself in, relieved to find the room empty. He quickly found the satchel and began to search through it. Like Hank, he stumbled upon the false bottom and quickly ripped it out. Unlike Hank, he found nothing there. Filled with rage, he flung the satchel across the room where it landed against a pair of black boots in the darkened closet. A quiet chuckle made Jack spin towards the sound.

"Is this what ye were lookin' for?" The man stepped out from behind the drape waving a fist-full of bank notes. His other hand held a pistol.

"*YOU!*"

"Yes, Jack . . . it's me."

"What are you doing here?"

"Well . . . I hear ye're plannin' on blamin' this bit of theft on a helpless blind man."

Jack was shaking with rage. "He's not helpless and he sure as hell isn't *blind!*"

"That's not my problem. Seems ye've gotten a bit greedy, Jack."

"What do you want? Money?"

The man grinned, shaking the wad of cash. "Looks to me like I've already got the money."

"What, then?"

"What I want is for ye to kneel down and put yer hands behind yer back."

"What are you going to do?"

"I'm going to truss ye up . . . and leave ye here." He put the notes in his pocket, stuffed the gun into the top of his boot, and picked up the length of sturdy rope he'd found at the stable when checking for

Martin's horse.

"You can't *do* that! Why would you do that?"

"So ye can have time to think, Jack," he said softly. "Now get on yer knees!"

Jack knelt, his legs shaking, fearing for his life, not daring to holler out for help. If he didn't get shot, someone would eventually find him . . . and he would have too many questions to answer . . . especially about why he was there in the first place. He might get accused of Martin's death and then all his plans would be for naught. "Please! I'm begging you! I'll do anything you want! I'll leave here and you'll never see me again!"

"Shut the hell up, Jack, or I'll be happy to shoot ye right now and be done with ye." He uncoiled the rope and bound Jack's hands behind his back, then pushed him over to the floor and hog-tied him to his feet. "Sure ye've been a pain in my bloody ass for too long."

Jack began to cry in earnest until a hand whipped across his mouth and blood dribbled down his chin.

"Let me fix that fer ye," he said sweetly, wiping the blood from Jack's face with a bandana. Then he stuffed it between Jack's teeth and tied it behind his head. "There," he said, patting Jack's shoulder. "All better now."

He chuckled as he tossed a handful of coins from Martin's pouch to the floor. He watched them roll around Jack's head before pocketing the rest. "I think there's about thirty pieces there, Judas. Don't be spendin' 'em all in one place," he said, tossing the empty pouch to the floor

Jack struggled against his bindings and continued to cry out in a muffled voice as Danny softly closed the door and whistled his way down the hall.

***

Kate sat alone in the caravan, trying to decide whether or not to join the rest of the family around the campfire. She was feeling better, at least physically. She was supposed to dance the traditional slip jig later with Saraid, Maureen, and Molly. It had been quite a surprise to her that she had come to love the Irish dancing, especially the slip jig. All that tapping and stomping the others did wasn't for her. The graceful steps of this dance had always been her favorite. Her tall, lithe frame leant itself well to the form; over the years, it had become her signature dance. The young women had insisted on learning the steps to accompany her as all of her old partners were now too feeble. She thought the dance much too refined for the likes of Saraid. Yet, if she was honest, and it strained her to admit it, Saraid had done well. She had spent months practicing in secret to achieve some semblance of grace as a surprise for Niall . . . and she had done it. Maureen and Molly had done this dance in the past, not to her standards, of course, but passably.

Kate rubbed the residual tightness in her forehead, fighting the desire to sleep again. Sighing, she thought about her argument with Niall, knowing there was nothing to be done about it. She was so unhappy, but what choices did she have? Dublin? The thought of leaving this place and going home was appealing but she didn't want to be alone. She had been in Clare for almost forty years. Her parents were long dead and two of her brothers had already gone back to England. Perhaps she would write to her brother, Peter, to see if she might be able to come back and stay with him and his family. Then she remembered that in his last letter, he had talked of moving to America.

Kate shook her head. *I would never survive an ocean voyage!*

Perhaps John could be persuaded to go to Dublin with her. Her most kindred son had nothing to keep him here but hard work with no reward, no standing in the right of property ownership. With his bearing and his love of literature, he would fit in so nicely with the learned gentry of the city. Of course, he would have to swear allegiance to the Anglican church. She was certain that if he did so, he would be able to find a suitable position at the university. He would certainly not be among the cretin working class of the factories.

She wished she could take Fiona with her, too. The child held so much promise that would never come to fruition here. She deserved good schooling. Though the Penal Laws were beginning to ease, Fiona, like all the other Catholic children, was still forced to hide her learning. James would never leave the farm that would be his one day. She nixed the idea of taking Liam and Bridget. She didn't have the energy to cope with such young children. But Fiona . . . she sighed, rubbing at the dampness in her eyes.

"Hello, Mrs. O'Brien."

Kate looked up and forced a tight smile. "Hello, Daniel."

"Have the others gone off to the campfires?"

"Yes. They left some time ago."

"Ain't ye comin' along, too?"

"I'm still trying to decide."

"Hey," he said, taking her hand. "I've been waitin' all year to see ye dance again! No one does a slip jig better'n ye!"

Kate chuckled in spite of herself. "Then I guess I'd better get my dancing shoes."

"Well, get a move on then! I'll walk with ye."

Kate's mouth twitched at the corners. Danny always managed to cajole her out of any bad mood. As they walked, Danny seemed preoccupied, so she thought about all the many struggles he'd had in his young life.

He and his widowed father had arrived from Kildysart years ago when Danny, who was barely into his teens, had found himself in some kind of trouble with a girl. Her husband had not hesitated to offer them a few acres of land, enough to get by on. Within two years, Danny's father had died.

Danny, then seventeen, had insisted that he could manage his father's small piece of land on his own. He was not much more than five-and-seven tall, but the hard work of the farm filled out his slight frame with compact muscle and wiry strength. Without assistance, he singlehandedly plowed, planted and reaped, working endless hours, days and weeks at a time without respite. It was only when the late fall and winter came and the fields lay fallow that he had the time or the inkling to socialize with his nearby O'Brien cousins.

Kate had been disdainful of the shabbily dressed young man who had insinuated himself into their evenings. She had begrudgingly added a plate to the table when her husband, and her own young men invited him to join them for a meal.

After a whiff of him and one look at his dirty hands, she had given him a stern look and pointed to the door. "You'll not sit at my table stinking of a barn and worse! Get out to the trough and clean yourself up."

Danny, rather than being offended, had given her a wide, dimpled grin and a deep exaggerated bow. "As ye wish, my lady."

Kate smiled, remembering how she'd watched him through the kitchen window. He had indeed gone to the trough and, without malice or pride, sloughed off his odorous shirt and dunked his head and upper body into the water. He'd come up sputtering and shaking the water from his curly head. He reminded her of Niall's dog, who did much the same when coming out of the river. Niall had laughed at his antics and held out a worn but clean shirt that he had long grown out of.

She'd listened to their conversation. "My mother can be a bit harsh," Niall had said.

Danny had replied, "Oh, I ain't worried none. Sure she'll like me soon enough."

And like him she did . . . eventually. Danny got under her skin in unexpected ways. He showed up one day with a handful of daisies he had picked in the meadow and gave her a slight nod of the head when he presented them to her. She was flummoxed and sputtering as she took them from him and placed them in water; but at dinner, she had given him a larger-than-normal portion of stew. He'd grinned at the small victory while she fought to keep a straight face.

Then there was the time that she was struggling with a basket of wet laundry while her own men had gone to get supplies. He'd whipped it out of her hands and helped her to lay them out to dry.

In bits and pieces, he'd finally made her laugh; and with that triumph, he'd picked her up and swung her around until she was screaming for him to put her down. Niall's father, had taken quite kindly to the scamp, who lightened the house with his good humor, and respected him in a fatherly way for his determination to keep up the small farm.

Yes, she thought now, *she had finally come to enjoy him . . . her rascal.* Especially when he danced. With his natural grace and quick feet, he could stomp with the best of them.

Kate had been so engrossed in her reverie that she was surprised when Danny spoke.

"Evenin' gentlemen, ladies," he said as they arrived at the O'Brien campfire. "I found this fair lass hidin' away and bade her join us with her dancin' shoes."

Kate slapped his hand playfully. "Now stop with the blarney, Daniel!"

"Mother!" John rushed to her side and took her arm as all eyes turned to them.

"What are you all staring at?" she asked, shrugging away from both men. "I was perfectly capable of getting here on my own, with or without my dancing shoes!" As she said the words, she realized that she did, indeed, feel better. Her speech and movements seemed normal.

Maureen looked to Saraid and Molly. "Guess we'll be dancin'

after all!"

Niall, who had overheard Maureen, asked, "What dancing?"

Saraid shook her head. "Nothin' for ye to concern yerself with, my love."

John asked, "Are you really feeling better, mother?"

"I'm just fine. No need to fuss over me." Kate took a seat with the other women who made room for her on the blanket. Bridget crawled into her lap, leaned her curly head against her grandmother's chest and sucked her thumb. Kate absentmindedly rubbed the child's head and leaned in to kiss her cheek.

Niall pointed to the center of the circle. "There's Connor. Time for the adult tales to begin."

Chapter Thirty-Two

The ring of individual fires cast a golden glow around the edge of the meadow. Fragrant wood smoke drifted aloft to mix with the moisture-laden air, creating a cloudy blanket overhead that obliterated the stars.

The children's story time had passed as well as the endless bawdy limericks. Now everyone was awaiting the final tale of the evening, narrated, as always, by the eldest of the O'Brien clan.

Connor O'Brien, descendant of the main line of the dynasty, was a masterful storyteller. His rich deep voice resonated easily throughout the meadow. Though eighty-three, he still held a proud upright carriage and had a full head of steel-gray hair. He used a shillelagh more as ornament than for assistance as he took his place in the center of the surrounding campfires. His crimson waistcoat shimmered in the firelight as he waited for silence to weave its way through the crowd. An iron rod bearing the O'Brien coat of arms, its three golden lions against a bright red background, had been driven into the ground beside him.

Connor began his short speech. "It seems that we have once again added to our ranks. As I look around, I see yet more O'Brien children among us, as well a few more Kennedys, MacConsidines, O'Caseys, McMahons, Quirks and Cosgroves. We also must pay homage to the losses among the O'Kellehers, the Powers and not least of all, our great friend, James O'Brien, who honored us all with his unfailing wit and undying faith in the Ireland of our forebears.

Each year we recite the mystical tale of Brian Boru, the High

King of Ireland, word for word. This is to assure that our heritage will not be forgotten by those who have heard it before and to preserve it for future generations."

Connor cleared his throat and began the tale:

> Centuries ago, Ireland was a great and beautiful land. It was filled with hills and forests, valleys green as emeralds, rolling on endlessly to feed the herds of cattle and sheep. Her soil was black and rich for farming; her many pristine rivers and streams filled with salmon fat enough to feed a hungry family.
>
> In the beginning, except for the royal courts, we were a scattered and primitive people whose clans settled far from each other. The men of Ireland were brave and stalwart. They were also artisans of precious metals, poets and great thinkers. The colleens of Lady Ireland were fair as the sky and beyond compare.
>
> It came to pass that the Norsemen, our barbaric enemies beyond the sea to the north, came in their mighty ships with tall sails and oars to trade with us. They were so enamored of all Ireland possessed that they chose, instead, to ravage her skirts. They cut down our forests to build more ships. They turned us into slaves in our own country, raped our women, took our gold and despoiled our land.

Patrick, walking alone, appeared out of the darkness and joined the rest of the family.

Niall nudged him and whispered, "Where's Annie?"

Patrick turned his mouth to Niall's ear. "We stopped for a pint at the Shamrock and the place was crazy. Seems like Jack is nowhere to be found. Annie had to give Jimmy a hand to settle the bunch waiting for their drinks. They were none too happy."

Niall shook his head. "People disappearing left and right. I wonder who's next." Niall looked more closely at Patrick and noticed the bruised areas on his face and nudged him again. "What happened to your face?"

Patrick looked away sheepishly. "Annie got a bit upset with me."

Niall was alarmed. "You didn't get rough with her, did you?"

"No! No . . . nothing like that."

"What then?"

"She just got a bit frisky is all."

Saraid looked up at Patrick and tugged on his tunic. "Are ye goin' to tell us all about it?"

"No, I'm not!" he replied with a hint of defiance.

Niall held up his hands. "Whoa, brother. She was only asking. No need to get your ire up." Aside from the tired expression on Patrick's face, Niall discerned a bit of difference in his bearing. "I'm taking it that it all went well?"

Patrick bowed his head, a grin spreading on his face. "Better than well–she was amazing. I think she really cares for me."

"Don't go getting carried away, now. Every man feels that way after his first time."

Patrick shook his head, remembering how she had so carefully led him through his ignorance. He felt his chest tighten and rubbed it idly. "No, it was more than that. She's really, really special."

Connor's voice continued to resonate over the camp:

> *Some years later, Teirgeis, the mighty warrior chieftain from Norway, came with a mighty fleet of over a hundred ships and thousands of warriors. He wanted to turn us into a Pagan empire with himself as Lord of all Ireland.*
>
> *Tiergeis sent half the ships to the settlement in Dublin, on the river Liffey, and overpowered the unsuspecting Irishmen. The rest of the ships sailed up the Boyne and established many settlements where Teirgis set up his headquarters near Alhlone, to the south end of the Lough Ree.*
>
> *The Danes, known as the "Black Heathens" for their dark body armor, decided they wanted Ireland, too, and so sailed up the River Shannon and built a new stronghold called "Limerick*

of the Mighty Ships." Many battles ensued between the Norsemen and the Danes, with the Irishmen trapped in the middle having to fight with one or the other to survive.

John returned to the group, his fists stilled clenched. He took Niall by the arm and pulled him aside.

Niall asked, "What's got you so riled?"

John turned his head aside, lowering his voice so Molly wouldn't hear. "Has Seamus talked to you?"

Niall shook his head and raised his eyebrows. "What about?"

"He wants to come to work the haying with us . . . said they'd sleep in the barn."

Niall chuckled, shaking his head. "Yeah, sure. I don't think the man's ever worked a solid day in his life. Haying would kill him."

"That's exactly what I told him."

"Did he accept that?"

"Not hardly. He started begging, and I told him he'd have to talk to you. Hey, don't be looking at me like that! It's the truth, you being the head of the family and all."

Battles and raids continued for hundreds of years. Villages were burned, their wares sacked, many slaughtered or enslaved and those who were left were made to pay heavy taxes. Royal Irish women were made to marry the Norse chieftains and many were carried off in ships to the Norse country. These heathens also destroyed the religious learning places and turned them into places of Pagan worship.

After many generations, the Irish finally began uniting. They learned how to build their own ships and how to navigate the great rivers. Finally, the Irish began to fight back and win some battles of their own. One great Irishman, Cellachan of Cashel, defeated the Dane, Sitric, and burned Dublin to the ground taking Sitric's riches away with him.

The crowd around the campfire cheered as they always did at

this part of the tale. Connor waited until they had quieted down again before continuing.

The greatest of our heroes were the mighty O'Brien chieftains, founders of the noble house of the Dalcassians in the 10th century. Brian mac Cennetig, son of Kennedy, whose mother was the sister of Conor, King of Connacht, was one of twelve brothers, most of whom died in battle. His brother Mahon, from whom the McMahons descended, became king upon the death of his father. Mahon and Brian fought side by side in many battles until Mahon's murder at the hands of the Norsemen.

Brian avenged his brother's death by killing Imar, the Osterman King of Limerick, and, at the age of thirty-five, took over this large center of trade and the rest of Munster as well. He went on to defeat the Norse King of Leinster and Sitric, King of Dublin.

In victory, Brian demanded that the other Irish kings proclaim him to be the one High King of Ireland. He took the name 'Brian Boru' from the town of Borime, where he set his royal seat, Kincora, on the banks of the river Shannon, near Killaloe.

He ruled Ireland's people peaceably for many decades.

Danny pulled Niall away from the group and motioned to John, Patrick and Roark to follow.

"What's going on, Danny?" asked Niall.

"Well, I took care of Jack fer now, but it means I'd better grab Hank and git while the gittin's good."

Niall asked, "What exactly did you do? Or shouldn't we ask?"

Danny described the events that had occurred in Martin's room. "I'm goin' to give the money to Hank so as he can have a stake. If Jack gets free, he'll have the law after me so I really need to go."

"What's he going to do about a ride?" asked Patrick.

"I'm goin' to grab Martin's horse. I don't think Martin'll be needin' it again."

"You don't know that," chimed in Roark.

"Then where is he?" asked Danny. "Nobody's bloody seen him since he left the Shamrock."

John was worried about him stealing the horse. "You get caught with a stolen horse, they'll be stringing you up!"

Danny chuckled. "Like I always say, they'll be havin' to catch me first."

He became known as "Brian of the Tithes" as he demanded monies from all the heads of the clans. He used these large sums of money for good. Brian built roads and rebuilt monasteries and schools. He sent many men far and wide across the European countries to buy books so that we could once again learn to read the Latin and Greek stories, histories and poetry.

Aside from being a great warrior, Brian was also a great and fair statesman. Rather than banish the Danes and the warriors from Norway, he allowed them to keep their strongholds and used them to help with trade and to utilize their natural resources.

Molly laid her hand on Saraid's arm. "My friend, I need to be askin' a favor of ye."

"Of course, Molly. What is it?"

"Ye know I wouldn't be askin' if we wasn't in trouble. Seamus—he wants me to ask if ye'd be willin' to put in a word to Niall for us."

Saraid's stomach clenched. "What kind of word?"

Molly began worrying the fabric of her skirt with nervous fingers, unable to meet Saraid's eyes. "We was wonderin' . . . and it shames me to be askin . . . if Seamus could work the hayin' with ye folks, and let us stay in the barn?"

Saraid wasn't sure how to answer. She'd caught a little of the men's conversation and knew how angry John was about Seamus. "Didn't he get hired on by anyone?"

Molly turned away from Saraid, her lips a tight line. "No. No one wants him. They all say he ain't reliable."

"An' knowin' that, ye want us to take 'im on?"

"Please, Saraid, we got no place to go."

Saraid twisted a blade of grass in her fingers and chewed on the end of it. She knew that the men folk had no respect for Seamus . . . and she couldn't blame them. She'd seen Molly struggle for years; always trying to keep a smile on her face as baby after baby stretched their meager earnings. Long months apart didn't negate their friendship or their loyalty to each other. She knew what Niall's answer would be but she would try. "Sure I can't promise anythin' Molly, but I'll ask."

"Thank you, Saraid," Molly said, hugging her. "Ye're my truest friend, always."

> *The Norsemen, jealous of Brian's power, set to wage another war with him. The Danes enlisted help from the Vikings from Normandy, Flanders, England and Cornwall. Fierce fighting men from the western Scottish islands of the Orkneys, the Hebrides and Shetlands joined the mail-clad Danes, too.*
>
> *Brian and his men from Munster were joined by the warriors from Meath and Connacht as well as the Christian Norsemen.*
>
> *The battle took place on Good Friday in the year 1013. Brian was now seventy-three years of age and his leaders begged him to stay away from the actual battle. He sat astride his mighty horse on top of a hill with his sword raised in one hand and a cross in the other.*

Many in the crowd had tears in their eyes. No matter how many times they heard the story, it was listened to with the reverence of a gospel rather than a mere tale. It gave them hope that they would survive the tyranny of British rule and rise once again as a people to prosper on their own land and govern themselves.

> *The battle raged from sunrise until sunset. Thousands of*

Irish in their leather tunics were cut down by the barbaric Norsemen who wore metal mail that was too hard for their meager weapons to penetrate. They were saved when Malachy, Brian's ally, arrived late in the day with fresh troops. The Danes were beaten back to the sea where they tried to escape to their ships, only to find that their boats had drifted away with the tide. Many were slaughtered and many more drowned trying to escape.

Brian had taken up refuge from the battle in his guarded tent. As he knelt there in prayer, he was betrayed by one of his own men, the heathen, Brodar, who made entry into his tent and slayed him.

Though Brian's men in turn killed Brodar, all was lost. Brian's son and heir, Murchadh, as well as Murchadh's heir, Turlough, were also killed in battle. They were laid to rest in Armagh near the tomb of St. Patrick.

After the battle ended, and most of their leaders had been killed, the troops disbanded and went home to their own tribes. Brian's ally, Malachy, was one of the few who survived. He took over power for the next eight years, but there was never again a king strong enough to unite all the people of Ireland.

The crowd was still as Connor bowed his head. Then he raised his eyes to them and shot his fists skyward. "We are Brian's legacy! We will not lose hope! The day will come when one of us will be strong enough to rise up and lead us to freedom! Then this beautiful land will once again be our own! The Catholics of Ireland will once again own their own land and prosper and do trade with other countries. We will rebuild our great schools and churches and honor our priests and teachers!"

The crowd cheered and the music rang out again through the camp. People began to dance, ignoring the tough bits of straw pricking their feet.

Maureen shook her head as she held out her hand to Roark, who helped her to her feet. "He's just amazin', isn't he?"

"A bit long winded but yes, he's a good one to tell the tale."

Maureen looked to Kate. "Are we still goin' to be doin' the slip jig?"

She nodded. "If you wish."

Niall turned towards Saraid. "I asked before—what's this about?"

The men helped Kate to her feet. Molly and Saraid also stood, brushing off their skirts.

Saraid looked away. "Nothin' for ye to worry about."

"What do you mean, *'nothin'*?" demanded Maureen. "Sure we've been workin' at this for months!"

Patrick joined in the banter. He'd obviously missed out on something. "What are you going on about?"

Molly beamed at the men. "We're to be dancin' the slip jig with yer mother."

Everyone began to laugh at the thought of them finding time to learn the intricate dance and to be accomplished enough for Kate to allow it.

"Forget it," Saraid muttered as she walked away from the group.

"Saraid! Wait!" Niall ran after her and grabbed her arm. "Why are you so riled? We're just teasing! Did you really learn the steps?"

"Of *course* I did! But I ain't gonna do it now."

"Oh, come on now. Since when can you not take a bit of teasing?"

Saraid looked out over the large circle of friends and family. The thought of embarrassing herself in front of everyone was frightening. "I wanted to surprise you, but I'll probably just be messin' it up and your mother will be findin' more fault with me."

Niall drew her into his arms and kissed her forehead. He drew her chin up to make her look him in the eye. "Come on, *Mo Ghrá*, dance for me. Just me. Don't look at anyone else. I promise I won't be laughing at you."

Saraid sighed. "I don't know . . . ."

Niall nuzzled her neck. "Please, Saraid. *Dance for me.*"

She sighed and shrugged her shoulders. "If ye really want me to, I'll try. I need my shoes."

They returned to the group where Fiona and James, with their tin whistles, were practicing their music with Patrick, John and Roark. John had a small harp and Patrick, with his pipe, bobbed his head in time with the music while Roark played his fiddle. Liam and Bridget chimed in with their rings of bells.

Kate was standing impatiently amid the other women while Saraid tied her soft shoes. As Saraid took her place, the music began, and the women arced their right arm over their heads, then raised both arms to the night sky and back to their sides. Kate, standing in front of the other women with her hands to her hips, began the easy graceful movements, doing a series of dance steps and kicks in front of the others. When she paused, Saraid, Molly and Maureen danced forward, duplicating the steps as they danced around her. People crowded around the circling women and hooted encouragement as the four women then danced in concert with each other, never missing a step. Though her pregnancy was showing, Molly managed to look graceful and keep in time with the others.

Niall was mesmerized watching Saraid whose breasts bounced when she leapt, and he smiled as her hips swayed.

She watched his eyes shine, aching with love for her, and she stood more proudly, her smile radiant, her feet sure and precise. Even Kate, as she did a turn, smiled at the women, pleased with all of them.

The music ended and everyone clapped, wanting a repeat performance. Kate just shook her head. "Once is all you're going to get tonight." Amid the groans and pleas, she looked at Saraid and smiled tightly as she wiped her brow. "I must say," she paused, knowing Saraid was waiting to hear a good word, "That was quite passable."

Niall was incensed, "*Passable?* That's the best you can do? She was bloody amazing and you know it!"

Kate shrugged and turned to John. "Will you walk me back to the caravan? I'm quite tired."

"Certainly." He took her elbow as they walked away from the meadow.

Niall was huffing. Saraid took his hand and kissed his knuckles. "Don't be worryin' yerself about it. For her to be tellin' me that I'm *passable* is a great thing. Sure it means I was much better than that!"

Chapter Thirty-Three

Annie and Jimmy had no sooner restored order and good humor in the tavern when a crimson-faced Jack stormed in. His eyes glittered with rage as he punched the air with his fists and shouted above the din. "WHERE IS HE?"

Noisy conversations and laughter ceased, followed by a nervous silence that filled the room.

Jimmy, who had been stuck for hours with the irritated crowd, bellowed back. "Where's *who*, ye bloody cur?"

Jack marched over to the bar and took a swing at Jimmy, who ducked to avoid the blow.

Annie flinched and cowered against the far wall of the tavern.

"Jesus, Jack," cried Jimmy. "What in the name o' God have ye got up yer arse?"

"You probably know full well what I've got up my bloody arse!" Jack continued to look around the now silent crowd. The man he was searching for wasn't there. "Where's Danny McMahon?"

One of Danny's kinfolk piped up. "What's it to ye?"

Jack marched over to the table of McMahons sitting in the center of the room and glowered at them. "I'm going to ask one more time. Where's Danny?"

The eldest at the table rose, his chair scraping against the rough wood floor. He towered over Jack. "I think we asked a reasonable question of ye, Jack. Why would ye be lookin' for Danny?"

Jack fumed, "He tied me up and stole my money!" He turned and marched off to the sound of their derisive laughter. He strode into the back room, emerging a moment later with a paper clutched in his fist. Marching back to the table where the McMahons were still chuckling among themselves, Jack shook the list in their faces. "Do you know what this is?"

"Sure I imagine you'll be tellin' us soon enough," said the senior McMahon as he turned to the others with a grin.

"You won't be thinking this is so funny when I pass my list on to Dublin! They'll be coming after the whole lot of you!"

A loud murmur spread through the tavern as clansmen debated what would happen next.

Annie's head shot up at the mention of the list. Patrick and all his men folk were on the list too. He would be in danger if Jack passed it on. Her mind spun. *I have to get that list!*

"Ah, Jack . . . " Jimmy muttered, shaking his head. Then, because he couldn't help himself, he raised his voice so Jack would hear. "What're ye *doin'* man?"

Jack spun and stared at the old bartender, shouting, "What?"

Jimmy shook his head sadly as he pushed a wet rag around the top of the bar, wiping up drink slop. "Sure ye just blew the lid off all of it now, din' ye?"

Jack closed his eyes, understanding perfectly what he had just done by showing the blasted list. He fought a wave of dizziness as he tried to assess the situation.

Seamus, bleary-eyed, sat silently at the end of the bar, well away from the threat. He turned in his seat to watch all that was happening. It was the most excitement he'd seen in a good while. His heart beat faster, waiting to see who the players would be in this little calamity . . . and which side they would be on. He alone saw Annie slowly inching her way across the room. *This should be interestin'!*

The McMahons rose as one as Annie inched closer to the table. Jack's cohorts, up to now an unknown bunch, stood up, too, prepared to defend Jack. The two groups of men began to push and shove at each other. As the scuffle intensified, Jack raised his arms to block a blow. His fist lost its grip on the list and it floated from his hand to the floor, sliding under a table.

Annie dove for it, huddling beneath the table to avoid the flying hands and feet around her. She folded it quickly and stuffed it into her bodice. As soon as there was space for her to move, she scrambled out from under the table and fled the tavern, running through the darkness to the glow of the campfires across the meadow.

Seamus chuckled as he drained the last of his pint. "Well, well, well."

***

Annie ran from fire to fire, growing breathless and more frightened as she searched the faces in the crowd for Patrick. She held her bodice close against the paper hidden there so she wouldn't lose it.

Finally, she found him. "There ye are!"

Everyone turned to see Annie standing there, wild-eyed and panting. She shifted her weight from foot to foot, trembling violently as she wiped the sweat from her face.

Patrick, alarmed, went to her and took her hand. "You look affright, Annie. What's wrong?"

His genuine look of concern calmed her some and she sagged against him with relief, whimpering. She looked up at him. "Ye're all in danger!"

"Annie, what is it?" he asked again as he led her to the group.

Niall, watching her closely, was alarmed at how distraught she was. If Annie was here, Jack must have been freed. "Annie, was Jack at the tavern?"

"Oh yes," she said, finally forcing herself to concentrate. She took a deep breath. "And fit to be tied he was!"

"What do you mean?"

"He's sayin' Danny attacked him and took all his money. Left him tied up, too."

"How'd he get free?" asked Patrick.

"I don' got a clue. Sure he just be sayin' that someone found 'im, and now he's gettin' a posse to go out and find Danny. He caused a big ruckus in the tavern with Danny's kin. Goin' to be trouble fer sure. I came as soon as I could get away."

Patrick nodded. "That's good Annie. We appreciate it."

Niall began issuing orders but Annie interrupted him. "An' somethin' else, too . . . ."

The men stopped. "What is it?" asked Niall.

"Maybe it ain't important, but I'm thinkin' it is."

"Go on . . . ." he said impatiently.

"When yer mam was havin' dinner with Jack, I had to get a tablecloth out of his desk drawer an' there was a list on top of the desk. Jack went an' got the list and was wavin' it round at the McMahons and makin' a stink about the names on it."

"What kind of a list?"

"I don' rightly know but it had all yer names on it." Annie reached into her bodice ignoring the gasp of the women, and retrieved the list. "I got it here!"

"Bloody hell," cried Niall. "How did you get this?" he asked, grabbing it from her.

Annie told about the scuffle in the tavern and how she'd managed to grab it and run.

Roark shook his head. "Did anyone see you?"

"I don' think so. Sure they was all busy fightin' when I ran out."

"You took an awful chance, Annie," Patrick said as he put his arm around her shoulder.

She looked up at him and smiled, putting her hand against his chest. "I done it fer *ye*, Patrick."

He bent his head and kissed her softly as the women around the fire looked on.

Niall looked over the list and shared it with Patrick and Roark. "We need to find Danny and warn him. Patrick, you go to Willie's wagon and see if Hank's still there. Roark, check through the crowd and see if Danny's still around. Give the signal along the way. I'll check the horse pen and see if he might have grabbed Martin's horse already."

Annie looked up at Patrick. "Can I come with ye, Patrick?"

He shook his head. "No . . . you stay here with Saraid. She'll watch out for you. Won't you, Saraid?"

"Of course!"

Molly snickered and Saraid shot her a look. "Do you have a problem with that, Molly?"

Molly's face reddened with embarrassment. The last thing she needed right now was to offend Saraid. "I got no problem," she replied meekly.

"Be sure that ye don't." Saraid turned back to Annie and took her hand. "Come sit with us."

Annie stood frozen where she was, having seen the look of disdain on Molly's face. She knew she had a reputation and shame made her want to run off. She prayed that Patrick hadn't seen the look. He would send her away for sure.

But he had seen. "Molly, this is my friend, Annie," Patrick said, loud enough for all of them to hear, as he guided her to the blanket. He spoke pleasantly but his eyes were steely. "Be sure to make her feel welcome, now. Do you hear me?"

"Sure," Molly replied, pasting a smile on her face. *How dare he bring this whore around my children?*

Patrick planted a quick kiss on Annie's cheek. "All right then. I'll be back soon enough." He walked over and joined Niall and Roark.

Roark asked, "Should we get some of the other men together?"

"Might not be a bad idea to put them on alert but have them stay put for now," replied Niall. He turned to Saraid, squeezing her hand. "We shouldn't be gone long. Stay here with the crowd. Use the signal if any danger seems near."

The signal, the call of a short-eared owl, was used by all of the clan to identify themselves if they approached another man unseen in the darkness, or as an alert to danger. Variations and repetition of the call signified the importance of a threat.

Before long, the women on the blanket heard the soft whistles and calls echoing throughout the meadow. They made themselves busy playing games and singing songs with the children, while trying to remain calm as they waited for their men to return.

Chapter Thirty-Four

Niall and Patrick split up, using the darkness behind the fires to quickly circumvent each side of the meadow. Silence and haste were more important than the discomfort of unseen brambles and branches that scraped their arms and legs as they made their way through the dense undergrowth.

Roark quickly made his way around the circle, careful to stay behind the clusters of folks sitting behind their campfires. He stopped for a moment behind each group, softly emitting the call one time to be on alert. With the acknowledgement of a returning call, he continued searching for Danny, knowing that their men would be prepared to respond if they were needed. His keen eyes kept sweeping the area as he went along and he became confident that Danny was not there. He ducked more deeply into the darkness near the river and headed towards the horse pen to meet up with Niall.

As he neared the pen, he heard Niall talking to Danny in hushed tones as they used the horses as cover. There were about forty horses there, some munching on straw, some with feedbags on their noses, and some just nickering quietly. Just as he signaled that he was coming, he caught the sound of a small stick breaking in the darkness, several feet behind him to his right. He dropped down to the ground peering through the brush, straining to see any movement. At the same time, he turned his face away from the sound, cupped his hands to his mouth, and emitted a sharper warning call to put the others on alert.

The horses sensed danger and began to fret, whinnying and

snorting. The few that were loose paced within their confines. The others, tethered to the fence posts, strained their necks against the ropes that bound them.

Niall grabbed the bit of Danny's horse. "You have to go right now," he hissed.

"What about Hank?"

"Don't be worrying about Hank! Just go! Head south but don't go to the cliffs. You'd be a sitting duck out there. Just take cover where you can and I'll find you. Wait an hour or so and we'll try to get Hank to you. After that, if we still aren't there, just go."

Just as Danny was about to mount his horse, another sound startled them and they stood still.

Two men came down the path towards the pen, one swinging a lantern, the other with a small bale of hay under his arm. They were singing drunkenly, laughing at their own rendition of a limerick they'd just heard at the Shamrock before the fight started. It was the Callahan brothers, coming to feed and check on their horses. Tommy, as usual, was staggering along. They entered the pen, Sean closing the gate behind them.

Niall held Danny back. "Wait a minute," he whispered. "They might be able to help." He quickly laid out a plan and Danny nodded. They moved unseen across the pen to the Callahans' horses.

By the river, Roark finally caught the movement behind the willow fronds that he'd been straining to see. There were three or four men who had crouched down as the Callahan brothers passed by them, just barely visible in the dim lantern light. He gave another signal to Niall who signaled back.

As Tommy and Sean came by them, Niall and Danny grabbed them from behind, covering their mouths so they couldn't call out. They pulled them out of sight behind the horses. The brothers struggled against them until they identified themselves and told them to remain silent.

Niall whispered, telling the brothers what was happening. "Are you willing to help us?"

Tommy sobered instantly from the shock. He and Sean quickly nodded that they would help.

Niall and Danny released their hold of the brothers. "Here's what you're going to do," he said quietly. "I want you to hurry and untie the horses on this side of the pen. When I whistle, I want you to start hollering and herd them toward the gate."

Tommy and Sean nodded silently and set aside the lantern and the bale of hay. They crept quietly through the darkness around the far end of the pen, whispering to the horses to calm them as they untied their ropes from the fence.

Niall, invisible in the dark, eased open the gate. He crept back to the brothers who had released a dozen horses that were prancing around uneasily. Danny quietly mounted his own horse in the cover of the willow fronds and eased into the middle of the pack of freed animals. He grabbed onto the ropes hanging from the horses' necks to either side of him, and held them tightly as he awaited Niall's signal.

Niall whistled sharply, startling the horses, and the Callahan brothers starting yelling and waving their caps. The panicky horses reared, snorting with fear. They ran from the sharp sounds behind them, toppling the lantern as they careened around the pen. In the frenzy, the lantern was kicked across the ground, coming to rest against the bale of straw, igniting it. As the bale flared, tufts of dry grass and straw that littered the pen also ignited, spreading the fire. The frightened horses sped through the gate, trampling brush as they careened down the path and through the trees.

Danny tried to rein in his horse to help put out the fire but Niall hissed at him. "Go!"

Danny's anguished eyes met Niall's. He hesitated only a second more before he gave his horse's flanks a hard kick and rode out, hidden in part by the straining beasts on either side of him. Riding low against his horse's neck, he passed only a few feet from the men hiding under the willows.

A shot rang out. Niall heard Danny's muffled cry as he let go of the other horses and sped down the path away from the fire.

The men in the woods began to holler. One cried out, "I think I got him!" The others screamed, "Look out!" They scrambled to get away from speeding hooves, taking cover behind the willows. Then they chased after the horses in hopes that they would find Danny injured or dead, ignoring the need for help behind them.

Roark let out a shrill series of whistles through the trees. He pulled his knife from his belt and began hacking at the ropes that held the remaining horses captive. Patrick and some of the other men from around the campfires came running, already alerted by the escaping horses that had run through the camp. Low flames and smoke were spreading quickly across the pen and igniting the base of some of the old fence posts where a row of stacked hay bales ignited into a brilliant ball of flame.

Tommy and Sean ran yelling to their own prize horses who were nearest to the flames, the smell of singed hair acrid in the air. Suddenly a flaming piece of ash landed on Tommy's horse's tail and it flared into full flame. Tommy screamed and, mindless of the danger to himself, grabbed wildly for the tail. He held it against his body, even as the big horse bucked and screeched with fear. Tommy hung on, smothering the length of the tail against his shirt with his bare hands. Sean stamped his feet against the straw and tried to hold his horse still as he cut his rope. The fire burned at their hands and feet. The skin beneath their shirts was blistering, but they were mindless of any pain.

The remaining horses emitted high-pitched screams as they bucked against the ropes that held them trapped on the burning straw beneath them. Niall and Roark both worked frantically at releasing them as their hooves kicked at them. Patrick and the others kept stomping at the quick- moving flames. Some, hearing the call and smelling smoke, had brought blankets which they soaked in the river, and spread over the flames. Others scooped pails of water from the troughs to throw at the horses' legs and tails and the smoldering straw that covered the ground. Still others brandished their knives and cut the low hanging willow fronds that were drying and igniting from the heat of the fire. The smoke burned their eyes and flames singed their soft boots and the hair on their legs, arms and beards as they worked feverishly.

A welcome bucket of cold water suddenly soaked both Tommy and Sean. Steam rose from the horse's tail to mix with the smoke and black cinders. The horse continued to neigh loudly but finally stopped bucking. Tommy and his brother sank to the sodden mess beneath them and sobbed.

It seemed to take hours but with the help of so many, only some long minutes had passed before the flames were under control. The fire was extinguished before it could spread to the dry detritus at the floor of the trees surrounding the pen. The charred straw was dragged away from the fences and covered with blankets that had been soaked again and laid dripping over the piles.

The men were breathless from the fear and exertion of putting out the flames. Some, like Tommy, wept with gratitude that not one horse had been lost. Some of the fencing was charred and still smoldering. To prevent a later flare up that could ignite the willows, it was torn down and dragged into one pile that was well away from the trees and covered with yet more wet blankets. Using axes, the men cut sturdy saplings from the woods and tied them to the remaining posts to rebuild the pen. The men began heading back to the camp to treat their burns after soaking their legs and shoes in the cold river.

Niall wiped the soot and sweat from his face with his sleeve as he looked around the pen. "We got mighty lucky."

"That we did," agreed Roark.

They walked over to where Patrick stood with the Callahan brothers.

"Are your horses all right?" asked Niall.

Tommy nodded but was still a bit dazed by the speed with which it had all transpired. His hands and chest were blistered and the front of his shirt was charred to ruin. Alcohol was still swimming in his veins and his head was aching from the adrenaline rush. Sean was less injured and more afraid of the consequences of what they had done. "What if they arrest us?"

Niall shook his head. "They'll be too busy looking for Danny to worry much about you. The fire was an accident. It did no real damage, so they'll probably let it pass."

Patrick shook both their hands. "Mind you, we're grateful and won't forget that you were a help to us today."

Niall took some coins out of his pocket and offered them to Tommy. "You did a good job today. Come by our wagon later and Saraid will give you some salve for your burns. For now, go get yourselves a pint and try to act as you normally would."

Tommy and Sean both chuckled and protested that the coins weren't necessary, but Niall insisted.

"Just try to forget about all of it."

Tommy, staring numbly at his hands, shook his head. "I don't think I'll be forgettin' about it fer a good long time."

He and Sean walked away with their charred lantern, talking softly to each other as they they wandered up the path.

"We've still got one thing to worry about," said Roark.

"Yeah. Now we have to worry if Danny got himself shot," replied Patrick.

"You know Danny," sighed Niall. "He'll probably yank the pellet out himself and save it as a souvenir."

Patrick shook his head. "He's going to get himself killed one of these days. He takes too many chances."

Niall nodded towards the path. "Let's go find Willie and see about Hank."

Chapter Thirty-Five

Fog rose like a wraith over the sea, smothered the rocks of the bay, and crept silently across the road into the meadow. In the lantern light, it curled down through willow fronds, snaked through the gorse and nettle and slithered across the ground. Outcroppings of rock and the nearby ring of caravans, their domed tarps blanketed in white, loomed like hulking apparitions.

Niall, with Patrick and Roark trailing behind him, signaled his approach through the heavy mist and Willie signaled back.

"I heard the ruckus," said Willie. "What happened?"

"No time to explain now. Where's Hank?"

"He's in the caravan."

"Jack's on a rampage. We have to get him out of here."

Willie shook his head as he motioned towards the milky shadows approaching them. Several men broke through the fog, walking in their direction, Jack leading the way. "Too late."

Jack, his damp ring of hair curling wildly, looked furious. "Where's Danny McMahon?"

Niall, poised, shook his head. "I have no idea."

Jack bellowed. "Are you honestly going to stand there and tell me that you know nothing about all this; that you weren't responsible for those horses getting free and Danny escaping?"

"We all helped to put out the fire, is all," said Roark, straight-faced.

"Would you have us leave the horses to die?" asked Patrick.

"I don't give a godly damn about the horses! McMahon robbed me and tied me up!" he screamed. Spittle flew from his mouth as he paced in front of them. "He's in cahoots with Hank for sure. They're probably both responsible for Martin's disappearance, too."

Roark scoffed at Jack. "That's a pretty big accusation."

Willie scratched his head. "What does Hank have to do with any of this?"

Jack wagged his finger at Willie. "You're involved with all of this too, aren't you?"

Willie shook his head, his eyes wide with innocence. "I have no idea what ye're goin' on about."

Niall, deadly calm, spoke quietly. "Actually, Jack, I heard a different story."

"What the hell are you talking about?"

"I heard that you threatened Hank over nothing at all . . . chased him out of Doolin hours ago."

"Really?" retorted Jack. "And maybe you're all in it together!"

"In what?" asked Patrick, acting confused.

Jack clenched his teeth and groaned in frustration. "Don't be acting so dumb! And don't think you can be playing me for a fool!" He paced in front of them waving his arms wildly. "You probably know exactly where Hank is, too!"

His adversaries all shook their heads in disgust.

Jack began muttering under his breath, knowing that nothing was to be gained by continuing the argument. "You'd better hope I don't find out just how deep you're into this." With that, he stomped off into the fog to continue his search for Danny, his silent posse following behind him.

Niall and the others were silent until Jack and his men were out of hearing range. "He'll probably be back."

Willie was tense. "That was a close call."

Hank popped his head up from within the caravan. "I should just be givin' m'self up," he cried.

"Ye'll be doing no such thing, Hank," Freddy whispered from beneath the wagon. "Ye done nothin' wrong."

Hank whimpered. "I don' want to be gettin' ye in no trouble."

A voice called out. "This yer horse, Willie?"

Hank ducked back inside the caravan.

The men turned to see a man emerge from the mist, leading Willie's horse by his rope. "He must 'a got cut loose with t'others."

The men all smiled at their unexpected good fortune. "Yes it is! I thank ye for bringin' him back to me."

"Ye want me to take 'im back to the pen?"

"No . . . that won't be necessary. I'll take care of it."

"Well . . . I'll be off, then."

"You have my thanks," said Willie.

Niall turned to Willie. "Let me use your horse."

"What is it ye're goin' to do?"

"I'm going to take a quick ride south—see if I can find Danny."

"What about Hank?" asked Patrick.

"He'll have to wait. Right now we've only got the one horse. If Danny's hurt, he won't be able to mind Hank."

Patrick asked, "You're going alone?"

"Have to," Niall replied. "It'll take too much time to round up the rest of our horses."

Roark spoke up. "How are ye going to find him in this damned fog?"

"I'll bring a lantern, use the signal. Danny will answer if he can. If he can't, we'll have to wait until morning and search again on our way home."

"All right," said Willie. "What do we do with Hank in the mean time?"

Patrick held up a finger. "I have an idea. Mother's always been kind to Hank . . . and she hates Jack. Why don't we hide him in mother's caravan for tonight and John can keep watch. Jack would never dare to ask mother if she was sharing the wagon with Hank or Danny."

His idea was met with silence until Niall finally nodded. "That could actually work. I'll wait here while you go ask her."

Patrick disappeared into the fog and crossed the clearing to where their own wagons were. There was still some commotion going on as the loose horses were being rounded up and taken back to the pen. He paused in the shadows when he heard Jack's raised voice arguing with his brother, John, and his mother. He waited until Jack continued on his way before approaching.

"What was that about?"

Kate snapped at Patrick from inside the wagon. "He and his little posse actually had the gall to search all our wagons for Daniel! What on earth is happening?"

Patrick was shocked that Jack had searched his mother's caravan, but it might work in favor of his plan. He explained all that had transpired and what they would like her to do. "I seriously doubt that he would come back and search here again."

John argued against it until Kate raised her hand for silence. "I'm not at all happy about this, I'll be awake all night . . . but foiling Jack will be more pleasurable than you can imagine."

John reached for Kate's hand. "Mother, you don't have to do this."

"Yes, I must. Daniel has always been a scamp, but he means something to me. We need to make sure that he's safe." She shook her head. "And Hank, I'll do what I can."

Patrick fought a smile. "So, you'll help?"

Kate's back stiffened as she looked at Patrick. "Yes," she snapped. She turned away from him and disappeared into the wagon to rearrange their belongings. "I'll make space for him," she called out. "Hurry!"

Patrick looked to John. "You'll watch over them, then?"

"Of course I will! Do you think I'd let anything happen to Mother?"

"No, I don't. I just need to know that we're all pulling together on this."

"Go, then. We'll be fine." John turned his back on his brother and climbed into the caravan to help his mother move things around.

Patrick hustled back to Willie's wagon. He told the others that he'd get Hank over to his mother for safe keeping.

Willie filled his saddlebags with some cotton batting and comfrey-laced salve in case Danny was injured. He turned to Niall and held up a small flask. "I'm putting this in too, just in case you need it."

Niall nodded and shook Willie's hand. "Thanks." He took Patrick and Roark aside. "You need to stay with the others . . . keep them safe. Tell Saraid I'll be back in an hour. That'll give me more than enough time."

Niall called out to his brother as the men were walking away. "Hey, Patrick?"

Patrick turned to see his brother smile. "Tell Annie she has our thanks."

Patrick raised his fist in a victory salute. Though he was anxious to get back to Annie, he and Roark took their time sneaking Hank, his bedroll, his precious fiddle and stool through the fog to his mother's caravan. Roark stayed with their wagon to see that Hank was safely settled, while Patrick headed back to the campfires to check on the women.

It was the first time he'd really been alone since he and Annie had left the cave. So many thoughts burned through his mind. He chuckled as he gently touched his sore cheekbone, remembering how Annie had railed against him in the cave.

Patrick was proud of what Annie had done for them. If she'd

been caught, she'd have paid heavy consequences. The list would help them warn and protect those named on it. He knew that, even now, the list that Niall had passed on to Connor O'Brien was certainly being passed from one hand to the next around the campfires.

He hoped that Annie wasn't feeling out of place with the other women. He'd been angry at Molly for her snipe, but he knew that Saraid and Maureen would watch out for her.

Thoughts of Annie warmed him and he knew he would miss her when he left Doolin. Tomorrow, they would be heading home. Could he really let her go? He was already aching to touch her again. As he reminisced about their night in the cave, his chest grew tight and longing filled him with a throbbing ache in his groin. He groaned and kept going.

Up ahead, the campfires glowed through the mist, burning off the lower edges of the fog. Music still floated softly around the site as if to ward off dangers that prowled unseen in the darkness.

Many of the crowd had decided to sleep on their blankets under the canopy of fog, safe in their numbers and the light of their dimming fires. Jack, still raging, stomped through the campsite looking for Danny and Hank.

When Patrick reached their fire, Annie ran to him and he swept her into a fierce embrace.

She filled with gratitude to feel the strength of his arms circling her, and tears filled her eyes.

"Are ye all right then, Patrick?"

"Ah yes, sweet girl, I'm fine." One hand grabbed a handful of her hair as he hugged her close. "Especially with your arms around me. And you? Are you fine, too?"

Annie sniffled, then beamed at him, laying her hand against his cheek. "Sure I be right fine, now. Saraid is a good and fair woman. She made me feel welcome."

Patrick smiled as he set her back down. His fingers gently grazed her cheek. "Of course she did. That's her way."

"Patrick?" asked Saraid, as she and Maureen walked over to join them. "Where are Niall and Roark?"

He spied Molly inching closer to listen to their conversation, so he guided Saraid and Maureen away from the blanket. He leaned close to Saraid's ear. "Where's Seamus?"

Saraid shrugged. "Last I knew he was headin' over to the Shamrock."

Patrick nodded. "I think he and Molly best be left out of this conversation." In a hushed voice, he told them all that had happened, including the fire, and the possibility that Danny had been shot when making his escape. "Niall's gone off to find him. Roark and I got Hank over to mother's wagon for the night. Roark stayed with them to get him settled."

"And Kate's all right with that?" asked Maureen.

"Surprisingly, yes." He relayed how Kate was going to hide both Hank and Danny, too, if he could be found.

Roark came striding up to them.

"Everything all right then, Roark?"

"Yeah. We figure hidin' Hank with Kate is the safest place for him to be while Jack's still after him."

Another shape approached them through the cloudy darkness. It was Seamus, staggering and stumbling towards them. He stopped when he realized that they were all staring at him. He looked up at them with bleary eyes, weaving where he stood. Molly ran to his side and grabbed his arm. "Ye're drunk again!" she cried. "Ye promised me ye'd not do that today!"

Seamus pushed her roughly off of him. Molly stumbled and would have fallen if Patrick hadn't grabbed her by the arm and righted her.

He hollered at Seamus. "What do you think you're doing, man?"

"Ain't none o'yer feckin' business, now is it?"

Roark pushed Seamus and the man fell. "Ye'll not be rough with her! She's yer wife, for Christ's sake! And pregnant besides!"

Seamus shrugged, unapologetic, as he struggled to get up. "Yea, she's m'wife an' I'll be treatin' her as I damn well please."

Molly, mortified and crying, went to Seamus to help him to his feet. "I din' mean no disrespect, Seamus."

He shook off her hand. "Sure ye're just like the rest o' these stinkin' folk. Thinkin' ye're better'n me." As he looked around the group, he spied Annie and grinned, showing his rotting teeth. He pointed a shaking finger at her. "I seen what ye did."

Annie froze. "Ye seen what?"

Seamus laughed, the sound ugly in the night. "I seen ye grabbin' that piece o' paper in the tavern. The one Jack was shakin' 'round."

They all looked at each other but kept silent until Patrick strode over to him. He grabbed a fistful of Seamus's shirt and yanked him to his feet. "Is that some kind of threat?"

Seamus continued to grin. "Ye can call it what'er ye like."

Molly turned to Saraid, begging for understanding. "Sure he don' know what all he's sayin'."

Saraid stiffened and stared at her friend with a mixture of anger and pity. "I think it would be best if ye got him back to yer wagon."

Seamus laughed. "I'm thinkin' I'm goin' to be stickin' right close to all of ye. Seems to me, if ye knows what's good fer ye, ye'll have some hayin' fer me to do after all."

Patrick opened and closed his fingers into fists, struggling to not put Seamus out of his misery, permanently. "Are you *seriously* trying to hold that over us?"

"I ain't gotta threaten nobody. All I gotta do is tell Jack what his little whore here done an' . . . "

Patrick yelled, "You bastard!" His hard fist drove Seamus right off his feet and he sailed into the air before landing hard on the ground, unconscious.

Molly wailed. "Stop, stop, stop! He can't help it!"

Annie gasped, wrapped her arms around herself, and ran to the edge of the clearing and wretched into the scrub.

They all turned to look at Molly, who now had her children circling her skirt. Seeing the disgust and pity in their eyes totally shamed Molly and she crumpled to the ground sobbing. Hanging on to their mother in confusion and fear, the children began crying, too.

Men from nearby campfires quickly approached to see what all the ruckus was about. "Ye need any help here?"

Patrick rubbed the pain from his hand and shook his head. "We're all right here, thanks."

Saraid sighed. As much as she wanted to just leave Molly there, she couldn't. She went to her friend, gently lifted her from the ground, and held her in her arms while she sobbed. Without a word, Maureen picked up the youngest of Molly's wailing children and herded the others, trying to calm them. Together, they took Molly and the children back to their wagon, leaving the men to deal with Seamus.

Roark huffed out a breath as he stared down at the drunk. "He's a useless piece of shit."

Patrick shook his head. "And a dangerous one at that. I couldn't let him say that about Annie." He looked around and suddenly realized she wasn't there. "Where did she go?"

"I don't know. Last I knew she ran off towards the scrub."

Patrick cursed and stomped around the clearing. "I have to find her."

"What are we going to do with Seamus?"

Patrick shook his head in resignation. "I'd say leave him here but that might not be a good idea. We don't know where Jack is. Let's get him back to his wagon."

Chapter Thirty-Six

The sound of hooves thudding against the ground was all that could be heard as Niall galloped through the night towards the Cliffs of Moher. Intent on his mission, he was oblivious to the smell of the nearby sea that hung heavy in the air. The lantern dangled from a long pole over the horse's back, the fog melting in rivulets against the glass globe, illuminating only a small patch of road. He knew that Danny wouldn't see the light through the thick blanket of mist, unless he was nearby and watching for it. Scrub pine and clumps of tall grass among the scattered outcroppings of rock provided few places to hide. The cliffs were only about four miles from the Doolin campsite, but the distance seemed immeasurable when you were searching for someone in the fog at night.

Every so often, Niall stopped and whistled into the fog, hoping for an answering call from Danny, or a sighting of his horse. He was more than half way there and, still, no response. The further he went, the more fearful he became that Danny had reached a bad end. He heard the sound of the high tide crashing treacherously against the steep rock face hundreds of feet below and knew that Danny would have gone no further. The danger of riding right off the cliff at night was too high. It would mean certain death.

When Niall reached a clearing at the top of the cliffs, the fog dissipated and he reined his horse to a full stop. He yelled out Danny's name and repeated the whistle several times. There was no response. "Danny, Danny, Danny," he muttered softly. "You crazy bastard. Where are you?"

His mind filled with thoughts of his cousin's laughing eyes and the ready smile on his freckle-strewn face. His recklessness sometimes belied the quick mind that got him out of trouble almost as fast as he found himself mired in it. Niall doubted that Danny would continue to cheat the devil without some serious consequence, but he dearly hoped that his luck had not run out. He wasn't ready to lose Danny just yet.

Niall dismounted and while holding the horse's reins, walked a short distance into the fog and whistled sharply again and listened hard. Nothing. He whistled again . . . still nothing. Feeling apprehensive, he began the ride back to the campsite, stopping and calling out, whistling and listening. Away from the cliffs now, he was surrounded by the utter stillness of the night. He was about half way back when he finally heard the nickering of a horse in the mist. He dismounted; and, when he whistled again, he heard a feeble echo come back to him. He quickly crossed the rough scrub and uneven limestone until Danny's horse was reflected in the light of the lantern.

"Danny!" Niall trampled through the brush until he found his cousin, lying on his back, his fist barely holding on to the reins. After quickly securing Danny's horse with his own, he dropped to his knees and ran his hand over Danny's head. "I've got you!"

Though Danny groaned loudly and the shoulder of his shirt was soaked with blood, he was still alive.

"Don't move!" Niall grabbed the saddle bag full of bandages and salve, and knelt beside Danny. In the lantern light, Danny's face was clammy and contorted with pain.

"I figured ye'd find me sooner or later," Danny rasped then cried out with pain when Niall turned him to his side to examine the wound.

Niall winced at the blood that had stained the ground beneath his body. He tore away the sleeve of Danny's shirt and, wadding it up, pressed it against the wound to staunch the bleeding. The cloth quickly soaked through. He pressed a clean bandage against it while Danny let out a wail between gritted teeth. After a few minutes, he looked again and, though the flow was slower, it was still oozing. "Jesus, Danny. You're losing a lot of blood."

"You got any whiskey?" he asked. "I'll be needin' me a drink before ye try to get that shot outta there."

"It's pretty deep. I'm going to have to use a knife."

"Still want that drink," he mumbled.

"Damn it Danny!" He grabbed the flask and held Danny's head as he poured some whiskey down his throat.

Danny choked and sputtered but he reached for the flask for another shot.

Niall pulled the flask back. "I'll need to pour some of that on your wound, once I dig the shot out of there."

"Yeah, well, I need more to cut the pain."

"Sorry, Danny. You'll just have to grit your teeth."

"Just knock me out, then."

Niall hesitated, wiping the sweat from his face. He didn't know if anyone had followed him out to the cliffs. He couldn't risk having someone hear Danny scream. He raised his fist and gave Danny a quick hit to the head. Not too hard, but enough to keep him out while he went digging for the ball of lead. He pulled his knife and ran the blade through the lantern flame. After wiping the soot off the blade with a clean piece of bandage, he dribbled some whiskey over it.

Taking a breath, he probed with his fingers to find the shape of the shot beneath the skin, then cut into the muscle. He heard the metallic sound of the knife tip against the pellet and slowly slid the edge of the blade under it. No matter how he tried, it was impossible. He couldn't draw it out without a curved implement. The knife would just continue to cut deeper into Danny's flesh. Niall tossed the knife aside and rummaged in the saddlebag for the salve. He rubbed some of it over his hand as well as a bit of whiskey before wiping them off with the piece of bandage. Then he slowly inserted his longest finger into the hole, crooked the tip of it around the lead pellet and slowly withdrew it. Niall wiped his bloody hands on the soiled bandage and laid the shot on it. Tearing another small piece of clean cloth, he rolled up the shot in it and tucked it into Danny's boot, knowing he would want to keep it as a souvenir. After cleaning his hands once again, Niall poured the rest of the whiskey into the wound. Danny had started coming to and winced loudly from the pain.

"Ye tryin' to kill me?" he yelled.

"Not yet, but I will if you don't quiet down. Hold still!"

Danny passed out again as Niall filled the bleeding cavity with the rest of the salve. He wrapped the remaining bandages over his shoulder and around his chest. Since he had nothing left to fashion a sling, he bound Danny's bent arm to his chest to keep the shoulder stable.

Niall knew that Danny shouldn't be moved, but leaving him alone and helpless until morning was too dangerous. If he laid him over the saddle, Danny would be draining blood all the way back to the campsite. "Now what do I do?" he asked aloud. Without much choice, he gently hoisted Danny astride his own saddle, holding him upright as best he could while he mounted up behind him. He held him in place, carefully navigating through the brush, back to the road. Towing Danny's horse behind him, he hoped that Danny would stay unconscious until they made it back to the campsite.

They were halfway there when Niall heard a whistle and the beat of hooves on the road. He stopped and whistled back as the hoof beats came closer. In the lantern light, he was grateful to see that it was Roark approaching.

"You found him! How is he?"

"He's in rough shape. He's lost a lot of blood."

"Is he gonna live?"

Niall shook his head. "I don't know."

"Let's get 'im back to the camp. Kate's ready for him."

The men rode at a steady, even pace. Even with two lanterns, the road was barely visible.

"What about Jack and his men?" asked Niall.

"They gave up about an hour ago. They're gonna wait 'til morning and head out to do another search. Jack is mad as hell, but he went back to the Shamrock."

Niall laughed. "To drown his sorrows?"

"Looks like," Roark chuckled.

"What about Saraid and the others?"

"Well . . . I was going to wait 'til we got back to tell ye. We had a problem with Seamus." As Roark explained what had gone on, Niall reined in his horse and came to a stop.

"Are the women all right?"

"They're still sittin' around the fire. Little ones were gettin' tired and fallin' asleep on the blanket, so James and Fiona took them back to yer wagon to bed them down. I think Maureen probably did the same with the twins."

"How about Annie?"

Roark shrugged his shoulders. "She was pretty upset and took off. Patrick's looking for her now."

Danny moaned and leaned back against Niall's chest. "He's starting to burn up. I'm sure this jouncing around isn't doing him much good."

"Can't be helped," said Roark. "Riding a bit faster might be smoother."

"You're right, let's go."

***

Annie ran through the campsite, her fear and humiliation choking her breath. Grateful for the fog, she stumbled along the rocky path and through the brush. She needed to hide not only from Jack, but from Patrick. How could she ever face him or his family again? Only hours before, she had been so happy, and now it was all ruined. She cried out with frustration and anger. How could Patrick ever want her again after Seamus had insulted her like that in front of everyone? They would never understand how she felt about Patrick because Seamus had spoken the truth. She was just a whore. The last thing she had seen was Patrick's fist hitting Seamus.

Annie tripped over an outcropping and landed prone on the ground. Not caring that her hands and knees were bleeding, she lay there in the dirt and sobbed, the ache in her chest unbearable.

Through the fog, not far off, she heard Patrick's voice calling her name. She couldn't let him find her. She didn't deserve him. She had to hide. Annie forced herself to her feet and once again ran blindly through the night.

In her haste to get to the sanctuary of her cave, Annie's bare feet slipped on the slick limestone rocks. She tumbled headlong down the uneven slope until her foot caught between two clints. She fell forward and struck her head, near enough to the water to feel it soak the ends of her hair. Her last conscious thought, as her fingers lay beneath the water, was that she would drown.

A few hours later, she awoke groaning from the pain and shivered from the damp air and wet clothing. She gently probed the painful lump on her forehead, her fingers coming away sticky with what she knew must be blood. Annie had no idea how long she had lain there on her back, her hair floating in the water, but she realized she hadn't drowned.

The night had cooled, the fog giving way to a heavy mist that lay over her like a sodden shroud. The only sound echoing in the darkness was that of the waves as they lumbered slowly towards the shore. Even in the dark, she could tell that the tide was well past peak and receding. She'd been lucky. When she tried to sit up, she found that her foot was wedged between the rocks above her.

"Oh God," she cried as she tried to move her imprisoned foot. "Please don' let it be broke!"

Try as she might, with her head below her feet, she could not loosen it. She gritted her teeth and, cursing, managed to pull herself into a sitting position. Using her one good foot, she scooted herself up the hill so that she sat above her trapped foot. Annie sat there panting in the darkness, afraid to call out for help, tears streaming down her cheeks. The painful movements had wedged the foot deeper into the crevasse and she could feel the swelling with her fingers. Shivering, she resigned herself to the dark night, knowing there was nothing she could do until daylight. She prayed that it would be Patrick that found her. A keening wail escaped her lips as she envisioned him, the longing in her heart almost too painful to bear.

"Please, Patrick, please care enough to find me." Sobbing now, she ignored the pain in her arm and reached for the ribbon that held back her hair. Pulling it free, she wrung the water from her long locks and let the weight of it cascade about her back and shoulders, taking blessed relief in what little warmth it provided.

***

Jack paced back and forth in his room behind the bar, imagining all the things he'd like to do to Danny and the rest of those bloody O'Brien men. His stomach was churning and he had a splitting headache. He lifted the bottle of Irish whiskey and downed another slug that burned all the way down to his gut.

Everything he had worked so hard for was quickly slipping through his fingers. Because of his earlier outburst in the tavern, he had put his own life in danger. *Where the hell is the list?* If it got spread around . . . *I have to get out of here!* The suspicions of the clans as to his activities were one thing, but the truth of it—the proof of it—were disastrous. If he waited until morning, he would be seen and watched and no doubt followed. He'd never make it out alive.

There was only one way out and he was loathe to take it. He hadn't spoken to the bitch in years and had no desire to do it now. He'd successfully avoided her when she'd come around for these bloody festivals and that's the way he wanted it to stay. He could threaten her . . . say he would tell everyone that he'd seen her kill Martin. Jack rubbed his forehead. *Damn! Damn it all to hell!* His own mother had caused all this mess! She could bloody well help him to escape. Did she have any idea who he was? Would she even acknowledge him as her son? She would probably make him beg, but he was damned if he would grovel at her feet. If she didn't comply, he would expose her for the crime.

Jack stopped pacing and sank into the chair, tipped the bottle up and tossed down another mouthful of whiskey. His mind was beginning to spin. All he wanted to do was sleep, just rest his eyes for a few minutes.

"Jack?"

He started awake, his heart racing. "What?"

Jimmy stood a bit away from him. "Ye might want to think about gettin' yerself outta here."

Jack shook his head, trying to clear it and to focus his eyes. His stomach knotted as Jimmy's words penetrated his fuzzy brain. The bar was less noisy than before. "What time is it?"

"It's 'bout midnight."

"Any of my men still out there?"

"Nope. They's all left for the night."

Jack rubbed his face with his hands, still trying to get some life back into his dull head. "Who is still out there?"

"That Seamus feller was sittin' there at the end of the bar, but he was nigh on passed out so I tossed 'im out awhile ago. There's a few folks still at the tables, but I don' know any of 'em."

"Grab the notes out of the till and bring them here."

Jimmy did as he was told and returned with a wad of bills. Jack tossed a couple his way. "If anyone comes looking for me, you tell 'em I'm not here."

"What're ye goin' to do?"

"That's none of your bloody business!"

"Hey! I's just askin'!"

"Keep the place open another hour and then close it up."

"What'er ye say, Jack."

Jimmy stomped out of the back room, muttering to himself. He picked up the scattered empty glasses left on the tables, pocketing the coins left there as tips as he wiped up. He patted his other pocket to reassure himself that the extra notes he had kept from the till were still there. *Serves Jack right!*

In the back room, Jack looked around, gathering up the things he wanted to take with him. Most of it was junk he could live without. He rubbed his fingers over the china figurine that he had always admired, but left it. He could buy all the figurines he wanted when he got back to Dublin. He tossed his extra clothes into his satchel. Jack pushed back his chair and folded back the rug, exposing the flat hook that pulled away a small section of the floorboard. He pulled out the metal box hidden there. Jack opened it to reveal the banknotes and gold coins he had been accumulating for some time. He packed the box into his satchel and took one last look around the room. He knew he wouldn't be back. Swearing, he closed the satchel and picked up the lantern. He cracked open the back door, looking for any sign of his enemies, but all he could see was fog. He smiled as he eased his way into the enveloping mist and began walking towards the back of the hotel on the hill. He knew exactly who would help him. The bitch would help him or pay dearly.

Chapter Thirty-Seven

There was an ell of small rooms at the back of the Aran View Hotel that was kept as quarters for the staff. During the festivals, some of the workers would double up together and rent out their rooms to the revelers who could not afford the regular accommodations. The owners turned a blind eye to this practice if the hotel was full and allowed the staff to split the coin amongst themselves.

Jack staggered from one side of the path to the other, his vision blurred, as he made his way to the last door. He took several deep breaths to try to clear his head before he rapped his knuckles hard against the wooden door. After a moment, the door creaked open a few inches and a pair of small eyes peered back at him.

"What do ye want?"

Jack stared back at her with bloodshot eyes. "Hello *Mother*," he said sarcastically.

Roisin's eyes widened with shock. *It wasn't possible! How could Jack be the little one she had abandoned a life time ago?* "I think ye're mistakin' me for someone else."

Jack sneered at her. "No mistake, I assure you. Open the bloody door, damn it!"

Roisin, trying to remember where she had set her shillelagh, attempted to shut the door in his face. Jack was obviously drunk, and there was no telling what he would do next.

"Open this damned door, or you're going to regret it!" He pushed hard against the door and, easily overpowered, she stumbled back into the room.

"What is it ye want from me?" she cried.

"I want you to admit that you're my *mother*!"

She snapped back at him, "Why should I be admittin' such a thing to ye? How is it that ye even be thinkin' this?"

He brought his face close to hers. "I've known for a long time. Years ago, some sot came in to the tavern during a festival. He saw you out there and remembered you and my father and how you left us." He shook his fist at her. "Do you have any idea how that made me feel?"

The old woman laughed in his face. "Sure I've never had a care about how ye might feel! An' even if I did, do ye really think I'd claim the likes of ye as mine? You're despicable!" She drew saliva into a ball in her mouth and spat at him.

Jack writhed with anger as he drew back his hand and slapped her full on the face. She cried out as she crumpled to the floor against his feet, causing him to stumble.

"You bloody whore!" he yelled, wiping the spit from his face. He began to weave awkwardly around the room. Then he spied her shillelagh in the corner and picked it up, the age-old twining briars smooth against his skin. Striking his palm with the lead-filled knob, he came to stand in front of her. "You'll not be laughing much longer, you old bitch."

Stillness filled the air, thick and heavy as the fog outside. Jack stood over her with hate and power in his bloodshot eyes.

Roisin grabbed onto the mattress and took a deep breath before using all her strength to rise awkwardly to her feet. She shuddered and pulled her rainbow shawl more tightly around herself. Though frightened for her life, she raised her chin defiantly. "Ye goin' to kill me now, Jack? Looks to me like ye'll be the one not laughin' a'fore long."

Jack realized that as much as he wanted to take the shillelagh and strike her repeatedly, he needed her help to escape. She owed him that much.

"I saw you kill Martin," he hissed.

"Did ye now?" she asked very quietly. Roisin struggled to remain calm though her heart was pounding wildly.

"I did. I covered for you, too," he added, explaining how he had left Hank's cane at the scene. "I had intended to do the deed myself, but then you came along and did it for me."

Roisin shrugged. She knew it was pointless to deny it. "I been huntin' him down for a long time."

"What did he ever do to you?" he asked.

She debated about telling him the truth. "He hurt a lot of good Irish people . . . me included . . . but 'specially the young boys. I had enough of it."

The years of her life swirled through her mind. All the years she had run from one place to another, begging food and a place to sleep. Sometimes she worked in the flax mills in eastern Ireland, and sometimes she found families who would pay a few coins for help in their homes. She would tend their children and make up stories to lull the little ones to sleep at night, often weaving her own dreams and longings into them. Mostly, she just wandered from place to place, never belonging anywhere. She'd missed having children of her own to love. Later, she was attracted to the fairs and festivals, where she used her storytelling abilities to draw the children of others to her bosom. Their smiles and laughter delighted her.

Anything was better than staying with the husband who had betrayed her, forced her to bed with Martin Clancy for the few coins he'd tossed their way. Since she'd been barren in their marriage, her husband thought it didn't matter. However, a short while after Martin had gone on his way, she found herself with child.

Jack said, "Well, now you're going to help me."

"What is it ye're expectin' me to do?"

He smiled without mirth. "I expect you'll take me away from here, let me hide out in your wagon."

"An' if I don't?"

"Then, when the sheriff gets here in the morning, I'll let him know about Martin. And I'll laugh when they string you up."

"Ye're a real disgrace as a man, Jack."

He bristled. "And you're such a saint? What kind of a mother leaves her own child?"

Roisin struggled only a moment with her shame and then steeled herself. "I had no choice back then. If I'd stayed, I'd have killed ye both."

Jack's face grew livid with rage. "All these years," he cried out, heaving the cane across the room. "You been coming here and gathering all these children around you and telling them stories! Did you ever once tell me a story?"

Roisin snapped back at him. "No—I never did."

"Why did you hate us so much?" Jack was struggling not to weep. "Answer me that!"

Roisin saw the anguish in her son's eyes, yet she felt no compassion. She despised the man he had become. In her bitterness, she took great pleasure in telling him the truth. "Yer da weren't yer father."

Jack screamed at her. "What in bloody hell are you saying?"

Roisin looked at the shock on her son's face; and because of his dealings with Martin, who had stolen her life from her, she was glad for his pain.

She shook her head. "I'll not say more."

Jack grabbed her fleshy shoulders and shook her hard, loosening her coiled braids. "You damn well better tell me right now, you whore!"

Roisin, repulsed by his whiskey breath, screamed her rage back at him. "I weren't no whore! Yer da saw fit to sell me off for Martin

Clancy's pleasure! All for a few bloody coins!"

"That's a lie! Martin had to be much younger than you!"

"Do ye think that mattered to the likes of Martin? Or yer da?"

Jack gave her a withering look. "Do you honestly expect me to believe this?"

"As God is holy, it be the truth!"

Jack pushed her away, and she landed hard on the edge of the bed.

The anger in her voice became a hiss. "Once ye was born, I couldn't stand the sight of ye–or yer da." She remained seated and rubbed her sore shoulders as he staggered about the small room.

Jack settled by the one small window and stared into the darkness. Rivulets of water trickled from the panes like tears. He thought back to his childhood and his father's bitterness, how he'd punished him relentlessly for every small thing. Even now, the memory made a lump rise in his throat. When he could speak again, his voice had lost its bitter edge and grew maudlin. "Do you have any idea how many beatings I took on account of you leaving?"

Roisin shrugged resignedly, turned her back to him, and dragged her meager bag from under the bed. Vestiges of shame and guilt that she thought she'd put behind her long ago fought to overtake the anger she had clung to for so many years. She, too, spoke quietly now. "Sure there's nothin' I can do to change that now, is there?"

Jack shook his head to clear the cruel memories. "Did Martin know I was his son?"

She shrugged. "No reason fer him to. Far as I know, he never come back."

They were both quiet with their own thoughts while Roisin packed her few belongings. She spied her shillelagh where it had landed against the far wall and sighed. She would never be able to reach it before he could grab it from her. *Perhaps if he falls asleep,* "We won't be able to leave 'til the mornin'," she said evenly.

"I don't want to wait that long."

"Well that's just too damned bad, now ain't it?"

"Are you afraid of a little fog?"

"That, an' who's goin' to be hitchin' up the wagon? Sure I ain't doin' it!"

Jack paced the room again, knowing she was right. He couldn't do it himself and chance being seen. Dazed, he walked over to the lone chair and sank heavily into it. Rubbing his temples, he tried to clear his head so he could think. He needed a plan. When he shut his eyes, his head began to spin. He slapped his face trying to get the circulation going in his brain. All he really wanted right now was the oblivion of another drink but what if he passed out and she left without him? Jack spied Roisin's cane where it had landed against the wall. *What if she killed him while he was passed out? I have to stay awake!* He rose and walked unsteadily across the room to pick it up. Once seated again, he held it against the floor with the heavy knob under his palm. He looked at his mother and found her staring back at him.

"Go to sleep," he said quietly. "We'll leave early tomorrow."

Roisin stared back at him. Now that he had her shillelagh, she was trapped. She sighed, feeling the full weight of her long-held secret heavy on her chest. She lay back, drawing the quilt over herself. All these years . . . she'd thought she was free of him.

Now she had to save him if she was going to save herself. Tears coursed slowly down her wrinkled cheeks as she fought blaming herself for the monster Jack had become. Maybe dying would be easier. Exhausted, her eyes fluttered shut as she prayed to her God for forgiveness.

Chapter Thirty-Eight

Patrick wished it would rain. Anything would be better than trying to find Annie in the heavy, oppressive air that hung over Doolin. His leather tunic stuck to his body like a second skin. He pushed his wet hair away from his face and tried to wipe the moisture from his arms but there seemed to be no help for it.

He had seen no glimpse of Annie's bright red hair, and no one he'd asked had seen her. He arrived at the Shamrock to find Jimmy locking the door.

"Jimmy! Have you seen Annie?"

The man shook his head. "I ain't seen her for hours, now. Last I knew she was runnin' out the door."

"Do you know where she lives?"

Jimmy shrugged. "She an' her mam got an old shanty a ways up the coast. Sure it's the first one ye come to."

"Thanks, Jimmy. If you *do* see her, tell her I'm looking for her."

Jimmy nodded and wagged a finger at Patrick. "You be careful out there," he admonished. "Jack's losin' his feckin' mind. If'n he catch 'er, no tellin' what he'll do."

Patrick headed out again. His lantern, providing only a glimmer of light, was of no use in the murky darkness. To continue walking along the edge of the rocks that tumbled down to the sea was too difficult and foolhardy. He wanted to scream. What was he going to do? He stopped and called out her name, praying she would answer him. The only sounds permeating the fog were of the waves hitting the rocks and the faint sounds of music from the distant campsite. Where would she hide? Suddenly it came to him: *The cave!* Why hadn't he thought of that right away? Patrick's heart was pounding with hope but as he peered into the fog, he knew that he had no frame of reference to find it in the dark. Disheartened, Patrick turned around and headed back towards the camp, using the distant music as his guide. He prayed she would be safe until morning when he would search for her again. He wasn't going to leave Doolin without knowing that she was out of harm's way. Maybe he could persuade her to come back home with him.

His little house was better than most but not really a home for a family. Did he want a family with Annie as his wife? He stopped and closed his eyes, trying to picture it. Patrick sighed and realized that he had never shared any part of his life with anyone but his family. He was used to being alone. He shook his head, finding no answer. Patrick sighed, knowing that his mother would probably never accept Annie. Nor would John. Maybe he would talk to Niall about it when he got back.

As he approached their wagons, he saw little activity around the caravans. John was alone, building a small fire, a pile of bloody bandages at his feet.

"What's going on?" asked Patrick.

"Patrick! Thank God you're back. Danny's a mess."

"Where is he now?"

"He's in mother's caravan. I'm trying to get rid of these," he said, pointing to the bandages.

Patrick squatted down and began feeding pieces into the fire. He quickly averted his face from the stench as the bloody cloths ignited and spewed rancid fumes into the air. "Is he going to make it?"

John shrugged, tossing another piece of bandage into the flames. "I don't know. He's lost a lot of blood. If he makes it through the night, I'll be more hopeful. We'll take him to Doc O'Hickey in Ennis on the way home."

"And Hank?"

"He's in there too," John said, pointing to the caravan.

Patrick chuckled. "And how is mother doing?"

John shook his head. "She's an amazement! She seems no worse off from the spell she had. She's got the two of them under a quilt and she's planning to stay awake tonight, to keep an eye on Danny. I told her I'd do it, but you know how she is."

Patrick nodded. "That I do." He looked around and could just make out James and Fiona, asleep atop their bedrolls under Niall's wagon. He pointed to them and asked, "Are Liam and Bridget inside the wagon?"

John looked over to the wagon and nodded.

"Where are the others?"

John gestured towards the meadow. "Niall and Roark went to check on Saraid and Maureen before heading over to the meeting. They're late, but Niall set it up, so he has to be there in case of any disagreements. We were all supposed to meet up earlier, but things got out of hand."

Patrick sighed. "Niall has taken on quite a lot. There's bound to be some ruffled feathers."

"Isn't that the truth!"

John looked at Patrick's face in the firelight and saw tension in his usually calm visage.

"Where have you been, Patrick? Are you all right?"

Patrick picked up a small pebble and tossed it into the darkness. "I've been looking for Annie. She ran off after Seamus laid into her. Where is he, anyway? I could kill that bastard!"

John nodded his head in agreement. "He's a real pisser, he is. They took him back to his wagon so he could sleep it off. He's going to use that list against Annie to get a job out of us. Molly's mortified, but she's going to stick by him."

"He may end up dead for it." Patrick closed his eyes. "Annie may have saved our necks with that list. It took a lot of courage to get it to us."

John sat back on the ground and wiped the sweat from his face with his bandana. "I agree with you." It wasn't often that he and Patrick opened up to each other. "So you and Annie got together?" he asked stiffly.

Patrick sensed John's disapproval but couldn't keep the smile off his face.

"I take it you enjoyed yourself."

Patrick nodded and stared into the fire. "It was a whole lot different than I thought it would be. I was thinking it would be about me just feeling her tits and poking at her." Patrick felt a deep clutch in his chest and bowed his head as the memory of her washed over him again. How wrong he had been! He thought about her patience, her joy and her fury. He thought about how soft and wet she'd been around him and on his fingers, how coaxing, how demanding and, oh, so accepting of him. Even now, he was aroused just thinking about her.

John punched his arm. "Hey boyo, come back! You're adrift. Has she tangled up your mind?"

Patrick felt the flush creeping up his neck and got to his feet. "Yeah, she has." He stared through the foggy darkness, discouraged that he hadn't found her.

When John said nothing more, Patrick rose to his feet. "I'm going to head over to find Niall and see what's going on with the meeting."

"Be careful," John whispered into the fog.

***

John poked at the fire to burn off any remnants of the bandages. He thought about Patrick and Annie . . . and Niall and Saraid. He didn't usually think about it much, but he realized in that moment that he was envious.

He really hated working the farm. Being dirty and sweaty and tired all the time was taking its toll. His joints ached on rainy days. The thought of doing it for the rest of his life, without respite, was a cross he didn't want to bear. He was only thirty-three, but he'd already begun to feel like an old man.

They all worked so hard every day that there wasn't really much time left over to want to do anything but sleep. Or was that an excuse not to think about a better life? He had the companionship of the family for meals and sometimes the dancing afterwards.

The fire was just about out, and John stared transfixed at the embers. The loneliness he felt in that moment surprised him. He'd never met a woman that he cared about being with, except to relieve himself on occasion. He knew that unless he left the farm and went off to a city, his prospects were slim for finding a different kind of life or a proper mate to share it with. Did he want to leave County Clare? He knew that his mother had been giving some thought to going back to Dublin. Now that his father was gone, she found neither comfort nor joy in her children or her grandchildren. But leave her home? He vowed to be more of a comfort to her while she struggled through her pain.

What would he do if he left his home? He would love to be a teacher but that was not possible—not unless he renounced his faith. Could he do that? His father would turn over in his grave.

It seemed that the only thing that truly gave him pleasure was his books. His mother had been only too eager to encourage him to read and cherish the wagon full of books that she'd brought with her from Dublin. Books of fiction, poetry, Greek and Latin histories, biographies, books on philosophy and the Anglo Bible. He had loved all of them.

His father had bellowed over the Bible and refused to allow it into the house. He produced his own Catholic version, insisting that he use that instead. His mother had argued for days until he finally tired of it and agreed to a compromise. She could keep hers, but he never wanted to see it again. She packed it away in her trunk, but everyone surmised that his mother read it when she was alone.

His mother had been thrilled when he showed her the first clumsy poem that he had written himself. His brothers had laughed at him, but his mother had always encouraged his literary pursuits. His father hadn't berated him, but neither had he praised his efforts. He'd merely nodded and patted his shoulder before walking back to the fields.

When the scribe had come to record the birth of Fiona in his big neatly written tome, John had showed him his own journal. In it were his recordings of odd bits of information about the family and the land. The man had been impressed, and his mother was so proud of him.

Eventually, his father saw the use of his skills and requested that he keep a proper year-to-year journal of farm information: climate, crops, yields, profits, and taxes paid. John had jumped at the chance to please the man. His mother helped him to set up the books, and he took great pleasure in keeping the records. Over the past years, the journal came to be referred to many times by his father and his brothers when referencing rainfall, last frosts, early snows, crop successes and failures, breeding cycles, and head counts of the livestock. He realized that he had found his niche when the others would consult with him before ordering seed or making decisions about the herds.

Still, he ached for something more. Something, *someone*. Sighing, he decided to make use of his time as he kept watch over his mother's caravan. He rekindled the fire and turned up the lantern to have more light before retrieving his wooden box from under the wagon seat. Opening the hinged cover, he took out his journal, quill and ink, and prepared to write about some of what had happened over this long weekend.

Using the box as a desk, he scanned the pages he'd written just before leaving the farm. His mother's recollections of her early life in Dublin made him admire his father all the more. John wondered if, deep down, his mother had regretted her choice. He knew that she had suffered disappointments. Clare was no match for the well-populated, genteel society of Dublin, but overall, he thought she and his father had been happy.

He smiled recalling the story that his father had shared so many times about traveling to Dublin with *his* father, Charles. Because there was a payment dispute over their wagons filled with flax, James had, with a twist of fate, met Kate, and his life had never been the same.

His father had repeated events and conversations so many times that it was easy to write it down like it was a story of its own. He'd also asked Paddy and his mother to fill in some of the tale. He knew it by heart. He flipped back through the pages until he found the passages he was looking for.

It made him chuckle every time he read it. Perhaps someday, Niall's children would read it and understand all that had really happened in their family years before they were ever born.

Chapter Thirty-Nine

Journal Entry
South of Killaloe
1738

James heard his father, Charles, shout across the stubble of the flax field. "That's it for me!"

He watched his father walk the short distance down the dirt path to the river Shannon, knowing from his hitching gait that pain was grumbling through his spine.

The back-breaking job of pulling up the four-foot plants by the roots, and tying them into stooks, had been done several weeks before. The bundles had been laid out over the field for close to a month for retting. Each day, the damp underside was turned over to bake in the sun. As the process broke down the outer straw-like husks, the cores would rot, making for easier removal of the long, silky fibers.

Moments later, he and Paddy, the new hire, joined him by the river. He set his hand against his father's shoulder. "Well, Da, I think that's the last of it."

Charles nodded silently. He removed the sweat-sodden rag from around his neck and dunked it into the cold wet of the river. He lay it, dripping, against his face. After a moment, he dunked it again and, draping it around his neck, eased his lean body down onto a wide stump and stretched out his legs. As he watched the southerly flow of the river, he felt the tension ease *from his body.*

Each year when the bundles were ready, they were taken to the factories for the making of linen. The only nearby factory had closed its doors earlier that year, meaning that the crop would need to be hauled all the way to Dublin. From there, it would be shipped to the weavers in Northern Ireland or sent to the thread and twine company on the western edge of Dublin itself.

Charles shook his head. "If I'd known about the factory closing sooner, I wouldn't have bothered planting the crop." Even though the round trip to Dublin with the heavy wagons would be arduous and take most of a week, he was too stubborn to give up the profit on his crop.

Charles looked out over the nearly barren verge, his eyes clouded with sadness. He sighed as he rolled up his shirtsleeves, revealing forearms tight with sinew. "The last of it, truly. When we return from hauling this crop to Dublin, we'll set this land to pasture and fill it with cattle."

Paddy made the sign of the cross. "Thank God for that!" He dunked his hands into the river to cool the burning blisters that were bleeding in places. "I don't think I could manage another day of this."

James laughed. He stared at the exhausted young man who had never done a lick of physical labor before coming to stay with them. "We'll toughen you up yet, Priest!"

Paddy was fresh to Ireland from a seminary in France. The O'Brien estate was secluded enough for Paddy to be disguised as a hired man during the week and still be able to secretly practice his vocation to the townspeople on Sundays, or when needed. The loyal Papists, grateful to have a man of the cloth nearby, would keep his secret.

Paddy looked back to where the heavily laden wagons were lined up, ready to be hitched up to horses at first light. "Flax has to be the ugliest plant I've ever seen."

"Ahh," said Charles, his brogue thick. "Perhaps now, but you should see it in the springtime. Sure the entire field is covered with masses of blue flowers. T'is enough to make a man believe that the sky had come down to sit on the ground. Nothing prettier in the entire world."

Paddy looked at the plants that were still standing along the far edge of the field. "Why didn't we cut down the rest?"

James looked across the field. "We'll harvest those in a few weeks when the seed pods turn yellow. Some of the pods will be used to make linseed oil and some to make medicine. They makes a great poultice for fever or aching joints."

Just before dawn, as the eastern sky lightened to gray, Charles led the caravan of horse-drawn wagons north along the river to Killaloe. Three of the long wagons were weighed down by bundles of flax that were piled high and hung over the sides almost to the road. The fourth wagon, driven by James and Paddy, held their bedrolls and the provisions to hold the men over for the three-day trek to Dublin and back.

Damp river mist hung over them, muffling the sounds of the heavy, metal wheels turning over the rutted road. The mist had begun to evaporate as they arrived in Killaloe, but the town was still quiet.

Signs of life came from the open door of the bake shop, where the yeasty smell of warm bread drifted out to them. The only other activity came from the forge, where the smithy was already pounding a red-hot piece of iron against his anvil. Fishing boats were bobbing in the river, awaiting the fishermen to fire their engines and head downstream to the estuary for salmon.

Charles reined in his horses and steered his wagon to the side of the road. "I'm hungry!"

They made a quick stop at the bake shop and stood near the old, much-repaired wooden bridge, debating its strength to carry them to Ballina on the other side. From there, they would head northeast over old trade routes until they reached Dublin.

Deciding to err on the side of caution, they crossed one wagon at a time. As they waited their turn, James nudged Paddy as he pointed to the hill behind the town. "Too bad for the fog. I could show you Kincora."

"Kincora?" asked Paddy.

"It's nothing but ruins now, but it's where Brian Boru had his palace."

Paddy nodded, knowing some of the history of the O'Brien family. "I'm sorry to miss it."

Weary and aching, the men finally reached their destination in the early afternoon of the third day. They were relieved and happy not to have met with any ill circumstances along the way. They spent hours in a long line of wagons at the warehouse on St. Thomas Street until it was their turn to unload their crop.

Charles, in no mood for nonsense, bickered with the foreman about the quality of the crop and what they wanted to pay him. "This is a prime crop," he said, his voice rising. "Every bit of it!"

He yanked a stalk from one of the bundles and cutting away the husk from the shaft, peeled back the root. He laid the silky strands over his fingers and held them in the face of the foreman to show how they glistened pale yellow-white, clean from end to end.

The foreman stared at Charles and his men with hard eyes, taking in their soiled clothing and disheveled appearance. Thinking that they were just another bunch of ignorant farmers, he determined to pay only the price set by George Langdon, the owner of the warehouse. "All right, then," he said. He made out a new invoice and handed it to Charles with a smirk.

Charles looked at the invoice, written in Latin, and rage filled him. He grabbed the foreman by his shirt and pulled him close. "You still think you can cheat me!" he roared. "You've written off half the amount that I've brought! Do you think I can't read, man! Doesn't matter if it's Latin, English or Gaelic! I can read as well as you! Probably better!"

The foreman was taken aback. Charles had indeed surprised him with both his nerve and his intellect. "You'll have to take it up with Mr. Langdon," he sputtered, as James pulled his father away from the man.

James, at twenty-eight, was a man in his own right. Taller and heavier with muscle than both his father and the foreman, he stepped between them and scowled down at the foreman. "And where might I find this Mr. Langdon?"

The paunchy old man looked James over and then took a step back. With James's piercing blue eyes and clenched jaw, he saw a confident man who was not intimidated by the likes of himself. He had no desire to do battle with him. "His office is over on the Weavers Square," he stammered.

James told his father to stay with the wagons, that he would find Mr. Langdon. "If you go, you'll lose that temper of yours and we'll get nothing."

Charles sputtered in frustration but, too tired to argue further, agreed to let James settle the dispute. After they pulled their wagons to the side, making room for those behind them, James unhitched one of the horses to ride bareback into the city.

* * *

Having never been to Dublin, James was flummoxed by the narrow, winding streets and the sheer number of people in the slums on the north and west side of the River Liffey. This is where the Catholic Irish of the city had been banished to live. The streets, filled with falling-down tenements, beggars in rags, and people fighting over space, suffocated him. No green hills here, he thought, marveling that people could breathe in such squalor and stench. Once on the other side of the river, it was like emerging into another world altogether.

There were wide streets with tall, stately homes abutting the quays of the river, as well as businesses, churches and government buildings. Parks, music halls and a new hospital gave credence to the rumored wealth of the Anglicans who had taken over the city. There was new construction going on everywhere, old buildings being torn down to make way for the new. Glass panes adorned the windows and street lamps lined the streets.

Hackneyed coaches and smaller private carriages sped down the streets transporting well-dressed travelers about the city, while walkers crowded the promenades along the shops. The men wore well-fitted waistcoats with colorful ascots and snug britches, their legs covered by silk stockings and feet shod in low-heeled shoes. Some wore their hair piled high and powdered or under flowing white wigs. Most of the younger men wore their hair tied sleekly back at the nape.

Clusters of women, protecting their complexions with colorful parasols, went shop to shop as they chattered amongst themselves. They wore long dresses with ribboned flounces and ruffles coming from their sleeves, jeweled chokers at their throats and fancy hats on their upswept hair.

James had never seen anything like it. He felt like he had entered a dream world far removed from the reality of County Clare. As he rode slowly past the Marsh Library, trying to read the shop signs, a small Ringsend carriage flew past him, almost colliding with his horse.

James shouted as his mare reared and he hung on tightly to the horse's mane so as not to be thrown. "What the bloody hell do you think you're doing!" His temper flared and he set out to chase after the carriage until he saw it stop in front of a building in the next block. The signage above read 'Langdon Shipping and Weaving'. He shook his head at the irony of it.

Pulling up on the reins, he watched as a tall, young woman, obviously in full temper, jumped without effort from the carriage, not bothering to smooth down the lacy bonnet that had blown askew on her head.

Unlike most of the women on the street, her light brown hair was a short mop of curls, softly framing her stern face. She yanked down the front of her snug-fitting red jacket and tugged at her cuffs before gathering up her navy skirt and petticoats. She stomped into the office building, her floral parasol jutting out from her free hand.

James chuckled, realizing that his heart was beating fast in his chest. He ran his hand over the mare's head. "That girl's got spunk, whoever she is! I don't envy whoever is going to get the tail end of all that temper!"

He dismounted and secured his horse to the hitching post. I think I'd like to see this battle.

He listened to the young woman shouting at someone inside the building and decided to wait until the noise abated before entering.

Chapter Forty

Journal Entry
Dublin
1738

Kate accosted her brother. "Where is father?"

Peter replied condescendingly. "Father had to step out. What-ever is the matter?"

She stamped her foot, her voice rising with her displeasure. "I can't believe that he is giving the account keeping to you!"

"Accounting is no job for a woman. You need only concern yourself with your tea parties and dances. Make mother and father happy by finding yourself a husband and being a proper young woman."

Kate's face flushed hotly. "How dare you! I did better with mathematics than you did!"

Peter shook his head. "But it is I who went to Trinity College, not you."

She banged her hand against his desk. "I have just as much education as you*!"*

Peter laughed in her face. "Being tutored at home is hardly worth the same!"

Women were not yet allowed to attend the college. Undeterred, Kate had argued with her parents for months until they gave in and hired a retired professor to tutor her at home. She had a love of learning that far outweighed her desire for social pursuits and a mind that was clearly astute at mathematics. She thought it only natural that she would be the family accountant and was clearly furious to be refused her dream.

"You're a pompous ass!" she yelled as she turned on her heel and stomped toward the door.

At that moment, James opened the door and she crashed into him in an angry huff.

She fell back and landed on her backside at his feet, her skirts flying above her knees, her face florid with anger and embarrassment.

James couldn't hold back the sudden laughter that sprang from him as he reached a hand down to assist her to her feet. He couldn't help but notice the slim ankles and gently curving calves of the long legs beneath her silk stockings. That and the brief sight of lace-ruffled petticoats caused a stirring in his loins before she hurried to pull down her skirt.

"Well now," he chortled, his eyes slowly taking in the rest of her. "Aren't you a lovely sight for tired eyes?"

Kate's eyes narrowed to slits as the lilt of his brogue washed over her. She quickly took in the shaggy-haired stranger with his untrimmed beard. He had broad shoulders and long muscular legs that were clad in soiled shabby britches. It was more than obvious to her nose that he hadn't bathed recently.

"You'd do well not to laugh at me!" she sneered. She slapped his hand away and quickly sprang to her feet, brushing the dust and wrinkles from her skirt. Her golden brown eyes were fierce with indignation.

"Dare indeed," James said as he reached out and straightened her bonnet and tried without success to still the rapid beating of his heart. Neither could he wipe the silly grin from his face. His eyes sparkled with amusement when, without a second thought, he blurted out, "Would you be free for a bit of lunch?"

Kate's years of disciplined breeding abandoned her, and a quick intake of breath was followed by an expletive uttered under her breath. She turned icy eyes towards him. "Please remove yourself from this doorway at once," she hissed, "so that I may pass through!"

James bowed low and swept his hand toward the street. "As you wish, fair lady," he said, allowing her to pass by him. "And you be having a lovely day, now." He stood there chuckling and watched her storm across the busy street and into the park that was fenced in by a low stone wall.

He was still grinning as he walked to the front desk with the invoice papers in his hand. The young man seated there had an uncanny resemblance to the young woman who had just stormed through the front door. James boldly asked him if he was related to her.

The man took in James's disheveled appearance and wrinkled his nose at the odor emanating from him. In contrast, Peter Langdon was freshly scrubbed and clean shaven, his hair tied neatly back from his face. He was impeccably attired; brass buttons gleaming against his well-fitting black waistcoat, his burgundy and gray striped ascot knotted just so. "Why do you want to know?" he asked in a bored tone.

"Well," James said, "that lovely lass resembles you more than a bit. I'm thinking that I might be asking her to join me for a bit of tea."

"You must be daft," responded Peter with a snort.

"And just why would you be assuming such a thing?" asked James, his brow furrowed in silent insult. He was not easily discouraged from pursuing what he desired.

"Look, Mr. O'Brien, is it?" Peter looked at the name on the invoice that he took from James's hand. "I think you're in a little over your head here."

James squared his shoulders and raised one eyebrow. "Is that so?" *he asked quietly.* "You don't even know me."

Peter stared at him with undisguised distaste. "First of all, from the stink of you, you obviously need a bath. Second of all, my sister doesn't socialize with common Irish farmers beneath her station."

James grinned in spite of himself. "There's nothing to be done for the sweat that comes from an honest day's work or a long day's ride." *He stared at the slender, well-groomed man of about his own age and shrugged. He had probably never gotten his hands dirty in his entire life.*

Peter bristled at James for his insolence. "Let's get this business taken care of so you can be on your way."

"About that," *James said quietly.* "I'm looking for a Mr. Langdon. I assume that would be your father."

"My father had a meeting and will be gone for a few hours. I'm in charge so you can do whatever business you have with me."

James eyed the man, debating with himself. He really didn't want to wait. "Your man at the warehouse tried to pull a fast one on us but my father caught him out. He tried to pay us less than the proper rate. When challenged, he raised the rate but then wrote that we had two wagons when, in fact, we came with three. Here are both invoices, so anyone can plainly see."

"You can read?"

James chuckled to hide his temper which was simmering close to a boil. "Four languages. And believe it or not, I can also write. So if there's nothing else, how about if you pay me the proper amount and I can leave this place."

Peter begrudgingly read the invoices and decided to just pay him and be done with it. He counted out the banknotes and waved him off, ending the transaction.

James stood there and counted out every note to be sure the amount was correct. He doffed his cap and said, "Thank you kindly. It was a pleasure doing business with you."

As James reached the door, he turned to face the man again. "Just so you know, there are those of us across these many green hills and fields of Ireland that have more lineage to kings than all you Anglicans combined . . . even if we do grow potatoes."

James was proud of his heritage. His family had leather-bound volumes proving their ancestry all the way back to Brian Boru, the illustrious High King of Ireland. Granted, they were a few relations away from the direct line, but related none the less. He bowed to no one.

With that, James quietly closed the door and stepped into the busy cobbled street. The late afternoon sun was quite warm and there wasn't much of a breeze stirring between the crowded buildings.

He wiped the sweat from his brow with his sleeve and took a sniff at himself. *Well, I am a bit ripe at that!* Looking up and down the street, he spied a barber shop in the next block. He tied his horse to a post and entered the two-chair establishment. He began to read the slate on the wall that listed the services offered and was pleased to note that they provided a room for bathing. Reserving a space for an hour later, he sped back to his father to turn over the money and to ask for his wages.

When James explained why he wanted to stay in Dublin for a few hours, his father lost his temper and accused him of wasting his time and his well-earned money. James would not be denied, and Charles finally agreed to let him keep the one horse, with a promise to catch up with them on the road later.

James quickly set out to find a shop to buy some new clothing, even though it would probably empty out his pocket. He didn't care. Freshly bathed, shaved, and his dark hair neatly tied back, he made a striking figure. He was determined to meet up with the enchanting *young woman again. He knew that if he presented himself properly, he could charm her into at least sharing a pot of tea. He just prayed she was still in the park.*

As his good luck would have it, she was there, sitting on a bench reading a small book of verse. When he softly called her name, she looked up. She didn't recognize him . . . but she was charmed, though she struggled mightily against the fluttering in her heart. A bit later, James smiled to himself as they shared a pot of tea. He became determined to woo this woman until she agreed to marry him.

It took more than two years of chiding from his brothers and friends; two years of arguing with his father . . . and hers. For those two years, he made monthly treks to Dublin, sometimes being refused at her door. For two years, he stubbornly added to the cottage adjacent to the main house, stone by stone, to build her a proper home, never accepting that he could not win her heart. For two years he took no for an answer, but he never once gave up on his heart's desire.

In the end, it wasn't the promises James O'Brien made of undying love and adoration, nor the whimsical poetry uttered with his lilting brogue, that won her. It wasn't the flowers, nor his capricious laughter. Neither was it the promise of the rolling hills of County Clare that swept Kate off her feet. Rather, it was the famine of 1741 that struck Dublin hard and the resulting bread lines, riots, starvation and disease that engulfed the city.

James finally convinced the Langdons that to marry him was less dangerous than the uncertainty and fear that threatened Kate's life every day in Dublin.

Chapter Forty-One

It was past midnight when Patrick finally joined Niall, Roark and the other men at the secluded area on the outskirts of Doolin. The fog served to muffle their voices and distort the location of the gathering. Heavy mist had turned to fine drizzle, suffused with the scent of thyme that lay crushed in the wild growth beneath their feet.

In the spring, Niall had convinced Connor O'Brien that this meeting could be the start of something positive for the Catholic Irish. The Anglo Stamp Act had forced an additional tax burden on any exports from Ireland, ruining the chance of solvency for many of them.

Catholic clan leaders, rebels, and disgruntled Protestant Irishmen of Parliament from all the counties of Ireland had been notified by runners, sent by Niall. The message they carried was to meet in Doolin for the festival on the last weekend in July. There were calls for unity among the arguing factions to clarify their complaints and to try to find agreement on how best to handle them.

They were all tired, anxious about being discovered by Jack and the armed constables that the Irish referred to as Charlies. After the altercation at the Shamrock, they'd all realized that some of the constables had disguised themselves as regular members of the visiting clans and had quietly infiltrated the taverns and campsites. The constables had kept their eyes and ears open for any information that might be gleaned from a drunken slip of the tongue or outright traitorous act.

Though Niall had done much of the work to bring this meeting about, he deferred to Connor to run it.

Connor begged them all to quiet down. Like many of the Irish landowners, he had converted early on to the Anglican church to save his thousands of acres of land from English confiscation. Even so, he was loyal to the Catholic cause. His forebears had become the Earls of Thomand and, through the generations, they controlled most of the southeast of Clare; a total of over 85,000 acres. When, in the previous year, the eighth and last of the O'Brien earls had died without an heir, the land was passed to other earldoms. Connor held lease to over 3,000 acres of this land and was overseer of Niall's family's holdings.

"As I see it," said Connor, "the biggest problem is that these new owners don't even live here. They've gone back to England or on to Germany and France to enrich their holdings, leaving people like me to collect the rents and taxes. When the tenants can no longer pay the higher fees I'm supposed to evict them! It's a dirty trick to get more pasture land for all the cattle they're bringing in." He paused, then shook his head, his sadness apparent on his lined face. "I've done what I can to help. In many instances, I've been paying their tithes from my own coffers. It has come to be a burden that I can no longer afford to carry. Though it saddens me, after the harvest, I will have no choice but to carry out the evictions."

Ryan Regan, from county Roscommon, was mad as hell. "That's what they did to me and all of us Catholic farmers up north! They took all my land for pasture and put up bloody stone walls and fences to keep us out! They left me with just an acre that I have to pay for, and I'm supposed to feed my family with that!"

Connor explained to them that since Britain had eased the bans on the exportation of cattle, more and more of the farming acreage was being turned over to grazing land. The thousands of acres of flax that used to be grown on these acres to supply the linen mills were now useless, as trade with Europe and the American colonies was banned. The only market open to them was England, who now taxed them so highly that no profit remained.

"They're leavin' us with nothin' at all!" cried another of the men.

"They done the same to us in Limerick!" cried out James Shaughnesey, a young man in his late teens. His father had allowed him to come with him to the meeting, warning him not to unleash his anger. "How's folks supposed to feed their families when they got no tillage? There's hundreds of folks already wanderin' around starvin' with just the clothes on their backs!" His father gave him a look, but the young man was determined to share his views.

Another young man cried out. "They don't even have homes anymore! They're all holed up in mud hovels along the roads!"

Connor wiped the drizzle from his face and called for silence, reminding them in a low voice about the possible dangers afoot. "There are a few Anglo-Irish among us who are trying to help us through the Irish Parliament."

"Bah," scoffed Henry Brennan from county Galway. "How's a bunch of Anglos goin' to help the Catholics?"

Roark sneered and asked, "Are you talkin' about that fool, Henry Flood?"

Several men echoed his revulsion. Flood, a well known Protestant orator and statesman for county Kilkenny, was well-bred and highly educated. He had an inordinate knowledge of Irish history and had worked long and hard to develop a united Irish front in the Irish House of Commons. Independent Irish rule, as well as better trade and economic conditions for Ireland, were his goals. A corrupt Parliament became increasingly worried that he might succeed.

"Yeah," Patrick piped up. "He was fine until the Brits got nervous and gave him a paying job with the Privy Council to shut him up."

Connor sighed. "He really felt that he could work for the betterment of all of us from the inside. He wants better treatment for us, but he still thinks we need the English protection against outside invaders."

Niall chuckled. "And how did that work out?"

"We need to take matters into our own hands!" cried a voice from the back of the crowd. "We need to tear down those damn walls and give 'em our own demands!"

Niall turned his head toward the sound of the familiar voice and saw that Tommy Callahan and his brother were huddled with the other young men.

Shaughnesey stood with several of his young friends. "Ye're right! We ain't takin' it no more! Come to Limerick! We got a gang of us ready to make 'em pay."

Shaughnesey's father wacked his son on the head. "You keep still! Violence will win you naught!"

Willie piped up. "Are ye talkin' about the Whiteboys? What is it you're meanin' to accomplish?"

"We're plannin' to wreck their fences and ruin the grazin' land," replied another young voice. "Kill some of them cattle, too!"

One by one, more young voices joined in, all talking at once. Niall gazed at the younger men in the group, their frustration festering on their faces like mold on rancid cheese. He could see no hope in their eyes and was sorry for it. He could sense that they were fighting for their manhood as well as their land.

"We're postin' our demands, too! They gotta stop the evictions and lower the tithes on what little land we got left."

"Sure, an' they got to leave our priests alone, too! They get caught sayin' Mass, they kill 'em where they be standin'!"

"T'is a sad time when our priests have to hide in gullies an' the woods, an' sleep in holes in the ground!"

Roark scoffed at some of the more reckless of them. "What happens when you're recognized and strung up?"

Shaughnessy, ignoring his father, faced Roark and the others.

"They won't catch us! We're too fast. We all dress the same in big white shirts and hide our faces so they can't pick us out."

"Keep your voices down!" Connor hissed. All this noise would get them caught for sure if anyone was nearby. He looked around the crowd, hoping the lookouts would be able to warn them before they were discovered. "There are other ways to achieve our goals. I've brought someone here tonight who thinks we can accomplish more for ourselves without violence. His name is Henry Grattan. I'd like you to at least give him a listen." He motioned for the young man to come forward.

Henry gazed out at the unsmiling crowd. "I know that most of you have never heard of me, so I will firstly tell you a bit about myself." For a young man of twenty-nine, he had a confident bearing and a compelling resonance to his voice as he addressed the crowd. "Briefly, I was born in Dublin and educated at Trinity College. I was to go into the practice of law, but my interests became drawn to the inequities of the Irish people and your struggles against England. I have just been sponsored by Lord Charlemont to enter the Irish Parliament."

The crowd began to grumble. One of them cried out. "You're just another bloody Protestant out to get us!"

Grattan allowed them to express their objections for a moment before raising his voice.

"Listen to me!" When the crowd quieted some, he began, once again, to speak. "Not all Protestants are lovers of what England is doing to Ireland. I am, first and foremost, an Irishman. I was born here! I am working for the National Irish Party, not just to liberate the great numbers of Catholics, but to free our Irish Parliament of the chains of bondage to England."

Niall, liking the presence of the man, could only hope that he would be successful. "I'm not sure," he said, "that England is going to pay you much mind."

Grattan smiled. "I think you're wrong. And here is why. I don't know how many of you realize that England is in a battle, right now, with the colonies in America. The people there have risen up and decided that they aren't going to let England hold sway over them any longer. The colonies have joined together and they are fighting to be a free country in their own right. England has had to send a great many ships filled with thousands of soldiers to fight the rebellion there. The British are in the precarious position now of not having enough troops left here to wage a proper battle with Ireland, nor the monies to pay them. This is why they are pushing for more tax revenue."

"A few years ago," Grattan continued, "we had a man from the colonies visit Dublin, Benjamin Franklin was his name. He was well received at Parliament and wished to create an alliance with us against our common persecutor. As he travelled around parts of Ireland and Scotland, he was appalled at the conditions many of you are living in under the rule of rich landowners and noblemen. He said that they were the worst he had seen anywhere in his travels and far more wretched than any free man in the colonies had known. It was his thought that a united front against England might benefit us both."

Connor interrupted Grattan to add, "Upon Franklin's plea for help, thousands of Catholic Irishmen left Ireland to do battle alongside the American colonists and many Scotch-Irish Protestants from Ulster also left to fight with the British."

Patrick's mind kept drifting away from the conversation. He stared into the fog and conjured up Annie's face and her deeply dimpled smile. All he wanted right now was to be joined with her, to feel her soft skin against his body. He groaned as a sharp ache ran through him.

Niall nudged him. "What is it?" he whispered.

Patrick chuckled and just shook his head.

Niall had many questions for Grattan. "How do we know that they will actually do battle against the British?"

Grattan smiled. "They already have! On April 19th of this year, there were battles at Lexington and Concord in Massachusetts. They're calling it *'the shot heard 'round the world'*."

The men grew quiet with interest, anxious to hear more.

This caught Patrick's attention. He asked, "How did it start?"

"It seems that the British General, Gage, had been warned that the colonists were planning a revolt and had accumulated a large cache of weapons in Concord. He made plans to send Lieutenant Colonel Smith and Major Pitcairn with eight hundred men to attack, confiscate, and destroy the weapons. However, Paul Revere, one of the Sons of Liberty, set out on horseback to warn the colonists that the British were on their way. Before long, church bells were ringing, cannon and muskets were fired to spread the alarm. By the time the British soldiers arrived at Lexington, the patriots, only seventy men strong under Captain Jonas Parker, were ready for them and refused to stand down. Major Pitcairn ordered his men to shoot and the battle began."

Excitement rose among them. One of the skeptical men asked, "Did the colonists win?"

"No, sadly, they did not. A great number of them were slaughtered and many more wounded, but it only incited their thirst for freedom. When the British moved on to Concord, they found themselves attacked on all sides. The Minute-Men, as they are called, streamed out of the woods and trees and across fields and beat them back all along the road to Charlestown. By the time the battle was over, the British had lost more men than the Americans and the real war had begun."

"What about the Irish?"

"The Irish are fighting on both sides of the war, but have no fear of retaliation from the colonists. They are most grateful to us and they are on our side!" Grattan reached into the breast pocket of his waistcoat and withdrew a folded piece of parchment. He held it up. "I have here a letter, recently penned by Mr. Franklin himself, on behalf of the Continental Congress in America, acknowledging our Irish Parliament as being separate from the English and their gratitude for our support. I would like to read it to you."

The crowd, rapt now, was eager to hear that they were not alone in their struggles.

> *"Your Parliament had done us no wrong. You had ever been friendly to the rights of mankind; and we acknowledge with pleasure and gratitude, that your nation has produced patriots, who have nobly distinguished themselves in the cause of humanity and America. Accept our most grateful acknowledgments for the friendly disposition you have always shown us. We know that you are not without grievances. . . . In the rich pastures of Ireland many hungry parricides have fed, and grown strong to labor in its destruction. We hope the patient abiding of the meek may not always be forgotten: and God grant that the iniquitous schemes of extirpating liberty by the British Empire may soon be defeated."*

The words hovered over them like the fog. A fragile strand of hope began to weave through their minds, uniting their hearts, giving way to emotional murmurs throughout the crowd. Pride became as tangible as the drizzle soaking their skin, igniting a thirst for the where-with-all to accomplish the same freedom for themselves.

Niall asked, "So what is it that you're asking of us?"

Grattan responded quietly. "It is my hope that you will let us do our work in the Parliament to right things without bloodshed."

Young Shaughnessy broke the spell, speaking for the dissenting lads. "I still think we need to take up arms and fight a proper battle against the Brits."

A sharp whistle pierced the night. Without another word, lanterns were extinguished and the men quickly and quietly dispersed through the dark scrub. Distant shouts could be heard as they carefully made their way back to the safety of their fires and campsites.

As they approached their own fire, Niall whispered to Patrick and Roark. "Did you see the Callahan boys, joined up with Shaughnessy and his men?"

Roark nodded. "Shaughnessy must have invited them. They're determined to take things by the horn."

"What they're going to do is get themselves killed," added Patrick.

As they neared the campfire, they realized that the drizzle had finally stopped, and the fog was lifting. They looked about the site, counting heads, making sure that all the men had made it back to camp. Aside from a few that were just now hurrying up from the river bank, everyone was accounted for.

Maureen and Saraid had set a blanket in front of a large outcropping of limestone. They were sitting against it, Saraid's arm wrapped around Maureen's shoulder and Maureen's head against her sister's bosom. Both were snoring, an empty jug of mead on its side between them.

The men chuckled at the sight of them.

Roark piped up. "I think my colleen has had quite enough for one night." He carefully picked her up and draped her over his shoulder. "I think I'll be taking this one back to the wagon and get her to bed."

"Here, take a lantern so you don't break your neck."

Patrick paced, agitation showing on his face and in his posture. He could see stragglers coming through the scrub from the direction of their meeting place . . . angry men that weren't theirs. *Charlies,* he thought. *What if they found Annie before he did?*

"What is it, Patrick?" asked Niall.

Patrick looked about the camp, hoping that Annie would miraculously appear, but she was nowhere to be seen. "I need to find Annie . . . make sure she's all right. If Jack finds her first, there'll be hell to pay."

Niall looked around, took in the same band of Charlies coming back. "You might want to wait a bit . . . maybe until daybreak."

"That might be too late."

Niall shrugged. "She's probably holed up somewhere safe for now. No sense looking for trouble."

Patrick nodded his head. "She probably went to her cave. I hate to think of her out there, alone and frightened."

"There's probably still a lot of fog along the shore. You'll never find her in the dark. Let it be. It'll be daylight soon enough." He watched Patrick pace some more and rubbed his tired eyes. "I'll help you look in the morning but right now," he yawned, "I need to get some sleep."

Patrick nodded his agreement. "I'll take a walk back to the camp and check on Danny."

"John probably needs some sleep, too, so I'll stay with the wagon."

Niall sat on the blanket next to Saraid and drew her across his lap. She mumbled incoherently. She shifted her weight until she lay face down between his legs, her head against his stomach, her arms curved around his back. She once again began to snore softly as he leaned his back against the large slab of rock and shut his eyes. Sighing, he laid his arm across her shoulders and wished they were enjoying the softness of a bed instead of the hard ground. He couldn't wait until this long weekend was over so they could go home.

Chapter Forty-Two

Niall stirred, his back stiff from sitting for hours against the large slab of limestone, his legs numb from Saraid's weight sprawled over them. He shifted her body and flexed his knees several times to ease the cramping.

The fog and humidity had finally lifted, leaving the night air clear and cool. He looked up to see thousands of stars sparkling like shards of glass overhead, the moon drifting in and out of the last wafting clouds. The only sounds disturbing the silence were the chirping of crickets, the soft nickering of a horse and the lone hoot of a distant owl. The meadow, glimmering in the moonlight and by the scattered lantern light, lay trampled. Grasses and wildflowers, bowed in temporary defeat by the merry feet that had reeled and pranced over her honey-colored coat, filled the air with sweet scent.

Niall sat there enjoying the stillness, grateful that the noise and excitement of the long day were past. In the moonlight, Saraid's unplaited hair glistened with beads of dew as he stroked his fingers through it.

He gazed around and could see that there were only a few stragglers about, some sleeping off their pints, some tangled in sleep with their lovers or mates. The rest, he was sure, had wandered back to their wagons and caravans.

A contented sigh escaped his lips and he closed his eyes. Memories filled his mind of coming here with his family during his growing-up years, mingling with other clans and far-flung relatives. He thought about how all the struggles and losses they'd shared were diminished by the music, the dancing, and the sense of family.

For himself, the tales of his ancestors, especially the tale of Brian Boru, would always give him hope for a free Irish Republic. For now, though, there was so much uncertainty. So many were at the end of what they could bear. He worried that some, like Seamus, coveting what the O'Briens had, would set out to destroy their property and livestock. His family had not yet suffered any harm, but they were watchful all the same.

Their coffers were getting low, but they had enough to get by for a few more years. They had other money tucked away to buy back ownership of their acres once the Penal Laws ended. If they ended. This money would never be touched for any other purpose. Niall clung to the hope that his son, James, would have clear ownership of the land.

Connor, as overseer, had been fairer than most of the land barons. He continued to hold the deed to their land separate from his other properties. They were allowed to use the land as their own as long as they paid Connor the tax money when it was due.

Niall yawned deeply and laid his head back against the rock. In half sleep, he was a young boy, walking through spring meadows without a care. The distant hills, verdant with life, lay before him against a vivid blue sky. Cattle lowed in the pasture on one side of a stone wall, wooly sheep, ready for shearing, on the other.

Suddenly, he saw an old woman with a hooded cloak, walking toward him through the pasture. She was carrying a large bucket full of water and a bundle of soiled clothing under her arm. The crone set down the bucket; and when she unraveled the clothing, he saw that they were covered with blood. She threw back her head and began to wail as she plunged the garments into the water and tried to scrub away the dark stains. Then she looked directly into Niall's eyes and laughed maniacally as she upended the bucket. A gush of crimson water caromed over the ground toward him, rising and falling like a red tide.

Niall cried out, breath shuddering in his chest, as he fought his way out of the nightmare. She was the banshee—the *bean nighe*, and she was coming—for him! Panting, he struggled to deny what he had just envisioned.

Saraid awoke and shifted her weight against Niall's thigh. Her voice was husky from sleep and mead. "What is it? Did ye cry out?"

Niall took in several slow breaths to ease the racing of his heart. "No . . . it's all right. I just had a bad dream." He couldn't tell her the about his vision. The O'Brien clan were among only a few of the clans to whom the banshee ever appeared to portend death. He'd not have her worry about the old superstition.

She yawned deeply, her arm tossed carelessly across Niall's groin. "Where is everyone?"

Niall chuckled. "You don't remember?" he asked.

Saraid tried to bring the evening's events back to her mind but couldn't clear her head.

"You passed out while everyone was saying good night. I thought it best to let you be and enjoyed a few peaceful moments."

She sat upright and swatted his arm. "Does my chatterin' disturb ye, then?"

He laughed and pulled her close. "Not at all, *A Grá*. It's just been a very noisy and tiresome day. Wouldn't you agree?"

"Sure I'm thinkin' I had too much mead and don't remember it all. My head will be rememberin' it right enough in the mornin'."

They were both quiet for a moment. Saraid peered through the dimly lit night at the nearly deserted expanse of the meadow. "Where are the children?"

"Patrick took them back to the caravan a few hours ago," he replied. "They were all done in, too."

"Yer mother is watchin' them, then?"

"Yes, she's tending to Danny, and John is there as well."

"She seems to be feelin' better."

"Let's hope she stays that way."

Saraid closed her eyes and listened to the night sounds; small rodents foraging for food, the flapping of bat wings overhead, and a solitary pipe playing softly somewhere beyond them. "She's a hard one to please. She finds nothin' about me that's right."

Niall frowned in the darkness and rubbed her arm absently. "She's become a bitter woman. She had grand dreams for her life here. Being a farmer's wife wasn't what she thought it would be."

"Why did she marry him, then?"

"I imagine she believed the fine tales my father wove about the glories of Clare. For him, this was a grand place." Niall shrugged. "She thought she'd be landed gentry, like her family was in Dublin. Instead, she ended up with nothing but hard work. I think she felt abandoned when her family moved back to England. And losing her Anglican church didn't help, either. Practicing any religion here means a long carriage ride to find a church, Anglican or otherwise."

Saraid was pensive. She had no thoughts about organized religion and couldn't fathom Kate's feelings of loss over her rigid church. Niall, on the other hand, always found time to get a blessing from Paddy when he said a crude mass for the villagers in the barn.

Saraid came from a long line of poor Catholics who still clung to some of the pagan ways and celebrations. For her and Maureen, the highlight of this weekend was to take the children on the pilgrimage to St. Brigid's Well, in Liscannor.

The last weekend on July marked *'Crom Dubh'*, one of the four events celebrated yearly in honor of the saint. Brigid, pagan goddess of the Druids, was also called the Goddess of the Sacred Flame of Kildare. Many Catholics believed her to be the foster mother of the Virgin Mary. Saraid would miss the rituals at the well if they were unable to attend.

She murmured, "She's kind of stuck with the lot of us and our ways. Is that why she resents me so?"

Niall held her close, trying to tamp down the anger that he still harbored over the argument with his mother. "It doesn't matter, *A ghrá ma Chroi*. Things are going to be different when we get home."

Saraid looked into his eyes for clues. "What're ye meanin' by *different*?"

Niall paused. "I already told you. I'll suffer no more of her disrespect for you!"

"That, again! An' I told ye, I'll not let ye put her out! I'll never have a lick of acceptance if ye do this! An' what would the children be thinkin' of us?"

Niall shook his head, unable to comprehend her thinking. He looked to the eastern horizon and could see the first shadowed light of the approaching dawn. "Let's get back to the caravan and get what sleep we can."

Niall pulled her to her feet and picked up the lantern. "We can talk on it more on the way home. We've a long ride ahead of us and I've had a bit much for one day." He wanted nothing more than to lie beside her, rest his head against her breast, and sleep away the emotions and fears of the last hours.

Saraid sighed and leaned against him. He wrapped his arm around her waist to guide her on the path, the lantern casting dim light on their footfalls. The moonlight played against the willows along the river and throughout the camp, adding a soft glow to what was left of the night. Niall's hand slid down across her hip and came to rest on the fullness of her bottom, drawing her closer to his side.

Saraid wrapped her arm around his back as they meandered to the end of the path to the rows of caravans. Some people were still about, dousing their camp fires and checking the piles of belongings that would be packed up onto their wagons at first light.

"Niall?"

"What is it?"

"What're we to do about Seamus an' Molly?"

Niall looked away from her and said nothing.

"We'll be needin' to decide by mornin', won't we?"

"It galls me to have to consider it at all. I hate that man."

Saraid closed her eyes, hesitant to plead with him, but Molly was in such a bad way. "I know it angers ye, it angers me too, but I hate to see how she's sufferin' at his hand. Is there nothin' we can do?"

"It would be my wish that when he wakes, he'll forget everything that happened tonight and we won't have cause to worry about it."

She decided to change the subject. "Patrick is quite smitten with Annie. He won't want to leave here knowin' she's in danger. Jack was a crazy man tonight. No tellin' what he'll do. I wonder where she went off to."

"Patrick said he was going to look for her at first light. Let's hope all will be well and we can leave here in peace."

As they neared their caravan, Saraid yelped as her knee buckled. "Ouch! Sweet Jesus!"

Niall grabbed hold of her as she stumbled, hopping on one foot. "What is it?"

"I think I've cut my toe!" She continued to hop until he swept her up effortlessly and carried her to the back of the caravan, and set her down.

"Let's see what it is," Niall lifted her long skirt to her knees and raised her foot. In the lantern light, he could see a piece of broken sea shell, deeply imbedded in the bottom of her big toe. A thin trail of blood was flowing down along the bottom of her dirty foot.

"Doesn't that look mean," he said, carefully pulling away the shard.

Saraid flinched and whimpered with the pain, more blood oozing down her foot.

"*Hush*, you'll wake the children. Do we have any of that salt water left in the clam buckets?"

Saraid grit her teeth, trying not to cry. "The buckets are under the wagon." She clutched her foot in frustration, blood running over her fingers.

He came back a moment later with a bucket and a clean piece of cotton. "All right now, my love," he said gently. "This might hurt some, but we need to get it cleaned out."

She clenched her teeth and muttered an obscenity as he poured the salt water over the open wound.

"I'm sorry, but there's still dirt in the cut."

Before she could speak, he took her toe into his mouth and gently sucked on the cut and spat away the grit and blood. As he repeated the move, she squirmed. "Now cut that out! Get the honey and calendula so I can make a poultice for it."

Niall did as asked, retrieving a pot of honey and a small bag of calendula from her herb box. The combination would both soothe and fight infection. He watched as she crushed the herb against his palm and poured some honey on top, mixing the sticky concoction with her finger. "There," she said when the consistency was right, licking the excess from her finger.

He pressed the mixture against the cut, applying pressure until the bleeding stopped. The honey had seeped from his palm to run all over her toes and down her foot. After he tore the herb bag to make a bandage for her toe, he started licking the herbed-honey residue from her foot.

Saraid muffled a giggle. "What do ye think ye're doin'?"

He continued to apply gentle pressure to the wound, his tongue licking at the dripping honey. He gave her a sly grin as he ran his tongue along the inside of her foot. She tried to pull it away but he held it in place. "The bleeding stopped, but I think this—tastes delicious." He chuckled as he ran his tongue over the calloused ball of her foot, under her toes and then drew each one slowly into his mouth. He was smirking at her as he let his tongue play at the soft skin between each toe. She tried hard to stifle her laughter as his saliva left a honeyed trail against her instep.

Niall continued to play erotically with her toes, his lips and tongue lingering on her flesh. Saraid's smile wavered as she began to tremble, feeling a deep tug of arousal in the base of her belly. She dropped her head back, exposing her long neck, her hair trailing down her back. He righted himself and laying his hands on her exposed knees, leaned in and kissed her throat, and slowly rained kisses down, down, down over the crest of her breasts.

Saraid sighed deeply. Raising her head, she pulled his face up until she held his gaze. She kissed him with sultry invitation as she spread her thighs wide. In the silence, he struggled not to moan as he slid his hands slowly along the tops of her legs, his thumbs just brushing the inside of her thighs to the pulsing wet center of her.

He felt himself straining against his britches, his breath hitching in his throat. It took all he had in him not to just pull them down and plunge into her. It was what he needed to banish the apparition of death that still haunted him. He bent his face to her thigh and felt her tremble.

"Niall!" The harsh whisper came from the side of the caravan and they both started, the intimate spell broken.

Saraid let out a yelp as she yanked her skirt down over her bare legs.

Niall was seething. "What?" he hissed through his teeth.

Patrick came into view. He averted his eyes, realizing he'd interrupted something between them. "I'm sorry," he whispered. "He's bleeding again and he's burning up." He turned to Saraid but couldn't meet her eyes. "Do you have any herbs to remedy a fever?"

She quickly rummaged through her box of herbs until she found the echinacea, calendula, comfrey root and yarrow. "Quickly! Get some water to boiling." Grabbing her wooden bowl and pestle, she crushed a good amount of the aromatic roots and herbs, then poured some of the honey over it. She handed the concoction to Patrick. "Take the dirty bandage off and douse the wound with whiskey. Then rub this into the wound. It might sting some but it will help to stop the bleedin' and festerin'."

Patrick left as Niall returned with a pot full of hot water from the kettle that had been simmering on John's fire. Saraid crushed more of the same herbs and sprinkled them over the water. She stirred the fragrant mixture with frustration. "It works better if it steeps for a few hours but we shouldn't wait to begin." She held a piece of linen over the cup and strained a weak cupful of the brew. She stirred in a bit of honey, then handed it to Niall. "Get him to drink as much as ye can. I'll bring over more after this sets for a bit."

Patrick arrived at his mother's wagon as Danny, delirious with fever and mumbling loudly, squirmed to get away from the hands that were trying to help him. Sweat poured from his face and body, his hair dripping like rain, soaking his bandages and bedding.

"We need to gag him," said John, "or the whole camp will hear him."

Kate deftly stuffed a wad of clean bandage in Danny's mouth. John held him still as her fingers worked to ease the soiled bandage from the wound. Danny recoiled as she tugged where the bloody bandage was stuck to his skin.

"Good heavens," she whispered. "The redness is spreading." She poured whiskey over the wound. Danny uttered a muffled scream before he passed out and lay limp against her, his slick skin soaking her dress.

Patrick handed her the bowl and Kate gently rubbed the poultice to both the front and back of his shoulder. John held Danny up as Kate wrapped the clean bandages around him.

Niall handed his mother the herb tea. "Saraid will bring more of it over as soon as it's ready."

Kate nodded. "It's good that she knows what to do." Her fear for Danny overcame any feelings she might harbor against Saraid.

Niall climbed into the caravan and sat behind Danny to hold him in a sitting position. "We need to keep him sitting up if we're to stop the bleeding." A clean, folded blanket, covered with a cotton sheet, was put behind his back against Niall's chest.

Kate removed the gag with trembling fingers and held the cup to Danny's mouth but he wouldn't drink. "Hold back his head."

Niall gently pulled Danny's head and Kate dribbled a bit of the warm golden liquid down his throat. Danny coughed and half the tea ran down his chin. She repeated the process several times, holding a towel under his chin. "It's going to be a long night," she said wearily.

Now that the first wave of emergency was over, they replaced the rest of the bloody bedding with clean.

Niall gazed around the caravan. "Where's Hank?"

Patrick gestured to his own wagon. "He's under some blankets in my wagon."

Saraid arrived with the pot of steeping tea and held it out to Kate. She could see the strain on Kate's face. "Ye must be exhausted."

"Anyone would be tired with all this going on," she snapped.

Niall was about to say something when Saraid caught his eye and shook her head. She took Kate's hand in her own and spoke softly to her. "Why don't ye come to our caravan and get some rest. We can spell ye here for a while."

Kate withdrew her hand and stared hard at Saraid, looking for some unkindness in her eyes but found none. She sighed and turned her head aside, rubbing the tightness out of the side of her face. Kate was alarmed to realize that her stomach was quivering and the tingling that had wracked her body earlier in the day was returning. She drew herself up with concerted effort. "I shouldn't leave him now, but perhaps you're right."

"You'll do him no good if you're asleep on your feet," said John. "We'll take good care of him and keep an eye on the rest."

Kate closed her eyes for a moment, realizing how exhausted she was. Maybe that was the problem. She just needed to sleep and she would be fine. She suddenly felt like a very old woman. "Very well."

John helped his mother to climb down from the wagon. She held his arm as she walked unsteadily over to Niall's caravan.

"You've had a rough day of it, Mother."

"Mothers have many rough days. I'm used to it," she said wearily.

He helped her into the wagon, shifting Liam and Bridget to make room for her. He covered her with a blanket and kissed her forehead. "Get some sleep," he whispered. "We'll wake you if there's any change with Danny."

Her eyes were already closed, her voice thready. "Ma . . . sure tha . . . you do."

Patrick noticed that streaks of deep pink and orange were creeping into the pale grey of the eastern sky. With the absence of the heavy fog that had impeded his earlier search, he decided that he would once again try to find Annie. He was bone tired but he was determined. He approached Niall and John who were standing outside the caravan. "I'm off to find Annie," he said as he picked up the lantern.

"It's near daylight," John said. "No need for a lantern."

Patrick shook his head. "Annie has a special cave and that's probably where she went. It's black as pitch in there."

Niall squeezed his shoulder. "We need to decide what to do about Seamus."

Patrick shrugged. "I'd just as soon hang him, myself. Do what you think is right. I can't leave here until I find Annie." He turned his back on them and set out once again for Fisherstreet.

John was mildly surprised. "She's just a barmaid."

Niall shot him a look. "I wouldn't say that too loudly around Patrick. She's his first and she'll always be special."

Chapter Forty-Three

Patrick strode over the Burren, through the village of Fisherstreet, past the Shamrock and on to the coastline road. He was so consumed by his search for Annie that he couldn't appreciate the dazzling vista before him. The sun had broken through the low purple clouds of dawn. Within minutes, they had risen, fading to pale gray, yellow and white, with hints of pink and orange against a vivid blue sky. The colors reflected like a painting over the shimmering stillness of the sea. Crying gulls circled overhead and swooped low over the water and the crevasses between the rocks for food. Fishermen in their boats were trawling their nets between the shore and the distant Aran Islands for the first catch of the day.

He breathed in the salty air, trying to steady his inner turmoil. Taking care not to slip on the slick limestone clints, he tried to remember the way to Annie's cave. The wildflowers gave him a hint and he veered closer to the descending fall of rocks. Nothing else stirred him as he picked his way over the uneven landscape. Patrick's frustration mounted as he realized that by now he must surely have passed the hidden fissure. Turning around, he retraced his steps and caught a glimpse of bright red in stark relief to the rocks below. He stared in horror as he realized that what he was seeing were long strands of hair being ruffled by the breeze.

"Annie!"

Slipping and sliding, fearing the worst, he made his way down the slope until he reached her inert body.

"Annie!" he cried out again as he pulled her into his arms.

"*A Stóirín!*"

She awoke to his voice calling her his little darling. "I can't believe ye found me!" She whimpered with pain and began to cry, clinging to him for warmth. "I'm so cold!" Her sobs rose as he tried to work her swollen foot from the rocks. "My foot!" she cried. "I think it's broke!"

"Hush, little one." The angry purple flesh was too swollen and tightly wedged to budge. Patrick held her close, rubbing her arms and back until he felt some bit of warmth return to her skin. He brushed her matted hair back from her face and tenderly kissed away her tears. He eyed the rock that imprisoned her and how it sat imbedded with the others around it, knowing he would have to move it to set her free. If he tried to push it straight away, the base of it would spring up against the one behind it, crushing her foot completely. His only hope was to push it to the side. There was nothing nearby to use as a lever.

"Annie," he said. "You're going to have to help me."

"How can I be helpin' ye if I can't move?" Anger and frustration mixed with fear as she began to wail again.

"Annie! Stop it! Get your wits about you!"

Annie, cringing at his reproach, stifled back a sob and nodded silently.

Patrick moved away from her and lay on his back so that his buttocks were close to the rock. He drew up his knees and planted his feet against the hard surface. He took her hand and spoke firmly. "I want you to wrap your arms around your knee and hold it tight. I'm going to try to push the rock away from your foot. I may not be able to move it too far, so when I say *now*, I want you to fall back and pull your foot free. Can you do that?"

Annie sniffed back her runny nose. Seeing the determination in his eyes, she straightened her back, preparing to do as he asked.

"All right then." Patrick took several deep breaths as he gripped the rocks to either side of him for ballast. He inhaled deeply, then, with held breath, began to push against the rock. The veins in his neck and forehead bulged with the strain. After an endless moment, he stopped, gasping for air. The rock had not budged an inch. "Damn it to bloody hell!" he cried, his legs quivering from the exertion.

Annie dropped her head onto her knees, crying silently.

When Patrick stopped shaking, he stood over Annie and trailed his fingers through her hair. "I need to go get some help."

"Please don' leave me!" Annie clutched his hand, fearful that he wouldn't come back and she would die here when the tide came back in. The thought of drowning terrified her.

Patrick knelt beside her and held her close. "I promise you, I'll be back!" He gave her a quick kiss and stood to climb back up the rocks.

"No!" Annie grabbed onto his ankle and wouldn't let go. "Please try again," she begged. Her voice choked on a sob, her eyes shimmered up at his.

Patrick sighed, unable to deny the fear in her eyes. "All right," he relented. "I'll try one more time."

He lay back down, this time on the other side of the rock, once again finding purchase against it with his feet. "If this doesn't work, you'll have to let me go for help, all right?"

She nodded silently, wiping her tears.

Patrick began to push, grunting and straining, sweat pouring from his body. He was just about to give up when, suddenly, the rock began to shift mere inches. "Now!" he groaned.

Annie fell back, her scream piercing the morning air as her ankle came away from the rock. The skin of her foot had been scraped away, leaving a raw, bleeding trail against the ground, but she was free. Patrick's legs collapsed, his muscles spent and trembling. Annie hitched herself over to him and fell across his body, holding him tightly.

"Oh Patrick! I knew you could do it!"

He held her as he stared up at the sky. After he finally calmed himself, he sat up and gingerly picked up her damaged foot. "Your foot's a mess."

"Sure I can't feel nothin'."

"That's probably a good thing, for now. Let's get you down to the water and soak it for a minute."

Patrick lifted her and carried her closer to the water, setting her down on a flat clint. She cringed as the cold salty water stung her raw skin and she bit her lip to keep from crying out. She tore at the soiled hem of her skirt, creating a makeshift bandage. Patrick took it from her and doused it in the water, rubbing away as much of the dirt as he could. They sat quietly for a few moments, each lost in their own thoughts. Suddenly, Annie pointed at something floating towards them just beneath the surface of the water. "What's that?"

Patrick reached out and grabbed the object. As he wrung the excess water from it, he realized that something about it looked familiar, but he couldn't place it. "It's just a hat." He tossed it back into the sea and they watched it bob on the surface until the current drew it away again.

"Annie, I have to ask. Why did you run away last night? I was worried sick when I couldn't find you."

She hung her head, hiding her face in the curtain of her hair. "I was ashamed of what Seamus said 'bout me to yer family."

Patrick sighed. "There was no need. We all know that he's nothing but scum. He's lucky I didn't kill him right there."

"Ye got no need to be defendin' me. What he said 'bout me was true enough."

Patrick took her hands in his and spoke softly to her. "Look at me."

She slowly raised her eyes to his. She was so full of longing that she could barely breathe.

He gently wiped away her tears. "I'm not ashamed of you."

Her breath released and she laid her face against his chest. They wrapped their arms around each other and sat silently for a time as the gulls continued to fly and screech overhead.

Annie wanted to beg Patrick to take her away with him, but she knew she couldn't leave her mother. He had become more than just a wish for a better life. His tenderness towards her raised a painful ache in her heart. She didn't deserve him, but dear Lord, she wanted him.

Patrick, too, was filled with conflict. He'd never cared for a woman before. He hadn't really wanted to think about this moment, of saying good-bye. Much as he hated the thought of leaving her here, he wasn't ready to think about bringing her home to Killaloe, either. Every minute he spent with Annie deepened the anguish of leaving her. In spite of his feelings, he finally accepted the fact that he had no choice; he had to go home. His decision made, Patrick took the strip of wet cloth and bound Annie's foot and helped her to stand.

"Can you walk on it?"

Annie held his arm as she made an attempt to put her weight on it. Pain wracked her entire leg but she hobbled as best she could.

Patrick scooped her up. "I'll take you to my wagon. Saraid will have something to help it."

"Patrick, I got to git on home. Mam will be frantic, wonderin' where I got to."

"Is it far from here? I have to get back to my family to let them know you're all right." He couldn't bear to look at her, lest she see his pain. "We're fixing to go home this morning."

She felt the blood draining from her body. He had said the words. He was leaving. No matter what she had dared to hope, the weight of his words lay like an anvil on her chest, a final crushing of her dreams. She struggled to bring air into her lungs. "It ain't far," she whispered "just a short way from here."

"I'll take you home, then," he said quietly.

Patrick was silent as they made their way up the embankment to the road. As he walked along, he shifted Annie in his arms. Slight as she was, she was growing heavy. He began to feel the frustration of having too many things to worry about. They needed to get Danny to a doctor. They needed to deal with Seamus. Patrick was so deep in thought that he didn't hear the horse and wagon pull up alongside them.

Roisin called out to them. "Lovely mornin' for a walk, now, ain't it?"

As Patrick turned to face her, she saw Annie's bandaged foot. "Oh, my dear, are ye hurt?"

"Auntie Ro!" Relief filled Patrick. "Would you give us a hand?"

"What is it you be needin', dear?"

"Annie's injured her foot so she can't walk on it. A ride would be helpful. I have to get her home and it's a ways yet."

Roisin stiffened, her smile frozen in place. "Well, I'm in a bit of a hurry."

Annie was puzzled by her reticence. "Auntie Ro . . . it ain't out of yer way none. It's just up the road."

Roisin hesitated. She wanted to help them, but Jack and his satchel were hidden under a blanket in the back of the wagon. She looked cautiously behind her. Her lone bag separated Jack from the end of the wagon. If he didn't like it, too bad for him. She was sure that he was too scared to show himself. She turned back to the young people and nodded, patting the seat beside her. "Sure ye can sit here next to me."

"We could just as easily sit in the back," protested Patrick.

"No, no," Roisin replied. "Sit up here with me and keep me company. Ye can be showin' me the way."

Under the blanket, Jack was seething. He felt the wagon shift with their weight as they climbed onboard. *What the hell did she think she was doing?* He should have killed her when he had the chance. He gripped the ball of the shillelagh tightly in his fist. He might still do just that when they were far enough away from Doolin. Suddenly, it occurred to him that they were not heading east towards Ennis as planned. If she was heading towards Annie's place, then they were heading north towards Galway Bay! What was she hoping to accomplish by that? Somehow, the bitch was trying to outsmart him. He ground his teeth, straining to control his rage. *She would pay dearly for this!*

The wagon slowed to a stop when Annie pointed to the ramshackle shack she called home. Patrick helped her down from the wagon and tried to give Roisin some coin for her trouble. "We appreciate your kindness, Ro."

She waved off his hand. "It weren't no trouble at all." She patted Annie on the top of the head. "Ye be takin' care of that foot now, hear me?"

Annie nodded and gave the old woman a wan smile. Roisin clucked her tongue and coaxed the horse to continue down the road.

Annie and Patrick stood facing the rough abode. Annie was filled with shame as she watched the look on Patrick's face change to one of distaste. The shack looked so timeworn and gray, blending into the limestone around it. She'd have given anything to avoid this moment but there was no help for it. And what difference did it make since he was leaving her and going home? She wished they were back in the cave, making love one more time. She closed her eyes tightly to keep from crying again. There would be plenty of time for tears after he left. Inhaling deeply, she tried to draw courage into her body, but it was almost too much effort. Her foot had begun to throb and she needed to get inside and lay down.

"Well . . . I guess I need to be gettin' inside to check on mam. She ain't doin' so good since my da and brother got drowned."

"It's just the two of you?"

Annie nodded. "That's why I work at the Shamrock." She looked away from him as her cheeks flamed.

Patrick swooped her up into his arms and carried her to the shack, pushing the door open. The musty dampness and the smell of mead assaulted him. He set her down on a chair at the small table and looked around the bare room.

Annie's mother moaned from her place by the lone window. "Where in bloody hell have ye been? I ain't slept all night waitin' fer ye to come home! An' who're ye?" She demanded, pointing at Patrick.

Annie began to shake. The shame stabbed at her like a rusty blade, over and over again. "I'm sorry, I am, fer not bein here."

Patrick straightened and stared at the disheveled woman, biting his tongue to keep from cursing at her. "My name is Patrick O'Brien. Your daughter has had an accident. She's going to need you to help care for her."

"*Me?*" Her own misery was too overwhelming to worry about anyone else.

"Yes, *you!*" He walked over to where the woman sat and looked into her limpid eyes. "Annie won't be able to walk for a few days so I'm asking that you watch out for her."

"Patrick, don' . . . it's all right."

The elderly woman wrung her hands. She turned her head towards the window and lay her forehead against the cool, salt-smeared glass. "I ain't eaten since yesterday," she whimpered. "Ye was supposed to bring food!"

Annie snapped. "Since when is ye hungry? I usually have to force ye to eat!"

Patrick didn't understand the nature of their relationship and was hesitant to interfere.

Annie looked around the meager space and tried to remember if there was any food left. She had planned to bring home a full sack of food from the Shamrock's buffet, but with all that had happened with Patrick, she'd forgotten all about it. She rubbed her hands over her face. Her night of love was growing more costly by the moment. Rising and hobbling over to the small cupboard, she searched the empty shelves for some small offering. All she found was an near empty jar of honey. She took it down and brought it to her mother with a tin spoon. "This'll have to do 'til I can get to the village."

Patrick grit his teeth. How could Annie live like this? How was she going to care for her mother, or herself, if she couldn't walk? It wasn't like she had any neighbors to look in on them. Resignation filled him as he made his way to the door.

"Patrick?"

"I'll be back." Without a backward glance, he quickly left.

Annie wept as she watched him walk away, the ache in her chest as unbearable as the pain in her foot. She struggled to believe that he would return, hope a thin ribbon pulled taut against the reality of her despair. Annie laid down on her small cot, bunching her thin blanket under her ankle to elevate it. She set her arm over her face and tried to ignore her mother's whimpering. More weary than she had ever been in her life, and to escape the deep feelings of loss that sapped her strength, she gave in to needed sleep.

Chapter Forty-Four

The camp was in a state of chaos. Several wagons and caravans were making a hasty departure from the grounds as rumors flew about the arrival of the sheriff and a posse of Charlies. Wagons were being searched in an attempt to apprehend Danny and Hank. Both were wanted for questioning in the disappearance of Martin and for Jack, who was also among the missing. Angry voices could be heard throughout the camp as the searchers tossed blankets and belongings from the wagons. Those who fought the searchers had their hands bound and were led away to the Shamrock to be questioned further by the authorities.

As John was hitching his horse to his caravan, Niall was rolling up the tarp on the sides of his, tying it to the frame to provide light and ventilation for the children. He'd brought Patrick's horse back from the pen and tied it to the back of his wagon.

Suddenly, shouts could be heard and the Charlies rushed towards the bay. With the low tide, searchers had found a cane protruding between the rocks, Martin's name carved into the wood. As the officials began searching for a body, they were speculating as to whether he had fallen into the sea or met with foul play.

Willie pulled up alongside John's wagon, wary of the temper that was pouring off the man. "Is everything all right?"

"No! Everything is far from all right!" cried John. "We have to get out of here!" He paced back and forth beside his caravan, tearing at his hair.

Niall grabbed John's arm and walked beside him, trying to quiet him down. "Don't be hollering or you'll be drawing attention to us."

John shook him off and began sputtering again but kept his voice at a hiss. "We need to get mother to the doctor. Where the hell is Patrick?"

"I'm right here," Patrick answered as he came upon them. "What's going on?"

"Where have you been?" John snapped.

Patrick bit back a quick retort. "I've been helping Annie. I found her but she was hurt."

They all stopped what they were doing and stared at him.

Niall was the first to speak. "Hurt how?"

Patrick ran his hand over his face. "She fell down by the shore, and her foot got stuck between the rocks. I had to get her free so she wouldn't drown."

Saraid went over to him. "She's all right, then?"

"No, not really. She scraped most of the skin off the top of her foot and it's quite swollen. I need some bandages and ointment for it."

John clenched his fists. "Tell me you're not planning to go back there!"

Niall barked at him, too. "We have problems of our own here! Mother's had another spell and Danny's hanging on by a thread! We have to get them both to Doctor O'Hickey in Ennis."

"What are you saying about mother?"

John grabbed the front of Patrick's tunic in his fist, his face crimson. "While you've been off enjoying your little *floosie*, things have gone straight to hell around here!"

Patrick flung John away from him, his own temper rising. "I wasn't off enjoying anything! Annie was injured, and I had to get her home. And, don't you be calling her a *floosie*!"

"Enough!" Niall yelled.

Willie's horse neighed and pranced with agitation. Willie drew the reins taut to keep the horse in place and talked softly to calm him down. He asked Niall, "What happened to your mother?"

Niall explained that she seemed to have suffered another spell which left her unable to speak.

"Her face is distorted, and she's barely able to move her arm or leg on the left side. We're going to see what the Doc has to say." He turned to Patrick. "You're going to have to deal with Hank."

Patrick protested. "I need to go back! I promised Annie I'd bring them some food and some liniment for her foot."

Niall shook his head. "We need you here! There's no time to be going back. We have to leave straight away."

"But they have no food and she can't walk!" Patrick was more conflicted than he had ever been about anything. He knew his loyalty was to his family, but he had promised Annie that he would return. What would she think of him if he just left? He doubted that anyone would be checking on her or her mother for some time, if ever.

"That's just too damned bad!" cried John. "She'll just have to wait until someone comes looking for her. God knows there are probably plenty of men who'll notice if she's not around."

Patrick snapped. He raised his fist and went full-bore against his brother. It took both Niall and Willie, as well as Roark, who'd just arrived, to pull the two men apart. John's bloodied face was full of venom as he struggled against the arms that held him. Patrick, too, struggled but easily freed himself. He rubbed his hands through his hair, his heart agonizing over what he had to do. "Let me at least get word to Jimmy at the tavern to send food to them."

Saraid approached them with an alternative. "How 'bout if Maureen and I go? They're not lookin' for women and children. We weren't ridin' off with ye anyway 'cause we're goin' to the Well."

Niall balked. "I don't know if the Well is such a good idea. You can come back sometime when it's safer."

Saraid glowered at him. "Ye know this is important to me, and

I've promised the children we would go. Saint Brigid's celebration is this weekend, not later!"

"Da!" cried Fiona. "We really want to go! We've never been there."

James joined in. "We were meant to see the O'Brien crypt, too!"

Niall shook his head. Since Maureen was in agreement, there was no talking them out of it.

Patrick sighed with relief. He pulled his sack of coins from the cord around his waist and handed it to Saraid. "Use what you need to get enough food for a week or so. I'd say to give the lot of it to Jimmy to give to her, but I don't know if he can be trusted to do that."

Saraid tested the heft of the bag of coins. "Are ye sure? That's a lot of coin."

"Yes, I'm sure."

John shook his head. "Man, you are such a fool!"

Patrick glared at him. "Just shut your mouth!"

"How 'bout we just take the food right to Annie an' then I can tell her that ye couldn't come back?"

Niall threw up his hands in disgust. "You never listen! We're in danger here!" He shook his finger at her, his face stern. "I'll not have you putting my children in harm's way."

He turned to walk away from her, but Saraid grabbed his arm. She put her hand to Niall's cheek and turned his face to look at her. "Aside from that, would ye have left me injured and hungry when ye was first lovin' me?"

Niall blinked, and stood very still. In silence, he thought back to their early days and all they had gone through together. He had to concede that he would never have abandoned her in a time of need. When he spoke, his voice was quiet. "That's different."

Saraid smiled. "Is it?"

He pulled her to his chest, knowing that he had lost the argument. "Promise me that you'll be careful."

"Of course, I will!" She patted the sheath that hung from a cord at her waist. "An' I have my knife, if needed."

He shook his head. "Let's hope you don't."

Saraid removed some bandages and liniment from her stores and set them aside. Then she and Maureen transferred all the cooking pots and their bedrolls to Patrick's wagon to make room for all the little ones in the caravan.

The younger children were loaded into the back. Fiona and James sat astride the horses that would pull them along. They whispered to each other, wondering what was really going on.

The women climbed into the wagon and bid the men goodbye. "Let's be going then," Saraid said as she picked up the reins. Fiona and James nudged the horses flanks and they headed off across the Burren towards Fisherstreet.

Willie had a suggestion. "How 'bout if I take Hank? My wagon has already been searched. The Charlies are all down by the water so I can scoot out of here right now, and meet up with you in Ennis."

"I'm just too damn much trouble," Hank whined. "I should just be givin' myself up and be done with it!"

John began getting angry again. "Be quiet, Hank! With all the other trouble we've got right now, it just doesn't matter."

Freddie pleaded with Hank. "Just git in the wagon and shut yer mouth! We ain't leavin' ye here!"

Hank muttered as he limped around the wagon, holding his precious fiddle and his meager bedroll.

The others agreed and settled a frustrated Hank under a pile of blankets in Willie's wagon.

Willie saluted the men, snapped his reins, and took off at a good pace.

The others set about getting themselves on the road. Roark drew his wagon to the front of the line and would lead them out. He planned to meet up with Maureen and the twins at the Well. Niall was to ride with John. Danny lay unconscious in the back of the caravan under layers of blankets with his head towards the front. They had put a gag into his mouth in case he cried out. Kate, though she could not speak, nodded faintly, understanding what they were asking of her. She was to lie with her head at the back of the caravan. If someone wanted to search the wagon, they stood a better chance by showing that their mother was ill and not to be moved.

Just as they were pulling out, Seamus and Molly pulled in front of them, blocking their way. "Were ye plannin' to leave without us?"

"One could only hope," said Roark.

Seamus cast an angry eye at Roark before directing his conversation to Niall. "We made a deal—unless ye be forgettin'."

Niall, his voice tight, struggled to keep his anger down. "I'm afraid our deal will have to wait. My mother's quite ill and we have to take her to see the doctor."

Seamus stuck out his chin and sneered. "I think ye're lyin'."

John was seething. "We've no time for this!"

Niall gazed at Seamus, observing his bloodshot eyes and tremors. "We've no reason to lie to you. You can come for the haying, but it won't be for another week."

"What're we supposed to be doin' in the meantime?"

"Do whatever you like," said John. "Just stay away from the farm for another week."

Molly put her hand imploringly on her husband's arm. "We'll be all right. We'll just go next week." Seamus roughly shook off her grip and sulked.

Molly looked at Niall. "Where are Saraid and the children?"

Niall tried to think of how much time it would take Saraid to get where she was going. In the end, he decided not to say where they'd gone. "They've already started out." He hoped Saraid would be able to come up with a story if Seamus decided to go there.

"One week," said Seamus. "We'll be seein' ye next Sunday mornin', then." He didn't wait for a reply before snapping his reins and heading off towards the road.

Patrick pulled his big wagon up behind Niall's caravan. "I'm all set. Let's get out of here."

The three wagons stayed close together and headed south towards the cliffs and the road to Ennis. They had traveled less than a mile before the steady stream of wagons came to a halt.

"Now what?" muttered Roark.

Several wagons ahead of them were blocked by a crude barricade across the road. The sheriff's men were searching the wagons. Roark looked back at Niall and shrugged. "There's only three or four of them that I can see."

Niall nodded. He looked at John. "Do you have your knife?"

John pulled his knife from the sheath in his boot and slid the blade under his thigh. "I hope to God Danny keeps his bloody mouth shut!"

Niall placed his own knife into his boot, out of sight but within easy reach.

The minutes ticked by slowly as each wagon was searched and then passed through the barricade. Roark was next. One man held his horse by the bit while the others poked through the contents of his wagon.

One of Charlies spoke to Roark. "It looks like you have family belongings here. Where's the rest of your people?"

Roark answered politely. "They've gone in another wagon to the Well. I'm meetin' 'em there."

Satisfied that he wasn't hiding anything, they allowed him to pass through.

John eased his horses forward. The same man held his horses still while the other men approached the caravan.

"Where are you folks headed?" one of them asked.

"We're taking our mother to the doctor in Ennis," replied John.

"She's quite sick."

The man headed towards the back of the wagon as he spoke to the Charlies. "Sounds like a likely story. I think we should check it out."

Niall tried to stay calm. "I'd rather you leave her be. She's really not well."

The man's face turned smug. "I'll just see about that."

The man ripped open the tarp closure, startling Kate. She raised her head awkwardly and faced the man, her hair and eyes wild. She let out a feral scream from her distorted mouth, spittle running to her chin. The man sprang away from the caravan, uttering a frightened cry which Kate answered with another cry of her own.

The other men came running. "What's goin' on?"

"My good God!" he panted. "Don't go near that wagon!"

The other man asked, "What's the matter with her?"

Patrick, who had a bird's eye view of the scene, fought to keep from laughing.

Niall calmly said, "I told you . . . she's sick."

"Let them through!" the man cried, still fighting to catch his breath. "Get 'em out of here!"

Niall and John pulled away quickly before the Charlies could change their minds. They pulled over further down the road where Roark was waiting for them. They got out of the wagons to check on Kate and make sure that Danny was all right. A few moments later Patrick joined them. "That was a bit closer than I bargained for."

John chuckled. "Mother's all right now. She gave a perfect performance!"

Patrick nodded his head. "It looked believable to me! How's Danny?"

Niall poked his head into the front of the caravan. He uncovered Danny's head and removed the gag. He was soaked with sweat and uttering gibberish.

Niall tried to get him to drink some water but most of it dribbled back out. "He's still burning up. We have to get moving."

Roark looked around and noticed that the Charlies had not detained the rest of the wagons. "I wonder how Willie managed to get through the barricade."

Just then, they heard a horse whinnying far off from the side of the road. It was Willie. He had tried to navigate his wagon through the clints and gotten stuck.

"Speak of the devil," said Patrick. The three men reached Willie as he was dismounting from his wagon to try to pull the wheels from the ruts.

Willie cringed when he heard the men coming, then sighed with relief when he saw who it was. "Thank God!" he cried. "Sure I had no idea how I was to be gettin' us out of here."

"What on earth were you doing, Willie?" asked Niall.

"I heard about the barricade just as soon as I left the camp, so I thought I would try to sneak around them. I almost made it before getting stuck here."

Niall and the other men checked out the terrain and figured that the only way out was to lift the wagon. Hank and Freddie got out of the wagon to lighten the load.

Patrick sighed and flexed his already aching muscles. "Let me get it."

Niall joined Patrick at the back of the wagon. Together, they lifted the back end as the others pushed against the wheels, freeing them.

Niall and John led the horse and wagon back to the road. At that point it was decided that, in the event of more trouble on the road, Hank should ride with Patrick.

Hank said his good-byes to Freddie and Willie and once again disappeared under the blankets.

Willie, relieved to have less to worry about, thanked the men and headed out.

The others remounted their wagons and followed down the hard-packed dirt road as fast as they dared. A few miles later they reached the turn to head to Ennis. They could hear the surf pounding against the cliffs as the tide rose.

A short while later, Roark broke off from them and headed to Liscannor to meet the women. He waved as the others went by. "We'll all meet up with ye at the farm."

Chapter Forty-Five

The atmosphere surrounding the Shamrock was heavy with the smell of anxious sweat and fear. A half-dozen clansmen, cursing and protesting their innocence, were being manhandled by the Charlies as they were herded into the tavern for questioning. Distraught family members cried out and wrung their hands to no avail while waiting for their release. Two men were posted outside the door to prevent anyone from entering or leaving.

Saraid reined in the horses as they neared, not wanting to get too close to the troubling scene. She glanced at Maureen, cocking an eyebrow in puzzlement. Maureen shrugged and said nothing.

"I wonder what's goin' on," said Saraid.

"It doesn't look any too good. Perhaps we should just forget tryin' to go in there."

Saraid looked around, then called out to a man who was standing alone, away from the others. "Ye there!"

The stranger looked at her and nodded his head solemnly.

She didn't recognize him but there were many here that were unknown to her. "Can ye be tellin' me what this is all about?" she asked, waving her arm at the troubling scene.

"Tis nothin' but trouble," he replied as he approached the wagon. "They're draggin' in anyone who might know what happened to Martin. They just found his cane down by the bay."

"Surely they don't think any of us is responsible," said Maureen.

"They's just grabbin' at straws. They's still lookin' fer that McMahon feller, too."

Saraid thought the man seemed friendly enough. She asked, "Is Jimmy around?"

He nodded. "He is, but he's a might busy in there tryin' to keep a lid on the trouble. He's keepin' the ale flowin' an' hopin' no one gets too ornery." He pushed his cap further back on his head and wiped his brow. "Seems Jack's disappeared, too."

Saraid looked at Maureen and whispered, "Maybe I could just be goin' in and askin' about gettin' some food to take with us."

The stranger looked away but was straining to hear what they were saying.

Maureen was aghast. "Why would ye be takin' such a chance?" she hissed. "Ye could be gettin' us stuck here for who knows how long! Think about the children!"

"Patrick is goin' to be right angry if I don't at least try."

Maureen shook her head. "Sure I'll be bloody angry myself if ye even *think* about gettin' out of this wagon!"

Saraid sighed, frustrated over the turn of events. She beckoned the man to come closer and spoke quietly. "Do ye know the barmaid, Annie?"

The man chuckled, his eyes twinkling. "I think most everyone knows Annie."

Saraid cringed inwardly but maintained a calm expression. "Do ye know where she might be?"

The man shook his head. "She ain't been seen since the other night. I got no idea where she's off to."

"Do ye know if they're servin' food in there?" asked Saraid, pointing to the tavern.

The man shook his head. "They's closed for business 'til things get sorted."

The children were getting impatient and beginning to fuss. James and Fiona, even as they stroked the horses necks and spoke softly to them, were having trouble keeping them calm. Saraid felt unease growing in the pit of her belly. She knew that Maureen was right. Much as she wanted to help Patrick, she couldn't jeopardize the children. She turned to the man and asked if he knew where Annie lived.

He shook his head. "I think she lives up the coast somewhere with her mother but I don' have a clue just where."

"All right then. Thanks for yer trouble." Saraid was left with no choices. Patrick would have to deal with his own problems. Something about the man made her uneasy, though there was nothing threatening in his demeanor. She turned to Maureen, who was trying to calm the twins. "Looks like we best be on our way."

"Now ye'd be makin' sense!"

The man nodded and drifted back to the to the edge of the crowd. Though pretending to pay them no mind, he kept sight of Saraid as she snapped the reins, guided the horses to turn the wagon around, and headed down the coast road. When they had disappeared from view, he sauntered over to the Shamrock and whispered something to one of the guards, who rose swiftly from his seat and went into the tavern. He returned shortly with the sheriff who conversed quietly with the man, nodding his head as he spoke. He thanked him for the information and gave him instructions. The stranger mounted his horse and took off down the road in the direction Saraid had gone.

Another man standing away from the others had watched the scene unfold. He sounded a hoot above the noise of the crowd. Several clansmen, who had also been watching Saraid's conversation with the stranger, acknowledged the warning with a whistle of their own. Before long, they were mounted and slowly trotted away from the crowd. When they were out of sight of the tavern, they cropped their horses and galloped away in swift pursuit of the lone man who had followed her.

***

Saraid reached the Cliffs of Moher and made the turn towards Liscannor that would take them to Saint Brigid's Well. She thought about how Annie would be feeling before long, thinking that Patrick had abandoned her. Being distracted, she didn't hear the man galloping up beside the wagon until he came into view beside her. He grabbed the reins from her hands, pulling back on them to stop the horses. James and Fiona cried out as the horses reared. They both grabbed handfuls of the horses' manes and dug their knees into the horses sides to stay upright.

"What in bloody hell do ye think ye're doin'?" Saraid shrieked. Furious to be caught off guard, she reached in vain for the reins.

"Ye need to turn the wagon around," he ordered. "The sheriff wants to speak to you."

Filled with rage, Saraid grabbed for her knife as the wagon came to a stop. As he leaned over her to gather up the slack in the reins, she lashed out at his hand with the blade.

He yelped as it bit into his skin and backhanded her across the face, his bloody hand smearing her cheek. She fell across Maureen's lap, dazed. Maureen screamed at him to stop. "What would the sheriff be wantin' with us? We aren't doin' anythin' wrong!"

Saraid recovered quickly and lashed out again with the blade. She missed her target and this time the man used his fist. Saraid slumped over, her mouth bloody. The knife fell from her hand, as everything went black.

Just as James leapt from his horse to come to his mother's aid, Roark and six men of the clans roared onto the scene. Roark rapidly whirled his cat o' nine tails over his head, the sound of it whistling in the air. With a quick flick of his wrist, he aimed the thin bands of knotted cotton cord and it unfurled, circling the man's face and neck. Roark yanked the wooden handle and pulled the man from his horse. The man screamed with pain as the cords lacerated his skin and blood poured from his wounds. He struggled to get up and free himself, but Roark tightened his grip on the cat until the man lay still.

Liam, Bridget and the twins began wailing from the wagon, while Fiona and James cowered with fear.

"Are ye all right, Maureen?" Roark yelled.

Maureen nodded silently, tears flowing down her face as she helped Saraid to sit up.

Roark, filled with fury, dismounted and approached the man who lay still and bleeding in the dirt. He made no move to release the cat from around the man's neck. "What feckin' reason do ye have for attackin' these women and children?"

The man struggled to speak. "The sheriff told me to fetch them back to the tavern. He wants to speak to 'em."

Roark pulled the cat tight and set his foot on the man's chest. "What gave him cause to want to speak to 'em?"

The man groaned with pain but stayed silent. When Roark tightened his grip, the man winced, tears glistening in his eyes. "Stop! I . . . I told the sheriff they was askin' questions about Annie."

Roark's fist found the man's face and the man fell unconscious, fresh blood flowing from his cuts. He motioned to the other clansmen who had already dismounted. Together, they dragged the inert man behind a stand of scrub and bound his hands and feet. Roark unwound the bloody cat from the man's head and stuffed a gag into his mouth.

The women were overcome with relief. "Roark, what on earth is goin' on?" asked Maureen. "An' why are ye with these men?"

"They caught up to me on the road and said ye were being followed by this one," he said, gesturing to the man who was no longer a threat. His anger was palpable. "Do ye know why he was followin' ye?"

She explained how they had stopped near the Shamrock and asked the man some questions.

Roark's voice was more stern than Maureen had ever heard. "You need not be askin' questions of strangers! Especially now! Ye're lucky these others were watchin' and set out to keep ye from harm."

Saraid blinked away the cobwebs in her head and rubbed her cheek. She worked her tongue around her mouth and spat out the remnants of a bloody broken tooth. "We wanted to get food for Annie, but that didn't happen. I never thought . . . ."

"No sense worryin' about it now," muttered Roark. He paced around the wagon to check on the children, soothing them as best he could. "We need to get out of here."

Fiona asked, "Are we still going to the Well?"

Saraid drew in a breath and let it out slowly. She recovered and sheathed her knife and looked up at Roark. "Sure we'll be fine there. It'll be crowded with kin folk."

Maureen looked at her husband, her expression blank. "What do ye think about it?"

"I think Saraid is determined to have her way," he said in disgust. He coiled up his cat and looped it over his saddle horn. "She's right that there will be a crowd there. I'll be with you, too, so you'll be safe enough."

Roark thanked the men for their help and shook their hands. They bid them good-bye as they rode off to return to their voluntary post at the tavern. They would continue to watch out for their kinsmen until the matters there were settled.

Maureen nodded silently, secretly pleased that they would still be making their pilgrimage. The ancient rituals of Saint Brigid's Well were as important to her as they were to Saraid.

They left the bound man at the side of the road, tying his horse to the scrub. Someone would find him before long. They still had several miles to go and wasted no more time talking about it.

Chapter Forty-Six

As they neared the sacred site, lines of people crowded the road, slowing the wagons. Some were pilgrims with bedrolls who had held vigil through the night and were now heading home. Many others were still joining the procession, waiting to take their turn with their offerings and prayers.

Brigid was the patron goddess of the ancient Celtic Druids and many of the Irish people still honored the pagan ways. The Catholic Church had found it too difficult to convert the pagans from all of their long-held beliefs, so they made some of their goddesses, like Brigid, Christian saints.

There were many wells throughout Ireland that honored this revered saint, whose feast day was celebrated on February 1st. There were four other *Pattern Days*, as they were called, throughout the year. *Domhnach Crom Dubh*, the greatest of her days on the Celtic calendar, was celebrated on the last Sunday of July, with the vigil held the night before. There were many rituals performed, prayers offered up, supplications made. For many of the clan women, going to the Well was an added benefit of traveling to Doolin for the *Ceilidh* on that same weekend.

"What's that cross, Mam?" asked Fiona, referring to the large stone cross that stood majestically on a rise behind the site of the Well.

Saraid explained to all the children. "That's the cemetery where the ancient O'Brien men, Kings of the *Dal gCais*, are buried. They're yer ancestors."

James's ears perked up. He had an abiding interest in the legends of his people. "Can we walk through the cemetery?"

"Perhaps Roark will walk ye through while we go to the Well, though I think ye'd enjoy the Well, too."

Roark scowled. "I think it best we stick together."

James was disappointed. "What's so special about Saint Brigid, anyway?"

"Sure she's a great one," said Saraid. "She's the goddess of all high things: tall flames, the mountains, and healing. They also say that those with high minds who are very wise, and those who make great things with their hands, as well as the great poets, are blessed by Saint Brigid. In Kildare, in the east of Ireland, she's called the Goddess of the Sacred Flame, which rises high in the sky. The priestesses there keep the flame going at all times."

Fiona was spell-bound. "I wish we could see her."

Saraid chuckled. "Ye'll have to settle for a stone statue. She's dead many years, now."

Roark motioned them to the side of the road where many wagons were parked. "I think it best we take that bit of space," he said, pointing to an area where another wagon was pulling out.

The children jumped from the wagon and began running about, even as the adults admonished them to stay close. Saraid and Maureen retrieved their offerings from the wagon as Roark herded the children. Saraid handed a seashell to each of the little ones. "Ye save this now to give to Brigid." She handed Fiona a small piece of lace and took one for herself.

Maureen took a small bunch of rosemary and thyme that she had tied together with string and handed it to James, keeping another for herself.

Roark noticed a few men wandering furtively about the wagons looking to do a bit of thievery. "Ye go on ahead. I think I'll stay here and watch the wagon."

James asked, "Can I stay with you?"

Roark shrugged. "If it's all right with yer mam."

Saraid nodded. "The crowd seems to be thinnin' some, so we won't be too long."

Fiona had skipped on ahead, exuding excitement as she anxiously waited for them to catch up. She watched as the pilgrims walked single file, most of them barefoot, to the statue of Saint Brigid. One by one they knelt and prayed for personal healing of their aches and pains, then recited the prayer:

> *Go mbeannaí íosa duit, a Bhrighid Naofa, Go mbeannaí Muire duit is go mbannaím Féin duit: Chugat a thána mé ag gearán mo scéil chugat Agus d'iarraidh cabhair in onóir Dé ort.*
>
> *(May Jesus salute you, O holy Brigid, may Mary salute you and may I salute you myself. It is to you I have come making my complaint and asking your help for the honour of God.)*

Their voices continued, almost as a whisper, with recitations of the Our Father, the Hail Mary and the Glory be to the Father. Then they rose, reciting the Creed, as they circled the statue three times. The pilgrims then climbed the steps behind the well to the crypt of the ancient O'Brien kings, to the tall cross, and circled it while once again saying the ritual prayers. After they kissed the stone, they descended the stone steps into the Holy Well.

Saraid, Maureen, and the children followed the others in single file. When their turn came, Saraid knelt and closed her eyes. With the ailing Kate heavy on her mind, she prayed for her healing, hoping she would not be called upon to care for her. Kate would surely resent anything she attempted to do for her, making them both miserable. Saraid sighed knowing that, in the end, she would do whatever was needed for her family.

The Well house was made of stone and lit by candles. As they went down the steps to the *Ula íochtarach*, the lower sanctuary, they could hear the lapping water. The chill of the underground space was defused by the warm bodies within. The walls were decorated with the votive offerings made by the pilgrims. Shells, beads, pictures, candles, bits of cloth and rosary beads hung in disarray from the stones. One by one, Saraid's family added their own bits to the jumble.

Saraid closed her eyes, took in a slow breath, then let the air escape from her lips. Gooseflesh prickled her skin and she smiled, feeling the holy presence of Brigid surround her. She reached for Maureen's hand; and, as their eyes connected, they shared a sense of well-being.

There was an elderly gentleman standing by the Well with a mug of water that he offered to the approaching pilgrims. Drinking from the Holy Well marked the conclusion of the ritual.

Saraid put her hand on Fiona's shoulder and whispered, "They say there's a fish in the Well. If ye see it, yer prayers will be granted."

Fiona was very quiet as they left the dimness of the holy space and emerged into the sunlight. She looked to her mother. "I felt very odd in there."

Saraid put her arm around Fiona's narrow shoulders. "Odd how?"

"I felt shivery."

"It's a very sacred place. Ye were feelin' the spirit of Brigid."

The little ones, too, were subdued, as if they had been enchanted by spirits to be on their best behavior. They walked back to the wagon and found Roark and James sitting in the cool of an old oak tree, talking quietly.

"*Da!*" cried one of the twins.

Roark stood and held his arms out to the toddlers. "Did ye see the Well?" He scooped them up, one on each hip, and nuzzled their necks as he joined the women.

Maureen asked, "Did ye take James to the vaults?"

Roark shook his head. "Too many scamps around. Can we head home now?"

The women smiled at each other and at him. Their holy mission was complete. "Yes. Let's go home."

Chapter Forty-Seven

The O'Brien men drove their wagons through the countryside at a steady pace. The further they traveled from Doolin, the fresher the air became, the salty haze and barrenness of the Burren, nothing but a memory. When the road led them past Lisdoonvarna, Patrick longed to stop and soak away his agitation in one of the hot mineral springs, but there was no time for that. As they approached Ennistymon, the smell of brown earth baking under a hot sun filled the air under a clear sky, evoking other memories of home. The hillsides were dotted with small farms surrounded by acres of harvest-ready crops and people working in the fields.

They finally came to a deserted area in a copse of trees by a slow running stream. They pulled the wagons off the road, grateful for the leafy canopy that provided cooling shade and a modicum of breeze. The men dismounted to stretch their legs and check on their passengers, while the horses drank their fill.

"Let's get Danny uncovered so he can get some air," said Niall.

John went to the back of his wagon and helped Kate to sit up. He rolled up a blanket and put it behind her back, gently taking her hand in his. "Are you all right, Mother?"

She gave a small lopsided smile but didn't speak. She pointed to Danny who lay unmoving behind her and shook her head.

Niall and John climbed into the wagon while Patrick and Hank tended to the horses. They pulled the blanket away from Danny's face and felt the heat emanating from his body. Niall fought down his fear and pulled Danny up and rested him against his chest. The younger man was completely limp and moaning incoherently, his clothing soaking wet.

"We need to do something right now or he isn't going to make it," said Niall.

"Patrick!" cried John.

As Patrick came running, John said, "He's really burning up! We need to get him into the water to cool him down."

Patrick had misgivings. "I hope the shock of it doesn't kill him."

"It's his only chance," said Niall.

They passed Danny's nearly lifeless body out of the wagon and Patrick carried him to the stream. After the men removed his boots and clothing, Patrick lifted him again and waded into the stream. He didn't know if Danny could hear him but he warned him about the shock he was about to get. "This is going to kick your arse, Danny."

He knelt in the cold water and bent forward, submerging Danny who lashed out violently. Patrick held him firmly against his chest but Danny kept kicking as his head went beneath the water. After a long moment, Patrick lifted him out of the water and carried his dripping body to the grass. Danny was shivering uncontrollably.

Niall ran for a blanket and the men dried Danny as best they could and put him into some dry clothes. Hank was wringing his hands and whimpering. Niall lost patience with the man. "Get a hold of yourself, Hank! I don't have time to listen to your sniveling!" Hank turned and walked unsteadily back to the wagon and climbed inside.

"We need to get going before he dies on us," said Patrick, squeezing the water from his tunic. "I don't think . . . ."

"Don't say it!" cried Niall. "We'll get him to the doc and he'll be fine!"

Patrick looked at John, who shrugged. Though they wanted to believe Niall, fear gripped them both.

They got Danny back into the wagon and wrapped him in a dry blanket, settling him so that his head was within reach of Kate's hand. John put a wet cloth on his forehead.

"Mother, can you sponge his face as we go along?"

Kate nodded, raising her good hand. John put a small bucket of cold water from the stream beside her and patted her shoulder. "Thank you, Mother."

An hour later, they approached the busy market town.

Ennis, shortened from its original Irish name, '*Inis Cluain Ramh Fhada*', meaning island of the long rowing meadow, was the capitol city of County Clare. It sat between two branches of the River Fergus, just north of where the river flowed into the Shannon estuary. There were no walls around the city, which made it a godsend for Catholics who, after the Penal Laws, were forbidden from living in walled cities. It was a haven for travelers and for those doing trade.

Centuries before, the O'Brien kings had moved their seat of power from Limerick and had built a castle, Clonroad, on the island. In 1240, King Donnchadh O'Brien had built sprawling church grounds with an abbey for the followers of St Francis. It became a theological college where hordes of students came to study under the Friars, until the English dissolved the monasteries.

It was Sunday afternoon and people were wandering the town, enjoying the pubs and browsing the tidy shops. There was little space between the shops but for a few small alleyways.

The O'Brien men kept up their pace, the horses' hooves beating a steady clacking rhythm on the cobbled road as the wagons wove through the pedestrians and other wagons in the congested streets.

They continued on until they came to a solitary stone house with a firm thatched roof on a private parcel of land at the outskirts of town. It was surrounded by small trees and neat hedges of blackthorn. It was a far cry from the customary five-hundred-acre plot originally bestowed upon the doctors who tended the various clans. Doctor O'Hickey, too, had lost land to the Anglos. The brothers steered their wagons down the curved dirt drive coming to a stop behind the building where they would not be seen by passersby.

Niall jumped from his wagon and rapped the brass knocker against the wooden door. Dr. O'Hickey's wife, Martha, answered the door with a smile. "Well hello, Niall. What brings ye here on a Sunday?"

"We have some problems and need the doc right away."

A deep baritone voice called out from within the house. "Who is it, Martha?"

"Come in, come in," Martha said, motioning him into the parlor. She eyed the wagons and said, "My goodness, there be a lot of ye."

Niall smiled at the small, plump woman who never seemed to change. The ruffled edging on her cap bounced in time with her steps as he followed her down the hallway. The smell of antiseptic wafted through the rooms, mixing with the aroma of cabbage and ham simmering on the stove. Niall's mouth watered, and he realized that he hadn't eaten for many hours.

Dr. O'Hickey approached Niall with his hand held out in greeting. "Niall! Good to see you. What seems to be the trouble?"

The doctor's resonant voice belied his stature. He stood all of five-foot-six-inches tall, had a narrow frame, spindly legs beneath his britches, and thinning hair which he wore long. He peered at Niall over his gold-rimmed spectacles, which had found a perch on the end of his pointed nose. His eyes were sharp, though, and showed great intelligence. He, as well as his father and grandfather before him, had been the official physicians to a long line of O'Briens. They prided themselves on having knowledge of all the latest treatments and cures available at the time.

"Well," began Niall, "we seem to have more than one." He looked around a corner to the parlor and then whispered, "Are you alone here?"

The doctor nodded. "Yes. Being a Sunday, we don't get too many folks in. They know I like a day to myself. But not to worry. How can

I be of help?"

Niall sighed with relief. "We've just come from Doolin. My mother seems to have had some kind of spell . . . two of them, actually. They've left her disfigured in her face and her speech is slurry. Her entire left side seems stiff. And then, there's Danny. He's been shot and he's half dead."

Dr. O'Hickey turned to Martha. "Quickly! Get a bed ready for the lad." He turned to Niall and went with him to the door. "Where are they?"

"We put the wagons out back. We didn't want anyone to see Danny. The sheriff's looking for him."

Dr. O'Hickey chuckled. "The lad's been up to his old tricks, has he?"

They walked behind the building where the others were waiting. The doctor waved to John and Patrick and looked at Kate, who was sitting at the back of the wagon with her legs dangling over the side. "Good to see you, Kate," he said as he took her hand and studied her face. "Let's get you inside so I can take a look at you." He left her to John, who carefully lifted her down and took her into the house by the back entrance. To Niall and Patrick, he motioned to the wagon. "Is our young friend inside?"

They nodded and the doctor climbed into the wagon to take a look. He ran his hands over Danny's forehead. "Good God," he said. "He's burning up." He unwrapped the bandage to take a peek at the wound. He gently probed the shoulder and shook his head. "You were correct, Niall. He's half dead." He hopped out of the wagon and motioned to the house. "Quickly now, bring him inside."

Hank was told to stay with the wagons and keep a look out.

Patrick pulled Danny gently into his arms and carried him into the house to the room where Martha directed them. They helped to undress Danny and then the doctor motioned them out of the room. "Martha, dear," he called out calmly. "Get the kettle on to boil."

The brothers paced the floor of the parlor for a long time before the doctor came out to them. "All right, then. Tell me what happened and what you've done for him."

Niall explained things as plainly as possible, ending with the dunking in the stream.

"Well," O'Hickey replied. "It sounds like you've done all you could do for him. Saraid did well to use honey and herbs in the salve. Unfortunately, his wound is severe, and the infection is already pronounced. Musket balls are full of foul bacteria. I'll need to debride the tissue surrounding the wound.

"What's debriding?" asked John.

"It means the cutting away of the infected flesh. We are learning more all the time about fighting gunshots from treating battle wounds in the fields. I am fortunate that I receive correspondence from some learned military doctors."

The O'Brien men listened attentively.

"Once I cleanse the wound, I'll cut away the dead tissue and clean it with alcohol. Then I'll pack the cavity with sugar and cover it with a clean linen bandage. As the sugar forms a semi-liquid, it will be washed out with water, taking the infection with it. I'll need to do this several times a day until the infection clears." He shook his head. "That is, if he survives the night."

Niall trembled and clenched his hands together behind his back. "If he makes it through the night, how long do you figure it will take 'til he's well?"

Dr. O'Hickey shrugged. "I would say at least a month, perhaps two."

"That long?" asked Niall.

The doctor nodded.

Patrick wondered how they would care for him. "Can we take him home?"

"Absolutely not," said the doctor, his deep voice adamant. "We'll keep him here."

"Are you sure?" asked Niall. "Will it be safe?"

The doctor could only hope that it would be. "I don't think that anyone will come looking for him here. Martha and I will care for him. We'll send along a message to you when he is well." Then he sighed. "We'll send a message either way. You have to prepare yourselves for the worst."

Niall eyed his brothers and none of them could speak. The possibility of Danny dying was too much to fathom. He looked out the window and couldn't help but think about the Banshee, wondering if her warning had been meant for Danny. Then he sighed, knowing that the omen was for himself alone.

The doctor broke the heavy silence. "Now, let's go see about your mother."

After he did a cursory examination, he smiled at Kate. "Your heart is strong as an ox and your breathing is just fine." Then he excused himself and went to find his wife.

"Martha," he said, speaking quietly.

"What is it, dear?" She was standing in front of the stove, waiting for the water to boil.

"Can you bring me a flower from the garden and a bite of that ham you have cooking?"

She knew better than to question him. "Certainly."

He returned to Kate and told her to close her eyes so that he could test her other senses.

John held her hand as she complied. "I can already tell that your hearing isn't impaired."

Martha entered the room quietly with a bit of ham on a plate and a single yellow rose.

Doctor O'Hickey held the bloom under Kate's nose. "What do you smell?"

Kate breathed in through her nose and gave a lopsided grin as the fragrance tickled her nostrils. "A rosh!"

"Very good," O'Hickey replied. "Now I want you to open your mouth." He slipped the tines of the fork with the tidbit of ham into her mouth and Kate chewed the meat. "Haaam," she said, drawing out the word as she wiped a bit of drool from her chin.

"Excellent! You can open your eyes now."

Kate blinked several times, the bright light causing a bit of dizziness. She sought to cover her eyes, but the doctor held her hand. "Are you feeling a bit squeamish?"

Kate nodded. He reassured her that it should pass in a moment or two. He asked her to raise one arm and then the other, then to try to raise her legs. He could see the weakness on the left side for both. He turned to her sons and crossed his arms over his chest. "I believe she has had a mild bout of apoplexy."

Kate's sons showed their worry and John asked, "What on earth is that?"

"They say it is caused by a blockage in the arteries of the neck to the brain, specifically the carotid artery. Sometimes the effects are much worse than this. If normal blood flow in the brain is stopped, a hemorrhage can occur when the blood becomes trapped. Or, if enough blood is prevented from getting to the brain, it can cause dizziness and fainting. She could have lost her sight or her hearing, or even her state of consciousness. Complete paralysis is not unheard of."

"So what can you do?" asked Patrick.

"The course of treatment in severe cases is bloodletting but I don't abide with that. Certainly not for your mother."

The O'Brien men were aghast. John stammered. "You mean take blood from her head?"

O'Hickey nodded. "It's difficult to know if the problem comes from blood going to the brain or too much blood trapped therein. If we drain blood and the pathways to the brain are clogged, it can cause death."

The brothers were becoming more worried than calm. "So, will she be all right?" asked Niall.

The doctor shrugged. "Sometimes these spells are a forewarning of a larger attack. I can tell you that she probably has what is called high blood pressure."

"What can we do about that?" asked Patrick

"She needs to rest and to have calmness in her life."

Niall couldn't help his chuckle. "That isn't an easy thing to come by in our family."

"Well," the doctor said, "you'll have to try. She's all right for now. Since she is obviously in good health otherwise, the paralysis in her face and limbs will probably be only temporary."

Kate looked at the men, who were discussing her as if she weren't in the room. Angry bile churned in her belly, nerve endings tingling at the roots of her hair, giving her strength. She rose unsteadily, but unaided, from the chair. "Taaa . . . mmmee . . . *hooome*! *Now*!" Without another glance at any of them, she straightened her back and, determinedly dragging her left foot, limped from the room.

They stood for just a moment in stunned silence before John bolted after her. Niall hung back to pay the doctor, who refused to take payment of any kind.

"I am well compensated by you yearly, needed or not, and it is a privilege to care for you now."

Niall took a last look in on Danny, giving his good shoulder a squeeze. "We'll be back for you, Danny. You get well, you hear me?"

Danny lay silent and still, his breathing shallow.

Niall ran his fingers over Danny's damp hair, feeling disheartened and yet angry. "You stupid fool," he whispered. His chest tightened and a mist came to his eyes. "We love you Daniel McMahon. Don't you dare die on us!"

Chapter Forty-Eight

Annie sat at the table staring into the twilight through the open door, willing the sound of a wagon to approach, the crunch of a footfall on the stones, or a knock on the door to signal Patrick's return. Many wagons had passed by the shanty as families departed Doolin, but none had stopped. Voices had called out to others, but none said her name. Annie longed to run from her chair to the rough path that led to the road, but her aching ankle would not allow it. As the swelling pushed sharply against the bandage, she tied it yet tighter to hold it at bay. Her belly ached with a rumbling hunger that was difficult to ignore. Hours had passed, the stub of a candle had long ago burned out; yet she continued to sit, her head now resting on her arms on the table. There was nothing else she could do.

The only sounds in the darkness came from her mother, who muttered a litany of curses and complaints under her breath, berating Annie with harsh words for her stupidity and poor morals.

Feelings of worthlessness, guilt and shame wrapped her in a shroud of desolation. Just when she felt that she could cry no more, the deep ache of abandonment and loss would flood her anew, and the lonely tears would begin again. Night had fallen and still Patrick had not come back. Her mind tried to accept this with some shred of dignity, thinking of reasons why he could not return, even if he'd had a mind to. Her heart still clung to the faintest glimmer of hope. Strands of memories wove through her mind: walking hand in hand across the Burren, the wildflowers, the cave, his shy, yet burning desire for her. The tenderness they had shared after their frenzied lovemaking smoldered in her with a different kind of fire. Annie's chest ached with longing to give him the same sense of safety and peace she had felt in his arms. She yearned to lay her face against his neck and sigh with the feeling of finally finding the place where she belonged. Though it was mid-summer, she shivered. Hot wet tears streamed in silent misery down her cheeks, stinging the chaffed skin where she had repeatedly rubbed them away.

In the late hours when hope waned, she chided herself for believing in him. Had all she felt been just a desperate longing in her own heart to be saved from this wretched life? Hadn't he felt it, too? Or, had he just used her as so many others had, with no thought of a special bond and being part of a whole? How she longed to share this pain with her mother, to be comforted by her! Knowing that her mother had nothing to give her but shameful insults, Annie pulled a blanket from her cot and wrapped it tightly around herself. Her body rocked in the straight-backed chair, eyes tightly closed, whispering a prayer to a God she wasn't sure existed. How could God visit so much despair on one person?

At last her mother slept and the night became still and silent as a shadow. Even the receding tide had grown quiet with a barely discernible ripple against the rocks outside the shanty. Annie rose, slowly closed the door and limped to her cot where she succumbed to a fitful, exhausted sleep.

Even in slumber, Annie suffered. Dreams dark with fear of Jack's wrath, of hanging by her neck from some desolate tree for her crime, pursued her in the darkness. She ran and ran and ran over hard ground, her feet cut to ribbons, leaving easy to follow tracks of blood in her wake. The cave! She had to get to the cave. Only there would she be safe from Jack's treachery. Through the night she ran, but try as she may, the narrow entrance eluded her. Her muffled cries carried on the night air into the emptiness that surrounded her. From a great distance she could hear her mother's voice muttering at her in disgust.

"Shame on you!"

***

As the first gray promise of morning approached, a wagon lumbered down the road and came to a stop above the path to the shanty. The driver hesitated, looking up and down the quiet road before finally dismounting. Using her shillelagh, she carefully descended the rocky path and rapped her knuckles against the weathered door.

Inside, Annie's eyes blinked and a jolt of hope filled her. *Patrick*! She jumped from the bed and nearly stumbled as pain rocked her leg. She limped across the room and swung open the door, her smile freezing in place on her face. Not Patrick.

"Auntie Ro?" she asked, her voice thick from sleep. Pulling her matted hair back from her face, she asked, "What is it ye be wantin' here at the crack of dawn?"

Roisin's eyes darted to the road, then held Annie's gaze, her fear visible on her countenance. "I need help."

Annie burst into mirthless laughter. The absurdity of the situation brought her to near hysteria. Roisin grabbed Annie's arm and shook her angrily. "Sure I don't know what ye be findin' so funny, missy!"

"Oh, Auntie Ro! Ye be comin' to the wrong place if ye be needin' help from me!" She began to laugh again then sobered as she saw that Ro was serious. She held out her bandaged ankle. "I can't walk, an' we be starvin' here. I ain't even got a stale crust to offer ye."

Roisin bit back a retort. She hadn't survived the harrowing night by being stupid. "I'll make a deal with ye. I'll feed ye if ye let me hide out here for a bit and get some rest."

Annie stepped aside and allowed the woman to enter. Annie's mother stirred and asked who was there. Roisin walked to the disheveled woman and introduced herself.

Annie's mother eyed her warily, offering no hand of welcome.

"Mary Muldoon, I be.

Auntie Ro said, "I just escaped from Jack and I'm beggin' ye not to turn me out."

Annie's hand flew to her mouth as the blood drained from her face. "What're ye sayin'?"

"Yesterday, when I give ye an' Patrick a ride, Jack was hidin' under the blanket in the back of the wagon. That's why I told ye to ride in the front. I come here to tell ye that he knows yer here and might be back to get ye before long."

Annie struggled to understand. "How did he end up with ye?"

Roisin decided there was no need to tell them that Jack was her son. She still had some trouble accepting the truth of that. "He forced me to hide him in my wagon and git him out of Doolin. I was s'posed to take him to Ennis, but I feared being alone with him on that lonely stretch of road. He had my shillelagh so I couldn't defend m'self, neither. So, I headed north toward Galway instead. I knew I'd come across some travelin' folks that could help me."

She gestured to the stove before heading to the door. "Put some water on to boil. I'll get m' bag and I'll share what food I have with ye. Then I'll tell ye the rest."

Roisin lumbered back to the road and returned with a sack. She spread the contents on the table; bread, butter, a chunk of ham, the fragrance of which set Annie's mouth to watering. Roisin also held out a tin of loose tea.

Mary had risen from her chair and shuffled to the table. She grabbed at the bread, tore off a chunk, and stuffed it into her mouth. Her eyes closed as she chewed, but her mouth was so dry that she began to choke when she tried to swallow. Roisin slapped her back until she coughed to dislodge the crust. Annie sat her down and made her drink some water.

"No need to act like ye never ate before!" Annie cried, embarrassed by her mother's poor manners.

"Well if ye'd brought food home like ye was s'posed to, I wouldn't be starvin' now, would I?"

Annie blanched, her eyes filling again. "I already told ye I was sorry!"

"Well, ye got food now, missus," Roisin said as she prepared the tea.

Annie set chipped plates on the table and took a knife to the bread. The soft butter gleamed from its crock, its fragrance a bit rancid from the heat. The ham, too, wasn't as fresh as it could be and they cut away the gray bits with regret. Roisin pulled two apples from the sack and they cut them up, too. They savored their juicy tartness until all that was left were the cores and brown seeds.

"So how did ye get free of Jack?" asked Annie.

Roisin shook her head remembering the ordeal. "I come across some men who knew me from the story tellin'. They'd stopped on the side of the road to eat their meal. I tol' Jack I needed to relieve m'self an' he complained 'bout it, but what could he do? I tol' him there was men about and he should stay hidden. Then I went to the men an' told 'em that Jack was hidin' in the wagon an' forcin' me to take him away." She laughed at the memory of it. "They rousted him out faster than ye could spit! I give 'em money from Jack's sack of coin an' they said they'd keep him fer a time so I could get away."

The women chuckled as they pictured the sight.

Roisin continued. "I got my shillelagh back and took this, too," she said as she plopped a small sack of coins on the table. "It'll keep me goin' for a time."

"Now then, Annie," Roisin continued. "I think it best if ye leave here for a while."

"An' just where would I be goin?"

"I don' rightly know, but it ain't safe fer ye here."

"I can't just leave mam by herself!"

"Is there somewhere else she can stay for a while? Do ye have other family 'round here?"

Mary pounded her fist on the table. "I ain't leavin' my home! Ye can leave if ye want to, an' maybe ye should. Y'ain't much use to me anyway with yer whorin' ways! Ye bring nothin' but shame to my door!"

Annie's heart shattered at her mother's cruel words. "Ye can't be meanin' that, Mam."

"I do mean it. Just get on out an' leave me be." She rose from the table and went to her chair by the window and stared out at the sea. "Lookin' on ye makes me sick, it does."

Roisin looked from Mary to Annie and shook her head. "I don' rightly know how ye can be so spiteful, missus. Ireland's become a hard place and we all be doin' what we got to do to survive. How are ye plannin' to survive all alone out here if she be leavin' ye?"

"Sure it ain't none o' yer bloody business now, is it?" Mary knew there wasn't much hope of her own survival if Annie left, and she really didn't care. It would be a comfort to do without Annie hovering over her, taking away her mead. It cut her heart in two to say the wretched things she had just said to her daughter. Her own shame was calmed by knowing that at least Annie would have a chance if she left. Annie was young and strong and made of much tougher stuff than she was. She looked around the shanty, despising the place. Without her husband and her precious son, there was no laughter to be found anywhere. A single tear trickled down her cheek. She would be grateful when death found her.

Annie crossed the room and knelt before her mother, hugging the woman's thin legs. "Please don' send me away."

Mary pushed her away, her heart breaking. "Just be gone with ye! I don' want ye here."

"What will you say to Patrick if he comes?" Annie's cheeks were streaked with tears and she wiped her nose on her sleeve.

Mary's hand suddenly slapped Annie's face so hard that she toppled to the floor. "Ye stupid slut! Can't ye git it through yer thick head? He ain't comin' back! Ye don't deserve him! He's left ye here like all t'others done."

Annie lay on the floor retching, bits of her meager meal pooling around her face as she wailed with grief and shame.

Roisin struggled to pull Annie up from the floor and half carried her to the table. She wiped the vomit from her feverish face with a damp cloth and scowled at Mary. "May God in his mercy forgive ye."

"It ain't me that needs forgivin'!" Mary bellowed. A bolt of pain seized Mary's arm and wrapped her chest in a vise. She gasped as she clutched her breast and dizziness filled her head. She fell back panting, each breath a knife cutting into her chest.

Annie and Roisin ran to her and Annie sobbed her name. Mary looked at her with glassy eyes and feebly reached for her hand. "I din' mean it," she whispered. "Sure I just wanted ye to go and be safe." Her last breath escaped her lips like a sigh and she was gone.

Annie dropped to her knees, buried her face in her mother's lap, and sobbed. "Don't leave me!"

Roisin sat down heavily at the table and put her face down against her arms, her own tears streaming. Now she understood what Mary had intended. She raised her head and took a deep breath. "Annie?"

Annie struggled to her feet and stood silent, staring at her mother, marveling at the peace that had found its way to her face. The lines that had creased her forehead lay quiet and smooth, her lips slightly parted, the hint of a smile gracing them. Annie wiped her eyes and turned to Roisin. "She did love me, din' she?"

"Ye poor child, of course she did," Roisin whispered. "Much as it pains me to say so, we need to see about gettin' her buried so we can leave here. Do ye know anyone who can help?"

Annie shook her head, sniffling. "I know she wanted to be buried at sea, to be with my da and my brother."

"Do ye have a boat?"

Annie nodded. "Just a small row boat but it don' leak. I use it for clammin' sometimes. If ye can help me get her to it, I can row her out."

Roisin sighed. "All right then."

The two women worked in silence. They wrapped Mary's body in a sheet and tore strips from the end of it to secure her within it. They lay a blanket on the floor and rolled Mary's body onto it. Annie struggled with the pain in her foot, but grit her teeth. Finally, with several stops to rest, they managed to drag Mary's body across the rocks to the boat. They were both thankful that Mary weighed near to nothing. Even so, they were panting by the time they had settled her into the bottom of the boat.

Annie rowed out through the small waves for some twenty feet, while Roisin watched nervously from shore, fearing she would get caught up in the tide's undertow. Annie secured the oars and, standing, began to shift her mother's bound feet over the back of the boat. The rowboat rocked dangerously and Annie gasped, fearing she'd end up in the water herself. She sat for a moment and closed her eyes in prayer. She knelt in the bottom of the boat and pushed more of her mother's body into the water until only her upper torso remained. Touching her lips to Mary's bound head, she whispered, "Go in peace to join the ones ye loved. They'll be waitin' on ye."

As she heaved the last of the body into the choppy water, the spray soared above her head and rained down in a shower of twinkling prisms in the sunlight. Annie wiped the droplets from her face and watched the white sheeted mass float just under the surface for a moment before the current found it and pulled it into its embrace.

"Good bye, Mam. I'll try to make ye proud of me."

Back in the cabin, Annie silently re-bound her ankle. They went through the small living space methodically. Annie packed her few clothes into a bedroll and gathered up what few possessions would help them on their journey. Roisin loaded the spare blankets, the few cooking pots and eating utensils into the wagon.

"Where are we goin'?" asked Annie as she climbed into the wagon.

Roisin shrugged as she snapped the reins. "As far as we can. There's enough money in Jack's pouch to get by for a time."

They headed south past Doolin, away from Jack, the chaos, and away from Patrick. As they passed the Cliffs of Moher, Annie heard the waves as they crashed into the rocks below. The last days had made her feel much like the rocks, had they been a living thing, with the waves pounding relentlessly against them.

They traveled on in silence for several hours. Auntie Ro knew that Annie was suffering. Every so often she would gaze at Annie's pale face and it struck an ache into her own heart. She was grateful that Annie had stopped crying, but the silence was almost worse.

"Annie? I'm sorry for your trouble," she said, patting the girl's knee. "It must be hard."

Annie continued to stare straight ahead. The shadows under her swollen eyes had deepened, the animation that usually radiated from her face was gone, leaving emptiness in its place.

"You'll survive this, child."

After a moment, Annie shook her head. "Everythin' is gone," she whispered. "I have nothin' left of my life. My home, my family, my earnin's . . . everythin' . . . is just gone."

"Well," Ro asked softly. "How about yer young man?"

Annie bowed her head feeling the agony in her bones. "Patrick is lost to me, too."

Chapter Forty-Nine

Niall and his family left Ennis mid-afternoon. They had refused Martha's generous offer of a meal, but accepted hastily put together sacks of apples, bread, and cheese to eat as they traveled. They continued east over the last miles of hilly countryside toward Killaloe, passing one farm after the other; acres of hay, wheat, barley, oats and corn, filled with men working different stages of harvest. On the distant rolling hills, expanses of verdant pastureland confined cows, steer, and sheep behind neat stone walls. With the passing of each bucolic mile, the sweet fragrance of crops and the sharp tang of animal hide and dung drifted over them. Niall breathed deep and felt the tension finally ease from his body and mind.

The O'Briens made no stop in Killaloe. Instead, they took advantage of the last hour of sunlight and headed directly south along the Shannon for the final stretch of road to home.

Niall's relief was complete as his own land came into view. He'd never been more grateful for the sight of the iron gates, open like the arms of a mother, welcoming them to their own road. At the crest of the hill, he slowed to take in the panorama of all that was his.

A field of ripe corn with silken tassels led to acres of hay, undulating in great waves across the landscape. The broad limestone house, with its neatly thatched roof, glistened in the dying sunlight. It sat at the head of the rectangular formation surrounding a broad courtyard. On one long side was the stable with four open bays for the wagons. The large cow barn, its nearly empty loft overhead, occupied the other long side. The fresh hay that would be cut and baled within the next week, would fill it to the rafters. At the far end stood the chicken coop with its rows of hen boxes nestled within. The pig sty and dung heap stood even further away, behind the coop, where the wind would blow the stench away from the house. A long, single-storied workman's house was set farther down the property at the end of the dirt road that curved around the fields.

Niall drove his wagon around to the stable and pulled up short. He stared at the squawking chickens and crows competing for feed . . . with two small, naked children pursuing them.

The blood drained from Niall's face and he grit his teeth. John and Patrick pulled alongside him and stopped.

The two hired men, who were busy re-thatching a portion of the barn roof, heard them arriving and came down the ladder and headed for the wagons. Paddy Maguire, the old farm-worn priest, pulled his cap from his bald head and was the first to speak.

"You'll not be any too happy with what's happened."

Niall felt his neck tighten and his fists gripped the reins. "Where are they?"

Mickey Kearns, the younger of the two men, took off his cap, his unkempt hair spilled over his forehead. He pointed to the barn. "They showed up 'bout two hours ago and made themselves to home. Said ye hired 'em on for the hayin'."

"And that's not all," said Paddy nervously. "Sure Fiona won't be any too happy, either. Seamus helped himself to that chicken of hers. Before I knew what he was doing, he was cooking Biddie up behind the coop. It was the smell that got my attention." Paddy paused and shook his head. "By then, it was too late."

Fiona had raised the Guinea hen from the day it had hatched and had named her Biddie. She had tamed it enough so that it would actually climb into her lap and allow itself to be petted as she stroked its feathers. Biddie, afraid of the aggressive rooster, was taught to fly up into the low limbs of a young pine tree to protect it from harm.

Patrick and John both dismounted their wagons and looked to Niall, who continued to sit very still. Finally, Niall looked down at his brothers and spoke very quietly. "John, go settle mother. Patrick, come with me."

"What are you planning to do?" asked John.

"Don't know yet," he said, as he dismounted and walked towards the barn.

Molly came out the barn door with a babe on the crest of her belly and another naked child toddling beside her. She stopped short when she saw Niall and Patrick approaching. She tried to smile but uncertainty washed over her face. "Oh . . . Niall."

"Is that all you can say?"

Her face turned crimson. "What was I to do?" she whined. "Seamus has a mind of his own."

"Yeah, well," Niall spat out. "He's about to get a piece of mine! Where is that bloody bastard?"

"I don' take kindly to ye speakin' to m'wife like that," said Seamus, appearing from behind the coop with his two older daughters in tow. He was carrying a tin plate on which was the roasted chicken, holding it out of the girls' reach. Juices were flowing where he'd torn off a blackened leg. He chewed on it slowly, grease smearing his beard, as he regarded Niall.

Patrick ripped the leg from Seamus's hand and tossed it on the ground. "That chicken's name was Biddie!"

One of the little girls grabbed the chicken leg from the dirt and bit into it while the other child wailed and tried to wrest it from her hand.

Seamus laughed. "What? You name yer chickens?"

Niall grabbed a fistful of Seamus's shirt and the plate flipped out of his hand, landing in the dirt. "That chicken was my daughter's pet!"

"Well, how was I supposed to know?" he asked defiantly. "An' anyhow, ye got lots more where that one come from. She'll never know the difference."

Niall pulled back his clenched fist, ready to strike Seamus, when Molly cried out, "No!"

Molly set the baby on the ground and knelt to pick up the chicken, wiping the dirt off the hot skin with her skirt. She clutched the plate to her chest, protecting it from Niall's grasp. "Please don' take it. The children are so hungry." Tears coursed down her cheeks as she gathered the children to herself, her eyes begging for pity.

Niall struggled to get his temper under control. He didn't want to strike the man in front of his children. "I told you not to come here for another week," he said tightly.

"Yeah, well, we's got nowhere to go, so we's here. I reckon ye can manage to feed us for a few days 'til I start workin'."

Patrick didn't know what to say or do, so he stayed still, waiting for Niall to make a decision.

Paddy and the hired man stood to the side looking at the ground. They'd fretted for the hours that they had waited for Niall to get home. Niall had entrusted them with the workings of the farm while they were away and all had gone just fine until Seamus showed up with his gaggle of naked, noisy hellions.

Niall stared at Seamus, then looked to Molly. "Pack up your things and get out."

Molly gathered the children and hustled them into the barn with the plate of chicken.

Rather than putting together their meager belongings, she quickly pulled the meat from the carcass and parceled out small pieces of it to her girls. It was the first taste of meat they'd had in weeks. The children shoved it into their mouths with their dirty hands, barely chewing it before swallowing and begging for more. Molly took a partially chewed tidbit from her mouth and placed it on the youngest one's tongue. When the baby began to cry, she pulled down her shift and tried to get him to suckle. The fretful babe clung to her nipple yet wailed after a few seconds, tiny limbs flailing, when what was left of Molly's milk was sucked dry. Molly began to cry as she rubbed her knuckle into the chicken fat and pushed it against the baby's lips. She prayed that Saraid would talk Niall into letting them stay. She had to. Her baby boy was starving. A few good meals would go a long way towards building up her milk supply.

Molly hated to think what Seamus would do to her if his only son died. He would find a way to blame her for it, and then she would have yet more bruises. One of these days she was going to end up too weakened to survive it. She would take the children and run, but where would they go? She could never provide for them. Their life would be better if someone would just give her poor husband a chance.

Molly put a sliver of the fragrant chicken into her mouth and closed her eyes, savored the juicy tenderness of it. She gave up all thought of anything but her growling belly and stuffed her mouth with more.

Seamus was smug and brazenly pushed his luck. "We had a deal, an' we ain't goin' nowhere."

"Yes, Seamus, you are," Niall said. "If you aren't out of here in fifteen minutes, I will personally see to it." Niall turned and strode to the big house, his shoulders tight, fighting to keep his fists loose. If he struck Seamus now, he would kill him.

"I'd do as he says if I were you," said Patrick.

Seamus shrugged. "Maybe ye's forgettin' that piece of information I could be passin' on about Annie."

Patrick stepped closer and glared down at the smaller man. Seamus had no choice but to step back.

"Well guess what, Seamus? Seems Jack is gone now, too. You've got nothing to say to anybody, and who would believe a stinking piece of dung like you?"

The smile left Seamus's face while his mind raced. "Ye really goin' to throw Saraid's best friend out to starve while she be carryin' a babe in her belly?"

Before Patrick could answer, the rumble of a wagon and horses' hooves drew their attention. Saraid and her passengers rumbled into the courtyard with Roark riding beside them. When they stopped, Fiona and James dismounted and held the reins while the women unloaded the younger children, who took off running for the barn.

"What's Seamus doin' here?" Maureen asked.

Saraid shook her head and sighed wearily. "Looks like we got more trouble." The entire weekend had drained her; her cheek ached, her broken tooth throbbed, and the long ride home had left her lightheaded and half asleep.

Roark rode over to Patrick. "Everythin' all right here?"

Patrick shrugged. "Seems Seamus decided to arrive early and made himself at home. We were just trying to convince him that it was time to leave."

"Where's Niall?" asked Roark.

Patrick pointed to the house where Niall was coming out the door to meet Saraid. He was anxious to talk to Saraid, too. He needed to know about Annie.

Niall took Saraid by the arm. "I need to talk to you," he said tersely. Then he saw her bruised face. "What in hell happened to you?"

She could tell he was already upset so she tried to make light of it. "Just a bit of trouble on the road. T'is nothin' to worry about right now. We can talk on it later." She was too tired to get into an argument with him. "Tell me why ye're so angry."

They walked to the far end of the house before he spoke again.

"Not only has Seamus shown up and made himself to home, he killed Biddie and cooked her for their dinner."

Saraid was suddenly wide awake. "Oh no!"

"I've told them to get packing but he's a cocky bastard. I'm not sure what he'll do."

Fiona came running up to them. "Mam! I can't find Biddie!"

Niall looked at Saraid and gave a slight shake of his head.

Saraid turned to Fiona. "Maybe she's gone off to roost in her tree."

Fiona ran off again with James, the younger children following behind. Saraid rubbed her head, needing some chamomile tea to sooth herself. "We can't be tellin' her. She'll be heartbroken."

Niall nodded. "Time enough for that. The haying crew won't be coming for a few days yet. I don't think I can abide Seamus until then, nor Molly and her stinking brood."

"That's harsh of you, Niall. Those children don't know anythin' different. It's not their fault."

Niall's anger was simmering close to a boil. "Then whose fault is it?" he snapped. "Certainly not mine! Why should I pay the price of Molly's poor choices?"

Saraid flinched. She was filled with sadness and close to tears. "Molly's no longer the girl I once knew her to be. When we was young, she was full of life and sweetness. Now she's like a broken piece of crockery, all shards and no substance. Bad as he is, Seamus is all she knows."

Niall let out a disgusted laugh. "So she allows herself to get beaten and bullied and constantly with child? Where's the sense in that?"

"There is no sense to it except to survive the only way she knows how."

"Well, she'll have to sort it out someplace else. I don't want them here."

Saraid felt helpless as she watched him pacing back and forth in front of her. She thought about how different her life was compared to Molly's, and felt so very lucky. It was only fate that had provided her with the love of this man and the good life she had. It could easily have been herself in a barn with a brood of dirty children and a lout of a husband like Seamus.

"What's a few days in the end?" she asked. "Sure they'll just sit outside the fence an' ye'll still worry on it. Better to find something for 'im to do an' ye can keep an eye on him. We can't let them starve. But," she added, "ye do what ye think is best."

She turned and walked towards the open door. She wanted to make a poultice for her face. Her head felt ready to crack open. All she wanted was to lay down and sleep. She would speak to Molly later when she wasn't so tired. Then she spied Patrick rushing over to speak to her. She held up a hand. "Not now, Patrick."

"What do you mean, *not now?* It will take you one minute to relieve my mind!"

"There will be no relief for yer mind today, Patrick. We weren't able to get to her. I'll explain it to ye later."

Patrick threw out his arms in protest. "Tell me now! Why couldn't you get to her!"

Saraid sighed wearily, her shoulders slumped as she leaned against the door jamb. She turned and Patrick saw her bruised face.

"My God! What happened to you?" Patrick asked, trying to take her arm.

Niall stepped in front of him, blocking his path. "Leave her be!"

Saraid shook her head at Niall, tears of frustration dripped from her eyes. She reached out for Patrick's hand. "There was nothin' I could do." Sighing, she looked at Niall and, though dreading it, knew she had to explain.

"The Charlies took over the Shamrock and they were pullin' clansmen in to question them about Martin disappearin'. They closed the tavern so I couldn't go in an' talk to Jimmy an' there was no food to be had. There was no one I knew who could tell me where I could find Annie." Saraid paused and took a breath, dreading the rest.

"The one person I asked turned out to be one of them. We left, but didn't know that he followed us, until he tried to take over the wagon." She looked at Niall. "I used my knife to slash his hand and then he walloped me one. Then Roark showed up with some of our kin and saved us."

Niall looked to the sky, fighting anger, frustration, and disbelief. Unable to stop himself, he lashed out. "I *told* you it could be dangerous! But do you ever *listen*? Of course not!"

Saraid stiffened, insulted by her husband's rebuke, too angry to hear the fear in his voice. She turned to Patrick, her own voice raised. "Now, sure I'm right sorry, Patrick, but I could do no more." Without another word, she tossed Patrick his bag of coins and went through the door, letting it slam behind her.

Patrick was livid. And worried. What must Annie be thinking? His face grew dark as he stomped around the courtyard. He heaved the bag of coins toward his wagon, kicked furiously at the loose stones until dirt flew into the air like low muddied clouds. Annie would think that he had just walked away and abandoned her! He never should have left it to someone else to do what he should have done himself. It wasn't Saraid's fault. He started running to his wagon, scooped up the bag of coins, determination dripping off him in waves. He was going back to Doolin and that was that. He couldn't leave her injured and without food.

Niall screamed after him. "Where the hell do you think you're going?"

"I'm going to do what I should have done this morning! I'll be back tomorrow."

"Don't you dare leave here!" shouted Niall.

"I have no choice. I won't have her thinking that I just left her."

"You're crazy!" screamed Niall. He ran after the wagon but Patrick smacked at the horse's rump and they took off too quickly to stop him. "You crazy bastard!"

Niall stood there, alone and unsettled, breathing hard as he fought his frustration. His eyes filled and he struggled to stop shaking with rage. What was happening to them? He felt a cold presence surround him and fear began to gnaw his gut.

John came out of the house after all the commotion had past. Niall was sitting on the stoop with his arms on his knees, his head bowed.

John sat down beside him and didn't speak for a moment. Finally, he asked, "What is it?"

Niall sniffed and didn't answer. John just sat there quietly and waited.

After a few minutes, Niall raised his head and blinked at the setting sun. "I have this feeling in my gut that something really bad is coming."

"What do you mean?"

He turned to John and studied his face. He envied the man for his calm nature. John only lost his temper when thoroughly provoked . . . as he had in Doolin. But then, they'd all gotten riled up at one time or another over the weekend. He had looked forward to the serenity of the farm. Now, even the farm was in turmoil.

"I had this dream." Niall whispered, "The banshee came."

The hair on John's arms tingled. "It was just a dream."

Niall rose and stretched. "I'm not so sure."

Chapter Fifty

Saraid entered the house and slowly climbed the stairs to her bedroom on the second floor. As she passed Kate's room, she saw her sitting by the window, staring at the activity below. Though she wanted to ignore her, Saraid called out, "Kate? Can I be bringin' anythin' to ye? Would you be wantin' some tea?"

Kate shook her head, pointed to her half-filled cup. As she turned toward her, Kate squinted her eyes as she examined Saraid's face. She tapped her fingers to her own cheek. "Wha hap'n to you?" she asked slowly.

Saraid shrugged. "Tis nothin' of importance. Just an accident."

Kate pointed out the window and struggled to form her words. "Why Sea . . . mus here?"

"They came early for the hayin'. Niall and John are tryin' to decide whether or not to let them stay."

Kate shook her head. "No good."

"You're probably right, Kate. Not much to be done about it though." Saraid turned, walked to her room and lay fully clothed on the bed. Her aching body was soothed by the faint scent of straw in the tightly stuffed mattress, her eyes fluttering only once before she sank into deep sleep.

***

After discussing the dilemma surrounding Seamus and his family with John and Roark, Niall begrudgingly agreed to let them stay. He gave Seamus strict orders to camp in their wagon outside the gate until the end of the week, and to stay away from the chickens and other livestock. Food would be provided for them twice a day. They would have to be content with bowls of boiled potatoes, with butter and milk, and bread until Seamus could earn his keep. Though not fancy, the simple fare was nourishing and filling. They would not starve.

Seamus held his temper, but the indignity of being cast off the property filled his mind with thoughts of revenge. He vowed to make the O'Briens pay for humiliating him in front of his family. Who did they think they were anyway? He left Molly and the squalling children by the gate and walked the mile or so to the tavern in the village. He needed a drink. He *deserved* a drink after holding his temper while Niall spouted his feckin' list of rules. As he walked, he pondered all the ways he could make their lives miserable. His lips formed a tight smile as an idea came to mind. Before long, he was whistling and had a lilt to his step. *They'll not soon be forgettin' Seamus Flynn!*

* * *

Willie arrived after supper with Freddie in tow. He provided a keg of ale that he'd had filled at the tavern in town. The men gathered around the kitchen table while Willie tapped out generous amounts into the cups Niall provided. They spent a few hours discussing the weekend's events and what to do next.

"I passed Seamus on the road to town," said Willie. "He was headin' to the tavern."

Niall closed his eyes and shook his head. "That's all we need, him getting liquored up then coming back here."

"Was that Molly and the children with the wagon by the gate?"

John nodded. "Looks like we'll be stuck with them until after the crops are in."

Hank sat in silence, holding onto his ale with his head bowed. Inwardly, he felt no safer than he had been with Martin. His hands shook slightly as he raised his cup and drained it.

Freddie sensed his friend's turmoil, helpless to relieve his suffering. "Is Hank goin' t'be safe here?"

"Probably as safe as he'll be anywhere," Roark answered.

The men sipped their ale in silence for a while.

Willie said, "By the way, Niall, the blacksmith was at the tavern. George said he'd be by tomorrow with yer tools. He said he's got everythin' sharpened and he's bringin' a couple of new hay rakes, too."

Niall nodded. "Did he say anything about the things for the kitchen?" He had ordered a new cooking pot and tongs for Saraid.

"He didn't mention it, but if you ordered it, I'm sure he'll bring it. Where's Patrick?"

Niall grimaced. "He's gone back to Doolin to see about Annie."

John got up, opened a cupboard and pulled out a jug of whiskey. "I don't know about you folks, but I could use something a bit stronger tonight."

The others all drained their ale and held out their cups while John poured. They continued sharing their worries and complaints until the candle stub flickered and the jug was empty. There wasn't a joke or a song to be had among them.

Willie and the fiddlers finally said their good nights, retrieved their bedrolls from the wagon, and headed to the stable to bed down for the night.

Niall and John lingered in the kitchen after the others left.

"Mother seems a bit better," said Niall.

"That she does," replied John. "Now we just have to hope that Danny will pull through."

Niall stifled a yawn. "Maybe we can get the spalpeens to help us harvest Danny's crops when they finish here."

"That's a good thought. They'd probably appreciate the extra wages."

"We'll have to pay them out of our pockets."

John nodded, thinking on the accounts book. "We can manage it. He'd do the same for us." Then he had another thought. "Maybe Hank could stay at Danny's place and keep an eye on things there until Danny comes home."

"*If* he comes home. We'll keep Hank here until after the harvest. He can sleep in the stable and keep out of sight of Seamus for a few days."

They both sighed and then they chuckled.

"We're a fine pair," said John as he headed for the door. "I'll see you in the morning."

Niall slowly climbed the stairs. The whiskey had done its job. He was downright calm; and if he was any more relaxed, he'd be asleep where he stood. He undressed in the dark and climbed into bed, curling up against Saraid's back. He wrapped his arm around her middle and sighed with relief to feel her hair under his face. She murmured in her sleep and nuzzled in closer to him, reaching her arm back and laying it across his thigh.

He forced all thoughts from his mind except for the comfort he was feeling at that moment. Tomorrow would be here soon enough.

Chapter Fifty-One

Patrick drove the horse hard but it was near nightfall by the time his wagon reached Ennis. There was no point in trying to go any further in the dark. He found his way to Dr. O'Hickey's without difficulty and asked to spend the night behind the house. They wouldn't hear of him sleeping in his wagon. He looked in on Danny while Martha readied a bed for him. He ran a damp cloth over Danny's feverish brow, disconcerted by his pallor. Danny never moved or blinked.

Martha came into the doorway. "The poor lad's really struggling. He's thrashed out a few times, but then he seems to collapse from the effort. Tonight will tell the tale."

Patrick nodded. "We'll just have to pray hard that he makes it."

Patrick tossed and turned most of the night and rose at sunrise. Before leaving, he tip-toed into Danny's room to check on him and found the doctor sitting in a chair by the bed, fast asleep. Patrick's footstep made a creak in the floorboard startling the doctor. He sprang up and adjusted his spectacles. "Good morning to you, Patrick."

"How's the patient?"

O'Hickey leaned over Danny and felt his forehead. He peeled back the bandage on Danny's shoulder and put his fingers around the red skin of the wound. "He's not out of the woods yet, but he isn't as feverish as when you brought him in." Danny stirred and began to moan as the doctor cleaned the fetid discharge from the wound.

"It's all right, Danny," said O'Hickey.

Danny's eyes fluttered open, glazed with confusion and pain. He made a feeble attempt to push the doctor away, but Patrick held him in place.

"Easy, cousin." He continued to hold him down as the doctor applied a new bandage to the wound.

"I've sat here with him most of the night," said the doctor. "As bad as he looks, I think he is a little better."

"Will he make it?" asked Patrick.

The doctor shrugged. "If we can continue to keep the fever down, he has a chance. It'll be a few days yet before we can be certain of anything."

***

Patrick left shortly thereafter, making a stop to buy a supply of food at the only open eatery. Anxious about Annie, he made one more stop along the road to water the horse and relieve himself. He was tense as he arrived in Doolin. He passed the Shamrock, but it seemed to be deserted. He didn't know if that was good news or bad, but he didn't stop. He continued up the shore road until he reached Annie's shanty. He jumped from the wagon, calling Annie's name, and ran to the door. It was unlatched and banging against the frame. Patrick called out again, but no one answered him. Puzzled, he went inside to find the place empty. *Where was her mother?* A knot formed in his gut. There were no blankets on the beds, not a dish in the cupboards, nor a kettle on the stove. *Where could they have gone?* Something must have happened. Or maybe someone took them in. Either way, it didn't look like they were coming back. Patrick punched the wall with his fist and welcomed the pain in his knuckles. She must have thought he wasn't coming back. "Damn it to hell!" he cried. He strode back up the pathway, climbed into his wagon, and viciously snapped the reins. Jasper neighed loudly and began to gallop down the road. Anger and frustration roiled in him as he rode back along the coast road. He paused at the Shamrock, but there was still no sign of anyone. He sat for a few minutes trying to decide what to do.

Jimmy appeared from behind the tavern. "Hey, Patrick."

"Jimmy! What's going on here?"

Jimmy shrugged. "A lot of nothin' is what's goin' on."

"Where is everyone?" asked Patrick.

"They's all gone." Jimmy cackled with glee. "I heard Jack got waylaid by a bunch of fellas on the road. They said he more or less took Roisin by force, and made her drive him out o'here. She's a cagey one, she is! She got those men to help her escape. Don' know what happened to him after that but he's gone. Serves the feckin' arse to right, it does."

"I don't care about Jack," Patrick spat out. "What happened to Annie?"

"Annie?" asked Jimmy. "Sure I don' know nothin' 'bout Annie. I ain't seen 'er. She's prob'ly at home."

"No, she's not. I just came from there and she and her mother are both gone. The place has been emptied out."

Jimmy scratched his head. "Like I said. I don' know nothin' bout Annie. Can't imagine she's gone too far." He motioned to the tavern and dangled a key from his fingers. "You want to come in for a pint?"

Patrick hesitated for only a moment before climbing down from his wagon and joining Jimmy. The tavern was cool and dim and utterly quiet. A far cry from the last time he'd been there. Their footsteps echoed across the wooden planks as they walked to the bar. Jimmy pulled down two mugs and filled them with warm ale from the keg. Then he grabbed the Irish whiskey and poured a couple of inches of the amber liquid into two glasses. Jimmy tossed his shot back and refilled it, before he pushed the other glass toward Patrick.

Patrick swallowed the whiskey in one gulp and felt it burn all the way down to his gut. He coughed and his eyes teared up. He shook his head and took a swallow of his ale to ease the fire.

Jimmy laughed. "Y'ain't much fer the whiskey, are ye, now?"

Patrick coughed again and shook his head. "I don't usually drink much," he rasped. He held out the glass for a refill. "Today seems like a good day for it."

The two men sat there until after noontime sharing what was left of the whiskey. Eventually, Patrick began telling Jimmy about how he cared for Annie. His speech began to slur and he was becoming maudlin. Jimmy decided that they'd best eat something and went to the back room to see what he could find. He appeared moments later with a plate that held a hunk of cheese with a coating of dusky mold, some stale bread, and a bowl of pickles swimming in brine. One look at it and Patrick, staggering with dizziness, bolted for the door and heaved. When he finally stopped retching, he wiped the glaze of sweat from his face. He gulped in the salt air, trying to clear his head, and then carefully walked back into the tavern.

Jimmy was slicing the blue-gray fuzz off the cheese and tossing it into a bucket. "There we go," he said. "Good as new." He wiped the residue off the knife with a rag and set it next to the cheese. "Help yerself."

Patrick eyed the cheese carefully and decided that it looked all right. He sliced off a piece and took a chunk of the hard bread. It tasted like gooey sawdust and he swallowed some ale to wash it down. Once his stomach stopped aching, he stood. The world had stopped spinning and he felt some better. "I think I best be heading for home. I want to get there before dark."

Chapter Fifty-Two

The blacksmith arrived early Monday morning with his heavy wagon that had high sides and a peaked roof. Fancy gilt-edged script proclaiming 'George the Forge' over an anvil painted in black, adorned both sides. Beneath that, in smaller neat block letters, was painted: 'Killaloe, County Clare, Ireland'. George O'Casey sat high on a tooled leather seat that was well padded for comfort.

George, another Irishman who had given lip service to the Anglican church, was affluent with a good head for business. He was in great demand by rich and poor alike as everyone needed his services at one time or another. He had a firm reputation for doing meticulous work and for being fair in his dealings with everyone.

He arrived at the O'Brien farm sporting an elegantly patterned waistcoat over a plain white shirt, sturdy britches and heavy boots. On his head he wore a top hat of dark green with a white feather. "Top o'the mornin' to ye, Niall!" he said, doffing his hat.

"Good to see you, George." Niall attempted to be sociable despite the vague unease that continued to torment him after a restless night's sleep.

The first thing George did after he climbed down from the wagon, was to remove the spotless top hat, waistcoat and shirt, and set them neatly into a box beneath his wagon seat. After donning a leather tunic, he added a brimmed tweed cap that he tugged down over his brow to shade his eyes.

George's arms and shoulders bulged with muscle as he unloaded his portable forge and set it up outside the stable. He was barrel-chested and stood well over six feet tall, causing many to kiddingly called him 'The Giant'.

Niall followed behind with the new hay rakes and spades. George took off his cap, wiped the sweat of his exertion from his brow and ran his fingers through his wild mane of dark hair.

As George waited for the coals in the forge to heat up, he busied himself with a box of horseshoes and hoof-cleaning tools.

"I brought ye a new plowshare. The other wasn't fit for another sharpenin'. Sure it had a good crack in it."

"Did you bring the kitchen things for Saraid?"

George laughed, his dark eyes twinkling with good humor. "Do I look foolish enough to be wantin' an argument with that feisty wife of yours?"

Patrick arrived at the stable with Jasper, who was limping. He examined the new tools. "This is some rake," he said, examining the long thin tines. "Pretty sharp, too."

"Sure," replied George. "It's a little wider than the old ones but the same weight. You'll be able to toss twice the hay with this one. Save ye time in the end."

Patrick nodded. "I see you brought the new horseshoes. I think Jasper picked up a stone last night as he's lame this morning. I was just going to check him out."

Niall shook his head. "You should have checked it last night."

Patrick sighed, unable to ignore Niall's glare. "I should've done a lot of things," he snapped, "but I got back late and I didn't notice it in the dark."

Niall watched the play of emotions on Patrick's face and could plainly see that he, too, was worse for wear, tensed up and just waiting on a fight. "What happened?"

Patrick shook his head. "I don't want to talk about it right now."

George looked on in silence and decided to leave them to it and mind his own business. "I'll take a look at this one first," he said. He took the reins from Patrick's hand and ran a gentle hand down the white blaze on Jasper's face. Speaking softly to the horse, he led Jasper into the stable and put him in one of the stalls. With his back against Jasper's rump, he lifted up his hind leg between his own to examine the hoof. He continued to talk quietly to the horse as he pried off the shoe. It fell to the wooden floor with a clunk and a small stone followed. "There ye go, boy. Amazin' how somethin' so small can cause such a big hurt. Bet that feels better already."

Jasper whinnied and pranced on the unshod hoof. George patted Jasper's dark brown flank before retrieving a set of new shoes from the box. As he was fitting the new one, a sudden shriek came from behind the chicken coop.

Fiona came running, tears streaming down her face. In her hand she clutched a mass of feathers and bones still crusted with bits of charred skin and gristle. A dozen flies followed her in pursuit of what was left of Biddie.

"Da! Somebody killed Biddie!" she sobbed. "And they ate her!"

Fiona wailed inconsolably. Niall pulled her to his chest and tried to comfort her. "I'm sorry, Fiona."

George looked to Patrick for an explanation but he just shrugged, having no idea what the trouble was about.

Fiona wriggled out of her father's grasp, looking up at him in horror. "Why are *you* sorry? Did *you* kill her?" she demanded. "Why would you *do* that?"

Saraid came running with Liam and Bridget and shot Niall a pained look. They began to cry, too, when they saw the feathers and bones.

Saraid grabbed Fiona by the arm as she tried to run from them. "No, Fiona! Your da did no such thing!"

"Then *who?*" Fiona wailed.

There was utter silence.

Saraid didn't know what to say. She looked at Niall and saw the blame in his eyes. Never before had he looked at her this way. Lowering her gaze, she turned away so he wouldn't see the shame and anguish she felt. She knew that it was her own pleading on behalf of Molly and her children that had caused her daughter's pain.

Niall closed his eyes and pulled Fiona close. "Seamus didn't know she was your pet."

Fiona struggled to pull away from him. "*Seamus?* Why did you let him kill her at all?"

"Listen to me, Fiona!" he said, raising his voice to be heard above her wails. "We weren't even here! He got here ahead of us and his family was hungry."

"That's no excuse!" Fiona cried, striking out at him. "How would he feel if I killed something that belonged to *him*!"

Niall held her arms and leaned his face close to hers. "Don't talk like that," he said softly. He tried to be gentle as he spoke, though his own anger was roiling near the surface. He resented having to make excuses for Seamus's heinous act. All he really wanted right now was to bring serious harm to the bastard. "The problem is, he had no food of his own to feed his children, and they were starving."

Fiona was still trembling with grief, too young and too angry to comprehend anything more than her own loss. "He's going to be really sorry he killed my Biddie! Maybe I'll just kill *him*!"

"You'll do no such thing, Fiona," cried Saraid.

Fiona looked up and realized that John, Willie, Freddie and Hank were suddenly there, too, and they were all looking at her with pity. She crumbled into her father's arms, fresh tears running down her face.

Patrick leaned over and patted her head. "We'll get you another chicken, Fiona."

"I don't *want* another chicken! I want *Biddie!*"

Niall stroked her back and continued to talk softly to her. "There's nothing we can do to bring Biddie back. I've already talked to Seamus and he didn't know that she was your pet. I let him know how angry we are. They'll be staying away from the rest of the chickens and everything else from now on. There's nothing else we can do."

Fiona looked at the feathers and bones in her hand as she sniffled. "Can we bury her?"

Niall smiled and tugged on her braid. "Yes, we can. Let's do it right now."

He and Fiona walked hand in hand to the shed to get a spade.

Patrick felt sorry for Fiona. "That poor girl. What the hell was Seamus thinking?"

Saraid was trembling. "Sure he wasn't thinkin' at all now, was he?"

John sighed. "We should have just thrown him out of here and been done with it."

Saraid was bitterly sorry now for having defended Molly and the children. She'd known that Fiona would be upset but had no idea that she would suffer so. What was she to do? She needed to talk to Molly. Maybe she could persuade her to go somewhere else. In truth, she knew that they had nowhere else to go. They would starve out there on the road. Or Seamus would start stealing and get caught out. What would Molly do all alone with four children and another on the way? She took off her cap and pushed her hair away from her face. "I need to go see about our supper."

The men watched her walk away, all of them uncomfortable with the emotional displays and unable to do anything to help.

"Well," said George. "I guess I'll finish shoeing the horses." The men parted company, all trying to find something else to do.

* * *

The midday sun stood high in a brilliant summer sky, the air filled with birdsong, the smells of pasture and fields, and the aroma of the afternoon meal.

Liam and Bridget carried bowls and utensils to the long planked table under the oak in the courtyard. James pulled the cord on the bell hanging from a post near the pasture to announce mealtime. Willie and the fiddlers came from the stable with Roark, who was having his horse re-shod as well.

George went to the water pump and removed his sweaty tunic. Between the heat of the day and the hot coals in the forge, he was drenched in sweat. He cranked the handle and dunked his head under the cold water, then shook his sopping hair side to side, creating an arc of water over the courtyard. He splashed more clean water from the trough over his chest and arms, rubbing away his stink. Satisfied that he was clean, he retrieved a clean tunic from his wagon before joining the others for dinner.

John walked slowly with Kate across the courtyard and helped her get seated at the end of the bench. He filled half a bowl of stew for her and sat beside her with one for himself.

Chunks of lamb with coarse-cut potatoes, onions and carrots swam in a thick gravy that had been simmering for hours outside in a cast iron pot. Saraid had thrown in a tankard of ale and a handful of sage, thyme and parsley near the end and the savory aroma enticed everyone to the table.

Niall and Patrick came across the field from the workers' cabin. They had opened the doors at each end of the rough building to air it out. They'd swept out the remains of the old straw bedding and the cobwebs from the rafters, checking the thatched roof as they went along. Then they set out fresh bedding for the harvesting crew of spalpeens that would be arriving any day now.

Saraid sliced hot bread while Maureen took care of ladling up small bowls of stew for all the younger ones. The men grabbed their bowls and ladled their own stew from the kettle. Everyone attempted to keep up a normal conviviality as they ate; but soon, the silences between conversations lengthened. Eventually, everyone's mind seemed to drift to the problems and worries they each had in their own heads. They began pushing around the remaining morsels of stew with their spoons, appetites gone.

Saraid stood abruptly and gathered up the bowls, scooping the leftovers into a bucket. It was a perfect excuse to seek out Molly. She would give them the leavings and they would be grateful to have them.

The men rose almost as one, and went off to finish their chores. Each of them was eager to be relieved of the oppression that hung over the table. Kate had dribbled stew on her dress and John gladly took her back to the house to change. Even Hank was eager for a job to do so he could feel like he was earning his keep. Niall led Hank and Freddie to the vegetable garden. He set Hank to weeding, while Freddie sat on his stool playing his fiddle to keep Hank company. The cheerful music drifted over the fields, eventually wooing even the foulest of moods to dissipate on the wind.

Saraid took the half-filled bucket of stew and walked to the end of the lane to where she found Molly kneeling in the grass with her children. "What are ye doin?" she asked.

Molly started and got to her feet awkwardly, her cheeks filling with color. She rubbed absently at her belly and looked away from Saraid to hide her embarrassment. "I'm teachin' 'em how to catch grasshoppers."

One of the girls squealed and jumped up. "I got one!" the child exclaimed, and popped the live insect into her mouth. She quickly retched as the critter began to wiggle against her tongue. She stamped her bare feet and squealed as she rubbed at her mouth, spitting again and again to get rid of the horrible feeling.

Saraid was horrified. "Why on earth are ye eatin'' bugs?"

Shame filled Molly, but unable to lie to her one and only friend, she squared her thin shoulders and lifted her chin. She looked Saraid in the eye. "We may have to learn to feed ourselves."

Saraid held out the bucket of stew to Molly, who nodded and accepted it with a whispered, "Thank you."

Saraid looked around the quiet landscape. "Where's Seamus?"

Molly shrugged. "Sure I haven't seen him since he went to the tavern yesterday."

"You mean he didn't come back?"

Molly shook her head and turned away. Her shoulders shook with the effort of holding back her tears. She finally couldn't hold it in for another second. She slumped to the ground and gave in to shuddering sobs. "What am I to do?"

Saraid closed her eyes. Compassion for her friend overcame the anger that had brought her here. She sank down beside her friend and pulled her into her arms and let her cry. The children joined in, crying, too. They patted their mother with their dirty hands, trying to comfort her. "Don' cry, Mam," they chorused.

"Ye need to leave him, Molly."

Molly pulled herself away from Saraid's arms and wiped her face on her sleeve. "An' do what, Saraid? Where're we to go? Who's goin' to take care of us?"

Saraid flushed and remained silent. She had no answers.

They were still sitting there as a mournful, off-key melody wended its way to them from beyond the sight line of the trees lining the road. They all listened as the voice got louder until Seamus rounded the bend and came into view, staggering down the road. The children ran to him. "Da!" they exclaimed as they ran to him and clutched his legs.

Molly got to her feet, quickly wiping away her tears as she fixed a smile on her face. She and Saraid watched in horror as he roughly shoved the children away, causing them to fall. "Leave me be!" he shouted at them.

Molly cried out and ran to the children, who were sitting in the dirt, sobbing. The toddler, not knowing any better, tried once more to grasp onto her father's leg, only to be rebuffed again. Molly tried to gather the three youngsters to herself as Saraid strode to where Seamus stood, cursing at all of them.

"How dare ye treat your poor children like that!" She was going to strike him but the look of pure hatred in his eyes stopped her. She began to tingle with fear, knowing that if she did such a thing, Molly would pay for it, as well as herself.

He stood there struggling to maintain his balance. His voice seethed just above a whisper. "You! Get away from us! They's mine and I'll be treatin' 'em any damned way I want!"

Saraid looked to Molly, who was beseeching her with her eyes and shaking her head. "It's all right, Saraid. We'll be all right now that Seamus is here."

Molly turned to Seamus and raised the bucket. "Look, my love. Saraid brought us some supper. Isn't that a kind thing?"

Seamus tried to wring the bucket from her hand but she held on tight. "No, Seamus! We have no food!"

Seamus shoved at her. She stumbled and the bucket finally came free. He threw the bucket at Saraid and it landed at her feet, the gravy and vegetables spilling over her toes and into the dirt. "We don't need no charity!"

Saraid picked up the bucket in silence. There was nothing she could do. As she turned to go, Seamus called out to her. She stopped, but didn't turn around.

"Ye just be bringin' our pot of potatoes like we agreed on before."

Saraid's entire body trembled with rage as she strode back to the house. She was as angry with Molly as she was with Seamus. She would never lower herself to grovel to a man for anything! Nor could she even imagine letting a man treat her so badly.

God help me, she thought. *If he was mine, he'd have my knife in his gut*!

Chapter Fifty-Three

Two days later, Jake McCarthy and his crew of spalpeens came down the road to the O'Brien farm, his horses pulling the long flat wagon that would be used during the harvest. The wagon was loaded with their bedrolls, pikes and scythes, and the men were eager to work. The band of a dozen or more traveling men for hire were heard long before they were seen, singing their spirited songs to pass the time on their journey. Tenor, baritone and bass voices lilted over the hills accompanied by some playing penny whistles, filling the air with merriment and anticipation. A few of them had families in other towns, but most of the men were single. The monies they earned during the harvest would go a long way toward getting them through the winter months when food was hard to find. They were always happy to work at the O'Brien place. The wages were good, the food was better than at other farms, and the bunkhouse, offering a clean, dry place to sleep, was a blessing.

Niall was happy that they were arriving earlier than expected. The weather had held with no rain in sight. Brilliant sunshine bathed the crops that were near bursting with goodness and ready to harvest. The hay was ripe and pale green, the corn ears full and well-tasseled, and the the wheat heavy and ready to be sheaved and flailed.

Everyone worked the harvest, even the children. Long-planked tables were set up in the shade for the workers to take their morning and evening meals. In the afternoon, pots of cold, sweet tea and loaves of black bread and apple cake were brought to the men in the fields. Bowls of early apples and pears added sweetness and energy to the men, whose sweat ran from their bodies all day long.

Saraid decided to enlist Molly to help with meal preparations. It meant having to keep an eye on her unruly children, but giving Molly something to do might distract her from feeling sorry for herself and stop her tiresome tears.

After the evening meal, Niall gathered all the men together to go over the week's schedule. Seamus sauntered down the lane with his hands in his pockets and a piece of straw dangling from his teeth to join the men.

Niall felt nothing but regret as he introduced Seamus to Jake and his men. He knew that, somehow, Seamus would cause trouble.

The workers eyed him suspiciously. "He gonna be bunkin' with us?" asked Jake.

Seamus started to say yes but Niall overrode him. "No. He'll be staying with his family."

Seamus spat the piece of straw from his mouth and glared at Niall. "Why? Ain't I good enough to stay with them?"

The workers fidgeted, sensing trouble ahead, but kept their eyes on Niall. They weren't used to having to deal with any problems on this farm.

Niall sighed. It was going to be a long week. Using what patience he could muster, he looked Seamus in the eye. "Molly might need you, so it would be better if you stayed with your family." Niall turned back to the other men and continued to set up the schedule.

Seamus pursed his lips, seething inside, but kept his mouth shut.

"All right then," Niall said. "In the morning, Patrick and I will start all hands with picking off the corn. Once the dew dries, we'll start on the hay. Breakfast is at sun up. We'll start out directly after. Any questions?"

The men shook their heads. Jake shook Niall's hand. "Thank ye fer takin' us on again."

"It's always good of you to come," said Niall. "You always give us good value."

With that, the men turned as one and headed across the field to their quarters.

Seamus started to walk away and Niall called out to him. Seamus stopped but didn't turn around.

Niall said, "I want you here at sun up like the others."

Seamus spat on the ground and continued to walk towards his wagon.

* * *

Kate lay in her bed, propped up on pillows, while John sat on a chair beside her reading aloud. She was having trouble concentrating on the words while so many thoughts tumbled through her mind. Finally, she lifted her hand and gripped his sleeve.

John took her trembling hand in his. "What is it?"

Kate struggled to form the words and licked at the saliva that trailed from the corner of her mouth. "Is sm . . . some . . . thin wrong?"

"What do you mean, Mother?"

She struggled to pull herself upright. "I'm not stu . . . stu . . . pid. Some . . . thing isn't ri . . . right." She lay her head back on the pillow, exhausted from the effort of speaking.

John closed the book and set it on the table beside the bed, wondering how much he should tell her. He didn't want her to worry, but perhaps she should be aware of some of what was going on. Maybe it would help to ease his own mind if he spoke his concerns aloud.

"Of course, you aren't stupid. No one has ever thought that. You're one of the smartest people I know."

Tears welled up in Kate's eyes and she clung to John's hand. "Wh . . . whs . . . whas wrong? Are we in d . . . dan . . . ger?"

"I don't think we're in danger . . . but there are things happening that we don't seem to have much control over."

He told her some of what had gone on since they left Doolin, how gravely Danny was injured, how sorry they were for having agreed to let Seamus come for the haying. "Everyone is upset about Seamus being here, especially Fiona."

Kate shook her head and gripped the bedding. She felt helpless. And old. She looked out the window at the twilight and suddenly longed for her husband. He always managed to make everything turn out right. Her eyes fluttered against the tears that began to course down her face. "I wi . . . wish I co . . . could go home."

John gathered her in his arms and let her cry softly against his shoulder. He felt as helpless as she did. More than a small part of his heart wished that he, too, could leave this place. It had been a long time since they had been to Dublin. He wondered if they should think about going to the American colonies, but what would they do there? He sighed. He knew that his mother wasn't well enough to survive the long sea journey. They would be adrift with no family to count on if they ran in to difficulty. There was no help for it now, though. There was too much to do here, and he couldn't leave his brothers with all the responsibility. Maybe, after the harvest, he would give it more thought. Right now, all hands were needed to get the crops in before the weather turned.

* * *

Saraid lay in bed fingering her cheek, testing the soreness of the bruise. It was still smarting, even after she had rubbed it with some of her healing balm. Niall climbed into the bed beside her and faced the wall. It had been a long time since he had turned away from her in their bed. She grew edgy, needing comfort, but lay still in the darkness, trying to let him be. He would let go of his anger soon enough, but, right now, it carved into her like a knife. She took in a breath and held it, fighting the tears that wanted to flow. She quietly let the long breath ease out of her lungs and dragged in another. Finally, she turned and curved her body around his, lay her face against his shoulder, breathed in his scent. His skin was smooth and smelled like soap after the bath he had taken in the river. Niall tried to shrug her off. "Go to sleep," he said gruffly.

Saraid was stung by his words. "How can I be sleepin' if ye're mad at me?"

Niall didn't reply.

"Please . . ." she whispered. "I'll tell Molly they have to go."

Niall rolled over onto his back and lay his forearm across his eyes. He was too tired for this. "It's a little late for that now. We're stuck with them."

Saraid rolled away from him and stared out the window into the moonlit night. She hadn't told him about her altercation with Seamus that afternoon; and somehow, this didn't seem to be the time to do so. Why did trying to help someone have to bring so much trouble to everyone else? She would have to talk to Molly in the morning. The wellbeing of her own family had to be more important than their friendship. Molly had made her own choices, and she would have to figure out how to fix it herself.

***

Patrick tossed and turned for hours and finally gave up on sleep. He got up and sat on the wooden bench outside his cabin and breathed in the clean night air as it cooled his clammy skin. The stars twinkled overhead and the moon glowed, nearly full, casting soft light over the fields. He closed his eyes and saw visions of Annie, her face dimpled, sweet laughter tinkling from her full lips. He groaned with yearning and rubbed at the tightness in his chest. What was he to do? How could he find her? He was tormented with a deep sense of loss that he didn't think he could live with. Maybe after the crops were in he could go looking for her. But where could he look? Maybe someone else had seen her leave Doolin and could tell him in which direction she had gone. Surely, she had told someone where she was going. He knew that she didn't have the means to travel far. She'd probably find another tavern to work in. He shuddered, thinking of her life and what she was compelled to do to survive. It didn't matter. He would find her and tell her he loved her and bring her back to the farm. Did he love her? Yes, yes he did. What if she was angry with him for leaving her? What if she hated him and wouldn't have anything to do with him?

Patrick groaned with misery. He picked up a stone and flung it into the night. Then he flung another, and another, as the lump in his throat ached. Finally, disgusted with himself and his self pity, he stormed into his cabin and threw himself onto his bed begging sleep to come. *I thought love was supposed to make a man happy!*

* * *

Hank lay on his bed of straw and massaged his hip. The soft snuffling of the horses was the only sound in the darkness. Working in the vegetable garden had felt good at the time but crawling around on his hands and knees had left him lame. He was grateful to Willie and the O'Brien family for taking him in. To be free of Martin left him with an unknown future. As bad as his life had been, at least he knew what to expect. Facing the rest of his life without a plan for survival was daunting. He wasn't sure how long he would be allowed to stay here. Though he didn't want to be a burden, he had no idea how to take care of himself. There wasn't any call for a fiddler on a farm. He didn't have the physical capability to become a hired man. Now that he could no longer pretend to be blind . . . well, he could . . . but to what end? He wished he could leave here with Willie and Freddie in the morning but then what? He was smart enough to know that there was no point in looking for his family. If they were still alive, they were long gone.

He ached with loneliness and yearned for a family of his own. What he wouldn't give to feel arms around him! Every time he thought about Molly and how Seamus treated her, his teeth clenched. How could Seamus be so cruel to his own family? Molly was such a lovely thing. And those poor rag-tag children! If they were his, he would cherish them each and every day! The man didn't know how lucky he was!

When Hank finally drifted off to sleep, thoughts of Molly brought a small smile to his lips. His dreams were filled with a better life, a life without an aching body and an aching heart.

Chapter Fifty-Four

Roisin removed her shawl and sat on the edge of the narrow bed. "Are ye ailin', my dear?"

Annie struggled to sit up and reassure the older woman. "I don' think so . . . I'm just so bloody tired."

"Well," Roisin replied, gently pushing Annie back down to the pillow. "Ye've been through a mountain of grief in a short time. It's only natural to be feelin' like ye do."

Roisin climbed in beside her, sighing with relief as her head found the soft pillow. She was soon snoring softly, comforted by the warmth of the young body beside her.

Annie lay wide-eyed in the darkness with thoughts of their journey spinning through her head. They had traveled south for two days, leaving the sound of crashing waves and the Cliffs of Moher far behind them. They followed the coast road south through Ennistymon and Miltown Malbay, stopping only when they reached Kilmurry, to rest the horse and to replenish their meager stores of food. At night, they pulled off the road and slept in the wagon, thankful for the warm nights. With the onset of dawn, they ate a quick meal and set out again.

Over the years, Roisin had traveled much of Clare. She decided to follow the coastal road around Loop's Head, and continue southeast until they reached Kilrush. Once there, they would probably be far enough away to blend in with other travelers without undue suspicion. Annie had never been outside of Doolin and had to trust that Roisin knew what she was doing.

It was near dark when they arrived at their destination. Kilrush was situated on a creek that led to the estuary of the River Shannon. In the twilight, they could see the outline of masted ships moored at the quay and smaller vessels anchored in the bay.

Goods of all kinds were shipped in and out of the bustling town. At this late hour, the boats were quiet and the crews were done with their work for the day. Just beyond the bay, they found a brightly lit old tavern that was in good shape, serving simple fare to townspeople and travelers.

Both women were stiff and tired, looking forward to sitting in a chair and having a decent meal. Annie's ankle was much better after all the sitting she had done, and she had just the trace of a limp. When they entered the noisy tavern, Roisin's face lit up as the aromas assailed her nostrils. Ale, food, pipe smoke and chattering filled the crowded space. The patrons who glanced their way most likely assumed they were mother and daughter and paid them no mind.

They sat at a dirty table and waited a long while to get the barkeep's attention. Annie absently began stacking the gravy-smeared plates and utensils while they waited. The harried barkeep finally came over and began to clear away the pints and dishes as men grumbled for pints at the bar. His wiry gray hair was disheveled and carelessly tied back from a kind face. His brow was furrowed from trying to do everything by himself, but still, he found a smile for them.

"Sorry for the mess, ladies. My serving girl run off today and I've got no help."

Annie saw an opportunity and offered to take her place. "I ain't no stranger to tavern life," she said. "I can work as payment for some dinner." She looked to Roisin for agreement and the older woman nodded.

"If I can have me some tea," Roisin said, "I'll just sit and be grateful for it."

The tavern owner looked around the busy room and, with a nod of his head, quickly agreed. He was impressed when Annie jumped right in to clear tables, deliver food and pints. He noted that even though the girl looked exhausted and had a bit of a limp, she worked with no complaint. He was also pleased that his customers seemed to take to her and stop their complaining. An hour later when the dinner rush was over, he brought Annie and Roisin each a steaming bowl of stew, half loaf of bread, and a pot of butter.

Annie had no stomach for the stew but forced herself to nibble on some of the bread, dipping it into the warm gravy. Later, the owner came over with three mugs of ale, and sat in the remaining chair at their table. "You saved me tonight, so this is on me! I'm Dennis O'Malley by the way."

Roisin clutched the mug and took a long swallow. "Nice to meet you," she said offering her hand. "Tell me, Mr. O'Malley, would ye be havin' a room for two tired ladies?"

He smiled. "Just call me Dennis. As luck would have it, I got the one my bar girl cleared out of just this afternoon. I haven't had the time to change the linens yet, though. Any chance ye can stay for awhile until I get another girl?"

Annie looked to Roisin who shrugged.

"We can do that," said Annie. "Fer now, we're just needin' a place to lay our heads."

"It's yours then. So where're ye ladies from?" He asked.

Roisin hesitated. "We just come from the east," she lied. "We's travelin' to visit with some family in the north."

Annie's head was bobbing and she struggled to stay awake.

Dennis rose from the table and nodded towards Annie. "This one looks like she could sleep right here. Let's get her to the room."

Annie roused herself and they got their bags from the wagon. Dennis, small candle in hand, led them up the dim staircase to the room. Other than the rumpled bedding, the room was small but clean. A basin and pitcher stood on a small table with a clean towel and a clean chamber pot sat in the corner. "I'm afraid there's only the one bed."

Roisin smiled. "Sure it won't bother us none." *No indeed*, thought Roisin. For the first time in days, she felt herself begin to relax.

The next morning, Roisin and Annie marveled at how well and long they had slept.

"I feel like a right queen for this mattress," said Annie, stifling a yawn.

Roisin chuckled. "Well I guess it be time to get yer royal arse out of those sheets! I want to get some breakfast!"

Annie groaned but rose and dressed.

Leaving their bundles behind, they went downstairs and found a young girl collecting breakfast dishes from the tables and wiping up crumbs and spills. She looked up, a smile crinkling her vivid blue eyes as they walked through the room.

"Top of the mornin' to ye," she said, flipping her heavy black braid over her shoulder.

Roisin and Annie nodded and returned the greeting.

"My name is Lucy. Dennis said I was to fix ye ladies some breakfast."

"Where is Dennis?" asked Roisin.

Lucy pointed through the open doorway to the small bay where Dennis was sitting on a piling smoking his pipe. He looked perfectly content as he watched a sail boat glide over the calm water, while raucous sea gulls circled overhead in search of food.

"I could eat," said Roisin. "Annie?" she asked. "Eggs sound good to ye?"

Annie shrugged as she stared through the open door at the water. "Just some bread and jam for me. An' some tea, please"

"Have a seat, ladies," said Lucy. "I'll be back in no time."

Annie continued to stare out the open door. Thoughts of her mother made her heart ache. She closed her eyes, took a deep breath, and blew it out. Nothing to be done about the past.

Roisin tried to engage Annie in conversation but the young woman was reticent, her mind far away. She hoped the grieving would spend itself soon. She missed Annie's smiles.

"Here we are ladies," said Lucy as she set a tray on the vacant table next to them. She placed a plate of eggs and ham in front of Roisin and a bare plate in front of Annie. A loaf of warmed bread on a board was set on the middle of the table with tubs of jam and butter.

"I have an idea," said Roisin as she sipped the strong tea.

Annie finally turned her face to Roisin. "What's that?"

"After breakfast, how 'bout we walk around the village and get a taste for it? See if we might be safe here?"

Annie nodded.

The women walked along the wide road to where Dennis still sat enjoying the morning. The bright-hued shops they passed were bustling with activity. Some of the shop owners displayed a sampling of their wares on tables outside: tanned hides, fresh fish, bolts of linen cloth and thread, crates of produce, fresh baked goods, and balls of salted butter wrapped in linen casings.

As they approached the harbor, Annie shielded her eyes from the bright sunlight that danced over the calm water. There was barely a breeze, and reflections of the boats and coastline mirrored clearly on the surface.

"I've never seen the sea so still or smelled the air so lackin' of salt," remarked Annie.

Dennis chuckled. "That's 'cause this ain't the sea." He pointed beyond the bay where the waters opened to a vast expanse flowing to the west. "That there is the Shannon Estuary. We get folks come through here from the east and up north, some as far north as Killaloe, to do trade with Limerick and then here." He pointed to the west. "The Shannon meets with the sea at Loop's Head. Some of the ships head on north to Galway or some go on south to Cork or even over to England or France."

At the mention of Killaloe, Annie froze. Patrick! Did his people trade here? She wondered how far away he was. She had no idea what kind of farming his people did. Did they have cattle? It had never occurred to her to ask. Would he ever come here to look for her? As quickly as that hope had flared within her, it burned out. Why on earth would he? He had already left her.

They watched as brawny, bare-chested men loaded kegs of butter, corn and other grains, and some filled with fish onto the ships.

On other ships, pigs, sheep and cattle were being herded into pens for transport. The din of the livestock caused Roisin to remark, "From the sound of 'em, they must know they's headed for slaughter."

The thought of that turned Annie's stomach queasy and she fought to keep her breakfast down.

Dennis gestured to the ships with his pipe. "We send many a bucket of oysters out of here, too, along with boatloads of fresh fish. Ships go in and out of here all day long."

Suddenly, Annie gasped. Several large beings . . . they weren't like any fish she had ever seen . . . arced high into the air. Their long bodies glistening in the sunlight before plunging back into the water, their tail fins leaving barely a ripple the surface. Over and over they seemed to fly, then disappear while they circled the bay.

Dennis laughed as Annie, shocked by the sight, suddenly began sputtering. "What on earth are they?" she asked. "Surely, they can't be fish!"

"They're dolphins!" Dennis cried. "Bottle-noses they're called, on account of their long snouts. They're mammals, actually. Only place ye'll see them is around the estuary. They pretty much live here. Right friendly they are, too. Sometimes they, like these here, keep the boats company as they come in and out of the bay, an' they stay awhile to put on a show."

Annie couldn't take her eyes away from them. They all seemed to be in pairs, arcing perfectly together or chattering away in harmony when they floated in place with their heads above water. Her chest began to ache with longing. How she wished that she and Patrick could soar together like that. She could hardly dare to hope that, some day, she might see him again. Her eyes began to fill and she turned and hurried away from the quay.

Roisin sighed and turned to follow Annie. "I guess we'll be seeing ye later, Dennis."

Chapter Fifty-Five

The day dawned clear and bright, only a few harmless puffs of white clouds marring the vivid blue of the sky. Everyone gathered at the corn field right after an early breakfast. Everyone but Seamus. He arrived at the field mid-morning, looking worse for wear and still reeking the excess of ale he'd consumed the night before.

"Is this the way you earn your keep?" fumed Niall.

Seamus glared with bloodshot eyes. "What *keep*? Ye got no call to be carpin' at me! If I was stayin' with the men, I'd a been here on time."

Niall knew that arguing would be pointless. Throwing a sack at Seamus, he pointed to the row beside him. "Start picking right here where I can keep an eye on you."

Seamus grumbled under his breath as he slung the strap over his head, began tearing the ears of corn from the stalks and shoving them into the sack. His head was aching and he was angry at Molly for not waking him. In fact, he had no clue where she was at the moment, and that angered him, too. She'd tried to bar him from the wagon when he stumbled home from the tavern late the night before. Well, he'd shown her! He'd pulled her from the wagon and shoved her into the grass and told her to stay put. Her whining and carrying on would be the death of him. He couldn't remember what else had gone on because he'd passed out as soon as his head hit the bedroll. The only thing he was glad of was to wake without his brats screaming and arguing with each other. He'd had no breakfast, but he didn't think he'd have been able to keep it down anyway.

It didn't take long before he was sweating profusely, and he could smell his own stink as the alcohol leeched out of his body. Listening to the spalpeens singing up a storm as they worked irritated the devil out of him. He carried his sack to Niall's wagon and dumped his load. He noticed the bucket of liquid on the ground and hoisted it to his lips and gulped it down until he gagged.

"Tea?" he asked angrily as Niall, too, dumped his load.

"Of course, tea! It's what we drink while we work."

"Seems to me," sputtered Seamus, "that ye could be providin' somethin' a bit stronger for all this work."

Niall laughed derisively and shook his head. "You call this work? The real works starts in a few hours." He said no more and returned to his place in the field. Most of the men were now busy with their scythes, cutting down the barren corn stalks. Jake and his crew worked one side of the field, while the O'Brien men, Roark, and their own hired men worked the other. Saraid and Fiona followed behind the men on one side, Maureen and James on the other, bundling the stalks into stooks.

The cool morning had rapidly turned warm and they began wiping sweat from their brows. The women and Fiona left the heat of the field an hour later. They returned pushing a wheeled cart, parking it under a canopy of trees on the far side of the field. They set up more buckets of tea, brown bread and butter, and some early apples for the men to have on their break.

Horses were hitched to the wagons and driven to the barn. The corn was emptied into piles on the wood floor, where the women and children would begin the shucking process in the afternoon. After setting aside the best of the ears for their own consumption, they shucked the rest for chicken feed, tossing the husks and cobs into a bin used to feed the pigs.

The men were grateful for the food and a break from the heat.

After gobbling down their fill, some broke out their penny whistles, some sang, while the others bantered good naturedly.

Seamus tried to enter into conversation with the men, but no one acknowledged that he was sitting right there next to them. Not to be discouraged, he kept it up until Jake finally looked at him.

"Ah," Seamus said, sarcasm dripping from his voice. "So y'ain't deaf after all."

Jake stared into Seamus's bloodshot eyes, giving him a disgusted look. "What is it ye be wantin', man?"

"Wantin'? How about ye give me the same time o'day ye give to t'others?"

Jake shook his head. "How about ye work like the rest of us and earn your place?"

"What do ye think I been doin' if not workin'?"

Jake stood and looked down at Seamus. "I been keepin' an eye on ye, and I ain't too impressed with what I seen so far."

Seamus jumped up, about to start a ruckus, when Niall and his brothers arrived from the barn with the hay rakes. "What's the trouble here?" asked Niall.

"No trouble I can't handle," said Jake.

"Hey!" cried Seamus. "I ain't tryin' to start trouble! I was just wantin' to be one of 'em, is all."

Jake ignored him and looked to Niall. "Are we ready to start on the hay?"

Niall looked up at the nearly cloudless sky and nodded. "Take your men and get started. Leave six behind to rake. We'll swap them out in the afternoon."

Patrick and John followed them to the field. Niall looked back at Seamus, resentment filling him again. "Leave Jake and his men be. They've been working together for a long time and have their own way in the field."

"An' ye think I ain't good enough to work beside 'em?"

Niall put his hands on his hips to keep from wrapping them around Seamus's neck. "When was the last time you worked with a group for harvest?"

Seamus waved his arms in frustration. "I ain't never had no call to work with a bunch o' bloody spalpeens. I always just took care o' my own. Is that a crime?"

Niall stroked his forehead and squeezed shut his eyes, praying for patience. "Look, there's a rhythm to the work that keeps anyone from getting hurt. You can't just hack as you please. The scythes are sharp and need to be swung precisely. For today, you'll follow behind me and rake. If you can follow directions, we'll see what happens tomorrow."

Seamus began to tremble. He was being talked to like an errant child with no common sense. He longed to tell Niall and the rest of his family to go to the feckin' devil, but he needed whatever coin he could earn this week. He had only pennies left and God only knew when he'd find work again. If he didn't have so many mouths to feed, he'd be better off. God, what he'd give to be free of the lot of them! He still needed to ask one more thing. "So, now that I'm workin', where are we to sleep tonight?"

In any ditch you please, thought Niall. "After supper, you can take your wagon down behind the barn. There's plenty of room in the loft where you can sleep. You can spread out a couple of the old bales and you'll be comfortable enough."

"In the barn? The other men got a nice bunkhouse to sleep in an' I got to sleep in the barn?"

"Look!" shouted Niall, his temper finally getting the best of him. "The bunkhouse is full! We hadn't planned on you being here and there's no place else. Not for your entire family! Be happy to have a roof over your head!" He began to stalk off to the field when Seamus opened his mouth yet again.

"Oh, an' I s'pose we'll get our dinner at the trough?"

Niall spun around and got in Seamus's face, his voice a terse whisper. "Be happy that we're putting up with you at all! The only reason you're even here is because Saraid took pity on Molly! I'd just as soon hang you from the nearest tree and be done with you! God knows you wouldn't be missed!"

Seamus felt the blood drain from his face and clenched his fists. He needed to just shut up and he knew it. His feigned bravado was fast leaving him, and he resented the loss of power he'd felt he held over this family. Deep down, he knew that Niall was right. No one would miss him if he was gone. Molly only stayed with him because she had nowhere else to go. He resented that, too. *Stupid bitch! Why has my life turned out so bad? How come these people have so much when I got nothing left? If people showed me some respect, I could be as successful as anyone.* But for today, he needed to just lick his wounds in silence and get through the day.

"All right," he said meekly. "I'll do whate'er ye say."

Niall had expected another show of belligerence and was surprised at the change of tone. He wondered what was actually going through the man's mind and vowed to keep a close eye on him.

After their late morning break, the men followed Niall to the acreage where the tall green grasses swayed back and forth in the hot breeze. He squinted as he eyed the field, knowing that it should have been cut a week ago when the seed heads had started to form at the tops.

Jake lined up his men in tandem six feet apart. The first man started at the right side of the field, sweeping his scythe from right to left, close to the ground, creating a windrow to his left. The second man followed in his footsteps, using a wooden rake to spread and fluff the hay back over the cuts. The third man followed with his scythe, making an overlapping cut over the first row, and that, too, was spread and fluffed by the man behind him. Over the rhythmic swish of the scythes and rakes, one after the other began to hum, and soon to sing, to pass the tedious hours in the hot sun.

Saraid and Maureen returned to the courtyard to tend to the mid-day meal and found Molly stirring a pot over the fire. Kate was sitting apart in a chair under the oak tree, struggling to read from a time-worn book of children's stories. Bridget was cuddled in her lap sucking her thumb. Liam stood beside her chair turning the pages, and Maureen's twins sat on the ground at her feet.

Molly's brood ran circles around their mother as she tried to stir the cast iron pot.

"Get them away from the fire!" cried Saraid. "They're goin' to get burned!"

"They won' listen to me!"

Saraid snatched one of the little ones by the arm as Maureen tried unsuccessfully to grab at another when the imp scurried past her skirt.

"Stop it!" yelled Saraid as the youngster tried to bite her hand.

Saraid forcibly made the child sit on the ground, pointed her finger at her with a warning, "Stay there, or I'll wallop yer bottom!"

Molly wailed in frustration and the children began to cry. "Don't be yellin' at my children!"

Saraid marched over to Molly and gripped her arm. "Yer children are no better than the wild creatures of the woods! Have ye no control over them at all?"

Molly stood stock still, hung her head, and began to weep.

"An' all of ye stop with your bloody whimperin'!" Saraid lashed out with such venom that she shocked herself. She yanked the bandana from her head and wiped her face, choking back her own tears. She held her heavy braid away from her neck as she paced the courtyard, praying for a cool breeze to dry the sweat that ran in rivulets down her back. She took a deep breath to quiet herself before standing in front of Molly and speaking again. "Look," she said quietly. "This really isn't goin' well. Everyone is anxious because of Seamus.

I think it would be better if all of ye just leave here."

Molly's head snapped up, her mouth agape, her eyes pained. "What are ye sayin' to me? Are you tellin' us to *leave*?" She waved her hands at the sky. "Where would ye be havin' us go?" she cried. The children, seeing their mother's anguish, suddenly clung to her skirt, begging to be picked up. Molly tried to comfort them best she could but was too overwrought to be of much use to them.

Saraid's heart was struggling to be firm, to get the awful words said. "Ye need more help than we can be givin' ye. Seamus isn't anything *close* to a worker and ye know it. For my life, I cannot understand why ye stay with him when he abuses all of ye so!"

When Molly began to make excuses for Seamus, Saraid held up her hand. "Stop it! Where's the girl I knew so long ago? The one with some back bone and some fire in her gut?"

"You don' understand!" cried Molly.

"You're right on that!" Saraid shook her head and began to pace. "I started out no better than ye! I, too, had nothin'! Did ye ever see me snivelin' every minute of the day?"

Molly laughed with hollow bitterness. "How can ye compare us? Ye have everythin'! Seamus didn' start out bein' this way. He had goodness and smiles in him, and he took good care of us." The tears coursed down her cheeks; and she struggled to wipe them away with one hand as she rubbed her belly with the other, as if to calm the babe within her. The children kept whining as she tried to pry their fingers from her skirt. "It's the drink. It makes him ugly. He don' mean it."

"Then he should stop the drinkin'!"

"It's not that easy!" Molly snapped. "He tries, really he does, but then we lost the farm an' he coun't find work. I know he's ashamed of himself, even if he don' act like it. He's a proud man."

Kate had tried to ignore the arguing but it was too difficult. She began to shake and desperately needed to escape the noise and confusion. As she rose from her chair and began walking towards the house, a wave of dizziness washed over her and she swayed. Saraid ran to her side and put an arm around her waist to steady her.

Saraid called to Molly over her shoulder. "We'll finish this later."

Chapter Fifty-Six

After the mid-day meal, the men returned to the field and spent a few hours raking the drying hay into windrows. By the time they finished this task and took a short break, it was time to go back to the beginning and carefully turn over the windrows to expose the underside of the rows to the sun.

Hank sat on his stool in the shade by himself. Freddie and Willie had left for home the day before, so he was lonesome and had no one to talk to. As he watched the men work, he wished there was something he could do to help. He was left with nothing to do but watch the antics of Molly's children. He chuckled to himself and thought that they were quite the handful. He could see Molly's frustration mounting as she tried to pour drippings over the pig roasting on the spit, the girls tugging on her skirts.

"Step away, now!" she cried. "Remember what Saraid said to ye? Ye're goin' to get burned!"

Hank tried to think of some way to ease her troubles. *Well, maybe there is somethin'*, he thought. Rising, he walked the short distance to the stable to retrieve his fiddle. He sat back down, took up his bow, and began to play a lively jig.

The children squealed with laughter, ran to where he sat, and cavorted around him.

Molly started to call them back until she saw him smile at her and shake his head. She watched him for a few moments and then she smiled back at him.

His heart sang! Smiling at each of the girls until his jaws ached, he filled with joy over their attention. When he stopped playing, they stomped their dirty little feet and tugged at him, crying out for more.

"If ye sit down and quiet yer selves, I'll play some more."

"Play! Play some more!" they cried as they continued to jump up and down.

"Not until you be sittin' yourselves down and bein' quiet," he said in a no-nonsense manner.

The imps continued to whine and fuss and demand to no avail. Hank kept his resolve though it was difficult with all the noise they were making. Finally, he stood up.

"I guess ye're not wantin' to hear any more music!" He picked up his stool and began to walk away from them.

"No, no!" they wailed, grabbing at him. "Play some more!"

He was having a difficult time keeping a straight face. "Are ye goin' to sit down and be quiet?"

The girls looked to each other, not sure what to make of Hank and his fiddle. They finally accepted that he meant what he was saying. They quieted down, sat at his feet, and pulled the toddler down between them.

"Well, then. I guess since ye decided to sit and listen, I can play another tune." He gave them each a broad smile and stuck the fiddle under his chin. They returned his smile, showing grey uneven teeth, as he began to play another lively song. He could tell they were itching to move about, so he stopped for a minute. "Do ye know how to do a jig?"

They looked to one another, shrugging their small shoulders, not knowing what he meant.

"Ah," he said. "Has no one showed ye how to dance?"

They shook their heads.

"All right then. I guess it's up to me! Stand up now!"

They jumped up and cried out. "Play! Ye said ye was goin' to play!"

"Watch m'feet," he told them. The pain in his hip seemed to vanish as he did a simple jig in time to the music. "Now ye try it!"

He continued to play and danced around them.

The older two girls pranced and jumped, the toddler doing her best to imitate them, before they all fell down in fits of giggles. They rolled around on the ground and came up with bits of grass and dirt stuck to their sweaty bodies.

Hank laughed with merriment at their antics, his heart as light as a feather on a breeze. He couldn't remember when he'd had such fun! His hip finally begged for mercy; and he sat down heavily, wiping the sweat from his brow. "Ye done a great job!"

"Play some more!"

After a few more tunes, he slowed the music down and sang some of his favorite ballads. They sat at his feet and, one by one, their thumbs found their mouths. Within minutes, they began to lean against his legs and nod off. Tenderness filled him until his chest ached with it, and tears ran down his cheeks.

Molly was mesmerized. She had watched this odd little man, a leprechaun come to life, charm her children into submission with nary a cross word. She couldn't remember the last time any of them had taken a nap. She walked slowly to where he sat and saw the gentleness in his eyes as he looked up at her. Standing silently before him, she glanced from one child to the other, so deeply touched that her eyes brimmed. Finally she whispered. "I don' know how to thank ye."

Hank's face turned crimson. "It weren't nothin'," he said quietly. He shyly touched the unruly curls of the oldest child's head. "I enjoyed it even more'n they did."

Molly lowered her eyes. No man had ever treated any of them with such kindness. Certainly not Seamus.

"Well . . . " she said, feeling awkward. "I should prob'ly get back to the cookin'. Do ye want me to be takin' 'em off yer hands?"

Hank shook his head. "Why don't ye just leave them with me and take a rest for yerself? I'll not harm them."

"Could I just rest here and listen to ye play some more?"

Hank was flummoxed, his cheeks flaming again. "I . . . I'd be right honored to play for ye."

Molly lay on her back in the warm grass and closed her eyes, the swelling of her belly a soft mound beneath her smock.

Hank played some of the sweetest music he could remember and soon Molly, too, was asleep.

The sounds of wheels and hooves came across the courtyard, waking Hank. He wasn't sure how much time had passed, as he'd nodded off himself. He rubbed the sleep from his eyes and looked up to see Seamus glaring at him from the wagon.

"What in bloody hell is goin' on here?" asked Seamus gruffly.

Molly was startled back from her nap. She rolled onto her side and awkwardly got to her feet, as did the children.

"Da!" the children cried in unison as they jumped up and ran to the wagon. Molly brushed off her skirt. "Seamus! What are ye doin' here?"

"I come to get us settled in the barn. An' I asked ye a question. What are ye doin' with this man?"

"What on earth do ye mean, Seamus? Hank played his fiddle for the children an' I came to listen too, is all."

"Is that so?" asked Seamus. "I din' hear no music. Looked to me like ye was all just sleepin' together."

"For God's sake, Seamus!" cried Molly. "We wasn't *sleepin' together*!"

Hank rose from his stool, fear creeping up his spine. "She done nothin' wrong, Seamus. An' neither did I."

Seamus jumped down from the wagon. He grabbed Molly roughly by the arm and began pulling her away. He pointed an accusing finger at Hank. "Ye just stay away from my woman, little man."

"Seamus! Let me go! Ye're hurtin' me!"

"I'll let ye go when I'm damn good and ready," he shouted. He left the wagon where it was and roughly dragged her off towards the barn. The children cowed when Seamus yelled at them to shut up.

Hank began to shake, his anger at Seamus boiling up in him. He knew what it was to feel helpless and in pain at the hand of others. He took a step towards them but stopped when Seamus shot him a look full of hate. As much as he wanted to intervene, he knew his place. Molly was not his. She belonged to Seamus. There was nothing he could do.

Patrick and George, having seen the tail end of the incident, came rushing across the courtyard.

"You all right, Hank?" asked Patrick.

Hank nodded, his face coloring.

George spat on the ground. "That Seamus is the devil's own, if I do say so."

"Hank, you've been no trouble to us, but we may have to move you to another place."

Hank felt panic rising in him. "Where would I be goin'?"

Patrick answered. "My brothers and I were talking this morning about having you stay at Danny's. The place is empty now until Danny comes home. He's got no hired man to keep an eye on the property. We're afraid that squatters might help themselves to the place. Do you think you could do that?"

Hank shook his head. "I got no experience with takin' care of a farm."

"You wouldn't have to do anything. We're planning on spending some time there at the end of each day just to make it seem like someone is there. We'll bring you food so you won't be hungry."

George piped up. "I could stay there at night until the crops are in. That way he wouldn't be alone."

"That's a good idea," said Patrick. "How do you feel about it,

Hank? It would keep Seamus from bothering you, too."

Hank was torn. He liked it here at the O'Brien's farm. He liked seeing Molly every day, too. He sighed. Who was he foolin'? He had to forget about Molly. "All right, then," he said. "If ye be thinkin' it's for the best, I can't argue. Sure I'm grateful that ye're willin' to keep me around."

George grasped Hank's shoulder. "It'll keep ye safe, Hank."

It was decided that George would take Hank to Danny's place the next day while the men were in the fields. They would tell anyone who asked that Hank had decided to be on his way.

The workmen were starving. The aroma of roasting pig had been drifting over the field for hours. They hurried through the last task of the day, raking the windrows into loose ricks.

The large mounds, scattered across the field, would sit for the night, the insides protected from the dew that would form overnight.

Jake couldn't say enough about the new hay rakes. "Bloody good on ye, George! This rake cuts the work in half!"

George laughed. "Just be careful where ye swing that thing. Ye don't want to be stabbin' anyone!"

At the end of the day, the men were tired and covered with the detritus of the fields. They shook bits of hay and dust from their hair and clothing and took turns washing up at the pump before sitting down at the table. They had worked up a serious appetite and dug into the meal with relish.

Jake reluctantly made room for Seamus at the end of the table. While there was no effort to include Seamus in their bantering, they did their best not to antagonize him. Molly and the children sat at another table across the courtyard with the O'Briens, George, Hank, and Roark's family.

Before long, they had eaten their fill and the sun was setting. The night clouds hovering over the horizon turned into streaks of bright pink, orange and purple, forecasting another good day for the morrow. Lanterns were lit, and a keg of ale flowed freely throughout the evening, loosening tension and tired muscles. Soon, music from their penny whistles, pipes and fiddles was flowing, too. The men danced around the campfire, their voices filling the night air with both laughter and song.

Seamus sat in silence, taking it all in, but did not participate. He just kept refilling his mug with ale, and kept a keen eye on Molly and Hank. They were sitting well-apart from each other and seemed not to be paying each other any mind. His children, wearing some sort of smocks that looked too large on their thin frames, seemed intent on getting Hank to play his fiddle. He seethed at the charity of others. To his mind, it was another show of how he couldn't provide for his family. His resentment grew at the attention Hank was paying to them and how they seemed to forget that they had a father sitting by himself.

The exhausted but happy workmen picked up the lanterns and said their good nights. They traipsed across the field to their bedrolls, their laughter echoing across the moonlit landscape.

Seamus sat alone in the dim light and drained the rest of the keg, batting it off the table when he found it empty. He watched Molly gather up his children and head across the courtyard to the barn. His hands began to shake, his vision to blur, and a lone tear ran down his cheek. They had forgotten all about him. *Well*, he thought, *maybe he would just forget about them, too. Maybe he would take off and just leave them here.* He chuckled. *Wouldn't that be a pisser? Let them put up with her bloody whinin' and I can just disappear and make a fresh start without all these feckin' mouths to feed.*

Chapter Fifty-Seven

As the bright morning sun and dry air were working their magic, the domed ricks were turning pale gold. The men took their rakes and spread the ricks out into loose windrows, exposing the damp green underside of the piles to the sun. Soon, the air filled with a sweet, intoxicating aroma as the drying hay was fluffed in the sunlight.

Suddenly, one of the men stopped in his tracks, yelling and pointing to the entrance road of the farm. They all began cowing in fear and making the sign of the cross on their chests.

Niall's head turned to see what the trouble was. "God damn it!" he yelled and began to run. "Stay here!" he called out to Jake.

Patrick and John were quick to follow him, the hired men remained huddled together, only too happy to stay where they were.

A wagon was coming down the lane. Seated upon it were Doctor O'Hickey and his wife, Martha, both wearing white cotton bandanas over their noses and mouths. On the side of the wagon was painted one word: '*typhus*.' In the back of the wagon was a casket.

"Is it Danny in that casket?" asked Niall, holding a bandana across his nose. The stench emanating from the wagon was powerful.

The doctor nodded.

"How can that be?" exclaimed Patrick. The putrid smell made him gag and he spit hot saliva from his mouth as his stomach churned. He and John were both quick to cover their faces.

John yelled out in anger and disbelief. "What are you thinking, bringing this disease to our farm!"

O'Hickey raised his hand for silence. He climbed down from the wagon and drew Niall away from the others. Martha sat very still, saying nothing, as she watched Saraid and Maureen at the edge of the courtyard, holding the children back. They watched the doctor pull down his mask and whisper something to Niall.

Niall's head shot up in surprise as the doctor put his hand on his shoulder and continued to talk quietly. Niall only nodded and said nothing. Then Niall was pointing to the road and making gestures. The doctor walked back to his wagon and, grim faced, gave a silent parting wave to the others. He placed the mask over his face, turned the wagon around, and went back up the lane.

As the dust settled on the road, Niall walked back to the others and began issuing orders.

"John, where's Hank?"

John was livid. "What does it matter where Hank is?"

"Just get him!" Niall snapped. "Tell him to bring his belongings."

Patrick was frantic. "Danny's dead! I can't believe it!" he began to cry as he paced the courtyard.

"Patrick, please!" Niall yelled as he rushed toward the field. "Get the wagon hitched and get some spades. We have to bury him."

Saraid ran to Niall. "What's happenin'?" she demanded, grabbing his arm to stop him.

He could not meet her eyes. "Doc brought Danny back to us . . . just not the way we'd like."

Saraid shrieked. "You can't be meanin' that our Danny was in that stinkin' casket!"

Niall nodded and looked away from her when she began to cry. "I have to tell the men to keep working. We'll be back when we've finished burying him."

Saraid ran from him, wailing, tears streaming down her stricken face.

Niall's shoulders slumped as he walked with heavy steps back to the field where the men were standing mute and anxious. He drew Paddy aside, putting his hand on the older man's shoulder. "We need you to come with us for a burial."

Paddy nodded silently and made a quick trip to his room, returning with a small prayer book and a rosary that he hid in his pocket.

Niall went to Jake. "We need to go and bury our friend, Danny. I'll leave you and Mickey in charge of the men. George, will you stay and help them?"

George nodded and kept silent though a million questions swam in his brain. He had no clue what was going on, but there was something not right about any of it.

Niall turned to Roark. "I'd like you to come with us." Roark nodded and set aside his rake.

Seamus eyed the goings on in silence until Niall began to walk away. "One less o' ye to put up with," he muttered under his breath.

Jake grabbed Seamus by the back of his neck and shoved him towards the field. "Have some respect! Get yer feckin' arse back to the field an' do yer job!"

Seamus shrugged and chuckled as he sauntered back through the hay field.

The three brothers were silent, each in his own state of disbelief, anger, and mourning as they caught up to Dr. O'Hickey and followed the stench of his wagon to Danny's place.

Hank was mumbling prayers and trying not to think about the dead man as he, Paddy and Roark followed behind the others. Hank wondered if they were expecting him to help with the burial. He shuddered and began to whimper softly.

"It will be all right," Paddy said calmly, patting Hank's knee as he fingered his rosary beads.

The doctor stopped his wagon in the shade behind Danny's home. He looked around and, satisfied that there was no one lurking about, jumped down from his seat and reached into the back of the wagon. He dislodged a sack of putrid meat from under a blanket and tossed it as far away from the wagon as he could. He pulled down his mask. "We'll have to bury that," he said, as the others looked on in disbelief.

Martha tore the mask from her face. "Well thank God for that!" She held her arms out to Patrick who helped her down from the wagon. Pointing to the seat, she asked him to retrieve the pot that was under it. She took it from him and walked into the house without another word.

John yelled. "What in God's name is going on?"

The doctor climbed into the back of the wagon and began to pry the top off the casket.

The men all cried out as they backed away from the wagon. "What are you doing! What about the typhus!"

"Hush!" said the doctor. He looked to Niall. "You didn't tell them?"

Niall shook his head. "There wasn't time. I thought it best to wait until we were here. Let's get him out of there!"

Hank moaned, feeling faint.

Patrick and the others were all talking at once. "He's not dead?" asked Patrick.

Niall shook his head. "He's as alive as you are, but he won't be for much longer if we don't get him out of this bloody box."

Paddy fell to his knees. "I don't understand!" He was clutching his prayer book to his chest with one hand as he made the sign of the cross with the other.

"It's all right, Father," said Niall. "You'll not be needing to give the last rights today."

The priest scratched his head in confusion. "Then what am I doing here?"

Roark, silent up to now finally spoke. "I'm wonderin' the same myself."

The casket lid was tossed to the side, and there lay Danny, a weak smile on his face. He took in a huge gulp of clean air. There was a sheen of sweat on his brow and his hair was a mass of wet ringlets. His clothes, too, were saturated from being confined in the box for the long journey from Ennis.

Danny twirled a nail that was attached to a large knot of wood from the pine casket. "Sure that was a great idea, Doc," he said, his voice a barely audible whisper. "Kept me in air the whole time." He tossed the knot of wood and struggled to raise his good arm. "Now get me out of this feckin' coffin!"

Niall and the doctor carefully lifted Danny from the casket, mindful of his sling and bad shoulder. He was pale and pounds lighter, but alive and grateful for it. His knees buckled as they began walking him to the house. Niall scooped him up and carried him through the door to his bed. They put him into dry clothes, and he was asleep in minutes.

John shook his head. "Why'd you bring all of us out here if he's alive? And why was he in a casket?"

Doc O'Hickey removed his glasses, closed his eyes, and pinched the bridge of his nose. Now that they had arrived at their destination without mishap, the apprehension he'd felt on the trip drained out of him. In its place was exhaustion. "Someone came to warn me that the Charlies were heading to our place. We had to get him out of there quick and couldn't risk having him in the open. Thank the Lord I always have a casket in the barn! I had to make it look real in case anyone came along and wanted to see what was in the wagon. I grabbed that meat from the silage and put it in the sack. With that stink in the wagon, no one was going to come too close."

He looked at Hank who was silently wringing his hands. "Niall tells me that it's going to be your job to take care of him. Can you do that?"

Hank, surprised, shifted from one foot to the other. "Is he goin' to make it? I ain't no doctor."

"He's on the mend now. You'll need to help him some, but his fever is gone, and he just needs to rest for a few more weeks. Martha brought along the big pot of soup she'd had on the fire and some bread. You'll just need to heat it up and feed it to him."

Hank nodded his head and straightened his back. "I can do that." He was relieved to know that he wouldn't be there alone. He'd have someone to talk to. And it felt good to know that he was needed.

"Good," said the doctor, patting Hank's shoulder. He looked to the others. "All right then," he chuckled. "Let's get those spades busy and bury that damned box."

The men dug a mock grave and at the last moment tossed the rotten meat into the casket before lowering it into the ground. They mounded the dirt over the plot and tied together two sticks in the shape of a cross.

Niall drew out his knife to carve Danny's initials into the wood.

"Don't be doing that!" cried Paddy. "It's bad luck, and God knows, we don't need any more of that!"

Niall shrugged and sheathed the knife. Then he plunged the cross into the soft earth at the head of the plot. Paddy opened his prayer book and sang the Latin prayers for the dead in his sweet tenor, his rosary beads dangling from his hand. The others bowed their heads and, one by one, they began to grin.

Chapter Fifty-Eight

When Niall and the others returned home, they were alarmed to find only Jake, Mickey and George in the field, and Seamus sitting by himself on the verge.

"Where is everyone?" asked Niall.

Seamus shrugged. "They took off."

"What do you mean?" asked Patrick as he looked over the empty field. The rakes and scythes were in a pile at the cut line.

Seamus looked from one to the other, secretly gloating over yet another problem for the O'Brien men. "They got spooked by the stench comin' off that wagon and was afraid of gettin' sick."

John and Paddy joined them.

Niall looked back to Seamus. "Why aren't you out there working?"

Seamus shrugged. "I was just takin' a little time."

Niall clenched his fists. "That so? Well, your time's done so get your worthless arse back out there," he ordered before striding across the field.

"Well," said Seamus as he rose and stretched. "Seems to me, if ye're expectin' me to work harder now, my pay should be a whole lot more."

Niall stopped and turned back to Seamus, his eyes dark. "Don't you worry none, Seamus. You'll get exactly what you deserve. Now either get back to work or get out!"

Seamus shrugged and sauntered back to the field. He picked up the big hay rake and fingered the tines as he stared at Niall's back.

His thoughts were ominous as he began tossing clumps of hay into windrows.

Jake and Mickey stopped their work as Niall approached. Jake was apprehensive as he faced him. "I'm sorry, Niall."

Niall looked out over the field. It would be a daunting task to get the hay and the other crops in without the extra hands. "Any hope of getting the men to come back?"

Jake shook his head. "They was right spooked by that wagon. There was nothin' I could say to keep 'em here. They insisted on their wages, and I had no choice but to pay 'em out of my own pocket."

Niall looked at the western sky where the sun was hovering at the horizon. There was about an hour of daylight left. "I'll settle with you at dinner. Will you stay on?"

Jake hesitated.

Niall wanted to tell him about Danny, but was afraid that the information might be passed on to ears that didn't need to know that Danny was alive. "We're safe enough here."

Jake searched Niall's eyes and saw no deceit. In spite of his misgivings, he had to trust that Niall was being as truthful now as he had been in the past. He nodded. "I'll stay. You'll be hard-pressed to get all this hay in by the end of the week."

In gratitude, Niall laid a hand on Jake's shoulder. "Thank you. I'll certainly make it worth your while."

Saraid and Maureen, arriving with buckets of tea, pitched in with the haying, as did James and Fiona. The women, still ignorant of the truth about Danny, were in the throes of their own silent grief.

James worked beside his father. He grabbed a rake and began a new row, raking the scattered grasses into windrows like the others were doing. It was the first time he had been allowed to work alongside the men and he strove to work as hard as they did. His slender arms and shoulders began to tire as he worked his way down the row, but he grit his teeth, determined to finish. He wondered about all that had gone on earlier, but could tell from his father's demeanor that this was not the time to ask. There would be time enough for that later.

Fiona was raking, too, though she didn't like it much. Her arms began to sweat and small bits of hay clung to her skin, making her itch. She stopped to scratch and noticed that Seamus was watching her. Fiona's face reddened and she looked away quickly. When she glanced back again, he grinned, and she felt a chill creep up her back. She quickly took up the rake and dug into another clump of hay with a vengeance.

The fields, usually filled with song and banter, were now saturated with the sounds of their exertion. Everyone worked long and hard until the last remnant of light was a fading halo sinking behind the distant hills.

When darkness fell, the weary crew staggered back to the courtyard, shaking the loose hay from their clothing and hair, removing their shirts and tossing them into a pile. The cool night air was a balm on their sweaty skin. They were almost too tired to eat.

Niall tapped a fresh keg of ale and filled the cups the men and women held out. Their sighs were audible as they chugged the brew down their parched throats. One after the other they belched and refilled their cups before sitting down at the table. James held out his cup. Niall hesitated, then nodded, giving him half a cup full. "You worked like a man today, son."

James's weary face brightened and he stood as erect as he could. Though his muscles groaned in protest, his father's praise filled his heart with pride. "Thank you, Da." He lifted the cup to his lips and tipped it up too fast, squealing as the foam filled his nose. The others laughed and became silly as their exhaustion washed over them.

Niall topped an earthenware jug with ale and set it on the table before he finally sat down and blew out a breath.

Molly was grateful that she was not expected to work in the field. With so many small ones to keep an eye on, she hadn't had the time to prepare a hot meal. Instead, she set out a platter of cold pork left over from the pig roasted the day before. Another platter held chunks of hard cheese, loaves of bread, and fresh vegetables from the garden. A jar of savory honey was passed to dribble on the ham.

As everyone began filling their plates, Seamus tossed a crust of bread at Molly. "Ye call this a fit meal for a hardworkin' man?"

She flinched as it hit her cheek. Her eyes filled and she hung her head, ashamed that he would do this in front of everyone.

"Seamus!" Saraid cried. The foul mood she'd carried all day finally got the best of her. She gestured at his children as well as Maureen's and her own, who were chasing each other around the courtyard. "Ye've no right to complain! Takin' care of all these children was work enough for anyone!"

Gloom settled around the table, people picked at their food, and Seamus continued to mutter under his breath.

Niall's head was pounding and he exploded. "Seamus, you ungrateful *bastard*! I've had enough of you! I want you to go get your things and leave! *Now!*"

Seamus laughed. "Ye must be crazy! How can ye be tossin' out one of the only hands ye got left?"

Niall clenched his fists as he rose from the table. "I'm going to get your wages," he growled. "You have five minutes to get your things together or I swear, you'll not see another day!"

The men and women around the table sat in silent suspense. Molly held her breath, a wave of dizziness enveloping her. She dared not look at Seamus or anyone else for fear of what he would do. And what about her—and the children?

When Seamus realized that Niall was serious, his smugness dissolved to panic. He felt the blood drain from his face and shook his head to clear it. His hand trembled as he drained his cup. He reached for the jug and silently poured another cupful and drained that, too. Then, without a word, he rose and began walking to the barn.

Molly stood and began to follow him to gather their things. "Seamus . . . wait."

Seamus spun around to face her. "Where do ye think ye're goin'?"

"To pack our things," she replied, cautiously touching his shoulder.

He shook off her hand and continued to the barn. "Ye're stayin' here."

Molly stopped, paralyzed with fear. "Ain't ye takin' us with ye?" she whispered.

He looked at her with disgust. "Why would I be doin' that?" He waved his fist toward the table. "These people have ruined ye. I want nothin' more to do with ye!"

"Seamus!" she cried. "What about the children?"

"I don' want them neither," he hollered over his shoulder.

Everyone at the table began to talk at once. "You can't just leave them here!" cried John.

"What kind of a father are you?" demanded Patrick.

Seamus lowered his gaze as if thinking of an answer. When he raised his eyes, the only thing to be seen in them was cold hatred. Then he spied Niall walking across the courtyard with the pouch containing his wages, and his face filled with defiant rage. He yanked the pouch from Niall's hand and strode into the barn. Within minutes he returned astride his horse, bits of hastily tossed clothing sticking out from the folds of his bedroll.

Molly chased after him across the courtyard. "Don' leave me!" she cried, choking on sobs.

Seamus ignored her as he slapped the horse's hind quarter and galloped down the lane and through the gate.

Molly collapsed into the dirt and curled herself into a shuddering ball of despair, sobbing. The others stood mute, surrounded by conflicting feelings of relief, pity, and anger.

Saraid's guttural sigh broke the silence. *Is this ever going to stop?* She slowly walked to where Molly lay, her friend's pain overriding her relief to have Seamus gone. She knelt beside Molly and pulled her gently into her arms, stroking her hair and kissing her wet cheek. "It will be all right," she whispered, though even she didn't believe her own words.

Molly shuddered against her and wept. "What am I goin' to do?"

Saraid was too tired to have answers. She looked up into the darkening sky where stars had begun to twinkle. "I don't know. I think it best if we all get some sleep. We'll decide what to do in the mornin'."

Saraid looked over to where the men stood around the fire muttering and gesticulating their anger. Molly's children, frightened and silent for once, stood a short distance away with their thumbs in their mouths. Her own children and the twins were gathered around the table while Kate and Maureen scraped plates and set the dishes to soak in a tub of water. Liam took his penny whistle from his pocket and began playing a mindless tune. Soon, James began playing his, as well. Molly's children ran to the boys and as they began their wild dancing, their giggles created a lilting melody of their own.

Molly sat up, sniffled into her sleeve and wiped her eyes. She filled her lungs with the clean night air and let out a tremulous breath as she watched her children cavorting around the table. "They're good children, no matter what ye're thinkin'."

"I know," Saraid said. She helped Molly get to her feet and they walked back to the table.

***

Hours later, Saraid lay in bed staring into the darkness. Niall climbed into the bed and drew her into his arms. He laid his face against her hair and whispered. "You all right?"

Saraid shrugged but didn't speak.

Niall whispered against her ear. "I need to tell you something."

Saraid stiffened. *He must have come to a decision about Molly and the children.* "Can't it wait until the mornin'?"

"No, I'm sorry, it can't."

"There's nothin' to be done about Molly tonight."

Niall's arm tightened around her. "It isn't about Molly. It's about Danny."

Saraid sagged against him and her eyes filled. "I don't want to be talkin' about Danny tonight."

He rubbed her back and then drew his fingers over her mouth and whispered in her ear. "*He's alive.*"

She began to let out a shriek as his fingers firmly muffled the sound. She twisted violently to get away from him and jump from the bed, but he held her firmly against him. "I'm sorry! Now be quiet and I'll explain."

"*You bastard!*" she yelled against his fingers. Feelings of betrayal washed over her and she continued to struggle against his hand over her mouth. He finally let her go when she tried to bite him.

"Quiet!" he hissed. "You'll wake the whole bloody house!"

Saraid gave up her struggle and he let her sit up. She stared at him, hurt vivid on her face. "Ye're my husband! How could ye leave me sittin' in all this pain over him, and not tell me before this?"

Niall closed his eyes against the pounding in his head. "Doc said we had to make it look real," he whispered. "He was fairly certain that the Charlies were following him along the road. We snuck Danny into his house and then dug a grave and buried an empty box."

Saraid shook her head, her anger momentarily assuaged by relief that Danny was alive. "He's all right, then?"

Niall shook his head. "Not hardly. He'll be flat on his back for weeks. That's the real reason we took Hank over there. He's going to look after him until he gets his strength back. George is going to stay there at night in case there's trouble. I told them we'd send food over with George. I don't think Hank has any idea of how to cook a meal."

Saraid lay back against the mattress, too troubled now to sleep. It was all too much to think about. Her anger at Niall still simmered within her; her stomach knotted with tension. When he tried to draw her into his arms, she stiffened and rolled away from him. "Don't touch me," she whispered, staring into the darkness with damp eyes.

"Fine," he muttered as he rolled away from her and tried to settle himself. It was a long while before he could surrender his mind to the aching weariness that filled his body. A new kind of loneliness filled him. Never in their years together had he and Saraid ever lashed out at each other like this. He should have told her sooner. *But when?* The entire day had had him reeling. They needed to get the crops in. And now they had no workers. Maybe he should have kept Seamus on for a few more days. The look on Seamus's face when he rode away had filled him with unease. He shook his head and took a deep breath. *Don't think on it now,* he told himself. *Just sleep!*

A long while later, Saraid gave up her anger. Niall had tossed and turned for a long time but finally seemed to have settled down, the rhythmic sound of his snoring soothing her need for comfort.

Moonlight drifted in the open window, casting blue light over the room. It glinted off the gold of her wide wedding band. It was the traditional Claddagh pattern; the heart representing love, the hands for friendship and the crown for loyalty. The symbols were banded by a fine filigreed pattern. The soft gold could be carefully stretched or compressed to fit the finger of the wearer as it passed from father to son, mother to daughter. Saraid had not had a ring of her own, so Niall had had one made for her to match his own when they married.

It reminded her now of how the ups and downs of their life wove together, bound by love and the promises they made to each other, the importance of forgiveness.

Though she couldn't yet reach out her arms to him, she slid her feet across the sheet to his, to bridge the void between them. She heard him sigh, even as he slept. As she, too, finally drifted into sleep, the thin thread of a vision, of lost souls, began to weave its way into her mind.

Other visions came calling in the night. Niall tossed and turned, sweating with the exertion of running, running, and running to get away from the banshee's wails that chased him across the fields. He bolted upright, shuddering with fear, gasping to get a breath into his lungs. He wiped the sweat from his face and took several slow breaths to calm himself before laying back against the damp sheets. He laid there for a long time, just staring into the darkness.

Chapter Fifty-Nine

A deepening cloud cover over the western horizon marred the otherwise clear morning sky with shades of purple and gray, billowing and bleeding together, in a distant wind, creeping north. The men jawed over the panorama while they finished their mugs of tea.

"Looks like rain," said Niall. A headache already starting, he closed his eyes and rubbed his fingers against his temples to relieve the pain. He hadn't slept well. The eerie ranting of the banshee had haunted his slumber and Saraid's silent, cold shoulder had irritated him since waking. Niall blinked hard to clear his head. "I hope it holds off until tonight."

"You all right?" asked Patrick.

"Yeah, just tired."

Jake shrugged and gestured at the blue sky overhead. "I wouldn't worry none. Them clouds is so far off that we may not get it at all. Seems to be moving straight north."

Roark nodded in agreement. "Maybe we should get in the hay that's already down before we cut anymore."

Patrick shook his head. "It's still too wet. Once it's in the loft, any moisture in the ricks' cores will start heating up, and before long, it'll combust."

John nodded. "Then the entire barn will go up."

Niall agreed. "Best we can do is to spread the windrows and hope it dries enough by the end of the day. Haying is slow, tedious work and we can't rush it."

John eyed the field. "We can probably get some of the next field cut today. If it rains, it'll get wet whether we cut it or not. Might as well use whatever time we've got."

The others nodded, picked up their rakes and pitch forks and set out across the field.

Before long, James, Maureen and Saraid joined them. The women had each donned their husband's spare work shirts over their long skirts and put their hard-soled brogues on their feet to protect them from the sharp stubble of the field.

Saraid tore a piece of linen in two and handed one to Maureen. They tied them over their foreheads to absorb their sweat before picking up rakes and joining the men. There was more wind this morning; and it didn't take long before bits of drying hay and dust were floating cloud-like in the air, and some of them began sneezing and rubbing their eyes.

George arrived and set his wagon at the edge of the field. He walked over to Niall and pulled him aside while the others continued to work. "Danny's some better this mornin'."

Niall nodded. "Any fever?"

George shrugged. "He's a little warm, but he's not delirious."

"How's Hank doing?"

George pushed his cap to the back of his head. "He says he's happy to be some place quiet. He's makin' his own noise with that fiddle of his. Truth be told, I think he's actually missin' Molly's ruffians. Keeps talkin' about 'em."

Niall chuckled. "Hard to believe, but to each his own." He looked off to the horizon. The clouds were still moving slowly north but creeping no closer. "How about if you sharpen the scythes while we start raking out some of the windrows? We're hoping it'll be dry enough to gather it in by the end of the day."

George whistled. "That's a pretty big undertakin'! You'll be lucky to get half of it done."

"So, let's get started!"

George got out his whetstone and a pail of water, gathered up the scythes, and set to work.

After a few hours had passed, Molly walked over to the women, her youngest in one arm and a jug of tea in the other. Fiona followed with a sack of brown bread for their break.

Maureen saw them coming and cried out. "It's about bloody time!"

Molly kept her gaze down as she set the jug on the back of the wagon. Without speaking, she turned and quickly walked back to the courtyard. Another confrontation with Saraid was the last thing she wanted.

Maureen tore the bandana from her head. She wiped hay dust from her sweat-streaked face and loose bits of hay from her sleeves, muttering as it ground through the damp fabric and prickled her sweaty arms. She grabbed the jug and held it to her lips and let the cool liquid slide down her scratchy throat. "God, it's hot! I'm headin' for the trough!"

Saraid, weary and out of sorts, muttered after her. "What's the matter, Maureen? A little heat an' hay too much for ye?" She wiped her brow and took a breath. She had to stop thinking about Danny.

Maureen stuck out her tongue as she stripped off the shirt and submerged her head and naked upper body into the trough of cool water. Throwing back her head, she let the water stream down her breasts and over her back. She dunked her arms and furiously rubbed the itchy scratches where slivers of hay had pierced her skin, then submerged her shirt and bandana into the trough and wrung them out. She was still muttering as she buttoned her shirt.

Saraid pulled stray pieces of straw from Maureen's hair. "We'll go for a soak in the river later. I have some balm that will make yer skin feel better."

"Sure a few more days like this, and I won't have any bloody skin left to be worryin' about!"

Saraid nodded in agreement as she pumped more water into the trough. She dunked her face and wiped the excess from her eyes. "I don't know how we're goin' to get it all done if it rains."

Maureen looked out over the field. "Sure all we can do, is all we can do."

The men stood around the wagon slaking their thirst and chewing on the rich dark bread.

Niall looked over the field. Most of the windrows were now raked out and the sun was still shining. "You know, I think we might get it done after all."

"This field, any way," said John as he examined the calluses and blisters budding up on his palms. He knew they would fill up and burst before long and be bleeding before the day was done. He cursed softly. He wasn't used to spending so much time in the fields and he didn't like it much. There was no need of it when they had a bunkhouse full of workmen to do the job. He wasn't looking forward to the physical effort that would be required of him over the next weeks. He would prefer to be sitting in the shade writing in his journal or doing some reading. He sighed. No help for it now.

George set the last freshly sharpened scythe against the wagon. The metal blades glinted cleanly in the sun, ready for use. "There ye be," he said as he put away his tools. "How's the new rake workin' out?"

Niall replied, "It's almost too big for this part of the job, but it'll be great for tossing the rooks into the wagon."

Patrick brushed the crumbs from his hands, took up one of the sharpened tools, and began walking back to the field. The others followed behind him. "How about if we let the women and kids finish raking out this field and we start cutting the next?"

The men agreed and Niall hollered over to Saraid to do just that.

By the end of day, there was still no rain and more than half of the second field was cut.

After a hasty dinner, they went back to the first field. Some of them made windrows and the others, using their rakes, began rolling them into large loose haycocks for the night. If it did rain in the night, the middle of the piles would stay dry. The second field was neatly windrowed and would be spread again in the morning.

Niall looked out over the field with weary satisfaction. Dozens of haycocks dotted the landscape, the once green grasses dry and golden from the sun. "If the weather holds, we can fluff it out once more in the morning."

"Yeah," answered Jake. "By tomorrow night, it'll be in the loft."

Niall caught a small movement out of the corner of his eye in the woods beyond the stone wall at the edge of the field. The hair at the nape of his neck stood on end. Gazing into the twilight, he strained to see beyond the shadowed wall, but there was nothing there. The only sound came from the bats as they flew over the stubble of the field, searching for insects.

"What are you looking at?" asked Patrick.

Niall shrugged. "My eyes are playing tricks. I thought I saw something move in the woods."

Patrick stared across the field for a long moment. "I don't see anything."

Niall shook his head. "Probably nothing."

The men called it a night and each headed for his bed, knowing that another long day lay ahead of them.

***

Seamus ducked down behind the wall and held his breath. He'd almost been caught!

Damn ye, Niall! He hardly dared to breathe as he lay in the dirt and leaves, hoping the men would disperse and not come looking for him. He should have waited longer to come here tonight, but he'd wanted a last glimpse of his wife and his scrawny brats as they headed to the barn. He sneered. *They got no idea what I got planned for 'em.* Soon, he would be *free*! He couldn't afford to make a mistake now and have his plan ruined. After several long moments, he took off his hat and dared to peek over the wall, relieved to see that the men were separating and heading off to their own lodgings. He watched George get into his wagon and head down the road, his poled lantern lighting the way. He wondered where he was going, why he wasn't staying here at the farm. *No matter.*

***

Patrick lay on his back staring into the darkness. Strong as he was, he was sore and exhausted from the day's work. He'd had too much ale at day's end and his head was buzzing. So much turmoil! At least Seamus was gone. The more he thought about all the different problems, the more agitated he became and the more he longed for Annie. He turned onto his stomach and buried his face in the pillow, trying to push thoughts of her away. *Think about something else!* At least Danny was all right and back home where he belonged. He closed his eyes and Annie, with her silly grin, reappeared in his thoughts. His groin ached with longing and he pressed his erection into the sheet, willing it away. He was too tired to relieve himself. *Where are you, pretty girl?* Small as she was, her arms around him had brought him great comfort. He could use a little of that right now. When he'd gone back to Doolin and found her gone, the emptiness that had filled him had been as painful as any wound he'd ever had inflicted on his flesh. *Come back to me Annie!*

***

Molly and the children were bedded down in the loft, the door open to a welcoming breeze. She stared out at the twinkling stars. She could just barely hear the men still murmuring in the courtyard, and, soon, all was quiet. The blanket over the hay made for more comfortable sleeping than the bare wood of the wagon. She shifted to make room for the baby to suckle. With regular food, her breasts were fuller and producing more milk. The little one was now getting enough nourishment and was beginning to gain weight and fuss less. For this, she was grateful. She worried less now that the poor babe would starve. This child was close to six months old, but barely larger than a healthy newborn. She looked at her own thin arm as her bony finger stroked the baby's cheek. She and the children would starve, too, if it weren't for Saraid's pity. Molly didn't try to fool herself into thinking that it was any more than that. She and Maureen just didn't understand that the only difference between them was that they had married well. Not everyone was that lucky. Even Maureen's Roark was having hard times and was somewhat beholden to Niall and his family. He wasn't here on a lark . . . he needed the work, too. They still looked down on her, though. Any mutual respect between them was long gone. Seamus had seen to that.

Where are you, Seamus? She couldn't worry about him now. They just had to survive somehow. She looked at her children, asleep and angelic beside her . . . so young . . . so helpless . . . with no kind of life ahead of them. *Maybe they would be better off dead.* She shuddered at the thought and pushed it from her mind. She sighed and squeezing shut her eyes, knew she would accept Saraid's pity for however long it lasted. She shifted the baby to her other breast and dozed while the ravenous baby sucked hard. *Please God, help us,* she prayed. *I can't spend the rest of my life like this.*

* * *

Seamus was disappointed and angry that the hay was still in the field. How long did it take to make a few haycocks, anyway? He toyed with the idea of getting out his flint and starting a fire in the field. No point in that. He would have to be patient, lay low another day. *They would remember Seamus Flynn!*

His stomach grumbled with hunger. He hadn't eaten anything but berries since the day before and he was starving. Seamus peered through the darkness to the table in the courtyard, envisioning the dishes of food that he'd seen carelessly left out after dinner. He waited better than an hour until he was sure that no one would be wandering about before easing his way across the courtyard. He quickly swatted away the swarming flies, and filled his hat with chunks of bread and a couple of dried out chicken legs. Then he took a cup from the table and tapped the keg, swearing softly to find it empty. *No matter,* he thought. *Tonight I need to keep my wits about me.* Right now, food was more important than drink. He ran back across the field and through the woods to where he had hidden his horse and sank to the ground. Seamus gnawed on a chicken leg, chuckling to himself as he remembered how Fiona had railed at him for killing her beloved 'Biddie'. He jutted the clean bone to the sky. "Here's to ye, Fiona!"

Chapter Sixty

"You can't just go rushing off!" hollered Niall. "I need your help here!"

"Well, that's too bloody bad!" snapped Saraid as she loaded a hamper of food into the wagon. After another restless night, she was determined to see for herself that Danny was all right.

"I told you I was sorry!"

"You still lied to me," she said as she climbed up to the seat. "I'm goin' an' ye'll not be stoppin' me!" Saraid snapped the reins, and the wagon lurched forward before Niall could grasp her arm.

Niall slapped his cap against his thigh and spewed a litany of curses as he stomped around the courtyard. "Damn fool woman!" He yelled after her, his voice floating unheard over the dust of her tracks.

Patrick approached him from the barn. "Where's she off to, as if I need ask?"

Niall glared at his brother. "Stubborn wench is off to see Danny." He ran a hand through his hair as he slowed to angry pacing. He finally stopped moving and his shoulders sagged.

"She'll not be forgiving me any time soon. She just can't get it through her thick head that I couldn't tell her about Danny any sooner."

Patrick patted Niall's shoulder. "Maybe she'll be in better spirits after she sees him."

Niall nodded, then sighed. "She hasn't spoken to me since I told her."

"Leave it be. Let's get to work."

***

Saraid found it difficult to hold on to her foul mood as she rode the short distance to Danny's place. It was less than a mile, the road dappled with shade from the arch of maple and oak branches that lined the way. Goldfinch males, their bright yellow breasts visible as they flitted overhead, chittered their sweet song as they beckoned to their mates. Saraid couldn't help but smile as she breathed in the heady fragrance of honeysuckle that grew wild along the stone walls behind the trees, the rambling flowers dotted with bees. As she approached Danny's, she could see Hank sitting on an upturned log outside the door to the cabin.

Hank set the block of wood and his knife into a basket before rising to greet her.

She jumped down from the wagon and pulled a hamper from under the seat. "What're ye doin' there, Hank?"

Hank's cheeks reddened as he picked up an object from the basket beside him, holding it out to her.

"A bunny?" The small figure was finely worked and clearly a rabbit. She smiled in wonder as she rubbed her finger over the smooth ears. "How clever ye are."

"Yeah, well, I got a bit of smoothin' out to do yet. I got a lot of time on me hands so I's keepin' busy. Thought I'd make some toys for Molly's little ones."

"That's very kind of—oh! Danny!"

Danny, having heard her voice, stood grinning in the doorway, his arm in a sling. "How's my favorite lady?"

Saraid moved into his one-armed embrace and hugged him gently. She pulled away after a moment and stared into his eyes as she put her hand to his forehead. "I'm better for knowin' that ye weren't really layin' dead in that coffin! I had to come see for m'self that ye're alive. How are ye, Danny?"

"Better every day. Gonna take more'n a piece of shot to kill me."

Saraid gestured to the hamper. "I brought ye some apple cake and chicken."

"Sound better'n anythin' in the world. Let's go sit under the tree."

"Should ye be outside?" she asked as they walked.

Danny shrugged. "Ain't seen anyone around. I think it's safe. Truth is, I miss bein' outdoors."

Saraid brushed off the small table and sat on the weathered bench. She broke apart the cake and gave him a chunk, then unwrapped the cloth that held the cold chicken and offered it to him.

"How're ye makin' out with Hank?"

Danny looked over to Hank who was humming softly as he shaved curling pieces of wood from the block. "He's no trouble and truth be known, he's a help. It's hard to just sit around here all day with nothin' to do and no one to talk to." He swallowed a bite of cake and licked his fingers before grabbing a piece of chicken. "I hear Seamus is gone."

Saraid snorted. "That one! A sorrier piece of mankind was never born!"

"What about Molly?"

Saraid shook her head. "Don't know what we're to do about her."

At the sound of Molly's name, Hank limped over to the table with the bunny in his hand. "Hard not to hear ye say Seamus was gone. Is Molly all right, then?"

"She's strugglin' with it. Part of her is glad and part, not so much." Saraid sighed. "I don't rightly know what's goin' to happen to her. Niall doesn't want her stayin' with us."

Hank hesitated and then held out the bunny to her. "Would ye take this to her? Tell her I said it's for luck."

Saraid smiled as she took the bunny and gently placed it in her pocket. "That's right nice of ye, Hank. I'm sure it'll bring a smile to her."

Hank flushed and gestured to the cake.

Saraid nodded and told him to help himself. She suddenly had an idea. "Hank, how 'bout ye ride back with me and ye can give it to her yerself?"

Hank closed his eyes and pictured Molly in his mind. If the O'Briens were to put her out, this might be his last chance to see her and it filled him with sadness. In another lifetime he would swoop in and whisk her and the children away. He'd make a home for them and they would live a life full of happiness. He would play his fiddle for the children and laugh as he watched them dance about and clap their hands. He'd teach them manners. His eyes smarted and he shook his head, knowing he had nothing to offer Molly. No home, no work, no idyllic life. "No," he said slowly. "I'd rather ye give it to her." He turned and limped back to his seat by the door, picked up the block of wood and began, once more, to whittle.

Danny stared after him and then looked at Saraid. "What was that all about?"

Saraid whispered. "I think he has feelin's for Molly. It's so sad."

"What's so sad about it? Seems to me, he'd be just the one to solve her problems."

Saraid laughed. "How could he be takin' them on? He's got nowhere to take them!"

Danny stared at Hank and then let his eyes wander over his land. "I got plenty of room here."

"Are ye mad?" Saraid was astonished to hear Danny offer such a thing.

Danny looked into her eyes for a long moment before he spoke. "Once I'm well, it may not be safe for me to stay here."

Saraid's heart filled with panic. She couldn't accept the thought of him leaving and not being a part of their lives. Surely, there was some way to make him stay!

"Where would ye go?" she asked.

Danny looked over to the field where his crops stood ready to be cut and felt helpless to do anything about it. "I'm not sure, maybe France. I got an uncle in the Irish Brigade. He's there fightin' for the king–Louis XV–against the British. Or, maybe I'll go to America and join up with the revolution."

"Ye're determined to get yerself killed, then?"

Danny shrugged. "It might be safer than stayin' here an' havin' to live my life lookin' over my shoulder."

Saraid turned her face away from him. It was too much! "I have to get back. We gotta finish gettin' the hay in." She stood and after giving him a brief hug, walked quickly over to her wagon, tossing the empty hamper under the seat. "They're hopin" to get over here by week's end to cut yers."

Danny bowed his head. "George told me that all yer help took off 'cause of me."

"Don't you be blamin' yerself for it!"

He shrugged. "If mine don't get cut, it don't. Cows can eat from the field if they's hungry enough."

Chapter Sixty-One

It was mid-afternoon when Saraid arrived back home. The rich smell of beef roasting on the spit in the courtyard hinted of celebration. *They must be planning to finish the hay tonight.*

The brilliant sun and mid-day heat had quickly finished drying the hay that had been fluffed out in the morning, and the men had begun to roll the windrows into haycocks.

Maureen sat at the long table twining strands of hay into twine with James and Fiona. She shot Saraid an angry look. "An' where've ye been, miss high and mighty?"

Saraid winced. She had no idea if she knew about Danny yet. "No need to be so angry with me!" she huffed. "There was somethin' I had to do."

"Look at my hands!" Maureen said with disgust. "Thanks to ye, they're all cut and bloody. An' every time I get a length done it starts shreddin'!"

"Well, it would shred less if ye wet it first!" Saraid snapped at her.

"And how was I to know *that* since ye weren't here to tell me?" Maureen snapped back.

Saraid sighed, sorry to have made the job harder for her sister. She'd forgotten that she and Roark didn't grow hay; they grew an abundance of potatoes and wheat. In a few weeks, they'd all be traveling to their farm to help them with their own harvest. "Let me show ye," Saraid said with more patience than she felt. She gathered up an arm full of the hay and walked to the trough, Maureen following behind her. She pushed the long strands under the water and kept tamping them down until they grew heavy and remained submerged. She gathered them up again and brought the sodden mass back to the table, soaking her long skirt and smock.

Maureen plunged her hands into the pail of water beside her to soothe her blisters and continued to mutter under her breath. "Ye should'a been here to help us."

"Well, I'm here now." Saraid grabbed up several pieces of the wet hay. "Just keep it wet and it'll hold together better and not break." She began rapidly braiding and twisting the strands and soon had a long length of hay twine ready for use.

Maureen paid rapt attention as Saraid's nimble fingers made short work of the task. "Sure ye make it look so easy."

"Ye forget, I've had years of practice."

Fiona grumbled. "I don't want to do this anymore!"

Saraid gave her a sharp look. "Ye know this is a busy time for everyone. We all have to do our part."

"Can't we go back to the field now?" asked James. "I'd rather be with the men."

"Me too!" cried Fiona. "We could start stomping the haycocks!"

Saraid looked off to the field where more and more large mounds of rolled hay sat ready for the next part of the task. She shrugged. "Go ask your da if he's ready for that."

The children ran to the field, eager to do the fun part of the haying. Saraid and Maureen began to chuckle as the children climbed the haycocks, yelping and laughing. They jumped and rolled and slid down the sides, compressing the piles into tight mounds. At the end of the day, the mounds would be bound with the hay twine before being loaded onto the wagon and hauled to the barn.

"Where're ye goin', now?" asked Maureen as Saraid headed to the house.

"Be right back," Saraid called out.

A moment later, Saraid returned with a jug of mead. "Seems to me, we could use somethin' to get us through this bloody task!"

Maureen clapped her hands. "I'll be drinkin' to that!" She held the jug to her mouth and took several swallows of the sweet, spicy brew. "Delicious! What's in it? I taste cloves an'–what else?"

"A bit of chamomile and clover. Ye'd best slow down with that. It's pretty powerful."

Maureen reluctantly gave the jug back to Saraid and smothered a belch with her fist. "So, I take it ye went to Danny's?"

Saraid nodded. "I didn't know if Roark had told ye yet. That's why I didn't say anythin' before I left."

"Ye could'a told me yerself. I would 'a gone with ye."

There was mild accusation in her voice, but before Saraid could reply, Molly approached them, baby on her hip.

"Can I sit with ye?" She asked shyly, wary of being rebuffed. She was tired of being surrounded by rambunctious children and craved the company of the women.

Saraid took another swallow and set the jug down. She stared at Molly in silence for a moment, then shrugged and, making room for her on the bench, pushed the jug towards her. "Have some."

Molly set the sleeping baby on a shaded patch of grass and sat down. Her relief was palpable as she picked up the jug and sipped at the drink. "That's really good," she said, wiping her mouth with the back of her hand.

Saraid reached into her pocket, pulled out the bunny, and held it out to her.

Molly's eyes opened wide with delight. "Where ever did ye find this?"

"Hank made it for ye. To wish you luck," said Saraid, watching a glow come to Molly's face.

Molly didn't know whether to laugh or cry as she ran her fingers over the miniature. "This is so lovely! And Hank made this? For *me*?" she asked in wonder.

"Yes, he did. Looks like the man has hidden talent."

Maureen asked to see the bunny. She examined the workmanship and shook her head. "He's beyond clever. I've seen worse than this sell for a good price at the fairs."

Saraid nodded and smiled to herself. Hank might be able to make a living after all.

Molly took back the bunny and cupped it to her heart. She missed the little man's kindness to her and her children. It touched her deeply that he would think of her and wished she could thank him in person. "I don't know what to say," she whispered, taking another sip of the mead. As she tucked the bunny into her own pocket, she knew that she would cherish it forever.

***

John hadn't seen his mother at the mid-day meal. The only explanation he'd been given was that she was resting. He decided to check on her after he dressed his hands. His blisters were broken and painful, and he sought to bind them with salve and bandages before heading back to the fields. His hands taken care of, he climbed the stairs. He watched his mother as she lay on her bed with her face towards the window. "Are you awake, Mother?"

Kate turned to him and smiled weakly. "I am."

"Are you not well?" he asked, his brow furrowed with concern.

Kate turned back to the window "I'm all right . . . jusss very tired today." More than tired, she thought. Her legs were weak and she'd had to use a cane for balance when she'd climbed the stairs to her room. Her stomach was queasy. She'd been unable to eat much at breakfast and barely touched the meal Fiona had brought to her at mid-day. She suddenly felt chilled and pulled the coverlet more tightly around herself.

John couldn't help but notice her pallor. "Can I get you some tea?"

She nodded. "Mmmay . . . be some . . . pep . . . min' to se'le my stomach."

***

George was using the long-tined rake to spear the haycocks and toss them into the wagon, one on top of the other. They'd been at it for hours. Once the hay had been tamped down, they'd rolled it over the hay twine and bound it over the top. Then they tightly wrapped more twine around the middle and rolled it to the wagon. The loose bits of hay were raked into small piles that would be gathered up later. In between loads, they took to eating dark bread and apples dipped in salt to replenish the copious fluids that were sweating from their bodies in the high heat of the day. Several loads had already been hauled and stacked in the loft, two rows to each side with a narrow path to walk between them. The walkways would keep air flowing in the barn, allowing any heat to escape. This last load would make the stacks three high on either side.

Near twilight, the men decided that their bodies could do no more and the rest would be left until morning. They were hot, tired and sweat-soaked, not used to having so much work done by so few hands. No amount of tea or salt had slaked their thirst. When they were finally done, they raced each other to the river and dove into the cold wet of the Shannon like eager children.

Niall gave George's shoulder a shake. "Go get Danny and Hank and we'll celebrate!"

"Good idea," Patrick agreed. "Tell Hank to bring his fiddle. We'll get out a keg of poteen, too!" The home brew was far stronger than ale and they all felt they'd earned it.

While devouring chunks of rare roast beef, sucking the juices from the charred fat, they quickly emptied platters of boiled potatoes and roasted ears of corn, both dripping with butter and salt. Finally sated, they sat around the campfire with their cups brimming with poteen and mead. Tin whistles and harps played as they sang ribald limericks, told tales, laughed, and drank toasts to the harvest. The children all danced around the fire and ran about the courtyard with no one trying to quiet them. Hank brought out his fiddle and played lively jigs that they all danced to, until they began tripping over their own feet, laughing, and rolling in the grass.

Molly walked over to Hank and sat beside him on the grass. She pulled the bunny from her pocket and held it up for him to see. "This is so lovely," she said softly, smiling up at him. "I don' know how to thank ye for bein' so kind."

Hank was grateful that his blush would not be seen in the firelight. His chest constricted as he looked into her shimmering eyes. "Nothin' so special 'bout it," he whispered hoarsely.

"Don't belittle yerself, Hank," she admonished him gently. "No one has ever given me such a beautiful thing."

Hank didn't know what to say and even if he could find the words, he didn't trust himself to speak. He bowed his head and remained silent.

"Well," she said as she got to her feet, "I'd best be gettin' my brood off to bed." She hesitated and then wrapped her arms around his shoulders and brushed her lips against his cheek. "Thank ye, Hank."

As she walked away, Hank squeezed shut his eyes and let the tears run unbidden down his face. He should run after her, take her into his arms and tell her of the love he felt. But he couldn't do it. He threw his fiddle on the ground, buried his face in his hands, and wept.

***

Seamus watched the exchange between Molly and Hank from

his hiding place behind the stone wall. He could just make out the look on Molly's face in the firelight. She'd actually kissed the bastard!

"*Ye filthy whore!*" he muttered. "*How dare ye get wrapped up with that cripple.*" She was still his wife and had no right to be flauntin' herself at another man! He was shaking with rage as he watched her gather up his children and head for the barn, where he knew they would sleep at the far end of the loft. *His children, God damn it!* It took everything in him not to run down there and beat Hank to a pulp. But if he did, it would ruin all his careful plans. *God damn the bloody lot of them!*

Chapter Sixty-Two

CRACK! The lightning zigzagged down through the night sky, illuminating the entire farm in eerie white light. Thunder bellowed and the ground shuddered.

"Goin' to wake the bloody dead!" Seamus grumbled as he pulled his hat down to keep it on his head in the rising wind. Lightning continued to strike and sizzle around him, making his pulse race.

"God damned storm! How am I s'pposed to get this bloody hay lit in this feckin' wind?" He continued to curse, worrying that the storm would wake the O'Briens before he accomplished his task. He fumbled with his flint. No sooner would he get a spark then the wind would scatter the loose hay and blow it out.

A bolt of lightning streaked down not twenty feet from him. He yelped in shock, cowering on the ground with his hands over his head. When he finally dared to look up, he began to laugh.

"Well, if that don't beat all!"

The lightning had struck near one of the piles of compacted hay that had been left in the field and it was ablaze in the wind. Sparks and bits of hay went sailing over the field, threatening to ignite everything but were extinguished before they hit the ground.

How can I pick it up an' not get burned? Suddenly he had an idea. Praying that he wouldn't be seen, he ran to the tool shed and grabbed the new hay rake with the thin metal tines. He ran back to the smoking pile that was fast going to ash. He tossed more hay onto the embers to keep the flame alive.

Seamus stole a glance toward the house and cabins to make sure that no one was watching him. He needed only a few more minutes, then it wouldn't matter if they saw him, the damage would be done. They would never be able to stop the fire once it took hold. The entire barn would burn down with Molly and his brats trapped in the fire. He scooped up the burning pile and ran toward the barn, the flames beginning to fizzle as he ran.

"Don't you dare go out!" he hissed. He ran up the ramp to the loft and hurried past several bales to be away from the wind. He carefully set down the smoldering pile, got to his knees, and gently blew towards the dry bale. Sparks flew and within seconds, the bale flashed into hot full flame. He quickly stood up and backed away from the heat, laughing manically.

***

Smoke began wafting through the floor boards to the barn. The cows began mooing and shifting their hind quarters against each other while the horses in the stable began nickering and neighing nervously in their stalls.

Danny woke and blinked in the darkness, confused by his surroundings. In the light of the next lightning strike, he spied George and Hank nearby, and it sunk in where he was. With the next crack of thunder, Hank cowered into the hay and hid his head under a blanket while George sat straight up.

The horses didn't want to settle down. Danny rose and half staggered from stall to stall, stroking their necks and speaking calmly to quiet them.

"This is one bloody storm," said George groggily as he rose to help Danny calm the horses.

Danny yawned. "Yeah, an' not much we can do about it. Don't think we'll be gettin' back to sleep tonight."

They gave up trying to calm the horses, retreated to their bedrolls and listened to the storm as it raged around them.

* * *

Niall jolted awake with a gasp when the thunder boomed directly overhead. Bridget and Liam both started crying and Saraid climbed out of bed to comfort them.

Moments later, Niall caught a faint scent of smoke drifting in through the open window. He stumbled across the room to where the length of curtain was billowing. His mind was fogged from the whiskey he had drunk after dinner; and as he peered out, he could make no sense of the ball of flame that was traveling across the field towards the barn. Then he caught sight of movement behind the flames and was instantly sobered as a chill ran through him. He screamed, "*No!*"

"*Fire!*" he yelled into the night. The wind blew his voice back to him and he didn't know if it would be heard over the storm. He pulled on his britches as he ran down the hall to the boys' room. "*James!*" he screamed. "*FIRE!* Go ring the bell! *NOW!* FIRE!"

James jumped from his bed and ran down the stairs in his nightshirt. He followed Niall outside and ran to the bell that hung in the courtyard as his father ran to the barn. He began shaking the cord and the bell clanged over and over, all the while he screamed, "Fire, fire, fire!"

* * *

Molly and the children began coughing as the smoke billowed towards them. She realized that they were trapped and cried out for help. Their only escape was to jump from the loft. It was at least ten feet to the ground and Molly was terrified. She huddled with her children at the end of the loft and continued to scream.

***

Saraid stood in the open doorway, frozen, not knowing what to do. All their hard work was going up in flames. With the thunder and the clanging bell, she almost didn't hear the piercing screams for help. Then she realized who was screaming. "*Molly!*" She prayed that Niall would get to her in time.

***

Patrick, John, the men in the bunkhouse, and Roark and Maureen in their caravan had awakened in the storm, too, drifting in and out of a hangover daze. They were all slow to realize what was happening, and it took the men a few minutes to react and run to the barn.

With another crack of lightning and an immediate boom of thunder, the sky opened up and sent icy pellets of hail bouncing over the ground. The wind blew the flames and smoke further down the walkway of the loft, igniting everything in its path. Embers flew up to the thatched roof and it, too, began to smolder and flash to flame. The stone walls of the barn acted like an oven, holding in the heat of the fire. Seamus grinned like the madman he was and slowly backed out of the door.

Niall reached the barn door, cursing at Seamus, who was mesmerized by the flames. Niall's shouts alerted him, and Seamus spun around with the hay rake in his hands. Before Niall could raise his fist to strike him, Seamus jutted the hay rake at Niall's bare chest, just nicking his skin, to keep him at bay.

Niall stumbled backwards, landing hard against the barn door. "I'm going to *kill* you!"

"Not if I kill you first!" Years of rage and hate surged through him. Before Niall could regain his balance, Seamus lunged forward, stabbing Niall straight through his torso with the rake, the tines impaling him against the door. Three of the tines had pierced his midsection and one had gone through his arm. Seamus went still, not quite believing what he had just done.

Niall, stunned, looked down at the rivulets of blood that were trickling down his body. He didn't feel any pain yet, but he knew he was going to die. The tines had missed his heart but he felt the air begin to seep from his lungs and the damage to his intestines would be too great to survive. He raised his eyes in shocked resignation and faced Seamus, whispering, "Why?"

Seamus let go of the end of the rake. The handle bobbed up and down, tearing at Niall's gut, but held fast to the door. Seamus began to laugh. "Why? Because I'm sick t'death of people like you thinkin' ye're better'n me! Ye're *nothin!*"

Seamus heard angry voices coming through the darkness and ran from the barn. He wasn't sure he would make it across the field but it didn't matter. Even if they caught him, he had won! The barn would soon be destroyed, Niall would be dead, and so would Molly and his brats. One way or the other, he would be free of the lot of them.

Chapter Sixty-Three

As he ran from his cabin, Patrick spied George running through the smoke to the cows, and Danny shooing the horses from the stable. He yelled to Roark to help them free the animals. He caught sight of someone running from the barn but the image soon disappeared into the darkness.

John and Patrick came around the end of the burning structure at the same time and gasped when they saw Niall, his head bowed. He was bathed in sweat and fighting to stay conscious. Blood was running down his body and soaking his britches.

In the few minutes it had taken them and the others to get to the barn, it was too late to save Niall or put out the fire. The thatched roof was now fully engulfed in flames and would soon fall into the barn. The floorboards under the bales and the old wooden braces holding up the thatched roof were beginning to glow like hot coals.

"Who did this?" screamed Patrick.

Niall rasped, "Seamus."

"Where is he?" screamed John.

Niall shook his head, unable to answer.

John reached for the hay rake to pull it free, but Niall, grabbed onto him.

"Don't—not yet," he whispered. "I'll bleed . . . faster . . . if you take . . . it out . . . now."

Niall panted in shallow breaths. "Patrick, get . . . bandages. I don't . . . want Saraid . . . ." He stopped, grimaced from the sudden pain and cried out in a sob. "To see me . . . like this."

James had been standing there watching the scene unfold, too numb to react; but now, he ripped off his nightshirt. "Here," he cried. "Use this!" He stood naked and afraid as John and Patrick tore the nightshirt into wide strips and tied the ends together to make one long bandage.

The yelling from the men struck Saraid with dread. "Niall!" she cried. No longer paralyzed in place, she began running across the courtyard. The hail had turned to hard rain, transforming the courtyard into a river of mud. Fiona chased on her heels. Saraid grabbed Fiona's arms to stop her and sent her back to the house. "Stay with Gran and the children!"

Kate had struggled down the stairs and stood next to Fiona, who was trembling as she clung to the younger, wailing children. They stared through the rain and thick smoke, unable to see the horrific scene.

"Gran!" cried Fiona. "I'm so scared! What is happening?"

Kate's mind could make no sense of it. When Fiona pulled the younger children away from the door, Kate went out and began staggering, barefoot, across the muddy courtyard.

Saraid screamed. "*No, no, no!*" as Patrick grabbed her and held her back.

"We have to get him away from the flames before he burns to death!" cried John. He pulled the long tines from Niall's body and blood began spurting like a fountain from the wounds in his mid-section and back as he collapsed to the ground. John and Patrick dragged Niall away from the heat and flames as rain began pouring down through the gutted roof and the barn began to sizzle.

Patrick knelt in the mud and bound Niall's wounds as tightly as he could. In seconds they were stained red. Patrick helped him to sit up so he could speak.

"James . . . ," Niall whispered.

James knelt beside him, trying hard not to cry, and grasped his father's hand.

Niall forced his eyes open "The land . . ."

James wailed. "I don't care about the bloody land! I want you to live!"

"Take my ring . . . keep it . . . someday . . . for your wife . . . ."

James tearfully began to pull his father's wedding ring from his hand.

"*Nooo!*" Saraid wailed and pushed James aside. She threw herself over Niall's body and sobbed.

Niall struggled to reach out for her with his good hand and let it rest in her hair. He coughed weakly as a thin stream of blood oozed from his mouth. He whispered in her ear. *"Tá mo chroí . . . istigh ionat.* My heart . . . is within you."

Saraid pulled away from him and looked into his weeping eyes as her own tears washed over him. "Ye can't die! Ye can't be leavin' me like this!"

"Do . . . someth . . . f'me," Niall's voice slurred.

"*Anythin'*, my love!"

"Dance . . . for me . . ."

"*Dance?* Ye're dyin' an' ye want me to bloody *dance?* Are ye mad?"

"Please . . ." he pleaded, his eyes filled with grief. "It's how . . . I want . . . to 'member . . . you."

***

Molly's screams got louder. George and Danny, thinking that lightning had started the fire, were unaware of what was happening to Niall at the other end of the barn. Roark had just finished getting the last of the cows into the pasture when he heard Hank yelling for Molly to jump. The three men ran to Hank to help get Molly and the screaming children out of the loft.

Now Hank was screaming. "Ye have to jump, Molly!" Smoke was

pouring out behind her and there wasn't much time left before the flames reached them.

Molly was hysterical, clinging to the baby in her arms. "I can't," she cried.

"Yes ye can, Molly!" cried Roark.

"Make the children jump!" cried Hank. "I'll catch them!" He tossed his cane aside and held out his arms.

"So will I," yelled George. "*Jump!*" He held out his arms as Molly, weeping with fear, pushed the oldest child from the loft. George snagged the child in mid-air and set her on the ground.

Danny stood by, afraid and feeling helpless in his sling, doing the only thing he could; yelling for them to jump as the flames began licking at Molly's skirts.

"Now you, little one! Come on!" cried Hank to the younger child. "Hurry! *Hurry*, now!"

She tried to hang on to her mother's skirt, but Molly, desperate now, shoved at her until she tumbled from the loft, screaming. Hank made an awkward catch and fell to the ground but the child was unhurt.

"Molly!" screamed Hank as he struggled to his feet. "Ye're on *fire*! I don't want ye to die! I *love* ye! For God's sake *jump*!"

Molly looked down into his eyes and her heart ached. She held her baby boy tightly to her chest, took a breath and let herself fall forward out of the loft. All she could think was, if she died, her babe would be next to her heart. The hem of her skirt was aflame, and Hank felt the hair on his arms singe as he caught her. He fell backward to the ground with her weight on top of him, the babe between them. He landed hard, hitting his head on a stone, and laid there unconscious.

George pulled Molly off of Hank and rolled her over and over on the sodden ground to smother the flames that were burning her legs. Roark, with tears in his eyes, picked up the lifeless, crushed remains of the baby from Hank's chest and cradled him in his arms.

Once they were all safely away from the fire, Molly pushed her singed hair from her eyes and held the lifeless baby close. She doubled over as a searing pain knifed through her womb and she felt life's blood seeping down her thighs. Overcome with despair, she gently set the baby on the wet grass and lay beside it. Then she heard Hank moan and crawled to him. Weeping, she lay beside him in the mud, cradling him in her arms as her frightened children clung crying to her charred and bloody skirt.

***

Roark, Danny and George heard the screams at the other end of the barn and ran. As they rounded the corner, what they saw sickened them. Everyone was circled around Niall as he lay dying in Patrick's arms, blood running from his bandages in the rain. They stared in disbelief to see Saraid dancing slowly in front of him with her arms over her head.

Paddy, tears streaming, was there with his rosary, making the sign of the cross over Niall's forehead, lips and heart, mumbling the prayers of last rites.

"Who did this?" asked Danny softly. He clutched his stomach as it threatened to spew its contents in the mud.

"Seamus," they all answered.

"I'll go after him," Roark said as he ran for his horse.

Danny went to stand by James. "So, why in bloody hell is she *dancin'*?" he asked, anger spilling from him.

James stared straight ahead, tears streaming down his face, his voice barely heard. "My da asked her to dance."

Danny felt his throat closing up, couldn't speak. He put his arm around James's shoulders and held him close, his own tears running down his face. His dear cousin and friend, who had been a brother to him, was dying and he couldn't do a bloody thing to save him.

Saraid's arms and hips swayed to a melody that only she could hear. The years of their life together floated before her weeping eyes: the day, all those years ago when she had met Niall in Doolin; the music, the dancing, their laughter. Their intense passion had brought them love and children; the quiet smiles and tenderness that had blessed them both. How she wished she had reached for him earlier in the night, instead of holding on to her anger. To give him her love one more time. Now it was too late. All of it gone.

Niall wept as he watched her dance, overcome with fierce love and sorrow. He looked up at her with glistening eyes, tried to smile but his lips wouldn't move. As his eyes glazed, her body transformed into the young girl he had fallen in love with. Her swaying pendulous breasts lifted and firmed, her broad hips narrowed, her waist lost the thickening that had come with four children. His longing for her was more painful than the catastrophic injuries to his body.

Niall heard the sound of a fiddle playing sweetly nearby. He stared at the wispy image that appeared in the distance. As it came closer, he could see a beautiful young girl with long yellow hair, beckoning to him with her bow.

Niall whispered, "*No.*"

The Banshee, shrieking, transformed into an old crone in rags with stringy gray hair. She taunted him with her wails, until he could stand no more, and closed his eyes for the last time.

***

Kate stood alone in the driving rain, her clothes drenched and clinging to her body, her bare feet awash in mud, unable to comprehend the chaos around her. She watched as the barn burned, fascinated by the billowing smoke and the flames that shot through the roof into the night sky. She listened as Molly screamed, and the horses shrieked, and everyone was running and yelling. She absently pushed the wet hair from her face and stared dully at her son as blood poured from his body and the others gathered around him. She began to babble on and on and on. Then a crooked smile crept across her mouth as she watched Saraid dance. She began to hum and bob her head, slowly clapping her hands and lifting one muddy foot and then the other, in time to Saraid's steps.

Chapter Sixty-Four

John rose early and walked through the damp air to the still, silent house. He stood in the doorway of the sitting room and nodded to the black-clad women who sat in chairs beside the casket, rosary beads in hand. They had kept candlelight vigil over Niall's body for the last five nights. He gave them their leave and one by one they rose, the flickering candles splaying their grim shadows about the room. Weary, they passed through the door, each of them placing a gentle hand on his arm with murmurs of sympathy.

Alone, he took in the room that had been transformed into the mourning room for the wake. Someday, when the pain of it wasn't so great, he would write about it. For now, he forced himself to commit it all to memory. He gazed at the open windows where bunches of rosemary and thyme hung from black ribbon, in hopes that the drifting fragrance would diminish the stench of death. Pots of flowers adorned the mantle, hearth and tabletops for this purpose as well. Beneath the casket, hot water from the kettle had been poured over bowls filled with rose petals, the infused aroma rising to greet the many mourners who had converged on their home to honor Niall. As news of Niall's death spread, hundreds had come from all over Ireland, many camping in the fields to await tonight's burial.

He walked around the room extinguishing the candles that had burned down to the end of their wicks, absently flicking his fingernail against the spatters of wax on the tabletops.

At last, he stood before the carved oak casket, gazing at his brother for the last time. Niall lay against the pure white wool lining, his face still showing traces of the pain he had suffered at the end of his life. Laying his fingers on Niall's forehead, he smoothed away stray hairs that had fallen over his face.

He thought about Saraid and her now fatherless children. He thought about his poor mother, lying sick and incoherent in her bed, unable to process what had happened. Then his thoughts turned to Seamus, the cause of all their pain, and his grief became overshadowed with rage. He shoved at the chair in the corner and was met with a sudden sharp cry. He pulled the chair aside to find Saraid cowering there on the floor. He grabbed her by the arms and yanked her to her feet. "Saraid!"

She struggled to free herself from his grip but he refused to let go and began shaking her. "You need to *stop this*! Pull yourself together! Your husband will be buried later today and you need to show some respect for who he was!"

She stopped fighting him and began to weep silently. "I can't," she whimpered.

He shook her again. "You need to stand for his children. They have no one without you!" Pity mixed with his anger and he reluctantly let her go.

She spun away from him and ran to her room. She huddled in the corner, staring at the bed. The thought of laying there alone, never to feel Niall's warmth beside her was more than she could bear. She hugged her knees and lay her head upon them, and began to rock.

* * *

Doctor O'Hickey softly closed the door to Kate's room and left the house. He crossed the courtyard to join the family at the long table laid with breakfast. Martha's gentle voice floated over everyone as she poured tea from a fine china pot. " . . . mustn't give up hope."

O'Hickey took in all the faces that turned to him as he approached. So much emotion! Anger, disbelief, fear, sorrow, confusion. And now, he would bring them more bad news.

John jumped up from his seat. "How is she? Will she be all right?"

The doctor sighed and shook his head before sitting down beside Martha and accepting the proffered cup of tea. He sipped it thoughtfully before answering.

"She's had a terrible shock. The time she spent in the rain didn't do her any good either. Her lungs are quite congested. I think she has pneumonia. Her mind . . . " He stopped to compose himself.

John covered his face with his hands, trying not to weep.

Patrick swallowed hard. "She had these strange spells when we were in Doolin, but you thought she would be all right."

O'Hickey nodded. "Yes, but this is something else entirely. You need to prepare yourselves. I don't believe she has the strength to survive this. Even if she miraculously recovered from the pneumonia, her mind has left her."

As if to confirm this, they heard Kate wailing from her open window. John ran across the courtyard and into the house.

The doctor walked over to Saraid, who sat on the ground, hollow-eyed in her grief, with Maureen, who held her hand. He took her other hand and squeezed it gently. "I am so sorry about Niall. He was one of the few truly good men I have ever known."

Saraid rose, stared blankly at the doctor and left them. They watched as she walked with unsteady steps towards the river, a jug in her hand.

"How much is she drinking?" asked the doctor.

Patrick sighed. "Enough. Since Niall died, she's taken to disappearing—usually with a jug of mead. We've had to search for her more than once."

Maureen sighed and rose from the ground, brushing bits of straw from her skirt. "I'll go with her this time," she said.

"And the children?"

Patrick bowed his head, anger and helplessness filling him. "Saraid keeps pushing them away . . . wants nothing to do with any of them." He waved his hand in the air. "Fiona has had to help mind the younger ones—and she's none too happy about it. Maureen is doing the best she can to watch over all of us, but she has her own family to care for."

Martha shook her head sadly. "How is Fiona dealing with her father's death?"

Patrick shook his head. "She's more angry than anything else. She keeps threatening to find Seamus and kill him."

"Is there any news of where Seamus might be?"

Patrick ran his fingers through his hair. "No, not yet. Roark went out searching for him that night but with the dark and the storm, there were no tracks to follow. This morning we found the place in the woods where he must have been hiding out, but no trace of him but for some chicken bones. The people in the village are spreading the word, but there's no telling if we'll ever find him. For now, he's in the wind."

The doctor sipped at his tea. "What will you do about the farm?"

"We've had to sell off all but two of the cows. There wouldn't have been anywhere to keep them or enough hay to feed them over the winter. The two we kept will share the stable with the horses until the barn can be rebuilt."

"Is there anything salvageable of the barn?" O'Hickey asked.

"The stone walls need repair. The heat from the fire cracked and crumbled a lot of the mud holding it together. Some of it collapsed. All the wood is lost or too weak to trust. That will all have to be removed before we can rebuild the loft and the roof."

"That's a big undertaking. Will you have any help?"

Patrick nodded. "You know how it's done. The villagers will all come for a barn raising. We'll feed them and keep the ale flowing, and it will be done in a few days."

The doctor refilled his cup. "So now the farm goes to James?"

Patrick nodded. "And to Liam. The way things are now, they will have to share Niall's third of the property that was divided when my father died."

"Will you and John stay, then? James isn't old enough to take it over."

"I will." said Patrick. "I don't have anywhere else to go. Neither do Paddy and Mickey. John will have to speak for himself. I know that farming has never suited him."

"What of Seamus's wife?" asked Martha. "I hear she lost a child."

Patrick began to tremble. He thought of Seamus and the destruction he had wrought. So much hatred . . . and for what? "She lost two actually." He swallowed against the lump in his throat. "The baby she was holding was crushed when she landed on Hank." He shook his head remembering the blood and gore of the other. "She was carrying another but the fall . . . " His eyes teared up. "This perfectly formed little baby . . . no bigger than an apple . . . and no chance at all. Molly wrapped it in linen and we buried it with the baby."

"Where is she now?" the doctor asked quietly.

"Danny took her and the other children to his place. Saraid couldn't bear to have her here. Molly's legs were burned some. We sent over salve and bandages. Hank is taking care of her."

Martha began to weep softly. "What will become of them?"

"No telling," said Patrick. "Hank says he's not going to leave her as long as Seamus is still out there . . . but we'll see. I guess it's up to Danny how long he'll let them stay."

***

Maureen picked her way across the field, trying to avoid the sharp stubble of cut corn stalks against her bare feet. When she reached the river bank, she muttered under her breath. The love she felt for her sister was overshadowed by the disgust she felt in her gut. Saraid stood on the small pier swaying, the jug dangling from her hand. She couldn't believe this drunk, soiled, incoherent mess was the same woman she had always looked up to. Her disgust turned to alarm as Saraid set down the jug and stepped perilously close to the edge of the pier, her intent obvious.

"Saraid!" Maureen threw herself forward and grabbed Saraid around the waist just as she was falling into the river. The shock of the cold water had them both flailing, Saraid fighting to get free, and Maureen fighting to hang on.

"Let me *GO!*" Saraid screamed.

"NO!"

Saraid swung her fist, aiming for her sister's jaw but missed. Maureen changed tactics and let go of her slick arms and, instead, grabbed her by the end of her long braid. She kicked her sturdy legs toward the river bank, pulling Saraid backward through the water. Saraid went limp, crying, cursing and sputtering water.

Once they were out of the river, they lay side by side on the bank. Maureen took several deep breaths to calm herself, knowing that these were hard words she needed to say. As much as she grieved for her sister, the children needed her too much to let her continue to wallow in self pity.

"Will ye listen to me?"

Saraid reached for the jug but Maureen quickly kicked it into the river.

"Hey!"

"*Enough!* Just . . . enough. Ye have to stop this. I know it's hard. In fact, it's pretty much the worst thing ye'll ever have to bear. What do ye think Niall is feelin', looking down on ye right now? Proud of his feisty, lovin' wife, is he?"

Saraid pulled up her knees and laid her face against them. "How am I supposed to live here without him? It's just too hard to think about!"

"Ye have to think about the children. They don't understand any of this! All they know is that their da is gone and their mother doesn't want them near her. They're all sufferin'. Not just ye! Ye have to put yer grief away and hold them and love them and comfort them. I can't do it for ye! I have my own children to care for, not to mention the cooking and caring for all the others. I just can't do it all by myself!"

Saraid shuddered and pushed the loose strands of wet hair out of her face. The river looked so serene and inviting. Her torment was a bottomless hole of darkness tearing her heart and soul from her body. Tears rolled from her eyes as she finally accepted that floating away was not an option. "I don't think I can stay here . . . with Kate."

Maureen sighed. "I know . . . but she isn't goin' to last much longer. How about this? How about if after the funeral, ye and the children come home with us for a bit? Until ye get yourself settled."

"James won't leave the farm."

"He can stay with Patrick and Paddy. It'll be good for him."

Saraid stood up, contemplated the river, and sighed. She slowly nodded and held out her hand out to Maureen. They stood eye to eye for a moment and then embraced for a moment more.

Chapter Sixty-Five

As the sun sank in the western sky, Seamus hunkered down in the brush behind the stone wall, cursing his luck. He thought he'd have a good hiding spot to watch the burial but as the crowd on the hillside grew, he soon realized that he was trapped. He'd have to wait until the mourners left to make his escape in the dark. The horse nickered and Seamus yanked at the rope around his neck. "You be quiet! Last thing I need is bein' found out now!" Nothing had gone as planned. Molly had survived but he hadn't been able to follow as she'd been taken from the farm.

His stomach growled and he cursed his hunger. He'd had nothing to eat for two days and all he could smell was the tantalizing aroma of game roasting on the cook fires on the hillside. He shook his flask over his mouth but it was as empty as his stomach, not a drop left to quiet his tremors. He continued to curse his bad luck, sniveling at the injustice of his circumstances. "It ain't my fault!" he hissed.

* * *

At sundown, Niall's casket was borne up the hill to the family plot; Patrick, John, Roark, James, George, and Willie acting as pallbearers. Connor O'Brien, as elder of the family, was to speak after the ceremony.

Kate, too ill to leave her bed, was watched over by Martha.

Paddy, defiant and mindless of the laws, officiated openly in his worn black cassock. It was the first time in years that he was performing any of the rites without fear of reprisal. He had known Niall since his birth, loved him like a son, and was damned if he would let him be buried without proper ritual. His clear tenor sang the mass while tears flowed from his eyes. Throngs of townsfolk stayed behind the low stone wall that surrounded the gravesite, silent but for the quiet murmurings of the recitation of the rosary and the soft mournful sound of the pipes being played on the hillside.

Saraid stood silent between Patrick and John, determined to do what was needed of her. She would have years to grieve after this day was done. For now, this moment, she stood with her back erect, shoulders defiant, her face void of expression. She was seemingly unaware of the little ones as they scampered around the cemetery, their young voices full of life, oblivious of the pain in older hearts.

The night, void of stars, loomed over the farm like a shroud. Campfires, hours of food and drink, song and dance, were unable to distract from the shadow of this death. Hours later when it was finally over, the wagons, one by one, began heading up the road as daybreak peeked through the eastern sky.

Suddenly, a horse keened in the trees across the field.

Heads cocked, eyed locked and at once, they all whispered, "Seamus!"

John hissed. "The bastard's been here the whole time, watching us!"

Patrick growled. "He'll not get away this time!"

Roark ran for his whip as Saraid and the men ran across the field. They reached the copse to find Seamus trying valiantly to hold his horse by the rope around his neck so he could mount. The horse kept trying to back away, lifting his front hooves off the ground. Seamus began to curse, refusing to let go. "Ye feckin' horse! Stay still!" The horse was having none of it and reared up on his hind legs, pulling Seamus off the ground. He hung on for dear life even as the hooves hit his chest and he fell hard to the ground. He tried to roll clear, still clutching the rope only to be lifted into the air again, more violently this time. Unable to hold on, Seamus fell to the ground screaming and stared up powerlessly as the mighty hooves came down and crushed his skull. The horse seemed to know that he had nothing left to fear and backed up a few paces and snorted before standing very still, his hooves spattered crimson.

The men stood silent, unable to believe how quickly it was over; Seamus a bloody mess on the ground, no longer a threat. Patrick gently held the horse in place.

Danny spoke first. "I guess I should go tell Molly."

Saraid nodded. "She may want to see the body before ye bury him. Then she'll never have to wonder if she's been told the truth." *And I'll never have to wonder where ye are or have yer blood on my hands.* She turned to walk away but stopped as her son spoke.

James stood very erect, his voice clear. "He'll not be buried on my land."

Everyone stared at the young man. Then, one by one, they nodded and put a hand to his shoulder. Arrangements would be made to remove the body from O'Brien land.

John closed his eyes and sighed. His need to punish Seamus would go unsatisfied. But perhaps it was better this way, better for all of them for Seamus to die at God's hand, not theirs.

***

O'Hickey rose from the table and walked to Patrick, placing a firm hand on the grieving man's shoulder. "We need to be getting back home." He opened his leather medical bag and brought out a small brown bottle of liquid. "This is for Kate . . . to ease her torment. I'll write down the dosage for you." He pulled a small piece of parchment from his bag along with his quill and ink.

When he was done writing the instructions, he packed his things away and buckled up the straps. "There's really nothing else I can do here right now, but if the need arises, you can send for me."

Patrick embraced the smaller man and took what comfort he could from it.

After they left, Patrick wandered out over the stubble of the field to his own cabin. The sun sat easy on his shoulders and warmed the chill he had felt in the house. He sat heavily on the bench outside the door and leaned back against the smooth stones. Looking out at the charred remains of the barn, he knew that the nightmarish memories of the fire would always be with him. It would be years before they recovered . . . if they recovered. Part of him wanted to leave this place and never come back.

He turned his gaze in another direction and saw nothing but green fields and low stone walls under a brilliant blue sky. Birds chittered in the trees overhead, sheep baaed and grazed on the hill behind the coop where the chickens clucked and pecked for grain. In another field, the two remaining cows grazed lazily, swishing their tails. Everything was as it should be.

He thought about Annie and his chest ached. How he wished she were here with him. Maybe someday, he would find her again. Or she might come here looking for him. How could he leave if that chance for happiness was here?

Patrick took out his tin whistle and began to play a gentle melody, filled with both the ache in his heart and the hope he still clung to. As it floated on the air over the land he loved, he knew that he would stay, for Niall, for James, and for himself.

Epilogue

February 1776

John read over the last entry in the journal that held the family tree:

> *Kate O'Brien, wife of James, died August 5th, 1775, Killaloe, County Clare, Ireland.*
> *Cause of death: pneumonia.*

John shrugged off the vague guilt he felt for not telling the entire truth. He refused to write 'insanity' as a cause of death in this sterile volume that the scribe had brought to him last spring. Was it only last spring? It seemed that years had passed instead of several months.

Profound regret still coursed through him when he thought about the last week of his mother's life. If he had taken her away from here all those months earlier when she'd asked . . . .

He sighed . . . no help for it now. She had suffered so much, and been so afraid, that it had been a blessing when she had finally succumbed to the pneumonia. John closed the record book and set it aside. He then opened the family history volume and wrote a passage about what had happened with Niall's family. It was still difficult to write.

> *After mother's burial, Roark and Maureen packed up their children and belongings to go home. They had stayed long after the two weeks they had planned, and still had their own crops to get in.*
>
> *Saraid was, by then, too overwrought with bitterness to stay on the farm.*

Maureen took pity on them and decided that perhaps, with some time away from here, she would recover enough from her grief to get herself settled again. And so, another wagon was filled with Saraid and the three younger children, to follow them home.

James remains at the farm with Patrick.

He turned the page and made one final entry:

February 11, 1776

Today, I, John O'Brien, son of James and Kate O'Brien, am leaving the family farm for good. There is nothing left here for me. I have never felt a calling to the land as my father and brothers have. My passion has always been found in the written word and I am poorly suited to live this farmer's life.

I am heading for Dublin where I have found a position at the grand library of Trinity College. I look forward to an unending supply of good books to read! Perhaps one day I will be qualified to teach.

I will leave these leather bound volumes of the O'Brien history and records in good hands. Patrick has promised to keep them safe for Niall's son, James, as he (James) is now the true heir of the family holdings. It is my hope that, in generations to come, someone will read these volumes with interest and fascination to learn where they came from.

Sincerely,

John O'Brien

John covered the pot of ink and, after cleaning his quill, packed them into his satchel along with a blank volume to keep for himself. Maybe one day he would have a family of his own and begin recording their own journey. He could only hope.

After loading his belongings into the wagon, he searched out Patrick and found him eating his mid-day meal. He set down the tomes before filling a plate from the cast iron stove and joined him at the table.

Patrick looked up from his meal. "Are you all set to go?"

"That I am." He explained about the books while he buttered a chunk of bread. "All the farm records are up to date. You'll need them for the accounting with the overseer in June."

Patrick nodded. "Not going to be much to account for but expense this time."

"True enough, but it still needs to be done."

Patrick was trying not to be angry about John leaving, but the truth of it was that John hated it here and he had to accept it. It would be hard to take on all the responsibility for the farm, but it would keep his mind busy. The harder he worked, the less time he would have to think about . . . he pushed the thought from his mind.

They walked out to the wagon and John held out his hand to his brother. Patrick grasped his hand and pulled him into a fierce embrace. "You'll come back to visit, won't you?"

John hesitated. "Maybe at the end of summer before the university starts the fall term."

Patrick nodded; but, somehow, he felt that he might never see him again.

John looked around one last time. "Where's James?"

"He wanted to go check his traps. He's determined to find something for dinner out there."

John chuckled. "I guess he's tired of your cooking."

"It's not that bad!"

John laughed and shook his head. "Give James my best. Tell him to write to me." He snapped the reins and the horse began to trot across the courtyard and up the drive to the road. Patrick stood there watching until the wagon was out of sight.

The air was cold but clear, Patrick's breath floating into the air like a cloud. There had been little snow this winter, and the ground around the new barn was still charred from the fire, evoking terrible memories. In the spring, when the rains came, the earth would be washed clean and new growth would come. He thanked God for small blessings. For now, it made it easier to get to the stable to feed the animals. They rarely got much snow here in the east of Clare because of the Gulf Stream off of the west coast of Ireland.

The new barn stood ready for cows and hay. The uncut field had been harvested late but would still provide some nutrition for the animals that remained. If everything went well, they would be fully running again by fall.

Patrick retrieved one of the volumes that John had left for him. He sat in the afternoon sun with a blanket wrapped around his shoulders and thumbed the pages, amazed at all John had written. His fine, clear writing had filled page after page with the events of the last year. All the doings in Doolin: the dancing, the music, and the story telling. He'd written of the Dance Masters and their fiddlers: Willie and Freddy, Martin and Hank, Martin's death and all that had followed. He'd written about his mother's spells, the Callahan brothers and their horses, and the fire where Danny had been shot. There was even a mention of Jack and the Shamrock tavern . . . and Annie. His breath caught. Not nearly enough words to explain what Annie had meant to him.

He closed his eyes and leaned back with his face to the sun. He realized that he had dozed when the sound of wagon wheels coming down the drive woke him. His eyes were bleary as he stared into the afternoon sun. It looked like John's wagon but he looked to be pulling another horse behind him. He couldn't be sure. He shook himself, stood, and began walking across the courtyard.

"Did you forget something?"

John smiled broadly and gestured to the back of the wagon. "I brought you a present."

"What do you mean?"

"Go look," said John as he climbed out of the wagon. "I found her walking along the road. Her wagon broke a wheel."

Patrick went to the back of the wagon and peered at the figure in a hooded cape, shivering under a blanket, a worn cloth bag beside her.

She sat up and held her breath as she peered out with the blanket covering part of her face. Her heart stopped and then it raced at the sight of Patrick standing there.

When he stared without comprehending who she was, she uncovered her face and removed her hood, letting her bright red hair tumble out.

"*Annie!*" Patrick stood there gaping and then whispered. "Is it really you?"

She nodded, clutching the cape around her body.

"Where have you been? How did you get here?"

John grasped his shoulder and gave him a shake. "Well, don't just stand there, she going to need some help getting down." He untied Annie's horse, and led it across the courtyard to give them some privacy. His heart was lighter knowing that Patrick wouldn't be alone here.

Patrick could make no sense of it. *Why would she need help?*

Annie held on to the side of the wagon and rose awkwardly, wrapping her arms across her chest. Her eyes flared briefly. "Ye din' come back fer me," she stated with timid accusation.

"I did, too!" he retorted. "I sent Saraid to tell you I couldn't come. She was to bring you food and coin to tie you over until I could come back! As soon as I found out that she never got there, I headed straight back, but you were gone!"

Annie's heart thudded in her chest. "Ye came back?"

"Yes I did!" he said angrily. "Where were you? I've been half mad all this time!"

She shook her head. "It's a long story." Then she grinned down at him. "Ye missed me, then?"

Patrick stormed around the wagon, throwing his arms wide. "Damn fool woman! Of course, I missed you! What do you take me for?"

Annie felt relief pour through her and her heart ached with love. He *had* come back! He *did* care! Her old playfulness came to the fore as she tried to keep a straight face. "Ye're soundin' a bit angry there, Patrick."

"I *am* angry, you bloody fool!" He was ready to throttle her.

Unable to stop herself, Annie began to laugh with joy. Patrick's face went white and then red as he hissed at her. "Don't you dare laugh at me!"

That he had repeated the exact words she had flung at him that day in the cave only made her throw back her head and laugh louder. After a moment, she got control of herself and wiped her eyes. She stood before him and spread the heavy cape away from her body.

"Will ye have us, Patrick?"

He stared at the round curve of her belly with shock. "I don't understand," he whispered. "You're having a baby?" Confusion and then resentment filled him. "When did that happen?"

Annie smiled at him, her dimples lighting up her face. "It happened in Doolin, Patrick, in the cave."

"You're having *my* baby?" Incredulous, he ran his fingers through his hair and then put his hands on his hips as he counted off the months in his head. *This can't be happening!* He wanted so much to believe her. "When is the baby coming?"

She sensed his doubt and, with the life she had led, could hardly blame him. "The baby should be comin' in May. It be yers, Patrick, I can promise ye that I been with no other man."

Patrick hesitated only an instant before he held out his arms and carefully lifted her down. He clutched her to his chest and wept into her hair. "I thought I lost you."

She held him with all the tenderness and strength she could

muster. "It's all right now, Patrick. I'm goin' t'make bloody sure ye never lose me again."

Acknowledgments

Writing is a solitary experience. Getting to the point of publication is not. I have found that it takes the proverbial village to get to the finish line. Along the way, I met and worked with an amazing group of like-minded women.

Special thanks go to Joan Shapiro, a poet and educator, who has supported my writing efforts for several decades. Her faith carried me through several years of doubt. She invited me to join one of her writing classes and it was there that I met and worked with a small group of women who became my first readers and long-time writing friends. These women elevated me both intellectually and spiritually.

Thank you to my classmates for their support through several revisions. Barbara Bergren, Ellen Karadimas, Donna Smith, Sarah Karstaedt, Sarah Olson and Terri Klein. Barbara Bergren, recently published herself, deserves a second thank you for answering all my tedious publishing questions with patience and grace.

Mystery writer Jenny Milchman, was kind enough to read a chapter—even though it was out of her genre.

Linda Conrad, a pressed flower friend from Pennsylvania, had read it a few chapters at a time as I emailed them to her. She found many errors in spacing and punctuation and offered to proof it for me. I mailed the first bound copy to her. She sent it back filled with post-its and told me to send it back to her after I had made the corrections. God bless her!

Finding the courage to let people read the first finished draft was scary. I had four copies bound and set them free. A dozen folks volunteered and pleased me to no end with their comments. Thank you Susan Gessay, my dear friend of many years, for letting me go on and on about the story and for your thoughtful critique. Thanks also, to Patti Levi, Susan Hayes, Cathy Nelson, and David and Pat Brannick. My daughter Michelle Macomber said it made her cry and that made me smile. My sister, Kathy and her husband, Dr John Andreoli Jr., gave me critical input about the difference between heart attack and stroke symptoms.

Writing the book was the easy part. Formatting frustrated me to no end. Twice, I quit and put it in a box for two years. After this last two-year hibernation, I was determined to get it done. After weeks of angst, I put out an SOS to my writer friends. I just couldn't do it. Before the day was over, I was contacted by Sharon Gresk who offered her graphic design skills to get me to the finish line. She also designed my awesome cover. Thank you Sharon!

A special thanks to June Bray for her fresh eyes and fine editing skills for the final editing of my manuscript.

My thanks would not be complete without acknowledging James, my Spirit Guide, who stood at my shoulder wearing his top hat. He directed and corrected much of my dialogue.

Author's Note

To my knowledge, there are no meadows in Doolin. I have taken great liberties with the topography to enhance the story line.

The lullaby that Saraid sings to Bridget is: *The Ballyeaon Cradle Song/Book* by Sne Uil Chellaigh.

The story that Roisin tells the children around the campfire is: *The Leprechaun* by Robert Dwyer Joyce.

The letter that Ben Franklin wrote to the Irish Parliament was taken from: *EIR History/The American Revolution in Ireland: Franklin's Irish Front/* by Matthew Ogden, https://larouchepub.com/eiw/public/2011/eirv38n12-20110325/49-55_3812.pdf

Bibliography

There is an enormous amount of information online about all things Irish. There were also a few books that I found that were superior in their breadth of information.

The Emerald Isle And Its People, Mark Morris, Passport Books, A division of NTC Publishing Group. Lincolnwood, IL, 1995.

The Story of The Irish People, A Popular History of Ireland, Seumas MacManus, assisted by several Irish scholars, Konecky & Konecky, 72 Ayers Point Rd., Old Saybrook, CT, Fourth Revised Edition, copyright 1921, Seumas McManus. This edition published in cooperation with the permission of the Devin-Adair Company, Greenwich, CT.

To School Through The Fields, Alice Taylor, St Martin's Press, 175 Fifth Ave., NY, NY, 10010, 1988.

Printed in Great Britain
by Amazon

54798741R10260